A CHRISTMAS KNIGHT

BY
KATE HARDY

*For Benita Brown. With many thanks for the story about her
wonderful GP father and the milkman's horse.*

DID YOU PURCHASE THIS BOOK WITHOUT A COVER?

If you did, you should be aware it is **stolen property** as it was reported
unsold and destroyed by a retailer. Neither the author nor the publisher
has received any payment for this book.

First published in Great Britain 2010
Harlequin Mills & Boon Limited,
Eton House, 18-24 Paradise Road, Richmond, Surrey TW9 1SR

© Kate Hardy 2010

ISBN: 978 0 263 87933 9

Harlequin Mills & Boon policy is to use papers that are natural,
renewable and recyclable products and made from wood grown in
sustainable forests. The logging and manufacturing process conform
to the legal environmental regulations of the country of origin.

Printed and bound in Spain
by Litografia Rosés, S.A., Barcelona

1673126

A CHRISTMAS KNIGHT

BY
KATE HARDY

THE NURSE WHO SAVED CHRISTMAS

BY
JANICE LYNN

MILLS & BOON

THE MAGIC OF CHRISTMAS

A time when families are made and hearts are healed

The only thing on nurses
Abby Arnold and Louisa Austin's Christmas lists
this year is to find that perfect someone to sweep them
off their feet before the first snowflakes begin to fall.
Can this year be the most magical of all and make
all their dreams come true? Find out in…

A CHRISTMAS KNIGHT
by Kate Hardy
This Christmas Knight is gift-wrapped—
not only in shining armour, but a doctor's coat
and a heart-melting smile!

THE NURSE WHO SAVED CHRISTMAS
by Janice Lynn
Spend this Christmas with the
ER's very own Dr Delicious—Dirk Kelley!

Praise for
Kate Hardy:

'THE CHILDREN'S DOCTOR'S SPECIAL PROPOSAL
is just as the title promises. Kate Hardy delivers a superb
romance that resonates beautifully with the reader. Bravo,
Ms Hardy!'

—*bookilluminations.com*

'THE GREEK DOCTOR'S NEW-YEAR BABY is
romantic storytelling at its best! Poignant, enjoyable and
absolutely terrific, with THE GREEK DOCTOR'S
NEW-YEAR BABY Kate Hardy proves once again that
when it comes to romantic fiction she's up there with the
very best!'

—*cataromance.com*

'SURRENDER TO THE PLAYBOY SHEIKH: I spent a
lovely morning with this book, and I'd advise you to do
likewise. Get it. You'll love it. An unrestrained…Grade A.'

—*goodbadandunread.com*

'PLAYBOY BOSS, PREGNANCY OF PASSION: This
story features a strong heroine who gains strength from
her family and a hero who realises the importance of love
and family before it's too late. Add in their captivating
romance and it makes for one great read.'

—*RT Book Reviews*

Kate Hardy lives in Norwich, in the east of England, with her husband, two young children, one bouncy spaniel, and too many books to count! When she's not busy writing romance or researching local history, she helps out at her children's schools. She also loves cooking—spot the recipes sneaked into her books! (They're also on her website, along with extracts and stories behind the books.) Writing for Mills & Boon has been a dream come true for Kate—something she wanted to do ever since she was twelve. She's been writing Medical™ Romances for nearly five years now, and also writes for Modern Heat™. She says it's the best of both worlds, because she gets to learn lots of new things when she's researching the background to a book: add a touch of passion, drama and danger, a new gorgeous hero every time, and it's the perfect job!

Kate's always delighted to hear from readers, so do drop in to her website at www.katehardy.com

Recent titles by the same author:

Medical™ Romance
NEUROSURGEON…AND MUM!
THE DOCTOR'S LOST-AND-FOUND BRIDE
FALLING FOR THE PLAYBOY MILLIONAIRE*

The Brides of Penhally Bay

Modern Heat™
RED WINE AND HER SEXY EX†
CHAMPAGNE WITH A CELEBRITY†
GOOD GIRL OR GOLD-DIGGER?

†Château Lefèvre linked duo

CHAPTER ONE

'LET me get you a coffee, and then I'll take you round and introduce you to the team,' Essie, the charge nurse, said with a smile.

'Thanks. I, um, brought some biscuits for the staff-room,' Louisa said, handing her a large tin.

'Thanks very much.' Essie beamed as she peered at the lid. 'Chocolate ones, too. Excellent. You'll fit right in.' She gave Louisa a sympathetic look. 'The first day's always the worst, isn't it? Like being back at school.'

Louisa smiled back. 'I've been doing agency work for the last three months, so you'd think I'd be used to change. But, yes, you're right. It feels like the first day at school, when you don't know anyone and you don't know the routine—well, as much of a routine as you get in the emergency department,' she finished. No two days were ever quite the same.

'You'll be fine,' Essie told her warmly. 'I've rostered you onto Minors—but if anything big comes in, I might need to borrow you for Resus.'

'That's fine,' Louisa said. As a nurse practitioner, she was able to see patients through from start to finish for the less serious problems—from taking the medical history through to doing the clinical examination, ordering and interpreting tests, diagnosing the ailment and organising a treatment plan for the patient. She loved the responsibility and the feeling that she was in charge of her own day, but she also enjoyed the busy, hands-on role in Resus, working as part of a team.

'Dominic's the senior registrar in Resus today. He's our resident heart-throb,' Essie said with a grin. 'He looks like Prince Charming.'

Heart-throb. Jack had been a heart-throb, too. But he'd been very far from being Prince Charming. He'd walked out on Louisa just when she'd needed him most. So much for promising to love, honour and cherish her. Jack had left her—and Tyler—because he couldn't handle the idea of having a son with Asperger's. As soon as Jack had heard the paediatrician say the words 'autistic spectrum disorder', he'd closed off, and Louisa had seen it in his eyes. She'd known that her marriage was cracking beyond repair, and there was nothing she could do to stop it. Less than two months later, he'd moved out and asked her for a divorce.

She could cope with Jack's rejection of her; but she'd never, ever forgive him for rejecting their bright, quirky, gorgeous son. And she'd taken notice of the old saying, ever since: *Handsome is as handsome does.*

Essie didn't seem to notice Louisa's silence. 'He's been here for eight years now. He joined us as a wet-behind-the-ears house officer, and worked his way up.' She sighed. 'Though he's not one for settling down, our Dominic. Women used to fall at his feet in droves, but nowadays he doesn't even date—he's completely wrapped up in his work. Pity, because he'd make a fantastic husband and father.'

Louisa had already spotted the photograph on Essie's

desk; the charge nurse was smiling for the camera, looking blissfully happy with her husband and two children. It seemed that Essie was the type who wanted everyone to be as happy and settled as she was. Well, she *was* happy and settled. She just wasn't in a two-parent family.

'Marriage isn't for everyone,' she said quietly.

'You're not married, then?'

'Not any more.' Not that she wanted to talk about it. Though, given the photograph on Essie's desk, she could offer the perfect distraction. 'But I do have a gorgeous son. Tyler.' She took a photograph from her purse to show the charge nurse.

'Oh, he looks a sweetie. And he's so like you.'

'He is,' she agreed with a smile. 'I'm really lucky.' And she meant it. Tyler was the light of her life, and she loved him with a fierceness that she knew probably made her protect him too much.

'So how old is he?' Essie asked.

'Eight. He started middle school last week—so this summer was the least disruptive time to move here from London.' Louisa took a deep breath. 'Actually, that's why I started today, not last week—I wanted to give him a few days to settle in to his new school first.'

'It's always hard, changing schools, whether you're from the local first school or not,' Essie agreed. 'Though I'm sure he'll soon make friends.'

Louisa would be very, very surprised if he did. Tyler was self-contained in the extreme. Having Asperger's meant he saw the world in terms of black and white, with no shades of grey. Other children quickly noticed that—especially as Ty was a walking encyclopaedia on his favourite subjects, and wouldn't hesitate to correct anyone instead of just letting it go for the sake of social harmony. She'd tried to help him, inviting children home for tea after school—but Tyler had never been invited back. Probably because most of the time, when someone came over, he'd lose interest in whatever game they were playing, disappear up to his room and start drawing. 'Maybe,' she said.

'Give it a week and he'll be playing football with the rest of them,' Essie said cheerfully.

Louisa wrinkled her nose. 'He's not really into football.'

'Computer games, then?' Essie asked. 'Tell me about it. My eldest is glued to his console.'

'What Ty really likes is horses. I'm going to ring round the local riding stables to see if there are any places for lessons.' Louisa had read an article about how good riding could be for children with Asperger's; it was just a matter of finding the right stables, one that could accommodate Tyler without making a big deal out of things. And maybe he'd find it easier to make friends with children who shared his passion.

'Horses?' Essie looked thoughtful. 'Then you definitely need to talk to Dominic. He's got a horse. He's bound to know a good riding school locally.'

Louisa smiled politely, but she had no intention of asking a heart-throb for help. She'd already learned the hard way that heart-throbs weren't reliable—and she'd never, ever take any risks with her son.

Essie had introduced Louisa to everyone except the resus team when her bleep went off.

'Resus—and I'm needed,' she said ruefully, glancing at the display. 'Sorry. Can I leave you with Jess to open up Minors?'

'Sure. No worries,' Louisa said.

Her first case was a seven-year-old girl who'd fallen and bent her fingers back the previous day; now her hand was stiff and swollen.

'I know I should've brought her here earlier. I thought she'd just banged herself and was making a fuss, and it'd settle down,' Mrs Aldiss said, chewing her bottom lip.

'That's often the case, after a fall,' Louisa reassured her. 'It's a tough one to call. Have you given her anything for the pain?'

'I've been giving her paracetamol, and I put an ice pack on her hand yesterday.'

'That's good.' She crouched down so she was on a level with the little girl. 'Hello, I'm Louisa—and you're being ever so brave, Pippa,' she said with a smile. 'Can I have a look at your hand, so I can see what's wrong and make it better?'

The little girl was white-faced, but she nodded.

Gently, Louisa examined her fingers. 'Can you make a fist for me?' she asked, showing Pippa exactly what she wanted her to do.

The little girl tried, but her sharp intake of breath told Louisa that it was just too painful.

'OK, sweetheart, you can stop trying now. You've done really well,' Louisa reassured her. 'I don't want to do anything that'll make it hurt more. But what I do want to do is see what's making it hurt so much, so I'm going to send you to X-Ray. It's not going to hurt, but they have special cameras there to take a picture of your bones so I can see if you've broken your finger or whether you've hurt one of the ligaments—that's the bit that helps you bend your finger.' She ruffled the little girl's hair. 'And once I know that, I'll know how to treat you. If it's just a little break, I'll do what we call buddy taping—that means I'll strap your poorly finger to the one next door, to help it mend.'

'If it's a big break, will she need a plaster on her hand?' Mrs Aldiss asked.

'It depends on the break. But I'd definitely recommend resting her hand in a sling. If you can just wait here for a second, I'll make sure Pippa's booked in with X-Ray and they know exactly what I want to see,' Louisa said.

Mrs Aldiss cuddled the little girl. 'And we'll have a story while we're waiting, OK, honey?'

Louisa swiftly booked a slot in X-Ray, explained what she was looking for, and then went back to her patient. Pippa's mother was clearly near the end of the story, so Louisa waited for her to finish. 'You're very good at that.'

'It's Pip's favourite. I've read it that many times, I know it off by heart,' Mrs Aldiss said.

Louisa smiled at them and took a sticker out of her pocket. 'I'll see you again after you've gone to X-Ray, Pippa, but in the meantime I think you deserve one of my special stickers for being really brave.'

'Thank you,' Pippa said shyly, brightening slightly at the sight of the glittery badge.

Louisa directed Mrs Aldiss to the X-ray department, then went to collect the notes for her next patient.

The morning was busy, with a steady stream of patients; when Pippa came back after her X-ray and Louisa pulled the file up on the computer screen, she was relieved to see it was a stable fracture.

'See this little tiny mark on here?' she asked. 'That's where you've broken your finger. So what I'm going to do is strap it to the finger next to it, to be a buddy to keep the poorly one straight.' Gently, she strapped up the little girl's finger. 'You need to rest your hand, sweetheart, so I'm going to give you a sling—that will help you keep your hand up and make the swelling go down, so it doesn't hurt so much. And I'd like you to come back in a week's time for another X-ray so we can see how well it's healing.'

'How long will she need her fingers like that?' Mrs Aldiss asked.

'Usually it's three or four weeks, and then another couple of weeks where you keep the hand rested—not too much exercise, and I'm afraid that includes using games consoles.'

'Just as well it's you and not your brother, then,' Mrs Aldiss said ruefully, 'or we'd really be in trouble!'

'It is your writing hand, Pippa?' Louisa asked.

Pippa shook her head. 'So I can still draw?'

'You can definitely still draw.' Louisa smiled at her.

'I'll bring you a picture when I come back,' Pippa said.

'I'd love that. I've only just moved to this department,' Louisa said, 'so I have a whole wall that's just waiting for pictures. I'll see you in a week, sweetheart. Remember to rest your hand as much as you can.'

Things had quietened down slightly, just after lunchtime, when Essie came into the office where Louisa was catching up with paperwork. 'The lull before the storm, hmm?' she asked.

'Probably. So I'm making the most of it and sorting out this lot,' Louisa said, gesturing to the notes and the pile of letters she was working through.

'Can I borrow you for a minute to meet the resus team? They're on a break—and very grateful for your biscuits, I might add.'

Essie continued chatting until they reached the rest room, and then introduced her to the resus team. 'This is Sally, our student nurse.'

Sally greeted her warmly, and then Essie motioned to the man who was sitting apart from the others, reading a medical journal.

'Louisa, this is Dominic Hurst, our senior reg. Dominic—Louisa Austin, our new nurse practitioner.'

Essie had described him as looking like Prince Charming. And that wasn't the half of it, Louisa thought. Dominic Hurst looked like a Pre-Raphaelite painting of a medieval prince, all dark flowing locks and fair skin and chiselled cheekbones and dark, dark eyes. Even dressed simply in a plain white shirt, sober tie and dark trousers, he was incredibly striking. No wonder women fell at his feet in droves. He was tall—just over six feet, she'd guess—and, at close range, those navy-blue eyes were devastating. Not to mention that beautiful mouth, which sent all kinds of crazy thoughts spinning through her head.

'Pleased to meet you, Dr Hurst,' she said politely.

He looked up from the journal and blinked. 'Sorry?'

'Dominic, I can't believe you're still working when you're on a break.' Essie rolled her eyes. 'You didn't hear a word I just said, did you?'

''Fraid not. I was reading.' He gave her a wry smile. 'Sorry.'

'This is Louisa Austin, our new nurse practitioner,' Essie repeated.

'Pleased to meet you, Nurse Practitioner Austin.'

Dominic's handshake was firm, precise and brief— and it felt as if an electric current was running through her veins. Which was crazy, because she never reacted like that to anyone. It hadn't even been like that with Jack, in the good days. So why now? And why this man?

'Louisa's looking for riding lessons, because her son likes horses,' Essie continued, and Dominic's expression turned wary.

Oh, for pity's sake, did he think she was going to use her child as an excuse to come on to him? Still, she wasn't going to be rude to him. 'He does indeed. He wants to be a knight when he grows up,' Louisa said, keeping her tone light.

If anything, Dominic's expression grew even warier. She didn't have the faintest idea why, but despite Essie's suggestion she wasn't going to bother asking him if he could recommend any riding stables locally. Clearly he'd take it the wrong way, so she'd be better off doing what she always did and sorting it out for herself.

Dominic Hurst might look like Prince Charming, but he definitely didn't have a charming manner. She sincerely hoped he was better in a work situation, for the sake of his patients and his colleagues. She made a polite murmur, and to her relief Essie stepped in again. 'Let me introduce you to Sasha and Ronnie,' Essie said, and swept Louisa over to where two women were making coffee.

Dominic took a gulp of coffee. Whatever was the matter with him? It was the poor woman's first day in the department and he'd been rude to her.

Well, not rude, *exactly*—he had at least acknowledged her and shaken her hand.

But the zing of attraction when her skin had touched his had thrown him, made him tongue-tied. Which was crazy, because he was never that boorish. Essie had even given him an opening, saying that Louisa was looking for riding lessons for her child. He could've given her Ric and Bea's number, because he knew they had a couple of spaces on their list. They'd talked about it last night, how people were cutting back on extras in the recession and riding lessons were expensive, and Bea had suggested that they should hold an open day to get people interested in the stables.

But then Louisa had said something that slammed right through him. *He wants to be a knight when he grows up.* Yeah. Been there, done that, and the absolute worst had happened.

Though that wasn't her fault and he shouldn't have taken it out on her.

He'd apologise later, and hopefully she wouldn't hold it against him if she was needed to work with his team in Resus.

Riding lessons. For her son.

Though she wasn't wearing a wedding ring. And there wasn't a tell-tale band of pale skin on her finger to say she'd removed it for work. He'd looked. And he was cross with himself for looking.

Dominic took another gulp of coffee, needing the bitter liquid to jolt some sense back into him. Louisa Austin was gorgeous, with beautiful grey eyes and long dark hair; she'd tied it back hygienically for work, but he could imagine what it looked like loose. Like waves of shiny silk. Her mouth was a perfect rosebud, and it sent a shiver of pure desire running through him, along with an insane urge to find out how it would feel against his own mouth. It had been a long, long time since he'd felt an attraction that strong and that immediate—and that was what had thrown him most.

He knew that it would be pretty stupid to act on that attraction. He wasn't in the market for a relationship; and, even if he was, Louisa had a son. Which meant that either she was already spoken for, despite the lack of a wedding ring, or she was a single parent who'd be wary of taking any risks in a relationship, for her child's sake, and would want someone responsible in her life.

Responsible.

Right.

Which was about as far from him as you could get: hadn't he ruined his brother's life, two years ago?

He needed to get out of here. Now.

'No rest for the wicked,' he said, striding over to the sink and rinsing out his mug. 'If we're to have any chance of meeting our targets today, I'd better get back out there and hope Resus stays quiet for the rest of the afternoon. Welcome to the team, Nurse Practitioner Austin.' And he left the rest room before he could do anything ridiculous. Like asking her to have lunch with him tomorrow so they could get to know each other a little better.

The rest of Louisa's shift turned out to be as busy as the morning, but she managed to get to the after-school club on time to meet Tyler.

'Hi, Mum.' He gave her the shy smile that always made her melt.

'How was your day, honey?' She gave him a hug.

'OK.'

'Best bit?'

'Lunch. We had pasta. It wasn't as good as yours, though.'

She really hoped that he hadn't actually said that to the dinner ladies. She could still remember the time they'd had Sunday lunch at her best friend's house and then, when asked if he'd enjoyed it, he'd very politely thanked Mel and gone on to tell her that her gravy was slimy and her potatoes weren't nice and crispy on the outside and fluffy in the middle like his mother's were. Luckily Mel hadn't taken it to heart, but Louisa had had to explain to Tyler that sometimes it was OK to tell a little fib so you didn't hurt people's feelings. And even after she'd finished explaining, he still didn't get it. 'Let's go home and make dinner. Do you have any spellings or times tables I need to test you on?'

'No. Do you want to see the horse I drew at lunchtime?' He had his sketchbook out of his schoolbag as soon as he'd put his seat belt on.

She stared at the drawing in awe. 'It's beautiful, darling.' The horse was drawn in painstaking detail, and was incredibly realistic. Tyler really did have a talent for art—something she could only assume came from Jack's side, because nobody in her side of the family was arty. But there was nobody to ask, because Jack's family had severed all connection with them as soon as Jack had left—and for the same reason.

Though it didn't bother her any more. She knew that she and Ty were better off without them. Her parents accepted Tyler as he was and gave him enough love for two sets of grandparents. They didn't need the Listons.

Tyler disappeared to his room as soon as they got home, and Louisa knew exactly what he was doing. Putting his drawing in a plastic wallet, labelling it and adding it to his database. One good thing about having a son who was obsessed with order was that she never had to tell him to tidy his bedroom. It was always immaculate. Smiling, she busied herself preparing dinner, and when everything was ready she called him down, careful not to let the new potatoes, chicken or vegetables touch each other on Tyler's plate.

He chattered happily about horses all the way through dinner; and then it was the usual routine of washing up while he had a bath, nagging him to clean his teeth, and giving him a kiss goodnight.

Carefully, he turned the kitchen timer next to his bed to twenty minutes. 'I'll put my light out as soon as the alarm goes off, Mum,' he promised.

And she knew he would, even if he was in mid-sentence. Tyler was one for sticking to the rules. 'See you in the morning, darling. Sleep well,' she said, giving him another kiss.

Then she curled up on the sofa with her laptop and looked up all the local riding stables, listing them with their phone numbers in her diary. She'd start calling them tomorrow. It was a pity that Dominic Hurst had turned out to be so formal and unapproachable—she would've appreciated some tips on choosing the right riding school. But she was used to doing things on her own, so she wasn't going to let it throw her.

And as for stray thoughts of a tall, dark, gorgeous and reserved medic with a mouth that promised sin…she'd banish them all from her head, because there just wasn't room in her life for someone like that.

Handsome is as handsome does.

CHAPTER TWO

Tuesday went without incident in Minors, but on Wednesday Louisa was called in to help in Resus.

'Essie tells me you're very experienced, so I'd like you to work with me, please, Nurse Practitioner Austin,' Dominic said.

She noticed again that he'd addressed her by her title rather than by her name. Was he just being like that with her because she was new, or was he like that with everyone? Then she remembered that Essie had called him by his first name. Better get things straight now, then. 'OK, but can we spend thirty seconds now to save us a lot of time when our patients arrive?' she asked.

He frowned. 'How do you mean?'

'It goes without saying that I respect your seniority, but I'm used to working on first-name terms. It's quicker, easier, and less of a mouthful. Would you mind?'

He blinked. 'OK, Nu—Louisa.'

'Thank you, Dominic.' She used his name deliberately. 'So what's happened?'

'Car crash. Three casualties,' Dominic explained. 'Both drivers are coming in with suspected whiplash, and the passenger has suspected multiple fractures. Ronnie and Sasha are going to treat the drivers, and I need you with me as lead nurse to treat the passenger—Sally will assist us.'

She nodded. 'How long have we got to prepare?'

'Five minutes. I'm going down to the ambulance bay now.'

She busied herself getting the trolley ready; when Dominic came back with the paramedic and their patient, the team swung into action.

'Rhiannon, this is my team, Louisa and Sally,' Dominic said calmly. 'They're going to help me look after you.'

'Hurts,' Rhiannon mumbled. 'Where's Gary?'

'Your husband's right here,' he reassured her. 'Ronnie's looking after him, and as soon as she's checked him over and made him comfortable, he'll be able to come and see you. And we're going to give something to help with the pain,' he said. 'I'm going to put an oxygen mask on you to help you breathe better, and then we're going to have a proper look at you, OK?'

On Dominic's direction, Sally gently cut through Rhiannon's clothes so he could do a full body assessment, top to toe. Meanwhile, Louisa hooked Rhiannon up to a cardiac monitor, put in a second line and started taking obs.

'Heart rate 135, respirations twenty-six, blood pressure 82/54,' she said. Tachycardia and low blood pressure pointed to major loss of blood—probably caused by internal injuries, Louisa thought.

'We need to get some fluids in. Start with a litre of Hartmann's, and get six units cross-matched for me,' Dominic said—and looked approving when he saw that she already had the saline solution in her hand.

Dominic had given Rhiannon painkillers to make

her more comfortable; but when her blood pressure didn't respond to the fluids and her sats started dropping, he glanced at Louisa. 'Can you do ABGs for me, please, Louisa? And, Sally, I need X-rays.' He listened to Rhiannon's chest.

From the bruising on Rhiannon's skin, it looked as if she had several broken ribs. No doubt Dominic wanted to check for pulmonary contusions. There were a lot of problems that could be caused by blunt trauma at high velocity, Louisa knew; with damage in Rhiannon's chest area, there could be trauma to the heart as well as the lungs.

'I think we need to intubate.' He held Rhiannon's hand as he explained to her what they were doing. 'You're struggling to breathe, sweetheart, so we need to help you with that and make sure you get enough oxygen. I'm going to put a tube down your throat so you won't be able to speak, but I'm going to give you some medication first so you won't feel it and it won't hurt—it'll make you more comfortable. I know you're feeling tired and it's hard to talk, so just squeeze my hand if you're OK with that—once for yes and twice for no.' He paused. 'That's a yes—that's my girl. We'll get you comfortable as soon as we can.'

Louisa was just drawing up the ampoules of anaesthetic when one of the drivers who'd been brought in came over to them, his face ashen. 'Oh, my God, Rhi! I'm so sorry. I couldn't avoid him—he just pulled out on me and there was nothing I could do.' He looked distraught as he stared wildly at Dominic and Louisa. 'I can't believe I've come out with just bruises, and Rhi's so…so…' His voice caught.

'Gary, isn't it?' Dominic said, somehow managing to

divide his attention and eye contact between his patient and her husband.

'Yes.'

'She was asking for you.'

'Can I hold her hand?' At Dominic's brief nod, Gary curled his fingers round his wife. 'Honey, I'm here, and I love you, and I'm so sorry.' He dragged in a breath and looked pleadingly at Dominic. 'Is she going to die?'

'Not on my shift,' Dominic said, 'though it might be easier on you if you wait outside. There's a vending machine just round the corner. I promise we'll come and find you as soon as we've got her stable and let you know what's going on, but for now we need to concentrate on Rhiannon here and treat her.'

Gary shook his head. 'No. I need to stay with her.'

'Unless you're a trained medic, it can look very worrying in here,' Dominic said gently. 'Especially as we're just about to intubate her to help her breathe. Trust me, we're going to do everything we can for your wife, but it will be much better on your nerves if you go and get yourself a hot drink and leave us to it for the next few minutes.'

'I'll come and get you as soon as there's any news,' Louisa promised. But she noticed that Gary was staring at his wife, looking stunned. In shock, she thought—not the medical kind, but the emotional kind. They needed to get him out of here. 'Do I have two minutes, Dominic, to show Gary where everything is?'

'Two minutes,' Dominic confirmed; the expression in his eyes told Louisa that he knew exactly what she was doing and approved. Which was a huge relief: he was much easier to work with than she'd expected. And he was sensitive with patients and relatives. Maybe she'd just caught him on a bad day on Monday.

'Come on, I'll show you where the drinks machine is,' Louisa said, slipping her arm through Gary's and guiding him out of Resus.

'I was coming down the hill. I wasn't speeding. I could see the other car approaching the junction, but he wasn't even indicating! And then he just pulled out in front of me. It was as if it all happened in slow motion. I could see we were going to crash, and I couldn't do anything to stop it. I slammed on the brakes, but it wasn't enough.' Gary shivered. 'We hit him and the car spun round. Rhi's side of the car was squashed against another one. And...' He covered his face with his hands. 'She *can't* die. We celebrated our twenty-fifth wedding anniversary last week. I can't... Not without her...'

Louisa got him a cup of hot, sweet tea from the vending machine—even if he didn't normally take sugar or drink tea, she knew it would help—and settled him in a chair. 'Gary, it wasn't your fault, and the staff here are really good,' she told him gently. 'We're going to do our very, very best. Now I have to go back and help Dominic treat Rhiannon, but I'll be back as soon as I can with any news.' She squeezed his shoulder. 'I know waiting's hard but hang on in there, love.'

'You're so kind. Thank you. And please—' Gary's face was stricken '—please, don't let my wife die.'

By the time Louisa got back into Resus, the medication had taken effect, and Dominic started to intubate their patient. She'd seen it done before, but never with this calm, confident efficiency—and he was amazingly quick.

Dominic Hurst was a superb doctor, she thought.

And she liked the way he'd made time to talk to his patient and her husband, clearly aware of how important communication was as a way of bringing down stress levels.

He blew up the cuff on the tube and turned to the other nurse. 'Sally, are they ready for us in Radiology?'

'Yes.'

'Great. Thanks for that. Can you bleep the orthopods, please, and let them know we have a patient with suspected flail chest? I want to have a look at the X-rays, so I'm going down to Radiology with Rhiannon.'

'Do you want me to give ITU a call, to put them on standby?' Louisa asked quietly, so Rhiannon couldn't hear her and start to worry. In her experience, it was best to involve the intensive care unit as early as possible, because cases of pulmonary contusions often led to ARDS—adult respiratory distress syndrome. And if there were multiple broken ribs, she'd need careful monitoring.

'Yes, please. And could you tell Gary I'm taking her to X-Ray? Not because he should worry himself sick, but because it means I can see the X-rays straight off and it'll save us some time. Tell him I'll come and talk to him as soon as we know more.' He smiled at her. 'Thank you, Sally. You've done a really good job. You, too, Louisa. Even though this is the first time we've worked together, it's felt as if we've been on the same team for years. Your old department must really be missing you.'

The compliment made her feel warm all over—especially as she hadn't expected it from him. And it was good to work with a doctor who appreciated the nursing staff rather than taking them for granted, especially one who bothered to give a student praise where it was due. She smiled back at him. 'Thanks.'

While Dominic went off to X-Ray with Rhiannon, Louisa contacted the intensive care unit to put them in the picture, then went in search of Gary to let him know what was happening.

'Is she going to be all right?' he asked. 'I'll never forgive myself if anything happens to her. And that stupid guy who tried to get into a gap that wasn't there, just to save a few seconds...' He was shaking, clearly near tears.

Louisa put her arm round him. 'I know, love. You said yourself there was nothing you could do, so don't blame yourself. The police will deal with the other driver.' Who'd also walked away without a scratch, according to Ronnie, but that wasn't something Louisa intended to share. 'We'll know a lot more when the X-rays are back, and Dominic will talk you through what Rhiannon's injuries are and how we're going to treat her. But for now we're keeping her comfortable. Try not to worry—and, yes, I know that's a lot easier said than done.' She gave him a sympathetic smile. 'Is there anyone we can call for you?'

'I... No.' He shook his head. 'I'd better call our daughter myself. She'll be devastated.' He dragged in a breath. 'I can't use a mobile phone here, can I?'

'In the corridors, you can,' she reassured him. 'The phone won't interfere with equipment there.' It wasn't the only reason the hospital preferred not to have people chatting on mobile phones—loud conversations disturbed other patients, and some ringtones sounded eerily like alarms on equipment. The blanket ban on mobile phones throughout the hospital had been relaxed, except for critical-care areas such as the emergency department, the coronary care unit and the special care baby unit, where equipment could be affected by electromagnetic interference.

'Thank you.'

When Dominic came back from Resus, he looked serious but calm. 'Gary, I've seen the scans and I'm sending Rhiannon up to Theatre where the surgeons can help her. She's got four ribs broken in two places, pulmonary contusions—that's a bruise on the lung and you often get that with broken ribs—and what looks to me like a cut to her liver.'

'So the surgeons can fix her ribs?'

'They might decide to let them heal without fixing them,' Dominic said. 'But the contusions are going to make it a bit hard for Rhiannon to breathe, so she'll be in Intensive Care afterwards until they heal—they can keep a close eye on her and make sure she's comfortable.'

'You mean she's going to be ventilated?' Gary's eyes widened. 'Oh, my God.'

'It looks and sounds a lot scarier than it is. It's going to be the best treatment for her,' Dominic reassured him. 'We're taking her up to Theatre now, and if you'd like to you can come with us, as far as the doors. There's a waiting area there, and one of the surgeons will come out and talk you through what's happening. The staff at the ICU—the intensive care unit—are lovely, and they'll be happy to answer any questions you have.'

They headed up to Theatre, Gary holding his wife's hand all the way.

'I'm so sorry, Rhi. I love you,' he said, clearly trying to hold back tears.

'They'll take care of her,' Louisa said gently,

putting her arm round his shoulders as Rhiannon was wheeled through the doors to Theatre. 'Is your daughter coming?'

'She's on her way.' He bit his lip. 'And I'm keeping you from your work.'

'That's OK.' If necessary, she'd work through her lunch hour to make sure that the targets were hit. People came before admin, in her book, and always would; and if she had to explain herself to the bean-counters, so be it. Nursing was about people, not numbers. 'I'll wait until she gets here.'

When Gary and Rhiannon's daughter arrived, Louisa explained what had happened and what would happen next, made sure they both had a hot drink, then headed back down to the emergency department. She was back in Minors as nurse practitioner for the rest of her shift, and her lunch break consisted of two minutes to bolt a sandwich so that she could catch up with the delay in treating her patients. When it was clear that she was still running late, she made a quick call to her mother to ask if she could pick up Ty from after-school club, and continued working steadily through her list. After she'd seen her last patient, she headed for Resus, hoping that Dominic would be there and that he knew how Rhiannon was.

'Shouldn't you have been off duty half an hour ago?' he asked.

She shrugged. 'It happens. I just wondered if you'd heard anything from the ICU about Rhiannon?'

'Yes, I have.' He smiled at her.

Without that reserve, he was truly stunning; her heart felt as if it had just done a somersault. Which was crazy, because she wasn't looking to feel this way about anyone. She didn't need a relationship to complicate her life.

'Do you have time for a quick coffee while I fill you in?' he asked. 'I could do with a Danish pastry.'

That sounded dangerously close to a date. Even though Essie had said he was wrapped up in his work rather than relationships, she didn't want Dominic to get the wrong idea. Especially as she was aware of how attractive she found him. 'Sorry, I can't. I need to pick up my son. Mum met him for me, but he hates it when I'm late.'

'Can I give you a lift home and tell you on the way?' he asked.

'Thanks for the offer, but my car's in the staff car park.'

'Then how about I walk you to your car while I tell you about Rhiannon?'

She nodded. 'That'd be good. Thanks. I'll just get my bag from my locker.' She hurried off to collect her things. 'So what did they say?' she asked when she returned and Dominic walked with her to the car park.

'Rhiannon's pulled through—the surgeons fixed the liver damage and stopped the bleeding. She's got an epidural in for pain relief, and she's going to be observed in ICU for a while to make sure she doesn't develop pneumonia.'

'Did they wire her ribs?'

'They decided against surgical correction of her flail chest, because the ventilator will make sure her lungs are working properly and aren't compromised by her ribs,' he said. 'As soon as the contusions are resolved, provided there aren't any secondary complications, she can come off ventilation. I popped in to see how she was doing and have a chat with Gary. They've warned him that her breathing is going to get slightly worse before it gets better—on the same principle that a bruise always hurts more the day after—but now he knows she's got a good chance, he's relaxed a bit.'

'His daughter's nice,' Louisa said. 'She'll support them both through it.'

He looked at her and raised an eyebrow. 'You didn't have a lunch break either, did you?'

'Yes, I did,' she protested.

He gave her a wry smile. 'Long enough to scoff a chocolate bar, hmm?'

'A chicken wrap, actually. I don't like chocolate.'

He looked surprised. 'You must be the first medic I've ever met who doesn't think it's a food group. And didn't you bring in a tin of chocolate biscuits the other day?'

'Yes—because most people like them.'

'So you're more of a savoury person?' he asked.

'I love cheese scones,' she said. 'And hot buttered toast with Marmite.'

'That's utterly revolting,' he said, pulling a face. 'So where did you work before here?'

'The London Victoria. It's where I did my training.'

'It's got a good reputation. What made you come to the George IV?' he asked.

'The nurse practitioner post was vacant—plus my parents wanted to retire to the coast. I know London's only an hour and a half from Brighton, but Ty adores his grandparents and I wanted to be able to stay close to them.'

'So your husband was able to move his job, too, or is he commuting to London?'

'Ex.' She took a deep breath. 'And Ty's father isn't part of our lives. At all.'

He grimaced. 'Sorry. That was nosey of me, and I didn't mean to stomp on a sore spot.'

She shrugged. 'It's OK. I guess the only way you get to know a new colleague is to ask questions.'

'True.' Dominic looked wary. 'And I owe you an apology from the other day. I'm not normally that rude.'

'I didn't think anything of it.'

'Yes, you did—otherwise you wouldn't have been so sharp with me in Resus this morning.'

She bit her lip. She had been a bit sharp with him. 'I'm sorry I was—well, snotty with you.'

'I understand why. Anyway, there isn't room for egos in our business. The patients should always come first.'

Her sentiments exactly. 'I think we started off on the wrong foot.'

'Agreed, and I'm sorry, too. For the sake of a decent working relationship, can we start again?'

She was all in favour of decent working relationships. 'Louisa Austin, nurse practitioner. Pleased to meet you.' She stretched out her hand.

He shook it; again, it felt as if electricity bubbled through her veins, but she ignored the sensation. This was *work*.

'Dominic Hurst, senior ED reg. Pleased to meet you, too, Louisa.' He paused. 'You said you were looking for riding lessons for your son. I assume Essie told you I have a horse? My best friend owns the stables where I keep him. I could have a word with him and his wife.'

'Thanks, but there's no point. He won't have a space.'

He frowned. 'How do you mean?'

'I've already tried ringing round some of the local riding schools and…well, their lists are all full.'

He looked surprised. 'We're in a recession and riding lessons are one of the first things that tend to get cut, because they're not cheap—instead of going twice a week, people go riding maybe once a fortnight instead.'

Just as she'd thought. Especially when the waiting lists had suddenly become two years long. Might as well get it over with now. 'The thing is, my son has Asperger's.'

He shrugged. 'And?'

'The riding schools I rang changed their minds about having places when I explained.'

'More fool them. Riding's really good for Asperger's kids. Being with horses helps them learn to understand non-verbal body language.'

Now that she really hadn't expected. She was more used to people being uncomfortable around Ty. Understanding like this was rare. 'Did you used to work in paediatrics, or do you know someone with Asperger's?'

'I know someone,' he said, 'and horses have made a huge difference to him. But I can remember his parents used to worry themselves sick about him, because he never seemed to make friends at school. I guess you probably do the same with your son.'

'All the time,' she admitted, caught off guard.

'Don't,' he said softly. 'He'll be fine. He might only have one or two really close friends, but they'll be good ones—and that's better than having hundreds of acquaintances you can't really rely on when life gets tough. And if he finds a job that matches the things he's interested in and doesn't involve having to deal with people whose minds aren't quite as quick as his, he'll shine.'

She blinked back the sudden rush of tears. How ridiculous. Just because someone understood, instead of making unfair judgements.

'Look, I'm going straight to the stables from here. I'll talk to Ric and Bea tonight, and then maybe you can come and have a look round at the weekend, meet the team, and see if Tyler likes the place.'

'That's very kind of you. Are you sure?'

'They do a lot of work with the RDA—Riding for the Disabled Association,' Dominic said.

Louisa's chin came up. 'Tyler isn't disabled. He just happens to have a diagnosis of Asperger's Syndrome.'

Dominic sucked in a breath. 'Sorry, I didn't mean it to sound like that. What I mean is, Ric and Bea believe in inclusion and it doesn't matter who you are or what your particular challenges are—if you love horses and want to ride, then you should have the chance to do it. Ric's parents owned the riding school before they retired and Ric took over, and they were the ones who started the RDA work at the stables. So Tyler won't be made to feel that he's a special case or anything—he'll be treated just like everyone else.'

Again, the tears threatened. How long had it been since people outside her own family and her best friend had treated her precious son just like anybody else? 'Thank you.'

'You're welcome.'

'He's eight,' she warned, 'and he's only ever ridden a horse at one of the farm park type places. He's a complete novice.'

'Bea's a brilliant teacher. She's great with kids and she's really patient with novices. I'll talk it over with her tonight. See you tomorrow,' he said as they reached her car.

'See you tomorrow. And, Dominic?' She gave him a heartfelt smile. 'Thank you.'

CHAPTER THREE

'WHAT happened?' Louisa asked.

Mrs Livesey was ashen with worry, cradling her two-year-old son. 'It's all my fault. The children were playing nicely and I was chatting to my friend over coffee—I should've been watching them more closely. Julian slipped and cut his head open on the piano. I put a cold wet cloth on it to try and stop the bleeding, but it wouldn't stop, so I brought him here.'

'That was the best thing to do,' Louisa reassured her. 'Scalp wounds always bleed a lot, so they often look worse than they are. Has Julian been sick at all, or had any kind of fit?'

'No.'

'Did he black out, or has he been drowsy since?'

Mrs Livesey shook her head.

'That's good,' Louisa said. She assessed the little boy's limb movements, then shone a light into his eyes; she was relieved to see that his pupils were equal and reactive. She took his pulse and temperature—both of which were in the normal range—and gently examined the cut on his head. 'It's clean—you did brilliantly there,' she told Mrs Livesey, 'but it's a little bit too deep just to glue it.'

'Glue it?'

'You'd be amazed at what we can do nowadays,' Louisa said with a smile. 'I'm going to put a couple of stitches in there, because it will heal better with less scarring.' She stroked Julian's hair. 'I'm going to put some magic cream on your head now to stop it hurting. But to make the magic work even better, we're going to have to sing a song. Do you know "Twinkle Twinkle Little Star"?'

'Yes,' the little boy said. 'Tinkle tinkle.'

'And can you waggle your fingers like starlight?' She demonstrated, and he copied her.

'Brilliant,' she said. 'And we'll get Mummy to sing, too, shall we?' From experience, Louisa knew that often parents needed as much distraction as toddlers. And Julian was giving a normal two-year-old's verbal response, which made Louisa fairly sure that the worst of his injuries was the cut.

Once the cream had numbed his skin, she got Mrs Livesey and Julian to sing with her, and gently but swiftly made sure the wound was perfectly clean, then sutured the cut.

'That was brilliant singing, sweetheart,' she told the little boy. She glanced up at Mrs Livesey. 'They're dissolvable stitches, so you don't have to worry about bringing him back to have them taken out. You need to keep an eye on him over the next couple of days; if he starts being sick, has a fit or is drowsy or just a bit unwell and you feel something's not right, come straight back. A mother's instinct is usually pretty sound and you know your child best.' She smiled. 'It's a lot to take in, so I'll give you a leaflet about head injuries.'

'And I have to keep him awake, right?'

'No, it's perfectly safe to let Julian go to sleep—he's

going to be tired from crying and the stress of hurting himself. If you're worried, try waking him after about an hour. I can tell you now, he'll be pretty grumpy about it, but that's normal. If you can't wake him easily, that's when you need to bring him back.'

She answered a few more questions and, once Mrs Livesey was reassured, Louisa gave Julian a shiny 'bravery' sticker and called in her next patient.

When she walked into the staff kitchen for a swift coffee break, Dominic was there.

'Good timing. The kettle's hot.' He smiled at her. 'Want a coffee?'

That smile was lethal, Louisa thought. Those dimples…no wonder her heart felt as if it had just done another of those odd little flips. But Dominic was her colleague. There wasn't room in her life for him to be anything more than that. And, even if there was, she'd got it so badly wrong last time that she was wary of repeating her mistake. *Handsome is as handsome does.*

She strove to sound normal. 'Thanks, that'd be wonderful. Milk, no sugar, please.'

'Same as me.' He paused. 'How's the little one you were giving stitches to?'

'He's fine.' She looked at him in surprise. 'How do you know about that?'

'I was passing through Minors earlier, and I heard you singing a magic song.'

She felt herself colour. 'Um.'

'Hey, don't be embarrassed. I'm all in favour of whatever it takes to make a child feel less frightened, and singing's great. I learned three magic tricks when I was a student, precisely so I could make a child concentrate on something other than the reason they came in to see me.'

'Magic tricks?'

He handed her a mug of coffee. 'What's this behind your ear?' He touched her ear briefly; it was the lightest possible contact but it made Louisa very, very aware of him. When he brought his hand away again, he was flourishing a coin between his thumb and index finger—which he then proceeded to flip between his fingers, one by one.

'That's very impressive.'

'It's called a Vegas coin roll,' he told her.

'That's going to beat the offer of a sticker every single time—especially for the boys,' she said with a smile.

'It doesn't take long to learn. I'll teach you some time, if you like,' he said. 'Actually, I was hoping to catch you today. Ric says they have a space, so come along on Saturday for a chat. Any time you like between nine and four—he or Bea will be around.' He fished in his pocket and brought out a folded piece of paper. 'This is their phone number, their address and directions to the stables from the centre of Brighton.'

She really hadn't expected that, and her breath caught. An unexpected kindness. 'Thank you. It'll mean the world to Ty. He's been obsessed with horses for years—but, living in London, we didn't really get to see horses unless we went out at the weekend to one of the farm park places.'

'And you thought that maybe he'd grow out of the obsession, get interested in something else?'

She nodded. 'Our paediatrician said these obsessions are very common with Asperger's children, and they tend to change as the children grow up. But he still really, really loves horses.'

'I'm with him, there. I met my horse when he was an hour old, and I fell in love with him on the spot.'

She could identify with that. The moment she'd first held Tyler, she'd felt a rush of love like nothing she'd ever experienced before—a deep, deep sense of wonder mingled with protectiveness and sheer joy. She knew that some mothers found it took time to bond with their child, but for her it had been instant and overwhelming—and the love had grown even deeper over the years. 'I'd better get back to my patients,' she said. 'And thank you again. I really appreciate it.'

On Saturday morning, Tyler was almost beside himself with excitement. She drove him to the stables, and Bea showed them around.

'Did Dominic mention about…?' Louisa asked quietly when they were in the tack room and Tyler was trying on hard hats.

Bea smiled. 'Yes. I assume he told you about Andy?' At Louisa's blank look, she continued, 'Ric's younger brother. He has Asperger's. Actually, he's in charge of stable management—Ric and I run the classes,' she explained. 'So you don't need to worry. We're aware of the challenges, but as far as I'm concerned if a child loves horses and wants to ride, my job is to help the child do just that. We'll work around the challenges together, because we're all on the same team.'

Louisa had to swallow hard.

Bea patted her on the shoulder. 'Riding's going to be great for him.'

'Will he be in a class?'

'I prefer one to one with beginners, at least for the first couple of months, until they're a bit more confident. But if he wants to come along to a class as well, once we've got him started, that's fine.'

'Dominic said you do RDA work.'

Bea nodded. 'We have half a dozen ponies that we use for RDA sessions—they're very calm and gentle. We run one class each day especially for RDA students. And it's not just about physical therapy, though of course riding's great for improving muscle tone and posture and helping to develop fine and gross motor skills. It's about life skills, too—being with the horses helps both children and adults with communication skills, taking responsibility and being part of a team. And connecting with the animals brings in a new element to their lives.' She paused. 'Really, Louisa, you don't need to worry. We'll take very good care of him. You can come and watch, bring someone with you, or even just sit in the car and read while he's having a lesson. Whatever makes you comfortable.'

'I'd like to watch. Not because I don't trust you,' Louisa hastened to add.

'But because he's your baby and you don't want to miss a thing.' Bea smiled. 'The first time they ride without being on a leading rein, it's like watching them take their first steps. It always makes me tear up as much as their mums.'

And then Louisa realised that Bea would take as good care of Tyler as she would herself; as the tension in her shoulders eased, she realised how worried she'd been.

'He'll be *fine*,' Bea said softly.

Tyler appeared before them, wearing a hard hat. 'It fits, Mum.' He beamed at her.

'Come on. I've got half an hour before my next lesson. Let's get Polo saddled up and you can have a walk round the paddock,' Bea said.

Tyler's eyes went wide. 'Really?'

'Really. Polo's going to be your special horse for a while, so let's get you introduced.'

Watching her son being led round the paddock put a real lump in Louisa's throat. And Tyler was glowing afterwards. 'I did it, Mum. I'm going to be a knight. Just like the man in the photograph.'

'The man in the photograph?' Louisa was mystified.

Bea looked at her. 'Ah. You didn't know.'

'Know what?'

Bea blew out a breath. 'I feel as if I'm breaking a confidence here. But I guess you need to see it.' She took Louisa and Tyler back to the tack room and showed Louisa the photograph on the wall in silence. A man on a white horse, wearing black armour and carrying a lance.

When Louisa peered more closely at it, she realised that the helmet's visor was up and she could see the rider's face. Someone she recognised. 'Dominic?'

'He still has Pegasus, but he doesn't joust any more,' Bea said.

Dominic was a knight—or, at least, he had been one. But, given that he'd been so open about the fact that he had a horse, and that he'd helped her arrange riding lessons for Tyler, why on earth hadn't he said anything to her when she'd mentioned how much her son wanted to be a knight? 'Why did he give up jousting?' she asked.

'I think it'd be better if he told you,' Bea said. 'It's not my place.'

'Was he hurt?' But she could see the mingled concern and awkwardness on Bea's face. 'Sorry, I shouldn't have asked that. It's not fair to you. Forget I said anything.'

'That's what I want to be. A knight,' Tyler told her.

'A knight on a white charger, hmm?' Louisa asked.

'The horse isn't white, he's grey,' Tyler corrected.

'He looks white to me,' Louisa said.

'White horses are *always* called grey, Mum,' Tyler informed her, rolling his eyes.

She ignored his impatience. In Tyler's mind, if he knew something, it followed that the whole world must know it, too. And in the same painstaking amount of detail.

'He's a Percheron. They come from Normandy in France,' Tyler explained, 'from a place called Le Perche. It's thought that Percherons are descended from destriers, but they're bigger and heavier than the medieval warhorses. Destriers were trained so you didn't have to use the reins, because your hands would be full carrying your sword and your shield.'

'Absolutely right,' Dominic said. 'Hello, Louisa.'

Louisa jumped. 'I didn't hear you come in.'

'Sorry. I didn't mean to startle you.' He looked at Tyler. 'And you must be Tyler. How was your first riding lesson?'

'Brilliant, thank you,' Tyler said politely. He peered at Dominic. 'And you're the knight in the picture, aren't you? Bea says your horse is called Pegasus. That's a cool name. How big is he?'

'Seventeen hands.'

'And how much does he weigh?'

'Nearly nine hundred kilograms.'

Tyler looked serious. 'That's quite a lot.'

'It feels like even more than that if he stands on your foot,' Dominic said with a wry smile.

'Does he live here?'

'Yes.' Dominic paused. 'You can come and see him, if you like—if that's all right with your mum.'

'Please, Mum? Can I?' Tyler's gaze was full of entreaty.

'He's very gentle,' Dominic reassured Louisa.

And *huge*, she thought, when Dominic took them over to the stables.

Tyler duly admired the horse, asking if he was allowed to stroke him and then, at Dominic's agreement, stroking the horse's nose. 'He's beautiful.'

'He certainly is,' Dominic agreed.

'Are you jousting this weekend?'

'No.'

His voice was even, but Louisa noticed the shadows in his eyes. Time to head off her son's line of conversation. 'Ty, we ought to—' she began, but Tyler spoke over her.

'But there's that picture of you. You're a knight. You had a lance and you were wearing armour, so you must be a jouster.'

'Not any more.'

'Why not?'

'Ty, you can't ask questions like that,' Louisa said.

'Why not?'

'It's rude.'

'But I didn't say a swear.'

How was she going to explain this? 'Ty, let's talk about this later, OK?'

'But I *wasn't* rude,' Tyler said, looking puzzled.

Dominic raked a hand through his hair. 'It's a fair

question. I don't joust any more because there was an accident and someone got hurt.'

He frowned. 'My mum's a nurse. She makes people better. Why didn't your friend go to see a nurse or a doctor?'

Dominic took a deep breath. 'It doesn't always work that way. Sometimes even a nurse or doctor can't fix things.'

'Oh.' Tyler digested the information. 'Do you miss jousting?'

'Ty, let's talk about something else,' Louisa pleaded. 'I dunno—what the horse eats, what kind of saddle he has?'

But her son refused to budge. 'If I'd been a knight and I didn't do it any more, I think I'd miss jousting,' Tyler said. 'I want to be a knight.'

'It takes a lot of practice and hard work,' Dominic warned.

'I don't mind. I'm going to practise holding the reins at home. Bea showed me how. All I need is a ribbon.'

'So let's go and buy the ribbon now,' Louisa said, seeing an opening. She caught Dominic's eye and mouthed, 'Sorry.'

He said nothing, and she stifled a sigh. So much for thinking he understood about Asperger's and the way it gave a child tunnel vision. Then again, Ty had obviously trampled on a really sore spot. He hadn't meant to: he just hadn't been able to pick up the visual clues that Dominic was uncomfortable and she hadn't been able to head Tyler in another direction.

'Time to say goodbye, Ty,' she said.

'Goodbye, and thank you for showing me your horse,' Tyler said politely.

* * *

Dominic leaned back against the stable door and watched them both walk over the yard. Hell. He hadn't been prepared for that one.

Do you miss jousting?

Yes, he missed it. Missed it like crazy. Holding the lance in his right hand and the reins in his left, then focusing on the tilt, urging Pegasus to a quick canter and then closing in, focusing on where he was going to land his lance. Speed, precision and skill: the kind of thrill that reminded him he was still alive.

Except he'd been a little too precise, the last time he'd jousted. Too fast. And he'd unhorsed his opponent. Oliver had fallen awkwardly, and the armour hadn't been enough to protect his back: he'd ended up with an incomplete spinal injury. An injury that had left him stuck in a wheelchair and ruined his career—because, as a surgeon, you needed strength as well as delicacy. And you also needed to be able to move round your patient. Stand up. Lean over. Oliver couldn't do that any more.

Hell, hell, hell. He'd taken so much away from his brother. His career, his hobbies, his mobility, his *joie de vivre*—Oliver was in too much pain, most of the time, to be full of laughter the way he'd used to be.

So giving up jousting had been the least Dominic could do. To make absolutely sure he never made a mistake like that again and someone else ended up badly hurt.

Pegasus whickered and shoved his head against Dominic's.

'Yeah. I know you miss it, too.' He made a fuss of his horse. 'But we just do steady hacking nowadays, OK? It's safer.'

* * *

On Monday, Louisa sought out Dominic at lunchtime. 'I've got something for you.'

'For me?' He looked at her in surprise.

She went over to her locker, took out a plastic wallet and handed it to him.

He looked at it; it was a sketch of a horse. And not just any horse. One he recognised. 'That's Pegasus.'

'Ty drew him for you yesterday. He just wanted to say thank you. For helping me sort out the lessons and for letting him make a fuss of your horse.'

'No worries.' He stared at the picture. 'Nobody's ever drawn my horse for me before. And he did this from memory, from seeing Pegasus just once?' At Louisa's nod, he blew out a breath. 'Wow. He's seriously good at this.'

'I'll tell him you liked it, shall I?' She looked pleased, too; clearly she was more used to people being put off by her son's directness.

'You can tell him I'm going to frame it,' Dominic said. 'And tell him thank you.'

'I'm sorry about the way he grilled you. He didn't mean to trample on a sore spot. He doesn't pick up—'

'Visual cues, and he has tunnel vision,' Dominic finished. 'I know. I'm used to Andy.' Andy had said the same thing, too: Why let the accident stop you jousting? He'd gone further, saying that Dominic giving up jousting wouldn't fix Oliver's back, so he was being completely self-indulgent and wallowing in it.

Maybe Andy and Tyler were right.

But Dominic still couldn't see past the guilt. Oliver would never joust again, or be a surgeon again. And that knowledge was hard enough to live with; harder still was the knowledge that his brother was in constant pain. Oliver had forgiven him, but Dominic still couldn't forgive himself.

'Are you all right?' Louisa asked, looking concerned.

'Old ghosts.' He shook himself. 'Ignore me. I'm fine.'

And that was the biggest fib of all.

Dominic had gone back into his shell, Louisa thought over the next couple of days. He was always perfectly polite and professional if she was working with him in Resus, but she was aware of his reserve. She tried to put it out of her head; they were colleagues, so it shouldn't matter. As long as the patients were treated properly, it shouldn't matter that he was reserved with her.

And then, on Wednesday evening, her car refused to start after Tyler's riding lesson. 'Oh, great.'

'Why won't your car work, Mum?' Ty asked.

'I don't know, love.' She sighed. 'I'd better call the roadside rescue people.'

She'd been waiting for nearly a quarter of an hour when Bea came over. 'Are you all right?'

'My car won't start. I've called the roadside rescue people—hopefully they'll be here soon and they'll able to fix it.' And hopefully it wouldn't cost a fortune; the expenses of moving had eaten into her savings.

'Come and sit in the kitchen. It's getting chilly out here. I'll get you a coffee,' Bea said, shepherding them inside and switching on the kettle. 'Ty, would you prefer juice or water?'

'Apple juice, please.'

She rummaged in the fridge. 'Sorry, love. I've got orange or cranberry. Or milk.'

'Nothing, thank you.'

'Always so polite. You have beautiful manners, Ty,' she said with a smile.

Tyler was busy drawing a picture of Polo when the roadside rescue people arrived.

'He'll be fine in here with me,' Bea said, ruffling Tyler's hair. 'He knows where you are if he needs you—right, Ty?'

He smiled at her. 'Right.'

When the mechanic had hooked up the diagnostic computer, Dominic came over. In faded jeans, riding boots, a white shirt with the sleeves rolled up and no tie, he looked incredibly touchable. 'What's the problem?'

'Spark plugs,' the mechanic said. 'Two of them. The problem is, they'll need specialist equipment to get them out—they're not a standard size and I don't have the right equipment to sort it out here. The manufacturer changed them on this particular model,' he said, rolling his eyes. 'It's not like the old days, when spark plugs were the same on every car. If just one had gone, I could've disengaged it for you and you would've been safe to get home or to the garage, but with two gone it's not safe to do that, I'm afraid. If you ring the main dealer now, they'll still be there,' he suggested, 'and they'll book you in so I can put your car on the back of the tow truck, and all you have to do is drop your keys through the door in an envelope.'

'Would you be able to drop us home afterwards?' she asked.

'Sorry, love. It's not covered by your policy. I would've bent the rules for you, given that you've got a little one, but I've got another callout waiting,' he said.

'Fair enough. I can call a taxi.'

The dealer's service department was just about to

close, but they duly booked her in for the next morning and asked her to drop the keys through their door.

She was about to arrange for a taxi to meet them at the garage when Dominic laid a hand on his arm. 'Don't worry about calling a taxi. I'll follow you to the garage and drop you and Ty home.'

'I can't impose on you like that.'

He shrugged. 'From what Tyler tells me, you don't live that far from me. And I'm finished here for this evening anyway.'

'Actually, I can drop the keys through the letterbox for you at the dealer's,' the mechanic added, 'if that saves a bit of time.'

'And it means you'll get home quicker—Tyler's routine won't be thrown out so much,' Dominic said.

That was the clincher. Ty. Although he coped much better with change nowadays than he had as a small child, it would still throw him. Routine was really, really important to him, and Louisa tried hard to stick to it. 'Thank you. Both of you. That's really kind.'

Louisa clearly wasn't used to leaning on anyone, Dominic thought, so she must've been a single parent for quite a while now. And she'd been adamant about Ty's father not being part of his life. Whatever had happened between them, it had obviously hurt her badly. Not that he could ask. It would be way too tactless.

When he pulled up outside the little terraced house they were renting, Louisa said, 'Would you like to come in and stay for dinner? It's nothing special—just pasta, garlic bread and salad—but you'd be very welcome.'

Tempting. So very, very tempting. He was about to say no when Tyler added, 'If you don't, then Mum will have to buy you flowers to say thank you for helping, and boys don't really like flowers so she'll fuss about it.'

He couldn't help laughing. 'OK, then, thanks. I have to admit, it'll be nice to have home-cooked food for a change.'

'Don't you cook?' Tyler asked.

'Not unless it comes in a packet with instructions for microwaving,' he admitted.

'Tut, and you a doctor,' Louisa teased.

'Can I show you my horse?' Tyler asked, the second Louisa had unlocked the front door. 'I got a commendation for it in Art today at school.'

'Well done.' Louisa gave him a hug and a kiss.

They both admired the drawing.

'Can I show you my other horses?' Tyler asked.

'Sorry,' Louisa mouthed.

'I'd love to see them,' Dominic said, meaning it.

Tyler showed him the drawings, one by one. Dominic was blown away by the detail, both of the horses and of the knights. 'You've got the armour exactly right, too.'

'It's called a harness,' Tyler said, 'but I guess you know that, because you have one.'

'Ye-es.' Not that he'd used it in two years. He hadn't even been able to bring himself to polish it. It was locked away in a trunk.

'Can I come to your house and see it some time?'

Dominic froze. And, just at that moment, Louisa walked into the living room. She'd clearly overheard the last bit because she frowned. 'Tyler, it's rude to invite yourself. And anyway, dinner's ready. Apple juice for everyone?'

Tyler led him into the dining room, which was small but neat. Just like the one in the living room, the mantelpiece was crowded with photographs: Louisa and Tyler, an older man and woman who he assumed were her parents, and a man who looked enough like her that he had to be her brother. Clearly she was close to her family. He'd been close to his, too; but his guilt had driven him away.

'I'd love a suit of armour,' Tyler said as he sat down. 'Grandad and me found a shop that sells suits of armour, when Mum and Nanna went to do girly stuff. Well, *bits* of armour,' he amended. 'I really wanted a cuirass, but it was too big for me and it was a bit expensive. Then we sat on the beach and had chips. And I found a pebble that looks like a horse's head. I'll show you.'

He rushed up to his room before Louisa could stop him.

She grimaced. 'Sorry. He's a bit impulsive.'

'I think most eight-year-old boys are,' he said. 'I know Oliver and I used to drive our mum crazy. He's a nice kid. And he's brilliant at drawing.'

Tyler rushed back in with the pebble, and Dominic duly admired it.

Dinner was simple but good; though it felt odd, being almost like part of a family.

'How was your day, Dominic?' Tyler asked.

The question really surprised him; but then he realised this was probably part of the evening routine; obviously Louisa was gently training her son in the art of social niceties to make his life easier as he grew older, just as Andy's parents had done with him.

'It was good, thanks,' he said. 'I patched up someone who fell off his bike and helped someone else whose heart stopped working properly.'

'What was the best bit?' Tyler asked, looking serious.

Dominic thought about it. 'Going to the stables. How about you?'

'My day was good. I got a commendation in Art, but the stables was the best bit. I like the smell of horses. And Polo's hair is all soft, except his mane, and that's like Mum's hair when we've gone swimming and it dries all frizzy at the ends.'

Dominic couldn't help smiling. 'Does yours go frizzy?'

'No, because my hair's short.' Tyler looked at him and frowned. 'But yours isn't, so yours must go frizzy, too.'

'I haven't been swimming for a long time.'

'You could come with us. We go on Thursday nights. And then we have fish and chips at Nanna and Grandad's. You could come with us tomorrow, if you like.'

'Sweetheart, Dominic's probably busy,' Louisa cut in.

'Sorry, your mum's right,' Dominic said. 'But maybe another time.' And, to his surprise, he realised that he meant it. It wasn't just politeness. He really would like to go swimming with them, then eat fish and chips out of the wrapper.

And the realisation that he wanted to get involved was even scarier. He should be wanting to run a mile: Louisa wasn't the kind of woman who wanted just a fling, and she came as a package. She was nothing like the women he used to date, who tended to be tall, leggy, blonde and exquisitely dressed. And yet she drew him far more than any of those women had. He wasn't sure what it was: her warmth; her selflessness; the way she treated everyone with kindness and courtesy? All he knew was that he wanted to get to know her better.

When they'd finished their meal, Louisa shooed Tyler upstairs for a bath.

'And I ought to go,' Dominic said. 'Can I help with the washing up first?'

'No, it's fine. It won't take me two minutes.'

'If you're sure.' He called up the stairs, 'See you at the stables, Ty.'

'Bye,' the little boy called back.

'Thank you,' he said as Louisa walked with him to the front door. 'I've enjoyed this evening.' He bent to kiss her cheek, but he misjudged it and somehow ended up kissing her on the mouth. It was the briefest, briefest touch, but it made his mouth tingle.

He pulled back sharply. 'I'd better go. See you tomorrow at work.'

'See you tomorrow,' she echoed.

When Louisa had closed the door behind him, she stood there for a while, just touching her mouth. It was the first time she'd been kissed by a man other than her father, son or brother for a long, long time; and the first time in years that she'd felt such a zing of attraction.

She liked Dominic. A lot. She liked the way he worked, the way he cared for his patients, the way he treated all his colleagues with respect, no matter how junior they were. The way he noticed if a student was struggling and would spend time afterwards explaining what he'd done and why—and she'd just bet he did exactly the same thing at the stables. He was patient with Ty without being patronising, and took Ty's quirks in his stride.

Not to mention the fact that he was spine-tinglingly gorgeous, too.

It would be very, very easy to fall for Dominic Hurst. But she had Tyler to think about. He was still young, and he needed more consideration than the average child; he found talking about emotions difficult, and was much happier with facts and figures.

So she'd better be sensible and keep things strictly professional between herself and Dominic. Anything more would be risking heartache—and not just for herself. This wasn't going to happen.

CHAPTER FOUR

DOMINIC had visions of Louisa all the way home, with her hair loose spreading over the water like a mermaid's; he'd just bet that she was a graceful swimmer. And he was cross with himself for not being able to get her out of his head. This was crazy. He didn't have room for a relationship in his life. He'd made sure of that, filling his time with work and his horse. When he wasn't at the hospital, he was at the stables. He went on team nights out with his colleagues, because he knew it was good for staff morale and helped to build solid working relationships; but he didn't do relationships. Before Oliver's accident, he'd never met anyone who'd tempted him to settle down—he'd been happy to keep his relationships light and just for fun. After the accident, he'd avoided personal relationships, not wanting to let anyone else down the way he'd let his family down.

Louisa Austin was different.

What was it about her that drew him so much? It wasn't just the way she was at work—kind, efficient and professional with patients and colleagues alike. And it wasn't just the way she was so selfless with her son. There was a calmness about her, a warmth, that made him want to stop driving himself so hard and just *be*.

He'd made a bad mistake, kissing her like that.

Admittedly, it hadn't been a passionate kiss. But it had been more than the friendly peck on the cheek he'd intended. And the softness, the sweetness of her mouth against his…it had made him want more. So much more.

'It's not going to happen. There are too many complications. We're just colleagues,' he told himself firmly.

But even so, he found himself seeking her out at lunchtime the next day. 'Can I steal some of your lunch break for a quick debriefing?' he asked.

'Sure.'

To his relief, she wasn't wary with him. So he might not have spoiled things between them completely.

'So which patient are we talking about?' she asked when they were sitting in a quiet corner of the hospital cafeteria.

'Um, not a patient exactly. I wanted to talk to you without half the ward as an audience—to apologise about last night.' He could feel his skin growing warm.

'It's OK. I know you didn't mean anything by it,' she said.

It had been accidental. But he couldn't take his eyes off her mouth. Which was crazy. He knew that neither of them was in the right place for a relationship. And he didn't do relationships, not since Oliver's accident. Nothing had changed.

But Louisa still drew him. He wanted to kiss her some more. Properly, this time.

He pulled himself together with difficulty. 'What did the garage say about your car?'

'They've got to order in a part. It should be done tomorrow.'

'I can give you a lift home tonight, if you like.' The words were out before he could stop them. But he could see on her face that she was going to say no.

'Thanks for the offer, but I can't make you go out of your way.'

This was where he should be relieved at the get-out, but his mouth was on a roll. 'It's not really out of my way. I have to go right past your place to get to the stables from here.'

'I need to pick up Ty from after-school club first.'

School was nearby, too. 'Not a problem.'

'Then thank you.' She looked relieved. 'I was going to ask Mum to bail me out, but I hate having to rely on my parents—it's not fair to them, asking them to help.'

'I'm sure they don't mind. And you seem pretty independent to me.'

'I try to be.'

He noticed that she turned the conversation away from herself after that; she was as cagey as he was.

But for some crazy reason he found himself smiling all afternoon.

When they met Tyler at school, the little boy seemed delighted to see him. 'Does this mean you're coming swimming with us tonight?' he asked.

'Sorry, I don't have my swimming things with me. I'm just giving you and your mum a lift home because her car's still being fixed.'

'We're going to take the bus to the pool and then Nanna and Grandad are going to meet us there,' Louisa explained.

'But you will come swimming with us another time?' Tyler asked.

'We'll see,' Dominic said, glancing at Louisa; her expression was unreadable.

'That's grown-up speak for "No",' Tyler said with a sigh.

'No, it means I don't make promises unless I'm absolutely sure I can keep them,' Dominic said. 'If I'm treating a patient, I can't suddenly stop just because it's the end of my shift. And that means sometimes I'm late for things or I don't manage to get there at all. And I don't like disappointing people, so I don't make many promises.' He smiled at the little boy as he pulled up outside Louisa's house. 'See you later—enjoy your swim.'

'Are you going to the stables now?'

'I am indeed.'

'Give Pegasus a pat for me,' Tyler said, scrambling out of the car. 'And thank you for bringing us home.'

'Pleasure.' The little boy was so earnest and always so polite; he found it touching.

'And thanks for being so patient,' Louisa added quietly. 'I do try to limit his questions. But I can't keep telling him off in front of people—it's not his fault that he finds social cues so hard.'

'He's a nice kid,' Dominic said. 'And you're doing a great job.'

He was still thinking about her when he was grooming Pegasus. 'The problem is,' he told his horse, 'I really like her. I like everything about her. She's bright, she's warm and kind, she's good with patients and staff alike. And she's gorgeous. Well, hey, you've seen her. Her mouth's like a rosebud, her eyes are the clear grey of a winter sky, and—'

'You're waxing a bit poetic there,' Ric said.

Dominic blew out a breath. 'Thanks for nearly making

me stick the hoofpick into my hand! Why are you creeping about the stables?'

'I wasn't creeping. You didn't hear me because your attention was focused...' Ric coughed '...elsewhere.'

Dominic grimaced. 'Well, thanks.'

'You were describing Louisa, I take it? She's nice.'

'And she has commitments.'

'Tyler, you mean?' Ric was utterly relentless. 'You get on well with him. I've seen you. So the problem is...?'

'She's not the type to do a casual relationship.'

'So try having a proper relationship for a change,' Ric suggested.

Dominic shook his head. 'That's not what I want.'

'Isn't it?'

Dominic didn't want to think about it, let alone answer the question, so he continued grooming his horse.

'It's time you forgave yourself,' Ric said softly.

'What if I let her down?' The question slipped out before Dominic could stop it.

But Ric didn't seem fazed at all. Didn't back away. Didn't make a big deal out of it. 'What if you don't?' he countered. 'Look at what you do every day. Do you let your patients down? No. If anything, you push yourself harder to make sure you don't. Do you let anyone down at the stables? No.'

'I don't have room in my life for a relationship.'

'Of course you do. If she deserves you, she'll understand you and you'll work out some kind of compromise. Just like Bea and me.'

'It's complicated.'

'You'd be bored with something easy.'

Dominic sighed. 'Have you got an answer for everything?'

'Yup. And if I haven't, Bea has.' Ric paused. 'Look, I've seen you together. You like her and she likes you. And you've got work in common—she'll understand about your job not being nine to five. Her son loves horses, so she'll understand that side of you, too.'

'It's a bad idea to mix work and pleasure.'

Ric ignored him. 'What's the worst that can happen? She'll say no? Then you can still be friends.' He regarded his friend. 'But I think she'd be good for you. She might teach you to be kind to yourself.'

'As you've known me since we were both in nappies,' Dominic said, 'I'll forget you said that.'

'Because I've known you that long, I'm about the only person who could say it to you.' Ric gave him a searching look. 'Except maybe for someone who's known you a teensy bit longer. Who worries about you, too.'

Dominic frowned. 'Have you been talking about me?'

'If someone rings me when I'm up to my eyes in paperwork and in a filthy mood,' Ric said, 'then I'm not really responsible for my mouth running away with me.'

Dominic narrowed his eyes. 'Mum or Oliver?'

'Irrelevant.'

'Oliver,' Dominic guessed, 'otherwise I would've had a parental summons to Sunday lunch and general smothering. What did you say?'

Ric sighed. 'Just that I agreed with him. That it's time you let people back into your life.'

'Don't be ridiculous. Of course I let people into my life.'

'Let people close, then. Someone besides your

family, me and Bea. And Pegasus agrees with us—don't you, boy?'

The horse whickered.

Dominic grimaced. 'Traitor.'

'We're worried about you,' Ric said. 'Because we love you. So just ask her, will you?'

'Yeah, yeah. If I get time.'

But Dominic thought about it a lot, over the next few days. Days during which the more he saw of Louisa, the more attracted he was to her. Just as he'd admitted to Ric, she was warm, she was kind, she was great with people. And those serious grey eyes drew him. Particularly when they were lit with laughter.

And maybe his best friend had a point.

'It's the team night out on Friday. Ten-pin bowling. Are you coming?' Essie asked on the Monday morning.

'I'm not sure yet,' Louisa hedged.

'If you can't get a babysitter, Ty could come and watch a film with my lot. They're going to have pizza, so he's very welcome.'

'Thanks for the offer, but—' Louisa began.

Essie patted her arm. 'It would do you good to have an evening out, plus it's good for team-building. Even Dominic always turns up to team nights out.'

The idea of seeing Dominic outside work, and not just at the stables—oh, help. But Louisa duly rang her parents that evening. 'Mum, I hate to ask, but there's a team night out on Friday and Essie asked me to go—I wondered if you could come over and sit with Ty for a couple of hours, if you're not already doing—?'

'Going out with your workmates would do you good,' Gillian cut in firmly. 'Of course we'll have Ty—he can have a sleepover at ours, and you can pick him up before his riding lesson on Saturday.'

'Thanks, Mum. I owe you.'

'Nonsense.' Gillian sighed. 'You're too independent, you know.'

'I don't want you to feel I'm taking you for granted.'

Gillian tutted. 'Don't be so silly. Of course you don't take us for granted. We love spending time with our grandson. I'd be very happy for you to ask me to babysit more often.'

Particularly, Louisa thought, if a date was involved. It was one of her mother's favourite subjects: how it was long past time that Louisa put Jack behind her and started dating again. Not that she intended to be drawn on that one. 'Thanks, Mum,' she said.

On the Friday lunchtime, Dominic said casually, 'I'm giving Ronnie and Jess a lift to the bowling place. So there's a spare seat in my car if you'd like a lift, too.'

'Thank you. That'd be nice.'

'So are you a demon bowler, Louisa?' Ronnie asked as they walked into the centre later that evening.

'I'm afraid I'm absolutely hopeless,' Louisa said. 'I've been about half a dozen times in my life—always for work, and I always come last.'

'We'll stick you on Dominic's team, then,' Ronnie said with a grin. 'That'll bring his average down and give the rest of us a chance.'

Dominic scoffed. 'I'm not that good.'

But he turned out to be brilliant. He scored strike after strike after strike. And, when Louisa had her third frame in a row without knocking down a single pin be-cause her ball had gone straight into the gutter, he disappeared briefly. By his return, two barriers had sprung up between the bowling lane and the gutter.

'That's cheating,' Aiden, one of the junior doctors, informed him.

'No, it isn't. The bumper bars are up on your lane, too, and Ronnie's a genius at zig-zag bowling,' Dominic retorted. 'So your team has just got an advantage.'

Louisa flushed when she realised what he'd done: now there was no way she could fail to knock down at least one pin. 'I feel like a baby.'

'No, it's to do with confidence,' Dominic said. 'Once you realise you can do it, you won't need the bars up.' He walked with her to the line when it was her next turn. 'It's a bit like tennis—your finishing position affects where the ball goes. Your last three frames, you ended up too far to the left, so try either finishing with your hand straight in the middle, or start off aiming very slightly to the right. Like this.' He stood behind her and guided her arm very gently.

Louisa was incredibly aware of the warmth of his body; she wished now that she'd worn a thick sweater instead of a strappy T-shirt, because she could feel her body reacting to his touch. Hopefully, as it was a special 'glow bowling' evening and all the lights were down except over the bowling lane itself, nobody else would notice the physical signs of her arousal.

'You can do this,' he said. 'It's like learning to put a line in. The first few times, when you practise on an orange, you don't think you'll ever be able to do it to a real, live person. And then suddenly it clicks, and after the first couple of times you do it in Resus, you wonder why on earth you thought you couldn't do it.'

'I suppose so.'

She did as he suggested, and to her delight she knocked three pins down.

'High five, sister,' he said with a grin, clapping his palm against hers.

She knocked another three down on her next go—again without her ball even touching the bumper bar.

'See? Leave them up until you're really confident, but you can definitely do it,' he said. 'All you needed was to believe in yourself.'

Her score still wasn't brilliant at the end of the night, but it was a personal best; and Louisa knew it was all thanks to Dominic.

After they'd eaten at the American diner next to the bowling alley, Dominic dropped off Jess and Ronnie, then drove to Louisa's house.

'Would you like to come in for coffee?' she asked.

How could he resist the chance to spend just a little longer with her? 'Thanks. That'd be nice.' But the house seemed silent when she opened the door. 'I thought you said your parents were babysitting?' he asked.

'They are. Tyler's staying with them tonight,' she explained.

Which meant that he and Louisa were alone.

And they could talk without worrying that what they said might be overheard or misconstrued.

He followed her into the kitchen and leaned against the table, watching her as she switched the kettle on and shook instant coffee into two mugs. Her movements were so graceful. She fascinated him.

'I enjoyed tonight,' he said.

'Me, too.' She busied herself adding milk, then finally pouring on the hot water.

'Louisa.' He walked over to her and took her hand. 'I might be speaking out of turn, here, but I can't get you out of my head. There's something about you that just draws me. And I'd like to start seeing you.'

Her eyes went wide. 'Dominic. I...' She shook her head. 'I don't date.'

'Because of Tyler? I already know you come as a package. And I'm certainly not expecting you to get babysitters so you can see me. I like your son and I think he likes me—so I'd like to get to know you *both* better. We'll take it as slowly as you like.'

She bit her lip. 'I haven't dated anyone since my marriage broke up.'

He needed to know. 'Very long ago?'

'Five years—Ty was three.'

'Your ex met someone else?' Dominic guessed.

'No.' She closed her eyes for a moment, then lifted her chin; whatever had happened, clearly it was a huge, huge thing for her. 'You know the "terrible twos"? Ty had them really, really badly. We didn't realise at the time that he had Asperger's. He couldn't tell us how he felt, why he needed everything to be in order—so he'd just scream. Most of the time it was something we couldn't do anything about...and he'd scream and he'd scream and he'd scream.' She sighed. 'Jack couldn't cope with the tantrums. And when the nursery suggested we see someone, and the GP referred us to a paediatrician who told us that Ty has Asperger's...he couldn't handle that his son was a bit different.'

Dominic was truly shocked. 'Jack left you because Tyler has Asperger's?'

'He couldn't deal with it.' She sucked in a breath. 'I might as well tell you the rest of it. Ty looks nothing like

Jack—he takes after my side of the family. And Jack asked me if Tyler was actually his.'

Dominic couldn't quite take it in. 'He accused you of having an affair?'

She closed her eyes. 'I *didn't* have an affair.'

'That goes without saying.' He realised his fists were clenched, and deliberately splayed his fingers. Apart from the fact that he had no idea where Louisa's ex lived, breaking the man's jaw wouldn't make things any better. 'You're not the type to cheat. What on earth made him think that?'

'It took me a long while to work it out.' She opened her eyes again. 'I think he just wanted to be able to blame the genes on someone else. I'm glad that Ty didn't inherit his father's personality. Though Jack wasn't like that when I met him. I'm not that lousy a judge of character—at least, I don't think I am.'

'You're not,' Dominic said. 'But you see the good in people.' She saw the good in him. 'What about his parents? Surely they…?' His voice faded as he saw her expression tighten.

'They sided with Jack. Which is why Tyler only knows one set of grandparents—*my* parents.' Her gaze connected with his. 'Don't get me wrong, I'm not telling you a sob story; I'm simply trying to explain why I don't date. Because I'm never going to put my son in a position where he can be rejected again.'

'I can understand that.' He shook his head in disgust. 'What kind of person would reject their own child? That's beyond me.'

'Me, too.'

'You're both better off without him.'

She gave him a wry smile. 'You're telling me. I fell

out of love with him the moment he told me why he was leaving. That's why I reverted to my maiden name—and I changed Tyler's at the same time.'

'And your ex didn't mind?' No way would Dominic ever have let himself be cut out of his child's life.

'He didn't want us,' she said simply. 'It made life easier for him, because he could pretend he'd never had a child. So now you understand why I have to say no.'

'I understand why you want to say no,' he said. 'But I'm so aware of you. And sometimes I catch your eye at work or at the stables and I think it's the same for you, too. There's chemistry between us.'

'Yes,' she admitted with a sigh. 'But I can't possibly act on it.'

Though she hadn't loosened her hand from his. Which was a good sign. He drew her hand up to his mouth and kissed the back of it, very gently. 'I like you, Louisa. And I happen to like your son. He's got a good heart and he's kind. Yes, he's very direct and he'll only talk about what he's interested in—if you try and head him off, he'll change the subject right back. Some people would find that hard to deal with, but I'm used to that already because of Andy. It doesn't worry me.'

Her eyes were very clear. 'Tyler likes you.'

'Good.' He paused. And she'd admitted that she was attracted to him. 'This thing between you and me—how about we keep it just between us, see where it takes us? And, as far as everyone else is concerned, we're just good friends.'

'You mean, have a secret affair?'

'No,' he said. 'I don't mean anything tawdry or hole-in-the-corner. I mean we'll keep it to ourselves until we're sure what we're doing and we're ready to let other people know that we're seeing each other.'

'Did she hurt you that much?'

He frowned. 'Who?'

'The woman who's made you wary of relationships.'

He shook his head. 'It isn't what you think. I used to be—well, I guess I had a bit of a reputation. All my relationships were short and sweet, just for fun, but it was always mutual. I simply never met anyone who made me want to change that and settle down. And then...' Then he'd caused his brother to end up in a wheelchair. Everything had seemed different after that. 'Life changed,' he said, knowing it was way too succinct but not quite ready to tell her the rest. 'I decided to focus on my career. Except now I've met you, and I can't get you out of my head. And you make me want to try to be...' He paused, trying to think of the right word. 'Different.'

'Different, how?' she asked. 'What's wrong with you as you are?'

A million things, Dominic thought. 'It's complicated. And I don't really want to talk about it right now.' He knew he was being unreasonable; she'd opened up to him, so he ought to do the same with her. But this was all so new. He wanted her to know him better before he told her about Oliver.

'So this is just between you and me.'

This time, he knew, she wasn't saying no. 'Just between you and me,' he echoed softly. He kissed the inside of her wrist, and his mouth tingled at the contact. He knew it affected her the same way, because he felt the shiver running through her. 'Louisa.'

She cupped his face with her free hand. 'I'm out of practice at this.'

'That makes two of us.' He turned his head so he could kiss her palm.

'Dominic...'

And then he was kissing her properly. A sweet, tender, exploring kiss that left them both shaking.

A tear slid down her face when he broke the kiss.

'Don't cry, honey.' He wiped away the tear with the pad of his thumb.

'I just...never expected this.'

'Neither did I. Work and the stables were going to be my life. Until you walked into the restroom. That's why I was so rude to you—it threw me,' he said.

'I thought you were being all formal and unapproachable.'

'No. I was trying to keep some distance between us because there was this huge zing of attraction and I really, really didn't want to fall for you.'

'Distance.' She gave him a pointed look, because his arms were still wrapped tightly round her.

'Epic fail.' He kissed her again. 'And *that* was because I need the practice.'

She laughed back. 'That's the worst excuse I've ever heard.' And then, just when he thought she was going to wriggle out of his arms, she kissed him.

Her mouth was sweet and soft and incredibly sensual, and that kiss blew his mind.

When she broke the kiss, he released her and took a step back. 'Distance,' he said. 'Because, even though I want to kiss you until neither of us can think straight, that's not a good idea. I'm not taking anything for granted, and we're most definitely not going to rush this. We're taking this slowly.'

'Agreed.' She handed him a mug of coffee, and lifted her own mug in a toast. 'To taking things slowly.'

'And seeing where it takes us. And keeping it just between us, until we're ready.'

Over the next couple of weeks, Dominic and Louisa snatched coffee breaks or lunch breaks together at work, getting to know each other; and they saw each other more out of work, too. Dominic gave in to Tyler's request to join their swimming session, one Thursday evening, even though he knew it meant meeting her parents—which made everything feel much more serious.

'Mum, Dad, this is Dominic Hurst—our friend,' Louisa introduced them. 'He works with me at the hospital, and he sometimes works with Ty at the stables.'

Dominic was half expecting a grilling about his intentions towards Louisa, but Gillian and Matt Austin turned out to be absolutely lovely, and he found himself relaxing with them, to the point where he accepted the invitation to join them for fish and chips following the swimming session—and insisted on helping to wash up afterwards.

He wasn't quite ready for Louisa to meet his family—there was a lot he needed to tell her, first—but he did invite her and Tyler back to his flat for a pizza one evening.

'Is that my picture?' Tyler asked, spying the framed sketch on the wall.

Dominic smiled. 'You bet it is. It's a brilliant picture.'

The little boy seemed to swell with pride. 'I drew

Pegasus from memory.' He glanced around the room. 'Do you keep your harness here?'

He'd known the little boy would ask that, given that Tyler had already drawn a copy of the photograph of him in his jousting kit, along with several other suits of armour. He'd even unlocked the box for the first time in months and checked that the plate hadn't rusted, so he wouldn't disappoint the boy. 'Yes. Want to see it?' he asked.

'Oh, cool!' The little boy's eyes were round with pleasure. Then he glanced at his mother, who'd raised an eyebrow. 'I mean, yes, please.'

His enthusiasm made it easy for Dominic to unlock the box.

'Oh, wow, that's amazing. I've only ever seen silver armour, even at museums,' Tyler said. He smiled. 'Black armour's right for you. Like Edward the Black Prince. He was a champion jouster. Are you?'

'I used to be.' When life had been different. But he didn't want to talk about that. Time for more distraction. 'Want to try it on?'

'Can I? Really?'

'It'll be a bit big for you,' Dominic warned, 'but sure. I'll be your squire and help you put it on. Did you know there are twenty-seven pieces in a set?'

Tyler nodded. 'And the squire used to clean the armour with sand and vinegar. Do you know what they had to use if they didn't have any vinegar?' He glanced at his mother, then whispered gleefully in Dominic's ear, 'They used wee!'

Dominic couldn't help laughing. 'That's gross, Ty!'

'I saw it on telly. And I looked it up in a book afterwards, so I know it's true.'

Just what Dominic would have done himself, at that age. Still smiling, he helped Tyler put most of the armour on.

'Wow, it's heavy.'

'Because it's eighteen-gauge steel,' Dominic told him.

'Look, Mum, I'm a real knight,' Tyler said when Dominic finished putting the armour on him, clearly delighted.

'Do you mind if I…?' Louisa waved her mobile phone at Dominic, obviously keen to take a photograph of her son.

'Sure.'

'Are you going to wear your armour again?' Tyler asked when Dominic had packed it away.

'I don't know,' Dominic said.

'Ty, you need to wash your hands before tea,' Louisa reminded him. As the little boy scampered out to the bathroom, she said quietly, 'Sorry about that.'

'I should've anticipated the question. And I could've lied and told him I didn't have my harness any more.'

'But you don't lie.'

'No, I don't.' Except for a lie of omission. He still hadn't told her about the accident. He closed the lid of the trunk. 'The pizza should be here any minute. Let's go and sit down.'

'Is this your family?' Tyler asked, looking at the photographs on the mantelpiece.

'My parents and my elder brother, Oliver,' Dominic said. The photograph was just over two years old. When Oliver had still been at the top of his game, a brilliant surgeon and a brilliant horseman. Guilt flooded through him.

'Mum's got a brother, too. I'd like a brother,' Tyler said reflectively. 'Or a little sister, even.'

Dominic glanced at Louisa, who'd gone very still.

Tyler shrugged. 'But I guess Mum would have to get married before she could have a baby.'

'I'm fine as I am,' Louisa said, though her voice sounded slightly hollow. 'Those are nice dogs.'

Dominic recognised the distraction technique for what it was.

And, to his relief, it worked. 'They're way cool.' Tyler looked longingly at the photograph. 'I'd love a puppy. A wolfhound puppy. That's what a knight would have.'

'We can't have a dog while we're renting. But if we buy a house next year, we might be able to have a dog,' Louisa said, ruffling his hair. 'But not a wolfhound. Something smaller.'

'Absolutely. Having lived with a big dog, I can tell you, if a Great Dane sneaks upstairs and settles on your bed in the crook of your knees, you always end up on the floor when he stretches out. Fudge here is a nightmare for pushing you out of bed,' Dominic said lightly, and to his relief the strain in Louisa's eyes eased.

Well, now he knew what Tyler wanted. A house with a garden, a dog, and a family.

But what did Louisa want? And—at heart—what did *he* really want?

Yet he knew he wasn't quite ready to find out the answers.

CHAPTER FIVE

THE following day found Louisa in Minors.

'I think I've got something in my eye,' Tim Kershaw, her patient, said.

Given how red and inflamed his eye was, she was fairly sure he was right.

'I did rinse my eye out, but it feels like I've got a boulder in there,' he added with a grimace.

A few questions elicited the information that he worked on a building site and he'd forgotten to put protective goggles on. To her relief, he didn't wear contact lenses and he wasn't allergic to any medication. 'What I need to do is have a close look at your eye,' she said. 'I'm going to put some drops in—they'll sting a bit, but then it'll stop hurting and I can examine you properly.'

Though the examination showed her nothing. 'I'm going to need to put some dye in your eye,' she said, 'to show up if there are any scratches. If whatever went into your eye left a scratch behind, it'll feel as if there's something still in there, even though it's gone.'

'I'm in your hands.'

The dye showed her exactly what she'd suspected. 'You've got a corneal abrasion,' she said. 'It'll clear up in a few days, but I'm going to prescribe you some antibiotic ointment and some painkillers. And I need you to wear an eye patch until you get the sensation back in your eye, otherwise you'll risk getting something else in it and you won't feel it so it could cause a lot more damage.'

When she'd finished fitting the eye patch, Tim smiled at her. 'Thanks. I already feel a lot better.' He paused, and his gaze flicked to her left hand. 'Um, can I take you for a drink tonight, to say thank you?'

'There's no need,' Louisa said with a smile. 'It's my job.'

'OK—as a way of getting to know you, then?'

Louisa kept the polite, professional smile on her face. 'It's very sweet of you to ask, but I can't.'

'Because I'm a patient and you're a nurse?' Tim guessed. 'But when I leave here, I won't be your patient any more.'

'It's not that,' Louisa said, thinking of Dominic. 'I'm already involved with someone. And it's pretty serious.'

Dominic, who was walking through Minors on his way to Reception, heard every single word. And he wondered just who Louisa had meant. Her son? Or—his heart skipped a beat—him? Over the last couple of weeks, the three of them had grown closer. He and Louisa had held hands at the cinema while Tyler had been glued to the screenplay, then gone out for a pizza and talked about their favourite bits of the film. They'd gone for long walks, crunching through autumn leaves while Tyler searched for conkers, or looking for unusual pebbles on the beach. And then there had been the afternoon when they'd gone to the pool and he'd raced Tyler, giving the little boy a head start. 'Because I'm bigger than you, so it takes me fewer strokes to get to the end, and I've been swimming for a lot longer than you have. Giving you a head start makes it fair—it's not me patronising you,' he'd explained. 'And if you beat me, it isn't because I've let you win: it's because you swam better than I did.'

He'd beaten Tyler the first two times. Just by a couple of strokes; although he hadn't wanted to patronise the little boy, he also hadn't wanted to wreck Tyler's confidence. And then he'd spent a quarter of an hour teaching Tyler how to breathe more efficiently between strokes, praising him for trying hard and gently correcting him until he'd got it right.

On their very last race, the little boy had beaten him by a single hand, and Dominic had whooped, lifted him up and spun him round in a victory dance.

Louisa had been close to tears. And, later that evening, she'd held him tightly. 'What you did today...that meant a lot to Tyler.'

'Me, too,' he'd admitted. 'I enjoyed it.' Though he hadn't examined his feelings too closely. They were too new, too far out of his experience, for him to want to analyse them.

Since that afternoon, they'd actually hugged each other goodbye in front of Tyler. And their goodbye kisses when he saw Louisa home after a team night out were starting to linger.

Pretty serious?

Maybe.

Though he was still far from ready to go public.

Apart from anything else, he hadn't told her about Oliver. And he knew he really had to tell her. Sooner, rather than later.

* * *

'Mum's found something way cool to do at half-term,' Tyler told Dominic at the stables on Saturday afternoon.

Dominic looked up from where he was cleaning his saddle. 'What's that?'

'We're going to see the jousting at Amberhurst Castle.' Tyler hopped from one foot to the other. 'I can't wait! Do you want to come with us? There's room in Mum's car.'

Oh, hell. How could he have forgotten? The last joust of the season, in the October half-term holidays, just before the ground started getting too boggy from the rain or too hard from the frosts.

Well, he hadn't actually forgotten. He'd deliberately blanked it from his mind. Especially as the joust hadn't been held at Amberhurst for the last two years.

'Thanks for inviting me, but I can't make it,' he said. 'Though you'll have a great time. There's always a re-enactment group camping in the castle grounds on the medieval weekends. You'll see the smith making the armour and the horseshoes; that's always good to watch.'

'Did you ever joust there?' Tyler asked.

Dominic shifted uncomfortably. 'Yes.' More than that, Amberhurst was his family home. He really had to get round to telling Louisa that; but he was trying to choose his words carefully. And there were other things he needed to tell her first.

'So you know the people who are jousting?' Tyler asked.

There was no point in lying. 'Yes.'

'And you jousted against them?'

'Yes.'

'Did you win?'

This was torture. Why hadn't Louisa got her usual second sense and come to the rescue? But she was chatting to Bea, with her back to him. 'Usually,' Dominic said, not wanting to push the little boy away but, at the same time, desperately needing a change of subject.

'So why don't you start jousting again?' Tyler asked. 'I know you said someone got hurt, but jousting's really safe now. It's not like when Henry the Second was killed by splinters from a lance going through his eye into his brain.'

'Back in 1559, you mean? I'm not *quite* that old,' Dominic said wryly.

But Tyler's focus was elsewhere. 'They have rubber bits on the end of the lances, and the end bit's made of really soft wood, so it splinters easily and absorbs some of the impact energy. And knights have better helmets now, the frog-shaped ones so they can see through the slit when they lean forward, but they sit up at the last minute to stop the splinters coming through.'

Dominic couldn't help smiling at Tyler's earnestness. The boy had certainly read up about the subject. But how could he answer the question without dragging up things he'd rather not talk about? 'Ty, I know this sounds like a cop-out, but sometimes grown-up things are complicated.'

'Grown-ups make things *too* complicated,' Tyler said. 'If you miss jousting, and your friends who do jousting miss you, it's obvious that you should do it again. Then everyone will be happy.'

If only it were that simple. Dominic sighed. 'I'll think about it, OK? I'm not making any promises.'

'Any promises for what?' Louisa asked, coming over to them.

'I asked Dominic if he'd come to Amberhurst with us, but he's busy,' Tyler said. 'And he says he'll think about jousting again.'

'About time too,' Andy said, coming in to the tack room and clearly overhearing the tail end of the conversation.

'Hmm. Well, I have a horse to see to,' Dominic said, regardless of the fact that he hadn't finished cleaning his tack. He needed some space. 'Catch you later.'

He thought about it for the rest of the day.

Jousting.

He'd missed it, badly. The speed and the thrill. And if Oliver could bear to have the jousting at Amberhurst again…would seeing his brother back in the saddle rub extra salt in his wounds? Or did he, like Andy, think that Dominic's sacrifice was self-indulgent and pointless?

There was only one way to find out.

When Dominic got home, later that afternoon, he picked up the phone and called his brother.

'You're jousting at Amberhurst?' Louisa asked, surprised.

'Yes.'

'But—I thought you didn't joust any more. What changed your mind?'

'Certain people nagged me about it.'

She bit her lip. 'Tyler?'

'He wasn't the only one.' Dominic looked at her. 'How would you feel about me borrowing your son for part of the day?'

'You're going to take him jousting? When Tyler tells

me there's a closing speed of *seventy miles an hour*?' She couldn't help her voice squeaking.

'Of course not. He's a novice rider—no way is he ready to handle a lance,' he reassured her. 'No, I just wondered if he'd like to be my page and hold my standard when I'm on the field.' He smiled. 'Actually, I've got a pretty good idea what his answer would be if I asked him. But I wanted to run the idea past you, first, to see how you felt about it.'

How did she feel about it? Panicky, fearful that her little boy could get hurt. But she also knew that it would do wonders for his confidence and his social skills, so she wouldn't stand in his way. And she appreciated the fact that Dominic had been thoughtful enough to take her feelings into consideration and ask her first. 'He'd be thrilled to bits. But that's all he'd have to do, hold your standard?'

'And give Pegasus a good-luck pat. Andy's going to be my squire for the day and check my armour; Tyler will be perfectly safe with him, staying next to the lances at the side of the tilting ground. He won't be anywhere near the horses—or the splinters when the lances make a strike.'

It was as if he'd zeroed in on her fears and answered them all. 'I don't know what to say.'

'Yes would be a good start. Oh, and that also means that you won't need to get a ticket for the event. You'll both be my guests.'

She shook her head. 'That's too generous.'

'Actually, it's entirely selfish,' he said. 'Because this will be the first time I've jousted since...' His voice caught.

'Since the accident?' All she knew about it was that

someone had been physically hurt; she had no idea who, or how badly, but it had clearly left deep emotional scars on Dominic. She took his hand. 'Do you want to talk about it?'

'No,' he said, and sighed. 'But I will, because I need to be fair with you. Just so you know what you're getting into. And I'll understand if you change your mind about coming to Amberhurst and you don't want to see me any more outside work—or even work with me.'

She frowned. 'Whatever it is, it can't possibly be that bad.' She was absolutely sure of that. The man she'd grown to know better was a good man. 'And I happen to like working with you. You're clear on your instructions, you treat the patients and staff with respect, and your mind works the same way that mine does.'

He took a deep breath. 'The accident was just over two years ago. Oliver—my elder brother—is now in a wheelchair. And it was my fault.'

She didn't understand how that could be, but she realised that he needed to tell her what had happened in his own time and his own way, so she remained silent.

'I wanted to beat him. We'd had this sibling rivalry thing going for years—he'd do something, and I'd try to better it. Though not in a nasty way,' he added swiftly. 'It wasn't putting each other down. I guess we pushed each other to be the best we could be. Being four years older than me, Oliver was always the trailblazer, but I was determined I wasn't going to be left behind; and, the better I did, he harder he blazed the trail because it spurred him on to be even better. I did think about becoming a vet, specialising in horses, but listening to him talk about his course when he was a student decided me: I wanted to help people, too, the way my brother did. That's why I became a doctor.'

'Was he an emergency specialist, too?'

'No, he was a cardiac surgeon,' Dominic explained. 'I thought about specialising in surgery, but when I did my pre-reg training I found that I liked the rush of the emergency department. I talked it over with Oliver, and he said that I'd be an excellent surgeon, but he thought the variety of the emergency department would suit me a lot better. And he was right. I love what I do.' He sighed. 'But this rivalry thing—it meant we had to be as good as each other outside work, too. Oliver used to play rugby. He was an Oxford Blue, and he could've made a career out of it, but he wanted to be a surgeon. So he used to play for a Sunday side, and coach the kids on Saturdays.' He dragged in a breath. 'For me, it was horses. I used to ride, do a bit of competition jumping and eventing, but then some of my friends joined this re-enactment group and dragged me along to see the jousting.' He smiled wryly. 'When I was Tyler's age, I was just like him. Crazy about horses, used to pretend I was a knight. I used to dress up with a bucket on my head and carry a mop around.'

She could just imagine it. He would've looked adorable.

'Then, at the re-enactment event, I discovered I'd never really grown out of it. When I got the chance to try jousting for myself...I loved it. I dragged Oliver along, and he couldn't resist it, either. He found a club in London and trained there. It's a buzz like nothing else. Speed, precision, and a special bond with your horse.'

'And yet you gave it up.' She was having real trouble understanding that. The way he talked about it made her think he'd loved the sport almost as much as he loved his job. 'Why?'

'It was the least I could do,' he said.

'How do you work that one out?'

'Oliver lost a lot more than I did.'

'What happened?' she asked softly.

'I unhorsed him in a joust.' He sighed. 'I knew I was better at jousting than he was—I'd done it for a few months longer than he had, and I'd kept up with my riding when he'd switched to rugby at university. And I knew it was risky for him—the most common injuries in a joust are broken fingers, which isn't exactly conducive to performing surgery. I should've been more careful.'

'But he knew that risk and it was his choice to accept it,' Louisa pointed out, tightening her fingers round his.

'It was my fault,' Dominic repeated.

'If someone's lance hits you, does it automatically mean you fall off the horse?'

'No. You should be able to deflect the blow—and, if you can't, you should still be able to hold on.'

'So it couldn't have been all your fault. And if someone comes off, does it automatically mean serious injury?'

'The armour should protect you, and there's padding underneath to minimise the bruising. But, in Oliver's case, it wasn't enough.' Dominic closed his eyes. 'I can see it even now, in slow motion. Just like it felt at the time—as if everything was happening underwater, every movement so much slower than usual. Oliver falling backwards off the horse, landing awkwardly—and I couldn't get to him in time to stop it happening. I was frantic, but the faster I tried to get to him the more everything seemed to slow down.'

Just like when a child took those first faltering steps and then toppled over and banged his head; she'd heard parents say that so many times in the emergency department. And she'd lived through it herself, with Tyler. She rubbed the back of Dominic's hand with the pad of her thumb, trying to tell him without words that she understood.

He opened his eyes again. 'The emergency services were there straight away, and they put him on a board—but they couldn't do anything about the damage. The surgeon told us that Oliver had an incomplete lower spinal injury. And that was the end of everything. You can't exactly open a ribcage and perform intricate surgery on a heart if you can't stand for more than a couple of minutes at a time.' He shook his head. 'I took so much away from my brother. And he's been in pain every single day for the last two years, because of me. I have to live with that knowledge.'

'I don't know what to say.' She moved closer and wrapped her arms round him. 'Except it's taken you a lot of courage to tell me this.'

'Courage?' He gave a mirthless laugh.

'It was an accident,' she said. 'It wasn't as if you set out to hurt him on purpose.'

'The end result's the same. I wrecked his life.'

'Has he told you that?'

'He doesn't have to. Before the accident, he was a brilliant surgeon and a brilliant rugby-player—and a pretty good horseman. Now he's stuck in a wheelchair. No career, no sports, nothing.'

Louisa racked her brains to remember what she knew about spinal injuries. 'If it's an incomplete injury, there's a chance he might be able to walk again.'

'At the moment, he can only take a few steps—and they hurt like hell. He's putting himself through an incredibly punishing physio programme. He's determined that he's going to walk again and drive again—he's having a car specially adapted.' Dominic's face tightened. 'But for the time being he has to rely on other people to haul him around. And he hates it. In the early days, he told me he wished he'd broken his neck and died, so he didn't have to struggle through all the pain…' His voice cracked.

She held him more tightly. 'It sounds to me as if he was angry and frustrated and lashed out at you because you're close to him—you're a safe person to yell at because you understand what makes him tick.'

'Maybe.'

'It's how you would be, too. And so would I,' she said softly. 'It takes two to joust, Dominic. And maybe Oliver had something on his mind, something that stopped him paying proper attention.'

'He was going to ask his girlfriend to marry him, that evening. He'd been carrying the ring about with him for a week.'

He didn't have to say any more; she could guess the rest. Oliver's girlfriend hadn't been able to cope with his disability, so the relationship had broken up: and Dominic blamed himself for that, too. 'If his mind wasn't on what he was doing,' she said, 'then he was just as much to blame as you, if not more so.'

But Dominic's expression told her that he didn't believe it.

He was even more damaged than she was, she thought. She didn't believe enough in other people, but Dominic had it harder, because he'd lost his belief in himself. And no amount of talking from other people was going to change his mind on that score. This was something he had to come to terms with himself.

Instead, she said quietly, 'Do other people at the hospital know?'

He shook his head. 'They know my brother had a bad accident, and I've taken life a lot more seriously since then, but they don't know the details.'

'Thank you for trusting me with something so personal. And I can assure you that I'm not going to be talking about it to anyone.'

'I appreciate that.' His voice was clipped; and she just knew that he was bottling up his feelings again.

'Does Oliver know you're going to joust again?' she asked softly.

'I talked to him about it, the other night. To see how he'd feel about it. If he'd mind.'

'And?'

'He said I was an idiot, and it was about time I stopped boring my poor horse with mindless hacking.'

'Hacking?' She looked at him, mystified. 'Isn't that something to do with computers?'

He smiled, and held her closer. 'No. It's exercising a horse out on bridle paths and in the country, rather than in a schooling arena. General riding, not training for jumping, etcetera.'

'Right.' She paused. 'So when are you going to ask Ty?'

'You're still happy for him to do it, even though I told you what happened with Oliver?'

'I think you're going to be completely paranoid about safety,' Louisa said, 'so he's going to be absolutely fine.'

She brushed her mouth against his. 'Come to dinner tonight. Ask him then.'

There was a look of wonder on his face. 'Seriously?'

'Did you really think I'd want nothing to do with you, once you'd told me?'

'Well—yes,' he admitted.

She stroked his face. 'It was an *accident*, Dominic. Did you go out deliberately to push your brother off his horse and break his back?'

'Of course not.'

'Well, then. I know you're blaming yourself, and I kind of understand why, but sometimes these things just happen.' She stole another kiss. 'If it had been the other way round, would you have blamed him?'

'No.'

'And would you have expected him to give up jousting and doing things he loved, just because you couldn't do them any more?'

Dominic grimaced. 'I suppose not. I know what you're saying, Louisa, but...' He shook his head. 'Every time I see the pain in his eyes that he's trying to hide from everyone else, something shreds me up inside. If only I hadn't been so keen to score points that day and make him admit that I was better than him at something. If only I'd just let it go.' He looked bleak. 'I just wish I could turn the clock back.'

'You can't,' she said. 'All you can do is learn from the past and move on. And maybe be a bit less hard on yourself.'

That, Dominic thought, was a lot easier said than done. But his spirits felt lighter after he'd talked to Louisa—sheer relief that she didn't think any less of him, now he'd told her the truth—and he duly turned up to dinner that evening. 'I need a favour from you,' he told Tyler. 'I asked your mum, and she says it's OK to ask you. I need a page.'

Tyler frowned. 'Why?'

'Because I'm jousting at Amberhurst. And someone has to hold my standard while I'm at the tilts. So I wondered if you'd like to do that. Be my page.'

'A real knight's page?' At Dominic's nod, Tyler let out a whoop of delight—and actually hugged him.

Dominic couldn't help hugging the little boy back. And when he glanced at Louisa, he could see her blinking back tears.

While Louisa finished preparing the meal, Tyler grilled Dominic on the exact duties of a page, and looked even more thrilled at the idea that he'd have to dress up accordingly. 'Your riding boots will do fine for footwear, but I'll get you leggings, a shirt and a tabard. If your mum gives me your measurements, I'll get it all arranged,' Dominic promised. Sensing that Louisa was about to offer to pay for the outfit, he added, 'It's a knight's duty to pay for the outfit of his page—and, in this case, a pleasure as well, because you're doing me a huge favour. Otherwise I'd have to ask Andy to be my page *and* my squire, and he's already going to be busy enough sorting out my harness.'

'I promise I'll do a good job,' Tyler said solemnly.

'There's also a bit in the show where I have to ride past the crowd and ask a lady for a favour,' Dominic added. 'So can I ask you, Louisa?'

'A knight's supposed to ask the woman he's in love with for her favour,' Tyler said.

Dominic and Louisa both froze.

'But I expect you'll ask Mum because I'm going to

be your page and you don't want her to feel left out,' he added.

Later that evening, when Tyler had gone to bed, Dominic kissed Louisa goodbye. 'I'm sorry about earlier. For a moment, I thought he'd guessed about us.'

'No. He was trying to put himself in my shoes. I think that all that social skills training he's doing at school and my back-up at home is starting to pay off,' she said lightly.

'Probably.' Dominic paused. 'How do you think he'd feel? About you and me seeing each other, I mean?'

'It's still early days,' she said softly. 'Let's wait awhile before we tell him.'

He nodded. 'You're right. Best to take it slowly.' But right now his heart felt fuller and lighter than it had in years—and he knew it was thanks to her. Her warmth, her selflessness, that air of calm. Maybe, just maybe, she'd help him to forgive himself. And maybe, just maybe, he could do something for her, too. Repair some of the damage that Jack had inflicted when he'd rejected her and their son.

CHAPTER SIX

AT LAST the day of the jousting dawned. Tyler was up at the crack of dawn, dressed in his page's outfit. 'My tabard's the same colour as Pegasus's caparison,' he told his mother proudly. 'And, look, it's got Dominic's silver unicorn on it, to show I'm part of his team.'

Louisa ruffled his hair. 'You look wonderful. Come on, we'll get you some breakfast.'

'I'm not hungry.'

Meaning that he was too excited to eat. 'Toast,' Louisa said firmly, hiding a smile. 'Or you'll feel all light-headed later—and you'd hate to drop Dominic's standard because you were feeling all wobbly, wouldn't you?'

Tyler sat down at the dining-room table. 'He's not Dominic when he's jousting, he's Sir Hugo. That's such a cool name. I'm still thinking about what mine's going to be.'

The little boy chattered nineteen to the dozen until Dominic collected them, and he continued to chatter all the way to Amberhurst Castle. 'Wow, Mum, look, it's a proper castle with turrets and battlements and every-thing!' He was almost beside himself with excitement.

The grounds of Amberhurst Castle were already crowded, with re-enactors wandering around in medieval garb and tourists milling about, eager to see the jousting.

'You can be let off page duties for a while, if you want to go and explore,' Dominic told Tyler. 'I need to go and see Pegasus, settle him down a bit.'

'Can I still wear my outfit?'

Dominic ruffled his hair. 'You bet.'

'What time do you need us back?' Louisa asked.

'The first joust is at eleven—so, maybe a quarter to?'

'Fine.' She took his hand and squeezed it. 'You OK?' she asked softly.

He took a deep breath. 'I think so. And nerves are good. It means you're not taking anything for granted and are less likely to make mistakes.'

She knew exactly what mistake he was thinking about. 'You'll be fine. And we'll be cheering for you.'

He lifted the end of her scarf. 'Better than that, you'll be letting me wear this, for luck.'

But the smile didn't quite reach his eyes. He was really nervous, she realised. Hearing that Tyler was busy scrambling out of the back of the car, she leaned forward and brushed her mouth briefly against his. 'That's for luck.'

'No better favour could a knight ask of his lady,' he said softly. 'And you *are* my lady, Louisa.'

Desire licked all the way down her spine, and she couldn't help a breathy little sigh. 'Yes.'

'Later,' he whispered, and she nodded. Her parents were meeting her on the field later, not wanting to miss their grandson's performance as a page; she'd ask them if Tyler could have a sleepover at theirs tonight. Because, once the adrenalin had stopped flowing, she had a feeling that all the guilt would come straight back and Dominic would really need her to hold him and soothe his soul.

Dominic checked his horse over, then checked all the buckles on his armour.

'And how many times have you done that this morning, little brother?' a voice asked behind him.

He whirled round. 'Oliver!'

'It's "my lord", to you. Tsk. Knights these days really have no manners.' His brother, dressed in medieval garb and wearing a crown, grinned broadly. 'Well, Sir Hugo. It's good to see you back. You OK?'

'Yes.'

Oliver arched one eyebrow.

'All right. I'm not,' Dominic admitted. 'I keep thinking about the last time I jousted.' And the guilt was almost paralysing.

'Listen. What happened—we can't change it. And, yes, of course I'd rather be out there jousting against you today instead of being stuck in this...' Oliver indicated his wheelchair '...but it's not going to happen and it's pointless either of us droning on about it. So you're going to get on Pegasus and you're going to joust as brilliantly as you always did and you're going to come first. Got it?'

Dominic wasn't so sure. 'I've been out of the field for a while.'

'Two years, three months and nine days,' Oliver said, 'if you're going to be boring about it.'

They both knew the exact number of days. Hours, even. 'In your shoes, I'd still be raging,' Dominic said.

'Done that, and it hasn't changed anything. Time to try something else and see if that works better. And it's time you stopped obsessing over it and moved on, too.' Oliver shrugged. 'So who's the young page next to Andy?'

'Tyler. The son of a friend.'

'Friend, hmm? When do we get to meet her?'

'I didn't say my friend was female.'

'You didn't have to. It showed on your face.' Oliver regarded his brother seriously. 'Does she know about the accident?'

'Yes.'

'And she's still around. Good. You picked some-one sensible. So when do we get to meet her?' Oliver repeated.

'When I'm ready. Don't be bossy.'

Oliver laughed. 'Big brother's privilege. Go out there and win for me.' He patted Dominic's arm. 'And I meant it. It's good to see Sir Hugo back. I've missed him.'

'So have I,' Dominic admitted.

'I'd better get back to the dais and do my lord of the manor bit. See you later. And I meant it about meeting your friend, too. And the page. He looks a nice kid.'

'Yes. He is.'

And then it was time to finish getting ready. Dominic made a fuss of his horse, scratching him behind the ears. 'Looking forward to this, boy?' he asked. 'And are we going to come out on top?'

The Percheron whickered and nudged him, as if to say yes.

Dominic grinned, and checked the saddle for the last time before Andy checked the straps of his armour.

He'd almost forgotten how much he loved this. There was no headier buzz than this: climbing on to the mounting block, getting astride his horse, and knowing that the joust was about to start. For the next few minutes he wouldn't be Dr Dominic Hurst: he'd be Sir Hugo de Amberhurst. He'd borrowed his stage-riding name from his Tudor great-whatever grandfather, whose portrait hung in the family gallery and whom everyone said Dominic resembled, right from when he'd been a toddler. Sir Hugo had been a legendary jouster, too, and Oliver had always teased him about being a throwback.

Automatically Dominic looked up at the dais opposite the jousting field. Oliver was sitting there, dressed in the costume of the lord of the manor, casually chatting to the people at the dais with him. The way they'd set it up, nobody who saw him would guess that the 'lord of the manor' was sitting in a wheelchair rather than on a throne.

Almost as if Oliver sensed Dominic's glance, he looked over, and raised his hand in a salute. A blessing. Wishing him well.

Dominic knew he didn't deserve it, but it warmed him.

'Ready, Sir Hugo?' Andy asked.

'Yes.'

'Good. Tyler—are you ready with the standard?'

'Oh, yes.' The little boy beamed and lifted up the banner.

'Come on, then, team,' Dominic said. 'Let's do it.'

Andy and Tyler walked out to the jousting arena. 'Introducing the one, the only Sir Hugo de Amberhurst and his horse Pegasus!' Andy called.

Dominic heard the cheers and clapping. 'On with the show, boy,' he said softly to Pegasus, and urged the horse into a fast walk.

* * *

Louisa, who had been taking photographs of Tyler while her father was in charge of the video camera, paused as Dominic rode out. She'd seen the photographs of him in his armour, but nothing had prepared her for how incredibly sexy he looked. The black knight on a white horse, carrying a dark red shield with a silver unicorn. No wonder most of the women in the audience had dreamy looks on their faces; and she had a feeling that she did, too.

'And the one, the only Sir Simon de Leigh and his horse Midnight!' The other knight's squire waved a gold-coloured banner with a blue boar on it; moments later, Sir Simon rode out on a black horse.

Both knights did a circuit of the arena in front of the crowd; and then Dominic reined back right in front of Louisa.

He reminded her of the knight in one of the posters in Tyler's collection—Waterhouse's *Lamia*, where the knight was looking down at the kneeling woman. And, lord, he was sexy. His beautiful mouth. The hot expression in his eyes as he looked at her.

And she wanted him.

Badly.

'May I wear your favour, my lady?' he asked.

It felt as if he were claiming her in front of the whole world, and she was aware of envious glances and murmuring from other women in the crowd. 'Yes, my lord.' She stood up, removed the scarf from her neck and handed it to him. It was a pretty one, lightly woven strands of copper and gold and russet with a fringe.

'Thank you, my lady.' He smiled and blew her a kiss, and she could feel the colour flooding into her face. Then he tucked the scarf in to his helmet; it glittered against the black metal, and the fringe fluttered in the slight breeze. He gave her another smile, and her heart fluttered as much as the scarf.

Sir Hugo and Sir Simon touched their right hands together in a show of friendship and a fair fight before riding to their respective ends of the arena.

The squires gave each of the knights a lance; they held it in their right hands, pointed upwards and slightly back. At a signal, they started to canter towards each other, lowering their lances as the horses picked up speed. Louisa was surprised at how fast it was—a matter of mere seconds before she heard a shredding sound and saw the ends of the lances bursting into splinters. All the while, her heart was in her mouth. Please, God, let Dominic be safe. Let him be able to concentrate and put the past out of his mind. Please let him be all right. Please don't let him be hurt.

'That's a strike on the breastplate for Sir Simon, three points,' the commentator said. 'And a strike on the shield for Sir Hugo, five points.'

The knights did two more passes, then at the end handed their shattered lances to their squires and rode slowly along the tilting rail so they could clasp their right hands very briefly.

'There's going to be a break between the bouts, so our knights are going to remove some of their armour now and give you a chance to meet the team,' the commentator said.

Tyler was proudly holding the standard by Dominic's side; Louisa took more photographs of him, then one of Dominic. The look in his eyes made a shiver of pure desire run the whole length of her spine.

'You've got people queuing up to talk to you, so I'll

see you later,' she said, and ruffled Tyler's hair. 'You did a brilliant job, darling.'

'I'm still on duty, Mum. You're not supposed to ruffle my hair,' he said, looking pained, and she couldn't help smiling.

When the meet-and-greet had finished, Dominic was able to shed his armour and join them for a wander around the castle grounds. He still looked like a medieval knight, wearing dark breeches, dark boots, an open-necked white shirt with billowing sleeves and a dark red velvet cloak.

Utterly gorgeous.

And all hers.

'This is the best day of my whole life,' Tyler said.

It was one of the best in hers, too.

Somehow Dominic ended up holding Louisa's hand as they wandered through the encampment. It felt so right, she thought. His bare skin against hers.

A shiver ran down her spine. Ty had had a wonderful day and was spending the night with his grandparents. So for once maybe she could stop worrying, let go, and just enjoy herself. Maybe tonight she could snatch one night of pure pleasure with a gorgeous, caring, attentive man. A man she found incredibly attractive, and she knew that it was mutual—the way he kissed her had become more intense over the last few weeks, and they'd both found it harder and harder to stop at just kissing.

Tonight, maybe they could take time out for *them*.

'Ty's staying at Mum and Dad's tonight,' she said softly. 'So I was wondering if you were busy.'

Dominic's eyes went wide, and he stooped to whisper in her ear, 'Do you mean...you're asking me to stay over?'

'Yes.'

He sucked in a breath. 'If you're sure—then, yes. Oh, *yes*.' His face was filled with the same wild, crazy joy that was bubbling through her entire body.

Tonight… She could hardly wait. Tonight, she and Dominic would explore each other properly. Thoroughly. And tomorrow she'd wake up in his arms. Sated. Warm. Happy.

The whole day sparkled. There was a second bout of jousting, and even though Louisa was secretly terrified by the speed and the potential for disaster as the horses galloped down the tilting rail, she knew how skilled the riders were and she enjoyed watching Dominic on Pegasus.

When the results were announced, Sir Hugo was at the top of the list—and he won the cup. She could see that Tyler was almost beside himself with joy when Dominic lifted him onto Pegasus and got him to sit there, holding the cup, while the photographs were taken. And then he beckoned to her. 'Come on. You have to be here, too. It was wearing your favour that made me win.'

'Go,' Gillian said, giving her a little push. 'And give me your camera.'

They stood either side of Pegasus, holding hands over the horse's neck, while Tyler beamed from his position on the saddle. How easily Dominic had made room in his life for Tyler. He thought about what would make the little boy happy: and yet Tyler's biological father hadn't been able to do that.

Dared she let Dominic further into their lives? Or should she still keep this just between the two of them?

Right at that moment, she wasn't sure. But one thing

she knew for definite. Tonight she wanted to fall asleep in Dominic's arms. Be close to him. And, when she glanced across at him, she could see in his eyes that he was thinking along exactly the same lines.

'This is the best day *ever*,' Tyler repeated as they walked around the stalls again afterwards.

'They're doing pony rides round the lower part of the grounds. Shall we go and see what the queue's like?' Dominic asked.

'Can we?'

'Sure.' He gave the little boy a hug. 'My treat, because you were the most brilliant page.'

'When are you jousting again?'

'When the season opens, next year—the ground needs to be dry enough and soft enough so the horses don't slip,' Dominic explained. 'But, if it's all right with your mum and you want to do it, you can be my page next season. Andy can start teaching you how to check the armour, too.'

Tyler visibly swelled with pride. 'I'd love that. Can I, Mum? Please?'

How could she resist? 'Sure.'

The queue for the pony rides wasn't too bad. They waited in line, then watched as Tyler was led round the field on the pony.

Louisa wasn't sure how it happened, but suddenly the pony was rearing and Tyler was falling off in a wide arc. Even as she started running, she knew it was too late, that she'd never get there in time to catch him. With horror, she saw that his hard hat wasn't on properly either— that it was falling at a slightly faster rate than he was. Dominic, too, was running—but even his longer legs and bigger muscles weren't enough to save the little boy.

It must've been only seconds, but it felt like eternity between the moment that Tyler hit the floor and she was on her knees beside him. 'Tyler!'

'Move the pony and keep everyone back,' Dominic directed the horrified stable girl who'd been leading the pony round the field. He pulled his phone from his pocket and Louisa was aware of him talking to the emergency services controller, but most of her attention was fixed on her son.

'Tyler, can you hear me?'

There was no answer; he lay there motionless. Unconscious.

All the worst-case scenarios flew through Louisa's mind. A broken neck, spinal injury, severe brain injury...

They couldn't move him, just in case they made things worse, but she desperately wanted her son in her arms. The child she'd nursed, that she'd loved from the very first second he'd been put in her arms, wet and slippery and warm. Her baby.

'Tyler. Wake up!' Her breath came out as sobs.

Dominic was checking him over carefully, without moving him. 'His ABCs are fine.'

'He's *unconscious*, Dominic!' she snapped.

'I know, honey. And the ambulance is on its way. Try not to pan—'

'How the hell can I not panic? That's my *son* lying there.' She hissed the words at him, knowing that she was being unfair but too worried and angry to stay calm.

Supposing Tyler died? She'd spent her time thinking of the man by her side, planning to make love with him this evening, instead of looking after her child. She'd been reckless with her baby, not paying attention, letting herself get swept away by her growing feelings for Dominic. Stupid, stupid, *stupid*. If she hadn't been so selfish, thinking of herself instead of her son, this would never have happened.

If Tyler died, if he was seriously injured and never recovered, she'd never be able to forgive herself.

Two years, three months and nine days ago. About the same time of day, too. Back then, Dominic had been on his knees as well, checking the vital signs of someone who'd come off a horse. Someone he really cared about.

The nightmare was back again. Except it wasn't just something he could wake up from. This was real.

When the jousting had gone well, he'd been so sure that life was going to be all right again. He was wandering around the place he loved most in the world, with a bright, sweet-natured woman by his side, and her son—a child he'd become increasingly fond of, the more he'd got to know the boy. And now the whole lot was unravelling right before him, just as it had when Oliver had fallen awkwardly off his horse.

Tyler was hurt. How badly, Dominic wouldn't be able to assess until the boy had recovered consciousness or was in hospital. But this was all his fault. Why had he suggested the pony ride? Why hadn't he thought to double-check that Tyler's hat was on properly? But instead he'd been thinking of Louisa, remembering the look in her eyes when she'd asked him to stay over. The promise of mutual pleasure and satisfaction and joy.

How had it all disintegrated into this mess—and so fast?

Right now, Louisa's face was blank with shock. Numb.

'Tyler,' she whispered. 'Tyler. Say something. Talk to me, darling. Say something.' Her voice was cracked with pain.

'Mum.' The word was barely a murmur, but they both heard it. 'Mum. My head hurts,' Tyler mumbled.

'All right, darling. Just lie still—there's an ambulance on its way and they'll have something to take the pain away.' Louisa wrapped her hand round his. 'Can you feel your legs?'

'Yes. They hurt, too.'

Thank God, Dominic thought. The time to really worry would be if the little boy couldn't feel anything at all. That would mean serious damage. He could still remember the look on Oliver's face, the panic in his eyes when he'd whispered, 'Dom, I can't feel my legs...'

Please, please don't let this turn out so badly.

Please let it be just simple concussion. No complications.

Please.

He checked Tyler's respirations, then took Tyler's other hand and checked his pulse. 'He's doing OK,' he murmured to Louisa. 'Where are your parents?'

'They were going to have a cup of tea in the castle café.'

No way could either of them leave Tyler to try and find them; but he could still take that worry from her shoulders. 'Give me their mobile number and I'll call them, tell them what's happened.'

Even though she was clearly frantic, her medical training stood her in good stead, because she remained calm and focused. 'My mobile's in my handbag. Use that. It's under "Mum mobile".'

He took the phone from her bag and found the number, and explained the situation rapidly to Gillian Austin. The Austins were there within minutes; as soon as he could see that Louisa had the support she needed, he withdrew slightly and called Andy.

'There's been an accident in the lower field. Tyler's hurt and an ambulance is on its way. Can you tell everyone what's happened and look after Pegasus for me? I want to go to hospital with Ty and Louisa.'

'Will do. Ring us when you know how he is,' Andy said. 'Ric or me'll come and get you.'

'Thanks, mate. I will.'

When the ambulance arrived, Dominic gave the paramedics a full run-down of what had happened and Tyler's condition. 'We're probably looking at concussion, but with that distance of fall I don't want to take any chances.'

'We'll put him on a spinal board,' the paramedic said.

Between them, they transferred the little boy to the ambulance.

'I'm coming with you,' Dominic said as Louisa climbed into the back of the ambulance.

'But you've got things to do here.'

'It's all sorted. You and Tyler are my priority,' he said, and climbed in beside her.

Louisa held Tyler's hand all the way to the hospital.

'I'm scared, Mum,' he said, his teeth chattering.

So was she. So scared that her entire body felt as if it were about to shatter into tiny shards. The back of her neck was burning with adrenalin and she could taste bile. But, for Tyler's sake, she forced herself to sound calm. 'I'm here, darling. Nothing's going to hurt you while I'm here.'

'And Dominic.'

'I'm here,' Dominic confirmed. 'I'm not going to let anything happen to the best page I've ever had.'

The journey felt as if it took seconds and days, both at the same time. Then at last they were in the emergency department at the hospital.

'Mr and Mrs Austin, would you like to wait in the relatives' room?' the doctor asked.

'This is Dr Hurst and I'm Tyler's mother, Louisa Austin,' Louisa said, her voice clipped. 'And, no, we wouldn't like to wait in the relatives' room, thank you. I promise we won't get in your way—we both work in an emergency department so we know what it's like—but there's absolutely no *way* I'm letting my son out of my sight.'

'Very well.'

The doctor checked Tyler over, and Louisa watched his face intently, looking for signs of things he wasn't saying. Did he think it was more serious than concussion? She clenched her fists in a vain attempt to stop herself shaking. But waiting grew harder and harder, and in the end she couldn't help asking, 'Do you think there it's just concussion or are there fractures?'

'We're sending him to X-Ray now,' the doctor said. 'I'll be able to tell you more when the X-rays are back.'

'And you'll ask Radiology for AP, lateral and Townes views?' she asked.

The doctor looked slightly wary. 'Yes.'

'That's what I would've asked for, too,' Dominic said. 'There's been no blood or fluid from his nose and ears, but he was knocked out. I have a very low index of suspicion on head injuries where children and the elderly are concerned, and I guess it's the same here.'

The doctor nodded. 'Mrs Austin, this is a completely routine exam. Tyler's talking and he's making sense, so that's a very good sign.'

Louisa lowered her voice so Tyler wouldn't hear. 'For now—you know how quickly children can deteriorate.'

Dominic wrapped his arms round her. 'Louisa, I know you've got all the worst-case scenarios running through your head, but they're all rare,' he said, keeping his voice equally low. 'The chances are, it's just concussion and nothing to worry about.'

'You don't know that. Not until the X-rays are back. And I need to go with my son.'

'Of course, Mrs Austin.'

She looked at Dominic. 'Mum and Dad were following us in the car. They'll be here in a minute. Can you wait for them and tell them where I am?'

'Of course I will.'

She went to the radiology department with Tyler, reassuring him and staying within his sight behind the screen as the X-rays were taken.

By the time they got back to the emergency department, her parents were there, talking to Dominic. She waved, but stayed next to her son, holding his hand.

It felt like for ever, waiting for the X-ray results to come back, but at last the doctor came over. 'I'm glad to say everything's clear, but I'd like him kept in overnight in the children's ward for observation, because of the distance he fell. That isn't a cue for you to start worrying.

I'm just being super-cautious—like your friend, I have a low index of suspicion for head injuries in children and the elderly.'

'Can I stay with him?' Louisa asked.

'Of course you can,' he said. 'I'll take you up to the ward myself and introduce you.'

'Thank you.' She blinked back the tears. 'I'm sorry I was stroppy with you earlier.'

'When it's your own child, you can't help it. I've got a six-month-old daughter,' the doctor said sympathetically. 'And my wife says I'm a nightmare—if Zoe gets the slightest sniffle, I'm checking her temperature and her breathing and thinking of all the differential diagnoses. The really scary ones.'

'Tell me about it,' Louisa said ruefully.

Once they were settled on the ward and Tyler had fallen asleep, Gillian said, 'We'll go and fetch some things for him—pyjamas and his wash things. And something for you to change into. I've got your spare key, love, so we'll go now and we'll be back as soon as we can.'

'Thanks, Mum.'

'And I'm staying,' Dominic said softly. 'At least until your parents get back. I'm so sorry, Louisa. If I hadn't suggested the pony ride, this wouldn't have happened.'

She swallowed hard. 'It wasn't your fault the pony reared.'

'No, but it shouldn't have happened. And why didn't someone check his hat?' He shook his head. 'I should've done that myself.'

'I thought Ty knew how to do it. He always sticks by the rules.'

'But maybe he was just so excited, he forgot. Again,

that's my fault. If I hadn't asked him to be my page, he would've been just a spectator. He would still have been excited, but he wouldn't have been sidetracked.' He shook his head. 'I'm so sorry.'

Louisa bit her lip. 'He's so precious to me. If anything happens to him…' The idea was so shocking that she couldn't breathe.

Dominic wrapped his arms round her. 'I'm sure it's simple concussion. I checked those X-rays myself, just in case anything had been accidentally missed, and everything looked fine. The doctor was just being very cautious and that's how I would've handled this, too—and it's how you would've expected it to be handled if the patient was a stranger instead of your son.'

She knew that was true, but she couldn't push the fear away. 'If something happens to him…'

'It won't.' He held her close. 'Of course you're worried. You're his mother and he means the world to you.' He paused. 'He means a lot to me, too. I wanted him to have the most fantastic day today, to make some really good memories—and I'm so sorry it's turned out like this.'

She felt a tear slide down her face and scrubbed it away. 'I feel so guilty. If I hadn't been thinking about tonight, about having you all to myself and…' Her breath hitched. 'This feels like payback.'

'No,' he said firmly. 'It wasn't your fault. And you and me…that'll keep. When Tyler's back on his feet.'

She said nothing, not having the strength to have a row about it, but she wasn't sure there could be a 'you and me' with Dominic. Not now. Because if she hadn't been so damn selfish and put herself first, her son wouldn't be lying here now.

And yet, at the same time, it felt so good to have someone to lean on. Someone to share the worries with. She'd spent so many years on her own, being strong; was it so wrong to lean on a shoulder when it was offered?

Torn between pushing Dominic away and sobbing on his shoulder, she took refuge in silence. Dominic sat quietly with her, just holding her, while Tyler slept. And finally Gillian arrived at the ward again.

'I brought your things, love,' she said. 'And I'll stay with you. We can take turns keeping awake and watching over him.'

'And that's my cue to go,' Dominic said.

Louisa frowned. 'But you came with us in the ambulance. How will you get home? We're miles from Brighton.'

'Don't worry, Andy or Ric will come and pick me up. And I'll call Essie, tell her what's happened and get her to arrange cover for you. They'll probably discharge him in the morning and I assume you'll want to stay with him for a few days.'

'I...' Louisa found herself shaking uncontrollably. 'Yes.'

'If anything changes,' he said, 'I want you to promise me that you'll call me. No matter what time of night or day it is. And I'll be there straight away.'

She swallowed the threatening tears. 'Thank you.'

'Promise me.'

'I'll call you.' At the intense look on his face, she added, 'I promise.'

He wrapped his arms round her. 'Hang on in there. He's going to be fine. And I'll speak to you tomorrow, unless you need me here before then.'

Louisa and Gillian stayed at Tyler's bedside, taking

turns to doze for a couple of hours while the other watched over the little boy. And, the next morning, just as Dominic had predicted, Tyler was discharged. Gillian drove them home and Louisa sat in the back with Tyler, holding his hand and thanking God that her little boy was safe. She'd never, ever put anyone before him again.

CHAPTER SEVEN

BUT, in the middle of the morning, Tyler was violent-
ly sick.

'Mummy, my head hurts,' he whispered.

'Worse than yesterday, or better, or the same?' she
asked, trying to keep her voice as even and controlled
as she could.

'Worse,' Tyler said, looking woebegone. 'It really
hurts.'

It wasn't uncommon for children to be sick after a
head injury, but she had a bad feeling about this. She
needed him checked over—right now.

'All right, sweetheart. Let's go and get you checked
over.' She called an ambulance, giving them full details
of Tyler's symptoms and the background.

All the way to the hospital, holding Tyler's hand, she
thought about it. Was it an extradural haemorrhage—
bleeding into the space between the skull and the brain,
caused by a rupture in an artery? The blood clotted and
caused pressure in the skull, which in turn caused headaches, drowsiness, vomiting and seizures; it could take
several days for the clot to grow and symptoms to turn
up. If Tyler had a clot...

He was sick twice more in the ambulance, and the

best she could do was wipe his face with a cool, damp cloth.

Please, let them get to hospital.

And let them be in time.

She'd never forgive herself if anything happened to her precious child.

Dominic was there to meet them in the ambulance bay. He took one look at her face and gave her a brief but fierce hug. 'You're in the right place, Louisa. Don't borrow trouble.'

The paramedics gave him all the information about the observations they'd taken, and Dominic examined Tyler swiftly. 'CT scan, I think,' he said.

Louisa swallowed hard. So he suspected a clot, too.

'I have a low index of suspicion with children and the elderly, remember,' he told her, clearly picking up on her worries.

It seemed to take for ever for the scan. And as soon as she saw the image on the screen, she knew. There was a definite clot.

Liam, the neurosurgeon, came straight down to see her. 'It's an extradural haemorrhage. We're going to drill burr-holes in his skull to release the clot, then we'll tie off the bleeding vessel. Try not to worry, because all the signs are good. His breathing is fine and his pupils aren't too bad, and there's no sign of any paralysis.'

But all Louisa could think about was the classic 'talk and die' scenario, where the patient appeared to get better and then collapsed.

Dominic nudged her. 'Louisa?'

She blinked, shaking her head. 'Sorry—I'm all over the place. What did you say?'

'Liam needs to know. Has he eaten anything this morning?'

'Two pieces of wholemeal toast with Marmite and no butter, and a large glass of milk—the same as he always has for breakfast. I think it all came up when he was sick.'

'That's good, because it means his stomach's empty,' Liam said. 'Now, stop worrying. He's in good hands, and you know that.'

'He's my baby,' she said, her voice a scratchy whisper.

'I'll take care of him, Louisa,' Liam promised.

She dragged in a breath. 'I need to tell Mum and Dad what's going on, but I can't leave Ty.'

'Give me their number, and I'll ring them,' Dominic said.

She took her mobile phone from her handbag and promptly dropped it because her hands were shaking so much. 'Sorry.'

He retrieved it for her. 'It's OK, honey. He's in good hands.'

'I can't stop thinking,' she whispered, 'about what could happen.'

He wrapped his arms round her. 'Go through all the muscles and all the veins and all the nerves, count backwards from a thousand in thirteens—whatever helps to fill your head and leaves no room for thoughts like that. What's your mum's number?'

'It's under "Mum home".'

'I'll call her now and I'll be up with you as soon as I can.' He rested a hand on her shoulder. 'Hang on in there. He's going to be fine. I promise.'

She swallowed the bile in her throat. 'You can't

promise that, Dominic. It's not under your control—or mine.'

'Liam's the best there is. I trust him. And that's why I can promise,' he said softly. 'Go to Theatre. I'll be there soon.'

She went up to Theatre with Tyler, and stayed while they gave him a pre-med and shaved his hair. 'You're going to be fine. I know the surgeon,' she reassured him, 'and he's brilliant. He'll sort it out and your head will stop hurting.'

But when the anaesthetist came to give Tyler the general anaesthetic and she was forced to wait outside Theatre, every second felt like a lifetime.

She was sitting with her head in her hands, praying silently, when Dominic joined her.

'Right now you need to be held, and that's exactly what I'm going to do—hold you.' He wrapped his arms round her.

She was shaking. 'Dominic, if he dies...'

'He's not going to die. He's in the best hands and your instinct was spot on. You got him here early enough for them to do something about it.'

How could he be sure? She wasn't. She didn't know anything, any more. All her years of nursing training meant nothing.

Part of her wanted to push him away. She'd promised herself she'd never ever put anyone before Tyler again, and here she was, letting Dominic wrap her in his arms like he had yesterday. Leaning on him.

But she was so scared. So very, very scared. And she needed to be held. She so desperately needed someone she could lean on. Dominic was solid and reliable and *there*.

'I spoke to your mum. Your parents are on their way right now.' He gave her phone back to her.

'Thank you.' She dragged in a breath. 'I keep thinking of the cases I've seen in the past. Cases where—where they...' She couldn't get the word out. Couldn't say it in case she made it come true. *Cases where they died.*

'Every case is different,' Dominic said. 'I know it's easier said than done, but try not to think about them. Tyler isn't going to die. Liam's a brilliant surgeon and he won't let that happen.'

He was still holding her when her parents rushed into the waiting area, asking questions at a hundred miles an hour; Dominic calmed them down and reassured them, the same way he'd reassured Louisa.

'Thanks for waiting with me until Mum and Dad got here,' she said when her parents finally sat down. 'And I'm sorry for keeping you from work.'

'You're not. Essie's got someone in to cover for me. I'm staying with you at least until Ty's out of Theatre.' He stroked her hair. 'And now that's clear, I'm going to get you all a hot drink. Don't argue. It'll give you something to do and stop the wait being so bad.'

The hot drink turned out to be sweet tea. She pulled a face. 'This is horrible.'

'Yes, but you know as well as I do that it's effective, so drink it—that goes for all of you,' Dominic directed. 'And it's occurred to me, Gillian and Matt—Louisa knows what the surgical procedure is, but you don't.' He grabbed a pad and pen from his pocket and drew a swift sketch to show her parents where the clot was. 'What the surgeon's going to do is drill some holes into the skull here, take out a little lid of bone, and then remove the clot and tie off the blood vessel so it doesn't bleed again.

It sounds an awful lot more scary than it is, and Tyler will be absolutely fine afterwards. He'll heal nicely.'

But the waiting dragged on and on and on.

Were there complications? Louisa wondered silently. Had something gone wrong? Was Liam going to come out of Theatre, looking drained and empty, and tell them that he'd done his best but he hadn't been able to save her son? Oh, God, no. Please don't let her lose him. He was the light of her life. Without him…

The thought was so terrifying that she couldn't breathe.

Every time she glanced at the clock, only a few seconds had dragged by. Each minute seemed like a lifetime; and each time she glanced up a little more hope seeped out of her heart. Her baby, her precious baby… How was she going to bear it without him? How could she carry on with a Tyler-shaped hole in her life?

When Dominic fetched sandwiches for them, she shook her head. 'I can't eat.' Swallowing would choke her.

'You have to eat,' he said, relentless. 'If you don't eat to keep your strength up, you're not going to be much use to Ty, are you? And he's going to need you after this.'

'What if—?' she began.

'No,' he cut in. 'Don't borrow trouble. These things take time. It feels like years out here and nanoseconds in Theatre. And it's better that Liam's thorough than if he rushes the job. It's going to be fine.'

At last, Liam and the neuro team came out.

And he was *smiling*.

Everything was all right.

Louisa closed her eyes and offered up a prayer of thanks.

'I'm delighted to tell you that the op was a success,' Liam said. 'I've removed the clot, located the bleed and tied off the blood vessel. I want him to stay in for a week, just while he's getting over the op, and then he can go home. He'll have headaches for a while, but he'll be absolutely fine. He's in the recovery room at the moment, coming round, and you should be able to see him in a few minutes.'

Her baby was safe.

Tyler was going to be all right.

All the worry and the fear stopped; and she'd been tense for so long, holding herself together, that she simply imploded. She burst into tears, sobbing out all the worry and the nightmares; and Dominic held her, letting her cry all over him.

'It's OK,' he whispered. 'You don't have to be brave any more. I'm here. I'm not going anywhere.'

Finally, she was all cried out; when she lifted her head off his shoulder, she saw that she'd soaked his shirt.

'I'm so sorry. I didn't mean to bawl all over you.'

'It's relief,' he said softly. 'You know that—we see enough relatives being brave, holding everything in, fearing the worst; and when they know everything's all right they know they can let go and that's when they start crying. Come on, let's go and splash some water on your face, and then you can see Ty.'

The coolness of the water against her skin made her feel better, and she'd managed to pull herself together by the time the anaesthetist came out to tell her that she could go in and see her son.

'Aren't you coming?' she asked when Dominic hung back.

He shook his head. 'It's not my place. But I'll come

and see him when he's settled on the ward. You know where I am if you need me.'

She could see from his eyes that he was sincere; he really would be there, if she needed him. Yet she still couldn't shake the feeling: if she hadn't got involved with Dominic and agreed to let Tyler take part in the jousting day rather than be just a spectator, this wouldn't have happened. Her attention would have been completely on her son, as it should've been, instead of partly on the man who'd tempted her to risk her heart again.

So maybe she should heed the warning and back off. At least until Tyler was old enough to look after himself more.

Which made her feel incredibly guilty about leaning on Dominic just now, letting him believe that there could be more between them—but, in future, they'd better stick to being colleagues.

Though Dominic didn't make it easy for her. He visited every morning before his shift, during every lunch break, and every evening at the end of his shift. On day three, when Tyler was starting to get bored and irritable and sick of being cooped up in bed, he produced a magnetic chess set and taught the little boy to play. 'Chess,' he said to Tyler, 'is the best game in the world. And, better still, you can play it any time. You can even play it long-distance—my brother and I used to play by email when we were students. He'd send me his move, and then I'd send him mine.' He grinned. 'Nowadays, we do it by text.'

And at the same time he nagged Louisa about eating properly, kept her in touch with what was happening on the ward, and brought in tubs of prepared out-of-season strawberries to tempt Tyler's appetite and, she suspected, her own.

Although Louisa tried psyching herself up to say to Dominic that they should stop seeing each other, she couldn't do it. Not when Tyler didn't stop talking about him. Plus she saw the way Tyler's face brightened as Dominic arrived, and the enjoyment mirrored in Dominic's eyes as they got out the chess board. How could she destroy that growing friendship and closeness? And Dominic never, ever missed a visit. He might get someone to call up and say he'd be late, but he was always, always there.

When Tyler was well enough to be discharged, Dominic continued his visits, except at her house rather than the ward. Every morning on his way to work he dropped in to start a game of chess with Tyler, and every evening on his way to the stables he called in, made Louisa a cup of tea and handed her a magazine or book to make her sit down and take a few minutes' break, and finished off the chess game.

Though she noticed that Dominic had stopped touching her. No hugs, no hand-holding, no resting his hand on her shoulder. And, whenever he left, he kissed her cheek. Not her mouth.

So had he, too, had second thoughts about their relationship? Yet, if that were the case, surely he would've stopped visiting Tyler? Not that she could ask. She didn't have the energy: and, besides, she wasn't sure what she wanted the answer to be. She was bone-deep tired, miserable and lonely, and she couldn't see a way through it. Not without having a heart-to-heart with Dominic—a conversation that she didn't want to start.

But eventually Louisa let her mother persuade her into

letting her look after Tyler during the day so she could go back to work. Gillian promised faithfully to call her if she had even the slightest worry about Tyler.

Although it felt strange to be back in the department, after two weeks off nursing her son, Louisa's first day back coincided with a cold snap and she didn't have time to think about anything except work. The waiting area was filled with people who'd slipped on the ice and put their hands out to save themselves, landed awkwardly and come to the emergency department in pain. Louisa was kept busy taking patient histories, getting them to show her with their good hand the position of their wrists when they'd fallen, and then sending them off for X-rays. Though she knew even before she sent them what the pictures would tell her: there was a classic Colles' fracture at the end of the distal radius.

For those who had fractures where the bone was in a good position for the break to heal normally, she put a backslab on and rested their arm in a sling. 'You'll need this to splint your arm for a couple of days until the swelling comes down, and then you'll see the fracture clinic to have a lightweight cast fitted,' she explained to her patients. 'You might need a second cast, a couple of weeks later, and you'll be in plaster for up to six weeks.' In two cases, the bone had moved so the patient needed anaesthesia and manipulation to get the bone back in the right place for healing. But in all cases she gave the standard advice to rest the fracture as much as possible, hold it above the heart, and make sure they didn't get the cast or backslab wet as they didn't dry out easily.

Her tenth patient of the day with a Colles' fracture was an elderly woman, and Louisa was careful to check about a history of osteoporosis.

'You know, you're the only one of my patients today who hasn't moaned about the ice,' she said as she examined Miss Castle's hand.

Miss Castle laughed. 'My dear, I've lived through far worse winters than this. Nineteen forty-seven was a terrible winter, with snow on the ground for months, and the drifts were thirty feet deep.'

'We certainly don't get snow like that nowadays,' Louisa agreed. 'That must've been hard to live with.'

Miss Castle nodded. 'Coming just after the end of the war—yes, it was tough. The power stations ran out of coal, so we had power cuts for five hours at a time. The gas pressure was so low that the light would go out and people had to be careful or they'd end up poisoned or with a huge explosion.'

Louisa thought of the last winter, and how only a few centimetres of snow had brought the country to a standstill. 'Do you remember much of it?' she asked.

'Oh, yes.' Miss Castle smiled. 'Apart from having snow feathers on the inside of the windows every morning, I remember we had to keep digging my father's car out of the snow—he was a GP. One day, it was so deep that we couldn't get the car out, so he borrowed the milkman's horse to see his patients. But the horse was used to his daily rounds and insisted on stopping and waiting at every place he normally stopped with the milkman!'

Louisa was charmed. Tyler would love that story, and so would Dominic. Maybe she'd tell them both that evening.

But then in the late afternoon Essie came in to see her, looking grim. 'I need you in Resus—there's been a bad RTA,' she said. 'A young lad's car slid on the ice and smashed into a tree. He seems fine, but the paramedics are bringing him in for a check over. The passenger, his dad, is in a bad way, though.'

'I'll come straight through.'

Dominic came in with the trolley after the handover. 'Eric Scott, aged 43. He was on the side where the car hit the tree, so he has multiple injuries—query spinal injury as well as the usual suspects from blunt trauma. No known allergies, not on any medication, and no medical conditions we need to be aware of. Not sure when he last ate, though.'

The anaesthetist was already on hand; once Eric Scott had been resuscitated, he'd be whisked up to surgery. Eric was laid flat, his neck stabilised with a rigid collar and tape.

The team swung into action to put him on oxygen, insert cannulas, get vital-signs measurements through a pulse oximeter and ECG and take blood samples. 'I want a litre of Hartmann's run in, cross-match six units, and blood samples sent for FBC, Us and Es, and glucose,' Dominic said. 'And I need someone to call Radiology and arrange X-rays—I want lateral cervical spine, chest and anterior-posterior pelvis.'

Eric was still unconscious; his blood pressure was low and his respiration rate was high. 'Looks like a thirty per cent blood loss—so I want a second litre of Hartmann's in after the first,' Dominic said.

Carefully Louisa cut through Eric's clothes to expose his chest so Dominic could examine him. 'Can you note this, Louisa?' he asked as he listened to Eric's chest. 'Sounds on both sides, might have cracked ribs but no sign of flail chest.' He glanced at the monitor. 'His blood pressure should be rising by now—he's losing blood from somewhere.'

Louisa glanced at the ECG. 'Dominic, he's in VF.' VF or ventricular fibrillation meant that electrical activity in the heart had become chaotic, so the lower pumping chambers of the heart were contracting rapidly and fluttering rather than beating. They needed to convert this back into a normal rhythm or they would lose their patient.

Dominic breathed out sharply. 'We're not going to lose you, Eric. Hang on in there.' He glanced at the team. 'Defib.'

He placed the gel pads and paddles in the correct position and checked the ECG. 'Still VF,' he confirmed. 'Charging at two hundred, stand clear—shocking now.' They waited ten seconds to see if the ECG trace changed.

'Charging to two hundred again,' Dominic said, keeping the paddles on the gel pads. 'And clear. Shocking now.'

Again, the ECG trace didn't change. 'Trying three-sixty now, Charging, clear—shocking now.'

But still there was no change. Dominic gave Eric 1 mg of adrenalin. 'CPR, Louisa, can you bag, please?'

She already had the equipment to hand. 'Five compressions, one breath?' she asked.

After a minute of CPR, they did a cycle of shocking again; there was still no response.

'I'm not going to lose you, I'm *not* going to lose you,' Dominic muttered.

They continued the cycles of CPR, adrenalin and shocking.

After twenty minutes, Louisa placed her hand on Dominic's arm. 'His brain's been without oxygen for twenty minutes. He's gone,' she said gently. 'You need to call it.'

'No. One more cycle,' he said.

But it was hopeless.

'Dominic. Call it,' Louisa said softly, 'or I will.'

She could see the muscle flicker in his cheek.

'Everyone else agreed?' he asked.

They nodded.

'Time of...' Dominic's breath hitched. 'Time of death, five thirty-two. Thank you for your help, everyone.' He swallowed hard. 'I'd better go and see the family.'

He looked drained and miserable. And he'd let her lean on him when she'd needed propping up; it was time for her to return the favour. 'I'll come with you,' she offered.

Dominic looked at her, and realised that she understood what was going through his head. That, since Oliver's accident, not being able to save a patient had always hit him harder. 'Thank you,' he said quietly. 'Just give me a second, can you?'

He lingered beside the body and put his hand on Eric Scott's shoulder. 'I'm so sorry. I did my best, and it wasn't enough. God bless,' he whispered, and dragged in a breath before joining Louisa outside the doors to Resus.

'His son's in the family room,' Louisa told him. 'Ian Scott, aged eighteen.'

'Eighteen? Poor kid.'

'He's been checked over and he's fine.'

'OK.' Dominic really, really hated this part of the job—where he took all the hope away from the relatives.

And it would be harder still for this family because there was nobody to blame, no stupid drunk-driver who'd been too arrogant and selfish to consider the lives of others before getting behind the wheel of a car. Just an accident on the ice, which nobody could have prevented.

He walked with her in silence to the family room. Eric Scott's wife wasn't there yet but his son was pacing up and down, looking anxious. As they walked into the room, hope filled his face. 'Is Dad…?' He stopped abruptly as he saw their serious faces. 'Oh, no. Please, *no.*'

'Come and sit down, love,' Louisa said.

'I'm so sorry, Ian,' Dominic told him. 'We did everything we could, but your father had a heart attack and we couldn't get him back.'

'No, he can't—not Dad.' Ian gave a sobbing breath. 'He can't be dead. I haven't even got a scratch. How can Dad be…?'

'That side of the car took the majority of the impact,' Dominic said gently.

'But he can't be dead. He can't be. He *can't.*'

'I'm sorry, love.' Louisa put her arm round him.

'I killed Dad,' Ian said brokenly.

'No, love, the accident killed him,' she reassured him.

'The car—I couldn't do anything. It was sliding and I couldn't brake, couldn't do anything.' He dragged in a breath. 'I wasn't driving fast, wasn't showing off. I just wanted to pick my dad up from work. It's his birthday.' The boy's face worked. 'My tutorial tomorrow morning was cancelled so I knew I could come home and surprise him, say happy birthday in person instead of phoning him. I was going to take him and Mum out to dinner tonight. He was so pleased to see me when he came out of the office. And now he's dead, and it's my fault, and… Oh, God, I wish I hadn't come home and I'd never, ever got behind the wheel of the car!' He collapsed into sobs on Louisa's shoulder.

Dominic crouched in front of Ian's chair and took the boy's hands between his. 'Listen to me, Ian. It was an accident, and it could've happened to anyone. We see lots of people in here whose car has hit a patch of black ice and they've lost control. Even really experienced drivers struggle on ice, so it's not your fault and you're *not* to blame.'

'How am I going to tell Mum?'

'I'll be here with you,' Dominic said. 'I'll help you tell her—but what you need to focus on is that your dad was unconscious, so he wasn't in any pain, and he loved you very much.'

'Do you have any brothers or sisters?' Louisa asked gently.

'No, there's just me.'

'You and your mum still have each other and you'll get through this together,' Dominic said. 'It's going to be tough and you're going to have bad days, but you'll get through this. You just have to keep remembering that this was an accident, one of those things that nobody has any control over.'

A few minutes later, Essie brought Mrs Scott in. She enveloped her son in her arms. 'Ian, the hospital called me and said you were in an accident. Thank God you're all right.' Then she took in the fact that he was sobbing, Eric wasn't there, and Dominic and Louisa weren't smiling.

'Eric?' Horror filled her face. 'No. *No.*'

'I'm sorry,' Dominic said softly. 'He never regained consciousness. We did our best to get him back but I'm sorry, we simply couldn't get his heart started again.'

While he comforted them, Louisa fetched some hot sweet tea and persuaded the Scotts to drink it—just as Dominic had made her drink the stuff after Tyler's accident, knowing that it really was the best thing for shock.

'Can I see him?' Mrs Scott asked.

'Of course you can,' Dominic said, and took her through to where Eric's body lay.

While she'd gone to sort out the tea, Louisa had asked Jess to make sure that Eric's body was covered with a blanket and his face had been washed, to make it easier for his wife and son to see him.

'Take as much time as you need,' Dominic said gently.

'I can get the hospital chaplain for you, if you like?' Louisa offered.

'No, I just want to be alone with him— Oh, Eric.' A tear rolled down Mrs Scott's face as she stroked her husband's forehead. 'How are we going to manage without you?'

'I'll be in my office if you need me,' Dominic said. 'Anything you need, just ask.' He mouthed to Louisa, 'I'm going to sort out the paperwork.'

She could see the strain in the lines around his mouth. Whether he wanted to or not, he needed to talk about this—and she was about the only person who could do this. She'd call her mum and warn her that she'd be late, stay with the Scotts for a little longer, and then she'd tackle Dominic.

CHAPTER EIGHT

DOMINIC stared at the computer screen, not seeing any of the words written there. All he could see was Ian Scott's face, the shock and horror mingling there when he'd learned that his father was dead. The way he'd blamed himself for the accident.

A feeling Dominic knew well: one he'd lived with for more than two years. He too had been in an emergency room while someone he loved had been in Resus, wired up to monitors. Thankfully Oliver had been so fit that his body had been able to cope with the trauma and his heart hadn't given out. Dominic knew he was lucky that Oliver was still alive, but he also knew that his brother, despite the brave face he put on it, was in pain every single day—and it had taken months of hard work to get him to the point where he was now.

He was still brooding when there was a knock on his door. He lifted his head. 'Louisa.'

'Don't say a word. Just drink it.' She handed him a mug.

He took a sip of what he discovered was disgustingly sweet tea, and gagged. 'Thank you for the thought, but this is—'

'Disgusting, I know, but shut up and drink it,' she cut

in. 'Essie just told me you almost never lose a patient in Resus and you take it twice as hard as everyone else. She doesn't know why, but I think I do, so just drink it.'

It was drink it or talk—so, despite the fact that he loathed the stuff, he drank the hot, sweet tea.

'It's brought everything back to you, hasn't it?' she asked gently. 'Being in Resus with your brother.'

There was no point in lying. 'Yes.'

'We see lots of people in here whose car has hit a patch of black ice and they've lost control. Even really experienced drivers struggle on ice.' She paused. 'So you don't blame Ian for the accident.'

'No, of course not. He's just a kid. He hadn't even been driving that long.'

'Can you hear yourself?' she asked softly. 'You could be talking about yourself. What happened with Oliver was an accident, too.'

'An accident that should never have happened. That wouldn't have happened if I hadn't been trying to prove a point.'

'But you don't know that, Dominic. Jousting's dangerous. It could've happened anyway.' She shook her head. 'It's time you let go and stopped trying to be perfect.'

Perfect? She had to be kidding. He knew he was very, very far from perfect.

'You're human. Are you going to beat yourself up for losing Mr Scott—even though he had multiple injuries and the senior consultant wouldn't have been able to save him either?'

'I hardly ever lose a patient.'

'I know you go above and beyond, Dominic. And I know why you do it—you're still trying to make up for what happened with your brother. But you're going to have to come to terms with the fact that nothing you do will ever be able to change the past. All you can do is move on and make the future a better one. You're still crucifying yourself—and it's hurting those who love you as well as hurting you. It's time you moved on.'

Her words hit him on the raw, and he couldn't help lashing out. 'You're a fine one to talk.'

'What do you mean?'

'The way you've been, this last couple of weeks. I know you're worried sick about Ty, so I've tried to give you some space, but you've been sticking up a brick wall between us. You're blaming yourself for the accident—you think it's your fault, and just because you asked me to stay over it's some kind of cosmic payback. That you have to decide between having your son or having a relationship.'

She didn't say a word: she just stared at him, looking stricken.

'I know your ex was a self-centred bastard who didn't deserve you or his son, but that doesn't mean that all men are going to be the same. It doesn't mean that you can't lean on me in case I let you down, because I never would. I've tried to be there for you without pushing you too hard—and that's the only reason why I haven't kissed you properly since the accident—but you're not going to let me close again, are you?' He shook his head, suddenly really angry. 'You've decided you know what's best for everyone. And you're not going to give anyone the chance to have a say in it, are you? You're playing God with everyone's emotions—Tyler's and mine as well as your own—and it's not fair.'

Her face went white. She didn't say a word, just walked out.

And what made it worse was that she didn't slam the door; she closed it quietly.

The anger within him died as fast as it had risen, and Dominic raked a hand through his hair. Hell, he'd really hurt her. He hadn't meant to do that; he'd just lashed out because she'd caught him on the raw. And, although what he'd said to her was true, he could've found a more tactful way of saying it.

He needed to apologise. Now.

Quickly, he logged off the computer and went to find her, but she'd already left.

He called her mobile phone, and a recorded voice informed him that her phone was switched off.

Which meant she was probably driving; and he knew exactly where she was going. Home to her little boy.

He rang the stables. 'Ric, I'm not going to make it tonight. Can Andy exercise Pegasus for me, please?'

'Sure. Is something wrong? Anything I can do?'

'Work,' Dominic lied. Something *was* wrong, but his best friend wouldn't be able to help with this one. This was something he needed to do himself. And he had no idea whether Louisa would even talk to him tonight, let alone open her heart and be honest with him—but he had to try.

It was too late for a florist to be open, so he went to supermarket and bought an armful of the nicest flowers he could find and then to the stationery superstore nearby and bought pencils and a sketchpad for Tyler. When he parked on the road near Louisa's house, he couldn't see her mother's car, so it meant that Gillian had gone home. Good. He liked Louisa's parents—a lot—but what he had to say was for Louisa's ears only.

He rang the doorbell and waited. Finally, she opened

the door, and frowned when she saw him. 'What are you doing here?'

'Several things. You know I promised Tyler I'd call in and see him every day to play chess with him, and I don't break my promises.' He handed her the flowers. 'And these are for you. An apology. I lashed out at you in the office and it wasn't fair of me. What you said…you were right. I'm trying to be perfect and I'm trying to make up for what I did to Oliver—and I can't do either.'

She looked wary. 'I didn't mean to be quite so harsh with you. And I'm sorry for walking out.'

'I think it's time we talked,' he said softly. 'Properly. And we need to be honest with each other.'

'Have you eaten?'

He shrugged. 'I'm not hungry.'

'Mum made a huge batch of chilli. It's in the fridge; I can heat some through for you.'

'No, you're fine.' He paused. 'Can I see Tyler now, before he goes to sleep—and then we'll talk?'

'OK.'

To his relief, she let him in. He spent a while playing chess with Tyler, talking to him about horses and admiring the pictures he'd drawn that day. And Tyler was delighted when Dominic gave him the sketchbook and pencils. 'I'll draw you on Pegasus.'

'I'd really like that,' Dominic said, meaning it.

'When I'm better, can we go swimming again?' Tyler asked.

'Sure we can.' Dominic smiled at him.

'And can I go back to the stables?'

A good question: and one he knew Louisa had been avoiding. He couldn't make the decision for her: it simply wasn't his place. 'You need to ask your mum that, not me,' he said gently. He stroked the fuzz of Tyler's hair, which had been shaved for the operation and was now starting to grow back. 'Time to get some rest, sweetheart. I'll send your mum up to give you a kiss goodnight.'

'Goodnight, Dominic.' Tyler hugged him. 'Love you.'

All the air whooshed out of Dominic's lungs. He couldn't say a word; he just hugged the little boy tightly back.

This was what it felt like to be a father.

He'd had no idea. No idea at all. It wasn't something he'd ever thought about, either before the accident, when he'd dated a string of gorgeous women, or afterwards, when he'd been too racked with guilt to think about anything else.

But now he knew. And it blew him away. This was something bigger than he'd ever felt in his life. That special feeling of knowing that you'd tackle any hurdle to make the child's life easier, no matter what it took; that you wanted to see him grow up into a man you'd be proud to call your friend. A fierce kind of protectiveness, mingled with fear and awe and wonder.

And then it really hit him.

He'd lay down his life for Tyler and Louisa.

And he wanted to be a family with them.

He wanted to be there for a whole string of firsts—Ty's first day at senior school, his first girlfriend, the day his exam results came through, his first driving lesson. All of it, the good and the bad—and even the tough times wouldn't be so tough because they'd be a family and they'd be there for each other.

Though whether Louisa would believe in him enough to let him do that was a whole different issue.

'Love you, too,' he said when he could finally speak again. 'Sleep tight.'

He found Louisa in the kitchen. 'Tyler's about to go to sleep—I said I'd send you up to give him a kiss goodnight.'

'OK. I'll go up now.'

Her eyes were huge with worry. About her son? Or about what he wanted to talk to her about? He cupped her face in his hands—and how good it felt to have her skin against his again. 'You're panicking,' he said softly. 'Don't. I'm not going to rant and rave. But we do need to talk. How about I make us both a coffee while you're tucking Tyler in?'

'Thanks. That'd be good.'

She returned to the kitchen just as he'd added milk to their coffee. 'Are you sure about the chilli?'

This wasn't just her natural hospitality, he knew. It was an avoidance tactic. 'I'm perfectly sure.' He looked at her. 'All I want to do is hold you, Louisa.'

'That's not a good idea.' She sat down at the kitchen table.

And he had a pretty good idea why: she was putting a physical barrier between them as well as a mental one. 'So I was right. You *are* backing off from me.'

'Tyler's still young. He needs stability in his life. I can't...' She shook her head and swallowed. 'This is a mess.'

'You're saying you dare not have a relationship in case it works out and he feels let down—as he was by his father?'

She closed her eyes. 'That's part of it. Which sounds so cowardly.'

'No, you're right to protect him—Tyler's only eight.

He does need stability.' He paused. 'But you and I—we agreed we'd keep what's happening between us to ourselves until we knew where this was taking us. So we're no threat to his stability.' He paused. 'You said that was part of it. What's the rest?'

She dragged in a breath. 'It sounds ridiculous.'

'I can't read your mind,' he said softly. Though he had a pretty good idea what was haunting her.

'Wanting you *and* Tyler. It's greedy. Wanting it all.'

'No. It's perfectly normal. A child and a relationship.' He took a risk. 'It's called being a family.'

She said nothing, and he couldn't read her expression at all. OK. One of them was going to have to be brave and call it. Clearly it was going to be him. 'Louisa, the accident happened. It has nothing to do with the fact that you asked me to stay over, that we were planning to make love together for the first time that night. It wasn't some kind of message to you saying that you had to give me up. It wasn't someone saying that you have to choose between us.' Had her husband given her that kind of ultimatum? Or had he simply rejected them both? Whatever, Louisa was clearly still hurting. 'You don't have to choose between me and your son. I know you come as a package. And I happen to want both parts of that package—you *and* Tyler.'

She cupped her hands round her mug. 'I don't know what to say.'

He could tell her what Tyler had said to him that evening, but he knew that would influence her decision. And he needed to know that she wanted him for himself, not just because her son had grown close to him. 'If you've decided that seeing me is a mistake because now you've got to know me better you realise you don't like me, or you don't find me attractive enough to go to bed with me, then fair enough. I won't be particularly thrilled about it—because I like you and I most definitely want to go to bed with you—but I'll accept your decision and I'll try my hardest to treat you professionally at work and be polite and friendly at the stables.' He held her gaze. 'But no other reason is good enough, Louisa. Be very clear about that.'

She dragged in a breath. 'You're pushing me, Dominic.'

'I know. And I'm going to keep pushing.' He wouldn't let her look away. 'Louisa. I like you. More than like you. And I need to know how you feel about me.'

Panic flittered across her face. 'This whole thing scares me. Before the accident, I thought I wanted to take things between us further.'

'That's what I wanted, too. So what's changed, apart from the accident?'

'I...' She shook her head in apparent frustration. 'I know what you just said, and logically I know you're right, but I can't get it out of my head. I keep thinking that it was karma. That if I hadn't wanted you so much, it wouldn't have happened.'

'That really isn't true.' He paused. 'Though I get where you're coming from. I've spent two years believing that it was my fault that Oliver had the accident, because I really wanted to prove I was better than him at something. I went over and over in my mind what happened: was the way I jousted against him any different from the way I jousted against anyone else?'

'Was it?' she asked.

'Probably not,' he admitted, 'but I don't know if I'll

ever be able to get the doubt out of my head. Or the guilt.'

'And it stopped you having a relationship with anyone.'

'Before the accident, I was too busy playing and enjoying life to settle down. Afterwards…I blamed myself for what happened and I didn't feel I deserved a relationship,' he said. 'Until you. You reached me in the way nobody else could. And when you asked me to stay over that night—it was like my birthday and Christmas and every red-letter day rolled into one. I wanted you just as much as you wanted me.' He paused. 'As far as I'm concerned, nothing's changed. I still want you. But I know you've been worried sick about Ty and I didn't want to push you and make you feel that you had to split yourself between us. That's the only reason I've been holding back. Not because I changed my mind.'

'You've been very patient. Thank you.' She bit her lip. 'But I don't know where we go from here.'

'Let me make it easier for you. We'll start with a question and I want a one-word answer. Do you like me—yes or no?'

'Yes,' she whispered.

'I like you, too. I want to see you, and I think you want to see me—but you're scared that it's all going to go wrong. That you're going to get hurt. That Ty's going to get hurt.'

She nodded.

'I don't have any cast-iron guarantees,' he said softly. 'But I would never intentionally hurt you or Tyler. So that's a start. And it feels like years since I held you— and I miss you. Louisa, please?'

Just when he thought she was going to refuse, she

scraped her chair back and walked round to his side of
the table. He pushed his chair back, scooped her onto
his lap and held her close, resting his forehead on her
shoulder so he could breathe in her scent. 'Louisa. I've
missed this so much.'

'I've missed it, too,' she said shakily.

He lifted his head, then looked her straight in the eye.
He could see longing mixed with fear and confusion. He
didn't know how to take the fear away. Or the confusion.
But the longing—he could do something about that.

Slowly, gently, he touched his lips to hers. A gentle,
sweet, reassuring kiss.

But once wasn't enough.

And then she was kissing him back and it was as
if someone had lit touchpaper. Her hands were in his
hair, his mouth was jammed over hers, and somehow
his hands had slid under the hem of her top and his
palms were flat against her soft, soft skin. He could feel
the peaks of her nipples against his chest, and he knew
that, sitting on his lap, she'd be just as aware of his own
arousal.

When he broke the kiss, they were both shaking.

'I'm sorry,' he said. 'I didn't mean to come on so
strong. I...' No. If he told her exactly how he felt, he
knew he'd scare her away. He had to be patient for just
a little longer. Take it slowly. 'I'm sorry,' he repeated.

'It wasn't just you,' she admitted.

Hope flared. 'So this thing between us—we're still
seeing where it takes us?'

'As long as Tyler comes first.'

He brushed a kiss against her mouth. 'Of course he
will. And I'll try to be patient. We'll wait until he gets
back on his feet before we take it further between us.'

There was something else he wanted to ask her, but not yet. They needed a little time. Time for her to trust her instincts again and let him as close as he'd been before the accident. 'I'd better go now. While my good intentions still have control of me.' He moistened suddenly dry lips with the tip of his tongue. 'I want you. Very, very badly. And I think we both know it could happen right here, right now.'

Her eyes were huge. 'Yes.'

'But it's not going to. The first time between us—I want it to be special. When Tyler's staying overnight with his grandparents and neither of us is going to be worrying about him. When we have the time and space to focus on each other, just for a little while.' He stroked her face. 'I want it to be something we both remember. For the rest of our days.'

CHAPTER NINE

OVER the next couple of weeks, Tyler's condition improved and the headaches stopped, to the point where Louisa was happy for him to go back to school. And although she and Dominic were officially 'just good friends' at work and at the stables, in private they drew closer. Dominic ate with her and Tyler every night, dropping in to see them between the end of his shift and going to the stables. Tyler learned not to time him exactly, because Dominic had explained to him that the time he arrived depended on his patient; but he always rang to say he was leaving the hospital, so Louisa didn't have to guess what time to serve dinner. And she was aware of how much her son looked forward to seeing Dominic in the evenings, talking about his day and playing chess and showing him his artwork. He never stopped talking about Dominic. And she'd noticed that Tyler greeted him with the same kind of hug he reserved for her and his grandparents, and that Dominic was just as affectionate back.

Dominic also called in on his way home from the stables, for a snatched half-hour of quiet time together when Tyler was asleep. Time when they lay full length on the sofa, wrapped in each other's arms, sometimes just relaxing in each other's nearness without needing to talk, and at other times talking about their hopes and dreams. He was the first person she'd actually told that she wanted to be nursing director some day; and he'd been incredibly supportive.

'You'd make a really good job of it. Though I think you'd have to change the role so you get some hands-on time with patients. If you were stuck doing nothing but admin, you'd miss the practical side too much.' He stroked her face. 'Though you'd also get to do more teaching, and I think that'd be right up your street. And you'd be really good on the PR side.'

She felt herself go pink with pleasure. 'You really think so?'

'Really. You're fantastic with people.' He kissed her lightly. 'You're an amazing woman, Louisa Austin. And I'm proud of you.'

She'd always thought that Jack had resented her work; then again, maybe Dominic understood it more because he worked in the same area, faced the same challenges. 'Thank you,' she said softly.

'You're welcome.' He stole another kiss. 'There was something else I wanted to talk to you about. Ty's desperate to go back to his riding lessons.'

She shook her head. 'He's not ready yet.'

He raised an eyebrow. 'You mean, *you're* not ready.'

'Same thing.'

'No, it isn't. Yes, he'll probably fall off again at some point, but he learned a pretty hard lesson about double-checking your equipment. He'll never make that mistake again. Next time he comes off, he might just have a bruise, or a dent in his dignity.'

'Or a broken arm.'

'At this age, they heal quickly. And he's just as likely to get a broken arm falling over in the playground at school,' Dominic pointed out. 'Think how many kids his age come in to our department and end up with a backslab.'

'I'm not ready for him to go back to riding yet, Dominic.'

'Life isn't perfect and sometimes you get knocked back, but you have to get up, dust yourself down and try again.' He held her closer. 'And the thing is, he'll know that if he does fall off again, you'll be there, you'll kiss it better, and you'll help him get back on the horse again. Just as you will when he encounters other difficulties in life.'

She looked at him. 'It's not as if you went straight back to jousting after Oliver's accident.'

'That was because my head wasn't in the right place.' He sighed. 'OK, so I'm being a hypocrite.'

'And pushy.'

He refused to let her wriggle out of his arms. 'OK. But it's the Christmas party at the stables, the third Saturday in December. He'd get a huge amount from it. And it'll help him bond with the other kids.'

'You're trying to pressure me.'

'No, honey. I'm trying to help you. Yes, I admit, there is a teensy bit of riding involved—but it's all very strictly supervised, and every single rider has an assistant. They look so cute, Louisa. The kids all wear reindeer antlers on their hard hats. It's all done indoors, so there's no worry about the weather. Then, when they've had a short ride, Bea puts music on and everyone has a bit of a dance or sings along, whatever they want to do. The less mobile kids can have their faces painted if they want—then it's food, a visit from Santa, and home. They each get a present from the pony they ride—and it's just lovely.' He paused. 'Ty would really enjoy it. And so would you. And your parents would love watching him.'

'I'll think about it,' Louisa said.

He stole a kiss. 'OK. That's all I'll ask. And I won't push any more.'

'Thank you.'

'I did have another question for you.'

'Involving the stables?'

'No, but it involves you and Ty.' This was the biggie. The equivalent of asking her to go public. Would she say yes or no? 'My brother's getting married. And, um, I wondered if you'd both like to come to the wedding as my guests.'

She was silent for so long that he knew what the answer was. 'OK. Sorry for pushing. Though I could reassure you that there won't be any horses involved.'

'It's not that.' Her eyes brimmed with tears. 'It's the fact you asked Ty as well.'

'Why wouldn't I?'

'You know how direct he is. He might say the wrong thing and upset someone.'

He kissed her lightly. 'He'll be much too busy having a good time with my parents' dogs. Though I admit that'll probably mean he'll step up the nagging for a puppy afterwards.'

She frowned. 'Your parents' dogs would be at the wedding?'

'Well, not at the wedding itself.' He smiled. 'But they'll be around.'

'He'd love that.' She bit her lip. 'But I think I'd better say no. He finds a big group of people he doesn't know a bit difficult to handle. We'd probably end up leaving early and that'd put you in an awkward position.'

Dominic really didn't want to make Ty feel uncomfortable; but he had a feeling that Louisa was using her son as an excuse. Meeting his family would mean going public about their relationship, and she clearly still wasn't ready even to consider it.

He'd just have to be patient for a bit longer.

'OK.' He kissed her lightly. 'I'd better let you get some sleep. See you at work.'

But Louisa couldn't sleep that night.

Dominic had asked her to his brother's wedding. Something that would be incredibly emotional for him; he hadn't said as much, but she had the feeling that he could do with someone to lean on. Someone to help him keep the regrets and the guilt at bay.

And he'd let her lean on him. Big time. He'd pushed a little—especially where Tyler and the stables were concerned—but, when she'd said no, he hadn't shouted her down. He'd let her know his opinion, but he'd appreciated the fact that she wanted to make her own decisions.

Time, she thought, for payback. To give him a little support, the way he'd been there for her throughout Tyler's injury and his convalescence.

She called her mother the next morning, before work, to ask a favour; and, although she fully intended to find Dominic before her shift started, she discovered that he was already in Resus, dealing with a patient with a heart attack. And she was kept busy in Minors with people who'd slipped on the ice and twisted their ankles, and then a chef with a nasty burn that needed a dressing; she sent him away with notes on what to do next and a follow-up appointment to check how well it was healing. Then she was kept busy with a builder who'd slipped from some scaffolding and his ankle was swollen and painful. She took a full medical history and asked exactly what had happened when he'd fallen, so she had a better idea of how he'd landed and whether it was likely to be a bone injury or soft tissue. Although she had a feeling it was more likely to be a sprain, she sent him for an X-ray to make absolutely sure it wasn't a fracture, and checked over a teenager with a piercing that had gone septic while she was waiting for the X-ray results to come back.

A quick check on-screen showed her that there wasn't a fracture.

'That's a relief,' he said, blowing out a breath. 'I couldn't afford to be off work for weeks now, not with Christmas coming up at a rate of knots!'

'You do need to rest it for the next two days, though,' she warned him. 'The best thing you can do is prop it on a pillow so it's level with your heart, and keep it up as much as possible until the swelling goes down. If you put ice packs on—wrap in a towel so it doesn't burn your skin—that will also help with the swelling and bruising. Painkillers should take the edge off it. After a couple of days you can start to use it again, but by that I mean *gentle* exercise, to ease yourself back in. No marathons, and definitely no more using the scaffolding as a slide, OK?'

He gave a rueful laugh. 'I'll remember that!'

'I'm going to put a tubular elastic bandage on your ankle to give it support and compression, though you need to take it off before bed.' She smiled at him as she fitted the bandage. 'I know I've just rattled on at you and it's going to be hard to remember everything I said, so

I'll give you a leaflet.' She quickly found the information leaflet on the computer, then printed it off.

'It's all on computer now?'

'It makes life a lot easier than finding fiddly bits of paper,' she said. 'Mind you, we always know where the sprains leaflet is. We see a lot of them in here—people who've landed awkwardly in sports, or slipped on the stairs or off a kerb. And don't start me on the evils of high heels!'

He laughed, ''Fraid I only do lace-up boots or trainers, love.'

'They'll be good support for you.' She saw him out, updated the notes and called her next patient.

How ironic that, on the day she really wanted to talk to Dominic, she didn't get a chance to have a break. She was kept busy in Minors for the rest of the day. Her last patient was a teenager who looked very sheepish and had a long, curly piece of wire sticking out of his thumb.

'I don't know if I dare ask,' she said.

'I was a bit bored in the first lesson after lunch,' he muttered. 'It's the spring from my pen. I wondered what would happen if I uncoiled it. I didn't know the end was going to be sharp.'

His mother ruffled his hair. 'You know now, love.' She rolled her eyes. 'I got a call from the school telling me he had a six-inch piece of metal sticking out of his hand, so could I please come and pick him up and I was having kittens that he'd hurt himself in metalwork! I did think about pulling it out myself, but Rob wouldn't let me. School said it was curved at the end and I should bring him here.'

'I'm such an idiot,' Rob muttered, his face turning beetroot.

'No, love, you're a teenager,' his mum said, patting his arm. 'It isn't the first time you've done something daft and it won't be the last—and your brother's the same. I'm just glad it's not a thick bit of steel stuck through your palm.'

'Does it hurt?' Louisa asked.

'A bit,' Rob admitted. 'Are you going to cut it out?'

'I'll send you down to X-Ray, and then we'll see what's there and know the best way to deal with it. Don't worry,' Louisa reassured him.

The X-ray showed that the wire was curved in slightly but wasn't too deep, so it wouldn't have to be cut out. 'I'll just snip most of it off with wire cutters,' Louisa said, 'to get it out of the way, and then I'll use forceps to take it out. It might sting a bit, but I'll be as gentle as I can.'

On the way to fetch the department's wire cutters, she bumped into Dominic. 'Hi. Busy day?'

'You're telling me.' He rolled his eyes. 'Why the wire cutters?'

'I have a teenager with a spring stuck in his hand; I need to cut most of it off to get it out of the way so that I can remove it properly.'

'Do you want me to do it? I know you're perfectly capable of doing it, but I'm a bit brawnier than you are—if the wire's thick, I can cut it more quickly than you can and that'll be less stressful for your patient.'

Typical Dominic, putting someone else first. 'Thank you. I appreciate that.' She took him through to Minors and introduced him to Rob and his mother. Dominic wielded the wire-cutters; the spring proved to be tough, and Rob gave a muttered 'Ow!'

'Sorry, Rob,' Dominic said as the spring came out.

''S OK,' Rob said. 'It's out now.'

Louisa checked the spring against the X-ray. 'Out cleanly, so you should be fine—your thumb might be a bit sore for a day or two, but you don't have to worry about infection. Let me clean that for you with a bit of antiseptic.'

Dominic chatted to Rob, keeping his mind off the fact that his thumb was stinging as Louisa cleaned the area with antiseptic. He was so kind, so caring, she thought. He had so much to give. And it was time she stopped keeping him at arm's length.

When Rob and his mother left, Louisa put her hand on Dominic's arm. 'Can I have a quick word?'

He looked slightly wary. 'Sure.'

'Last night…I was a bit hasty.' She took a deep breath. 'I still don't think Ty would cope too well with a wedding, but I asked Mum and Dad if they'd have him for the day. So, if the offer's still open—yes, please, I'd love to go to the wedding with you.'

Dominic sucked in a breath. 'As my friend, or as my colleague?'

'Not as your colleague,' she said. 'Or as your "good friend".' If he was going to introduce her to his family, then they'd do it properly. 'I was thinking as your girlfriend.' She wrinkled her nose. 'Well, I'm probably a bit too old to be called a girlfriend. Partner, then.'

In response, he wrapped his arms round her and kissed her soundly.

Obviously she looked shocked, because he laughed. 'Hey. You're standing under some mistletoe.'

'No, I'm not. We don't do anything more than tinsel and cards in the admin areas and a tree in Reception, and you know it.'

'Imaginary mistletoe, then. And I should warn you

that there's a lot of it about at this time of year. I might have to kiss you in all sorts of places.' His eyes glittered. 'Thank you. I know it was a big ask.'

'When is it, so I can let Mum and Dad know?'

'The Saturday after next.'

'What?' She stared at him in surprise. 'Dominic, haven't you left it a bit late? I mean, what about table plans and everything?'

'That won't be a problem. Two minutes on a computer, that's all.' He paused. 'Um, and it's not a day thing. It's a weekend.'

'A whole weekend?' She knew she was sounding like a parrot, but Dominic had left her too stunned to do anything else but repeat what he said. How could a man who was so organised at work be so hopelessly disorganised about his brother's wedding?

'Dinner with my family on Friday night,' Dominic explained, 'then the wedding itself on Saturday. And we'll stay over on Saturday night.'

'In a hotel near your family?'

'No. We'll stay at the castle.'

'Castle?'

'Amberhurst.'

She smiled. 'What a lovely setting. I didn't realise they held wedding receptions there or that you could book a room to stay there.'

'You can't.'

She frowned. 'I'm not with you. You just said your brother's getting married there.'

'It's a family tradition to marry at the church in the castle grounds and, with Oliver being the eldest son...' He shrugged. 'I guess it's the obvious place.'

She suddenly realised. 'You mean your family *owns* Amberhurst Castle?'

'Yes.'

She sat down, shaking her head in disbelief. 'Dominic, we went there for the jousting, and you never said a word.'

'I was going to tell you when we were there. I was going to introduce you and Tyler to Oliver and my parents—but then Ty came off the pony and there just wasn't time.'

She blew out a breath. 'Dominic, what else aren't you telling me?'

'Nothing. It's not a big deal.'

'Isn't it? I feel a bit out of my depth,' she said. 'Your parents own a castle. So that means this is going to be a society wedding—and, well, you've met my family. We're not posh.'

He looked surprised. 'Your parents are lovely. And it's not about being posh or any society stuff. It's just a quiet family wedding, at my family's home. And I can assure you, you'll fit right in. Just as I do with your family.'

He scooped her up, sat down on her chair, and settled her on his lap. 'The reason I didn't ask you about the wedding earlier was because Ty was still recovering and I didn't want to put any pressure on you, in case he wasn't well enough to come. I didn't want you to feel obliged to go to the wedding because you'd accepted the invitation and then end up spending the whole time worrying yourself sick about him. And you can change your mind about him joining us at any time—even on the morning of the wedding itself. It won't be a problem for anyone.'

He really wanted her there. He wanted to introduce her to his family. As his partner. And he'd included Ty.

'Come with me,' he said softly. 'I really want you there with me.'

'OK. But I need to know the dress code,' she warned. 'And what colour the bridesmaids are wearing, so I don't clash.'

'I'll text Oliver and find out,' he said. He rested his forehead against her shoulder. 'I'm sorry I didn't tell you before. I'm not very good at timing.'

'You're telling me,' she said drily, stroking the hair back from his forehead. 'And you'd better let me go before someone walks in and catches us in a clinch. We're meant to be concentrating on our patients, Dr Hurst, not snuggling up together at my desk.'

He stole a kiss, then let her wriggle off her lap. 'I think I need you to keep me on the straight and narrow.'

'What about the wedding list?'

'I've already ordered their present. But if you offer to wrap it for me,' he said with a smile, 'I'll be your slave. I'm hopeless at wrapping.'

'I can't imagine you being hopeless at anything,' she said drily.

And now she had to find an outfit suitable for a society wedding, and she'd have to go shopping on Saturday—the first Saturday in December, when the shops would be crowded with people brandishing Christmas lists. One of her least favourite chores. Especially as it meant that she'd miss out on spending precious weekend time with Ty.

But her mother came to the rescue. 'We'll have a look online—then I'll go into town tomorrow armed with your shortlist. You're the same size as me, so I can try them on, and I'll bring you the ones I think will suit you best and take the others back the next day.'

'You're wonderful. And I owe you a spa day,' Louisa said.

Gillian laughed. 'I'll hold you to that.'

But what her mother came up with the following day was nothing like the dresses Louisa had chosen with her on the internet. Gillian had picked a violet-coloured dress with a sweetheart neckline and strappy top, with an organza skirt that fell softly from the empire waistline almost to her ankles. There was a lilac pashmina to go with it, and an organza and feather fascinator in a perfect matching colour, and the prettiest underwear Louisa had ever seen—as well as a pair of black strappy shoes that she didn't think she'd be able to walk in, let alone dance in.

Oh, help. She hadn't even thought about dancing.

'Mum, this looks a bit…'

'I don't care. Try it on,' Gillian said firmly.

The dress fitted perfectly. The shoes were far more comfortable than they looked. And Louisa stared at herself in the mirror, surprised.

'You look gorgeous,' Gillian said. 'Wear your hair up, with a couple of strands down and curled to soften it.' She produced a box from her handbag. 'And wear Granny's pearls. They'll set this off beautifully.'

'Mum—thank you so much. You're wonderful.' Louisa hugged her. 'And I meant it about that spa day.'

'I'll look forward to that, darling.' Gillian hugged her back. 'So does this mean that we can stop pretending that you and Dominic are just good friends now?'

'We *are* good friends.'

'You're a bit more than that, love,' Gillian said.

Louisa blinked. 'How did you know?'

'Apart from the fact that mothers have a sixth sense about these things,' Gillian said drily, 'it's obvious in the way you look at each other.' She paused. 'He's a much, much better man than Jack ever was. He's reliable, he's kind and he adores Ty. I think you're good together. So does your father. And it's about time you had a bit of happiness.'

Tear pricked her eyes. 'Oh, Mum.'

'Don't,' Gillian warned, 'or I'll start crying, too, and then Ty will want to know what's wrong. Come on. Let's go and ask the boys what they think of your glad rags.' She tucked her arm into Louisa's. 'I'm so proud of you, the woman you've become. And I think Dominic's the right one. He's good enough for my girl.'

CHAPTER TEN

ON THE Friday evening of the following week, Dominic drove Louisa to Amberhurst for the pre-wedding dinner. He stopped in front of the gates, got out of the car and tapped a code into a discreet panel by the wall. The gates swung open silently and then closed again behind them as he drove through; the castle loomed in front of them.

When he eventually parked the car in front of the castle, Louisa felt as if her stomach was tied in knots. Now she had an idea how Dominic must have felt about meeting her parents. Would she measure up?

'They'll love you,' Dominic said.

She blinked. 'Did I just say that out loud?'

'Uh-huh.' He kissed her swiftly. 'Give it five minutes, and I promise you'll feel at home. My family's very normal. Well. Normal*ish*,' he amended. 'I suppose they're a bit eccentric.'

But he loved them. She could see that in his expression. So she was prepared to love them, too.

He insisted on carrying her case as well as his own. He set them down briefly while he tapped in a code into the panel by the front door, then opened the door and toted them inside. Immediately there was a huge amount of barking and four assorted dogs burst into the hallway.

'It's OK, they won't hurt you. They're more likely to lick you to death.' He stooped down and allowed them to leap about over him, and she followed his lead.

'Oh, you horrible lot! Benjy, Cody, Buster and Fudge, *heel*.' An older woman—Louisa recognised her from the photographs in Dominic's flat as his mother—came into the hallway. She was beautifully dressed and perfectly coiffured; Louisa felt a teensy bit daunted. But she had the same smile as Dominic, and her eyes were warm as she assessed the younger woman. She kissed Dominic. 'Hello, darling.'

He kissed her back. 'Hello, Ma.'

'You're just in time.' She smiled at Louisa. 'And you must be Louisa.'

'Hello.' Louisa smiled awkwardly. 'I'm so sorry, I'm afraid I don't know much about etiquette. Do I call you Lady Hurst? And, um, do I curtsey?'

'You call me Milly, and forget all the other nonsense.' Dominic's mother enveloped her in a hug. 'Welcome to Amberhurst, Louisa. And I'm sorry about this lot giving you such a noisy welcome.'

'It's OK. I like dogs.'

'Even Great Danes?' Milly asked, looking surprised. 'Fudge, *sit*,' she said in exasperation to the Great Dane, who'd sneaked forward and was busy sniffing Louisa's knees.

Louisa laughed and fondled the dog's ears. 'My son's desperate for a wolfhound. I've explained that we can't have a dog where we live now, but maybe one day we can have a dog. Something spaniel-sized, maybe.' She knew that Tyler would adore these four, from the little Jack Russell right up to the huge Great Dane.

'I'm sorry that Tyler wasn't able to come to the wedding,' Milly said. 'I was looking forward to meeting him. Dominic explained why and I completely understand. I remember when Andy was little; if there were too many people around it made him uncomfortable, so he'd go and sit with the dogs or the horses—and his parents used to have to go and search for him, worried sick that he'd wandered near the pond or something.' She shivered. 'Perish the thought. But maybe when it's a little quieter around here he might like to come and visit and play with the dogs.'

'Thank you. That's very kind of you.'

'Everyone's in the drawing room. Dinner's almost ready. Dominic, do you want to take the luggage upstairs? Louisa, I'm just going to give these monsters their dinner in the boot room to shut them up, but do come and have a glass of champagne.' Milly raised an eyebrow. 'Or do you need the bathroom first?'

'No, I'm fine, thank you.' Louisa couldn't help feeling a little shy, but Dominic had already started upstairs with the cases.

Awkwardly, she handed Milly the posh chocolates she'd bought in her lunch hour. 'I, um, wanted to bring something to say thank you for having me to stay, but flowers didn't feel right—not the day before a wedding when there are going to be flowers everywhere.'

'That's so *sweet* of you, but you really didn't have to bring anything. I know I have you to thank for the smile being back behind Dominic's eyes, and that's the best gift any mother can ask for. Her child being happy.'

Just what her own mother had said. And how she

knew she'd feel about Tyler's eventual choice of partner, when he grew up.

Milly looked away, but not before Louisa caught the sheen of tears in her eyes. She blinked them away rapidly and cleared her throat. 'And these are for me?' She peeked at the package and beamed. 'Oh, I *love* these. I know I'm going to like you, Louisa. A lot. You'll have to forgive me for being rude and not offering these to everyone else with coffee. These are going in my study.'

'Would that be in your "secret" chocolate drawer, Ma?' Dominic drawled as he caught them up.

'Which is kept locked.'

'And you think that's going to stop anyone?' He laughed. 'Oliver taught me how to pick that lock when I was nine. And Papa taught *him*.'

Milly rolled her eyes. 'You're terrible. The three of you. How I put up with you, I really do not know! Dominic, I'm going to give these monsters their dinner before they sneak into the kitchen and start trying to scrounge things from Cook. Take Louisa through to the drawing room.' She shooed the dogs further along the corridor, and they bounced joyfully before her, while Dominic ushered Louisa to the drawing room.

Dominic caught Louisa's hand as they reached the doorway. 'OK?' he mouthed.

'Fine,' she mouthed back. She liked Dominic's mother, and she was pretty sure she'd like the rest of his family, too.

The room was full of people. She picked out Dominic's father and brother instantly: they both looked so like him, with the same dark hair and navy-blue eyes, and of course Oliver was the only one in a wheelchair.

Dominic carefully introduced her to everyone,

including Oliver's fiancée, Mina, and her parents, plus several great-aunts and great-uncles. Louisa was aware that everyone was watching them as she was introduced to Oliver, wanting to see whether she'd be fazed by the fact that he was in a wheelchair, but she ignored the feeling of being watched and smiled at Dominic's brother before shaking his hand firmly.

Milly reappeared and handed her a glass of champagne before shepherding everyone into the dining room. The table was enormous, seating eighteen; and all the places were set. It looked exactly like one of the displays in the stately castles Tyler loved visiting, with furniture so highly polished that you could practically see your reflection in it, exquisite porcelain, solid silver cutlery and candelabra, and delicate hand-blown glasses in the deepest blue. There were flowers arranged in what looked to her like priceless antique vases, and the carpet was so thick that you actually sank into it. The walls were covered with paintings and the curtains were rich deep-blue damask. Everything screamed luxury and wealth.

And then she saw the photographs on the mantelpiece. In silver frames. A wedding photograph of Dominic's parents, graduation photographs of the boys, a photograph that was clearly celebrating Oliver and Mina's engagement, and one that looked like a multi-generational family photograph. But the photographs she really loved were the more candid shots of Dominic and Oliver as children, playing in the garden. In one, Dominic had a bucket on his head and a mop in his hand, clearly pretending that he was a knight.

'That's one of my favourites. Sir Hugo's first outing, when he was five,' Milly said with a smile, seeing what had caught Louisa's eye. 'And I love the one in his flat of the two of you with Tyler and Pegasus.'

Louisa knew the photograph she meant. The very same photograph that had pride of place in Tyler's bedroom. 'My mum took that one at the jousting. I'll have a copy made for you, if you like.'

'Thank you. I'd love that. It's the happiest I've seen Dominic for more than two years.' Milly paused. 'We had hoped to meet you at the jousting. But then there was the accident. It must have been terrifying for you.'

'It was. I'm just so lucky Ty's made a complete recovery.' Then Louisa bit her lip, remembering Oliver—who'd also been involved in a riding accident and would never make a complete recovery. 'Sorry, that wasn't very tactful.'

'But it was honest. And Oliver does at least have most of his independence. It could have been an awful lot worse. At least I don't have to cope with an Oliver-shaped hole in my life. That would be a lot, lot harder.' Milly patted her arm.

Louisa discovered that she was seated at the opposite end of the table from Dominic, next to Oliver.

'Can I help you at all?' she asked as Oliver prepared to transfer himself from his state-of-the-art lightweight wheelchair to the dining chair.

'Thanks, but I can manage.' He smiled at her, softening the slight abruptness of his tone. 'It was about time Dominic brought you to meet us. How's your little boy doing?'

'He's fine, thanks.'

'Is he back in the saddle yet?'

She took a deep breath. 'No. I'm not sure I'm ready for that.'

'Of course, it's your decision,' Oliver said. 'But he'll miss out on an awful lot.'

How could he say that, when he'd been so badly injured in a fall from a horse?

As if he could read her thoughts, he said softly, 'Once a horseman, always a horseman. I miss it.' He paused, his eyes growing serious. 'Dominic said he told you about the accident.'

'Yes.'

Oliver looked relieved. 'I'm glad he's talking about it. He refused counselling afterwards, but I think he needed it as much as I did. More than I did, probably. I used to play rugby, and I could've had a bad tackle at any time that would've left me like this. I wouldn't have held it against the person who tackled me, and I don't hold this against my brother.'

'He does enough of that for himself,' Louisa agreed.

He gave her a level look. 'Maybe you're the one who can help him learn to forgive himself. Because it wasn't his fault. It was a stupid accident, and I'm just as much to blame because I wasn't giving the joust my full concentration. I've told him that, but it didn't stop him wearing a hair shirt.' He sighed. 'I'm half-surprised he didn't decide to train as a surgeon to make up for the fact that I'm not one any more. But it'd be a waste if he did—emergency medicine suits him down to the ground.'

'He's an excellent doctor. And he said you were a brilliant surgeon.'

'I was,' Oliver said, with no hint of arrogance—just like Dominic, she thought, Oliver would make enough effort to excel at anything he did. 'But now I intend to be a brilliant GP. I'm retraining. So I'll still get to make patients better—but I'll get to see my patients over the whole of their treatment rather than simply fixing a valve in their heart and waving them off home to recuperate and having no idea whether their lives really are better after the op. And the hours are more family-friendly, which Mina will appreciate—I can do my fair share of changing nappies.' He shrugged. 'If life gives you lemons, you'd better learn to make lemonade—or you're going to wallow in misery, and I can tell you from experience that that's a complete waste of time.'

Milly made everyone change places between courses, so over the next course Louisa ended up sitting next to Roderick, Dominic and Oliver's father, who was incredibly sweet; and over pudding she was charmed by their great-uncles, Rupert and Ashton. After dinner, the women all withdrew to the drawing room again, leaving the men to their port; Louisa finally got to chat to Mina, Oliver's fiancée, who turned out to be incredibly sweet-natured. She and Oliver would definitely be happy together, Louisa thought.

When the men joined them again, Dominic sat on the arm of Louisa's chair, resting his hand on the nape of her neck. Although she knew this was all for show and didn't actually mean anything, she still couldn't help the little thrill running through her at his touch.

Finally people started drifting off to bed.

'Can I help you clear up?' Louisa asked Milly.

'It's all taken care of,' Milly said with a smile.

Of course. To run a house this size, they'd need staff. And Milly had mentioned a cook, earlier.

'But bless you for offering.' Milly gave her a hug.

'We've got a busy day tomorrow. I think we all need to try and get some sleep.'

'Yes. Goodnight,' Louisa said politely.

'I'll see you up,' Dominic said.

'I had a lovely evening,' she said as they walked up the sweeping central staircase. 'I like your family.'

'Good. They liked you, too.' He paused outside a door that she assumed led to her room. 'Um, there's something I need to talk to you about. Can we go inside?'

'Sure.'

He opened the door and flicked on the light. What she saw was a very masculine room—and her case was standing right next to Dominic's.

He looked awkward. 'I thought you were going to be in the room next door to mine, but we have the great-aunts staying and there was a burst pipe yesterday that's made two of the bedrooms uninhabitable, which means we're shorter on space than usual. I'm afraid my mother made a bit of an assumption. She's put us both in my room.'

Meaning that his mother thought they were already sleeping together. Louisa felt the colour shoot into her face. 'Oh.'

'Look, I've got a blanket in the back of the car—I'll go and fetch it. I can sleep on the floor.'

'Dominic.' She placed her hand on his arm before he could open the bedroom door again. 'I'm not going to make you sleep on the floor. We can share a room.'

Colour rose in his face. 'This wasn't some deep, dark plot, you know. I wasn't intending to share a bed with you this weekend. Actually, I'd been planning to take you to Venice in April. The most romantic city in the world, in springtime. And *then* I was going to seduce you.'

'April. That's quite a long time to wait.'

He shrugged. 'You're worth waiting for.'

She could see in his eyes that he meant it. And it melted her. 'Maybe it's time we stopped waiting.'

He sucked in a breath. 'Are you sure about that?'

'Very sure,' she said softly. She tipped her head back so that she could look at him. Lord, he was gorgeous. His pupils were so huge that his eyes looked black, there was the faintest shadow of stubble on his face, and that beautiful mouth… How could she resist?

'You're beautiful. Adorable,' he said softly, and bent his head. He brushed his mouth against hers, and when she leaned into him he caught her lower lip between his, teasing it and cajoling her into letting him deepen the kiss.

Desire spun through her; Dominic was irresistible. And, best of all, he was all hers.

He stroked his fingers under along the bare skin of her back, above the top of her dress. 'Your skin's so soft,' he said, his voice full of wonder. 'Louisa, I really need to touch you.'

She needed him to touch her, too; she could feel her nipples hardening and her breasts were aching. 'Then touch me,' she whispered. 'Please.' Just so he knew this was completely mutual and he wasn't pushing her into anything she didn't already want.

His hands were shaking as he lowered the zip and slid the straps from her shoulders. He dipped his head to nuzzle the skin of her shoulders, making her shiver in delight. She arched against him and his mouth traced a path of kisses along the column of her throat, then slowly along her jaw and up to her mouth, He kissed her again, his mouth sweet and sensual and offering more and more pleasure. She slid her hands into his hair and kissed him back.

He eased the bodice of her dress down towards her waist and his hand skimmed her midriff. She closed her eyes as his hand slip up further underneath and at last he cupped her breast, teasing the hard peak of her nipple between his forefinger and thumb and rubbing it against the lace of her bra.

He broke the kiss, his breathing uneven. 'Louisa, I want to see you.'

She knew what he was asking, and nodded. He slowly eased her dress over her hips, and she shimmied until the material hit the floor. There was a deep, intense look in his eyes as he unhooked her bra and let the lacy garment fall.

And then he looked.

He sucked in a breath. 'You're gorgeous.'

Desire kicked sharply through her. 'I need to see you, too.'

'I'm in your hands.'

Slowly, she removed his tie. Opened the buttons of his shirt, very, very slowly. Pushed the soft cotton off his shoulders. And stared.

It was the first time she'd ever seen him stripped to the waist; there was light sprinkling of hair over his chest, and he had perfect six-pack abs, which she knew came from riding and working in the stables rather than from pumping iron in a gym.

Feeling brave enough to touch him back, now, she stroked his pectoral muscles. 'You look like a Greek god.'

He laughed. 'Hardly. I'm just a man.'

Just? she thought. No, Dominic wasn't 'just' anything.

He was special. And she loved him. Really, really loved him.

Not that she could scare him by telling him that. Not now, when they were going to make love for the first time. Better to concentrate on a different truth: the fact that she really, really wanted him. Physically, he blew her mind.

She reached up and pressed a kiss against his chest, and he gave a sharp intake of breath. 'Do you have any idea how much I want you?'

'About as much as I want you, hopefully.'

His eyes widened. 'Oh, yes. I want you *now*,' he said hoarsely.

Common sense was forgotten; all she knew was that she needed this man to touch her and make her see stars. 'Yes.'

He dipped his head and kissed her throat in a way that made her arch back against him. He drew a line of kisses along her collar-bone, teasing the pulse-point and making her wriggle, and then slowly, slowly moved downwards. His mouth was warm and sweet against her skin, making her want more. Then, at long last, he closed his mouth over her nipple, sucking hard. She gasped his name in pleasure and slid her fingers into his hair, urging him on.

After that, things went blank for a while. She had no idea which of them moved first, which of them finished undressing the other, but then they were skin to skin, and it felt so good.

'If you want me to stop,' he said huskily, 'say it now and I'll go and have a cold shower.'

'If you stop now,' she said, 'I think I'll go insane.'

He smiled. 'You and me both, honey.' He stroked her

thighs apart, and sucked in a breath. 'Your skin's so soft.'
He cupped her sex, and she pushed against him.

'Don't tease.'

He pushed a finger into her, circling her clitoris with
his thumb.

She closed her eyes and a breath shuddered from her.
'Oh, that's good. Oh, Dominic. *Yes.*'

'Mmm. You're so responsive.' He stole a kiss, then
kissed a path down her body. Her hands fisted in his
hair as she felt his mouth on her, just where she needed
it most.

Her orgasm surprised her, unexpectedly fast and
fierce, and she gasped.

'OK?' he asked, looking concerned.

'Yes, I… It's been a while,' she admitted. 'I'm a bit
out of practice.'

'You're delightful,' he told her. 'Sexy as hell. And I
really, really want to make love with you.'

'Yes,' she breathed. 'Yes, please.'

He took his wallet from the table next to the bed and
removed a condom; he ripped open the foil packet and
rolled the condom onto his penis, then kissed her again,
his kiss sweet and yearning. At last, he fitted the tip of
his penis against her and slowly eased into her.

'Dominic.' She stroked his face. She knew he was
holding back, being gentle with her—but gentle wasn't
enough right now. 'I want all of you.' She shifted so she
could wrap her legs round his waist.

Dominic could hardly believe that this warm, generous
woman wanted him as badly as he wanted her. He felt
as if he was losing himself in Louisa. Her warm sweet
depths were wrapped round him, her eyes were all dark

with desire, and he couldn't resist dipping his head to steal a kiss. She slid her hands into his hair, drawing him closer, and kissed him back.

It was as if stars were exploding inside his head as he felt her body ripple round his, urging him on towards his own climax. He'd never felt anything quite like this before, such a pure and deep connection. All he could do was hold on.

But when his pulse had finally slowed to normal, guilt kicked in.

'I'm sorry. I shouldn't have taken advantage of you.'

Her legs were still wrapped round his waist, and she refused to let him go. 'You didn't take advantage of me. I was there with you, all the way.'

'This was supposed to be Venice in April. A four-poster bed, candlelight and Bellinis. I wanted to make it really romantic.'

'Some people,' she said softly, 'would think that an ancient castle is just as romantic. Including me.' She stroked his face. 'I wanted this as much as you did. And I've already made you wait for long enough.'

'You're incredible. You make me feel as if I can conquer the world.'

'You can.' She stole a kiss. 'And you don't feel quite so tense now. Are you still worried about tomorrow?'

'Being Oliver's best man? Yes and no.' He sighed. 'I mean, Mina loves him to bits. She's stood by him, even when he went through the ragingly angry stage and tried to push her away. Getting married is absolutely the right thing for them to do. But he's not going to be able to walk down the aisle with her. He's not going to be able to carry her over the threshold. It's things like that I feel I've stolen from his future.'

'He doesn't blame you. He told me last night, apart from the fact he thinks he contributed to it himself, it could've happened in a rugby match. And he really doesn't hold it against you. You're the only one doing that.' She paused. 'And you've given him something else. Did you know he's retraining?'

'No.' Oliver hadn't breathed a word to him. Given the state of his back, it had to be a desk job. 'What's he doing, taking over the estate management from Papa or something?'

'He's going to be a GP. So he gets to care for his patients all the way through. And, as he put it, it's family-friendly hours.'

'He's planning to have a family?' Dominic really hadn't expected that.

'Put it this way, he was talking about changing nappies. And whether they're able to have children of their own, or they need IVF or they decide to adopt, I think Oliver's going to be a very hands-on dad.' She stroked his hair away from his forehead. 'He reminds me a lot of you. He's got that same energy.'

'Yes.' And he wanted to be a hands-on dad, too. With a ready-made family—and maybe a little brother or sister for Tyler. And a puppy. A house, a garden, a family: Tyler's dream definitely matched his, and he hoped that it matched Louisa's, too.

Not that he intended to propose to her in bed. Or right now. He hadn't even told her he loved her—though he had a feeling that she might already have guessed that.

He kissed the tip of her nose. 'Though there's something I should tell you, Nurse Practitioner Austin. I'm really looking forward to falling asleep with you in my arms. And waking up with you.'

'Guess what?' Her face was all soft and sweet. 'I'm looking forward to that, too.'

And suddenly his plans for Venice didn't matter any more. Because this was just perfect. Everything he wanted.

CHAPTER ELEVEN

THE next morning, Louisa woke, feeling all warm and cosy, to find herself sprawled all over Dominic. Her head was on his shoulder, her arm was round his waist and her fingers were curving down over his hipbone. Her legs were tangled with his; and his arms were wrapped tightly round her.

'Good morning,' he said softly.

She felt herself flush. 'Have you been awake for long?'

'Long enough to enjoy you sleeping. You're delectable. And I love the way your skin feels against mine.' He shifted so he could kiss her. 'All's very right with my world this morning.'

So he'd stopped panicking about being Oliver's best man? Good. Hopefully he was finally starting to forgive himself.

'Does your hair take hideously long to dry?' he asked.

'Not if you have a hairdryer I can borrow.'

'Good.' He kissed her again. 'Because I really need to introduce you to my shower.' Three seconds later, he scooped her out of bed and carried her into the shower, laughing.

This was something she would never have done with Jack. And yet, with Dominic, it felt right. The intensity in his eyes when he looked at her, the sheer desire on his face: they sent a thrill through her. And was she deluding herself, or was it more than just desire? Could Dominic feel the same way about her that she felt about him? Did he love her back? The possibility shimmered in the air.

They spent longer in the shower than Dominic had planned and it was a rush to get her hair dried, but finally they made it downstairs. Louisa was glad to help out with all the last-minute tasks and checking to make sure that all the arrangements for the wedding were going smoothly. The flowers were breathtaking—the bold, clean lines of the calla lilies softened by the pretty star-shaped flowers of the tuberoses—and the marquee was filled with staff, setting the tables and checking the table plans and putting the place-holders in the right places.

Milly sent Dominic off with the dogs, saying that he needed to burn off some of his energy before he drove her insane with all that pacing around; and Louisa was drafted in to help amuse the five-year-old flower girl and three-year-old pageboy, telling them stories and teaching them new songs.

And then finally it was time to get ready for the ceremony. Dominic stared as Louisa emerged from the bathroom in her dress. 'You look fantastic,' he said.

'Don't sound so surprised,' she said drily.

'Sorry, I didn't mean to insult you. What I meant was, apart from last night, I've only ever seen you either in uniform at work or wearing jeans. You look lovely.'

'Thank you. You look pretty amazing yourself,' she

said. Formal dress suited him; and when he gave her a shy smile her heart skipped a beat.

'Do you have a wrap or something?' he asked. 'The church can get pretty chilly.'

She nodded, and fished out the lilac pashmina. He draped it round her shoulders. 'I really like your hair like that, too.' He dipped his head and kissed the back of her neck; the touch of his lips against her skin made a shiver of desire ripple all the way down her spine. 'Sorry,' he said. 'There's just something about you that I can't resist.'

The compliment made her glow, and she tucked her hand into the crook of his arm as they left the room and headed downstairs.

'You look fabulous, Louisa,' Milly said. 'That colour really suits you.'

'Thank you. You look lovely, too,' Louisa said, meaning it.

Milly was wearing a suit in sky-blue silk, with a matching hat and a corsage of tuberoses. She took another corsage from the box resting on one of the little tables in the hallway and pinned it to Louisa's dress.

'Thank you. They smell gorgeous,' Louisa said, breathing in the heady, exotic scent.

'Don't they just?' Milly smiled. 'So clever of Mina to choose them.'

Milly handed her a buttonhole for Dominic, a single calla lily, and Louisa carefully pinned it onto his lapel.

Roderick emerged from the kitchen. Milly cuffed his arm and wiped the tell-tale crumbs from the corner of his mouth. 'Honestly, *men*! Do they never stop eating?' she asked, rolling her eyes.

'I was hungry,' Roderick protested, 'and you know

what it's like at weddings. It takes ages before anybody gets fed, what with the photographs and the receiving lines and all that hanging around.'

'Just *behave*,' Milly said—and Louisa could see exactly where Dominic had got his irresistible little-boy grin.

Oliver was the last to arrive in the hallway, wheeling himself down the corridor.

Louisa saw the stricken look in Dominic's eyes, and slipped her fingers through his, squeezing his hand gently. 'Smile,' she said softly. 'Everything's just fine.'

He gave her a grateful glance and did so.

'So are we all ready now?' Milly asked, deftly pinning on Oliver's buttonhole.

'I'm nervous,' Oliver admitted, 'but I'm ready. Because Mina's about to make me the happiest man in the world when she walks down the aisle to me.'

Everyone else was looking at Oliver, but Louisa was looking at Dominic—and she saw him flinch. And, as they walked to the church, she noticed his steps starting to drag as they drew nearer.

'I think I need a breath of fresh air,' she said as they reached the beautiful old building. 'Dominic, would you mind…?'

'Of course,' he said, and stepped to the side with her. 'Are you all right?' he asked quietly.

She waited until his parents and Oliver had gone inside. 'I'm fine, but you're not. Talk to me.'

He rested his head against the cold stone of the porch. 'This is all so *wrong*. Oliver should be walking down that aisle, not wheeling himself down it. How can I possibly be his best man when I did that to him?'

'We talked about this last night. It was an *accident*.

Oliver's come to terms with the situation,' Louisa said softly. 'Now you need to do the same. There's nothing you can do to change it, so just try to make the best of it. Do you know what he said to me last night? If life gives you lemons, you have to make lemonade. And he's right. Look at the good bits. Your family's lovely. They adore you—including Oliver—and that's why he asked you to be his best man. Nobody else will do. And today's a really, really special day.'

'You're right,' he said, taking a deep breath. 'It's Oliver's day, and I need to put the past and the might-have-beens out of my head. And thank you for stopping me acting like a selfish jerk.'

'You're welcome,' she said.

He was still holding her hand when they walked into the church. It was full of white flowers, and the sun shone through the stained-glass windows, dappling the flowers with rich jewelled tones. The perfect winter wedding: all they needed was a tiny sprinkle of snow after the service, to act as confetti, she thought with a smile.

The tiny church soon filled up, and then the organist started to play the Trumpet Voluntary. All chatter ceased and everyone stood up, turning round to look at Mina. She looked amazing, walking down the red carpet in the aisle on her father's arm, the bridesmaids and flower girl and pageboy behind her. She joined Oliver at the top of the aisle; the vicar made the introductory speech, and when it came to the vows Oliver hauled himself out of his wheelchair. Clearly it was a struggle for him—Louisa could see the flash of pain across his face—but he was obviously determined to say his wedding vows to his bride while standing on his own two feet.

Louisa held Dominic's hand really tightly, and there

wasn't a dry eye in the congregation as Mina and Oliver made their vows and he kissed her before lowering himself back into his wheelchair. She could see Dominic blinking back tears when he returned to the pew after handing the rings over, and the lump in her throat grew even bigger when a woman started playing a violin solo and then a man with a gorgeous tenor voice started singing Louis Armstrong's 'Wonderful World' while Mina and Oliver signed the register.

The next few hours passed in a blur. Photographs, the champagne reception, a gorgeous meal and then the speeches. Dominic gave a very funny speech that had everyone laughing. But then he grew serious.

'I've always looked up to my big brother, right from the first moment I was able to toddle along behind him. Oliver's an amazing man, full of courage and strength and kindness, and I couldn't have wished for a better role model. I'm incredibly proud of him.' Dominic's voice cracked slightly. 'And I love him very, very much. So I'd like you all to join with me in wishing him and my new sister-in-law every happiness for the future.' He raised his glass. 'The bride and groom.'

When Louisa glanced over at Roderick and Milly, she could see them both wiping away a tear as they raised their glasses. And there was a suspicious sheen in everyone else's eyes, too, as they raised their glasses and echoed Dominic's toast.

'That was a beautiful speech,' she whispered to him, 'and you've really done your family proud.'

He said nothing, but held her hand very tightly through the rest of the speeches. Particularly when Oliver looked him straight in the eye during his speech and said, 'And I'd like to thank my best man. He's given me more than he knows, over the years, and I couldn't have asked for a better brother. I've been truly blessed in my family—and I'm so glad I can share that blessing with the love of my life, too.'

It was a public declaration from both of them. But would it be enough to break through the barriers Dominic had put round his heart? Louisa wondered. He'd heard his brother's speech, but had he listened to it—really listened to it—and understood that it was time to let the past go?

His face gave nothing away; and now wasn't the time or place for her to ask.

And finally it was time for the first dance.

Louisa had half-wondered if they'd skip the dancing, but clearly Oliver had other ideas. And when Dominic ushered her away from the table, she realised that the marquee led into the ballroom, where a band was set up at one corner.

They began to play the first notes of a song she recognised.

'"You Raise Me Up". What a fantastic song for a first dance,' she said. 'The lyrics give me goose bumps every time.'

It was a very, very, very slow dance, but Oliver and Mina managed it. And at the end of the dance, everyone cheered the bride and groom. Dominic had his arms wrapped round Louisa and was holding her really close; she could feel the tension running through him.

'You're supposed to dance with the chief bridesmaid now,' Louisa reminded him gently, 'while your mum dances with Mina's dad and her mum dances with your dad.'

'Yes, of course.' He shook himself.

'Go and be the gorgeous, charming man you are. For Oliver and Mina,' she said softly.

'As long as you promise to dance with me for the rest of the evening.'

She brushed a kiss against his lips and smiled at him. 'Absolutely.'

Dominic did exactly as Louisa had suggested. He danced with Mina's sister, chatted normally to her—and he was able to be charming, and all because he knew Louisa was waiting for him. With her, he felt different. He felt like a better person, not just the man who'd changed his brother and his family's life for ever. When he'd listened to the words of the song Oliver and Mina had chosen for the first dance, he'd realised that they fitted the way he felt about Louisa, too. She made him more than he thought he could be.

When the song ended, he noticed that his brother was sitting down; not so unusual, but there was a tightening round his eyes that made Dominic suspect Oliver was in an awful lot of pain. Quietly, he went over to him. 'Are you all right?' he asked, concerned.

'I just got married. I'm more than OK. And I had the first dance with my beautiful bride. That was the one that mattered.' Oliver smiled at him. 'I know what you're worrying about. Don't. All that physio and work in the swimming pool paid off. I'm not going to be stuck in bed for a week, recovering.'

'You're in pain right now.'

Oliver shrugged. 'It's worth it.'

Dominic took his hand. 'Oliver, I'm so—'

'Shh,' Oliver said. 'I know. And I'm fine—really, Dominic, I'm fine. I've been training with my physio for that dance for months, so I haven't knocked myself up. And I'm still going to carry my bride over the threshold tonight, except she's going to be sitting on my lap as I carry her.'

Guilt squeezed Dominic's heart.

'Dominic, listen to me. I'm not sitting here thinking about what I don't have—I'm sitting here, truly thankful for what I do have. This is my perfect day. I've just got married to the woman I love most in the world, in the place I love most in the world, with all the people I love around me. And I'm about to start a new career as a GP. I've got so much ahead of me, so much good stuff to come.' He paused. 'The past is the past. It's time you let it go, little brother.'

'How can I?' Dominic asked.

'Listen to your girl. She talks a lot of sense.'

'She talks a lot, full stop,' Dominic said wryly.

Oliver laughed. 'Then, between the pair of you, I bet it's hard to get a word in edgeways.'

'She lets me be silent, too,' Dominic mused. And it was true. With Louisa, he'd discovered that he could be himself. She knew the worst of him, and yet she hadn't pushed him away. If anything, she'd drawn him closer.

'She's lovely. And I'm glad you've found someone, Dominic. I've hated seeing you slowly shutting yourself off from people these past two years.'

'She's special,' Dominic said softly. 'Really special.'

'Be happy. That's all I want for you,' Oliver said, 'to be as happy as I am. Now go and dance with your girl before we both get maudlin.' Oliver smiled at him. 'And, just for the record, I meant everything I said in my speech. I'm proud of you.'

'I love you, Oliver,' Dominic said.

'I know. And I love you, too.' Oliver returned his hug, then patted his back. 'Go and dance with lovely Louisa. And stop worrying about me. *Really.*'

The band was playing 'The Way You Look Tonight'. Another song with more than appropriate words. There really was nobody like Louisa in the room. And the way she looked tonight…that'd stay with him for a long, long time.

Dominic went to claim his dance with her, and found himself singing along with the song.

'Why, Dr Hurst, I didn't know you had such a nice singing voice. Or that a die-hard rock fan like you would know the words to a Sinatra song.' Her eyes were sparkling.

'I grew up with this stuff.'

'My parents are more into the Beatles,' she said, 'though Mum once admitted that she had a crush on Andy Williams.'

'"Can't Take My Eyes Off You". That's one of Ma's favourites, too, though I prefer the Muse version,' he said reflectively. 'It has better guitars.'

She laughed. 'You *would* say that.'

Then the band switched to another slow number, Dominic drew Louisa close, swaying with her to the rhythm of the song. She wasn't wearing her wrap, so her shoulders were bare except for the two tiny straps. Unable to resist, he dipped his head and kissed her shoulder. Her skin was so soft and she smelled so sweet.

She gave a breathy little sigh and moved closer; and he felt his control fraying past the point of no return. He needed her, and he couldn't help himself; he traced a path of kisses up the sensitive cord at the side of her neck, drawing her closer still, and then finally his mouth was right where he wanted it to be, jammed over hers. Her arms were round his neck and she was kissing him back, her mouth warm and sweet and promising.

Heaven.

It took him a while to realise that the band were playing a more up-tempo number. He had no idea how long he'd been kissing Louisa on the dance floor; the only thing he knew was that he didn't want to stop—and he didn't want an audience.

'Louisa,' he whispered as he broke the kiss.

She looked dazed. 'Hmm?'

'There's something I need to tell you.' And he knew where, too. 'Let's go,' he said. 'Somewhere a little quieter. More private.'

She gave him the most sinful smile. 'What a good idea.'

It was all he could do not to turn caveman, haul her over his shoulder and carry her upstairs to his bed. But they left the ballroom discreetly. He led her down a corridor and out through a side door into the formal garden. 'Look up,' he said.

'Wow. I don't think I've ever seen stars that bright.' She smiled. 'And a full moon, too. It's pure silver.'

And the soft light made her look incredibly beautiful. He took off his jacket and slipped it round her shoulders.

She looked concerned. 'You'll be cold, Dominic.'

'I'm with you. So I'm warm where it matters.' He took her hand and placed it over his heart. 'Right here. Feel?'

'Yes.' She smiled at him.

'I love you, Louisa,' he said softly. 'I love everything you are. And it's not just that I'm being all sentimental after seeing my big brother get married. I've known it for a while—it was just a matter of finding the right place and the right time to tell you. And that's here and now. I love you.'

'Oh, Dominic.' Her eyes glittered in the moonlight. 'I love you, too. I never expected to feel that way again, but with you it's different. You make me feel…' She shook her head. 'I can't explain it. Not properly. But everything sparkles when you're around.'

Gently, he drew her back indoors, then scooped her up and carried her up the stairs. The second he'd closed his bedroom door behind her, he let her slide down her body until her feet were back on the floor and then kissed her again, this time more passionately. And then he realised that his curtains were still open. Unwilling to relinquish her, he danced with her to the window, humming 'Can't take my eyes off you', and shut the world out.

And then he had the sheer pleasure of undressing her, very slowly. He unzipped her dress and drew a line of kisses all the way down her spine as the material parted beneath his hands, then hung her dress over the back of a chair to stop it creasing.

Louisa undressed him just as slowly, stroking the skin on his chest and his midriff as she undid his shirt, and causing his blood pressure to spike as she released the button on his trousers.

He removed the final scraps of her underwear, loving the contrast between the roughness of the lace and the softness of her skin, then scooped one arm under her knees, picking her up so he could kiss her and carry her over to his bed.

She breathed his name as he laid her against the pillows, her face filled with desire and something else he knew now he could dare to name. And he knew that he felt it, too. He could let himself love Louisa. He could be himself with her. Give her all that he wanted to be.

He paused to slide on a condom, then knelt between her thighs. 'I love you,' he said as he eased into her. 'I really, really love you.'

'And I love you. You amaze me,' she said. 'I love who you are. Your gentleness and your strength. Even your stubbornness.'

He laughed. 'I'm not the only one who's stubborn.'

'Mule. That's me,' she teased.

He kissed her. 'You're the sexiest woman I've ever met—and you turn me on in a big way, my lady.'

'"My verray, parfit, gentil knight",' she quoted. 'Do you have any idea how gorgeous you look, dressed up like a medieval prince?'

'Any time you want me dressed up in my armour, honey, just say. As long as you take it off for me again. And grant me some very special private favours.' He pushed deeper into her.

'Oh, yes.' Her expression went starry. 'And that velvet cloak. I love that cloak. I've had some seriously X-rated fantasies about you in that cloak.'

'Good. Tell me about them,' he said softly. 'Because I think I'd enjoy acting them out.'

'Kiss me,' she whispered, and he dipped his head. Her mouth was so sweet, so soft and giving. So hot. And how good she felt wrapped around him like this; the feel of her skin against his made his blood heat.

He felt her body begin to ripple round his, and he broke the kiss. 'I love you, Louisa,' he whispered.

'I love you, too.' And he could see it in her eyes, at the exact moment that they both tumbled to a climax.

Afterwards, snuggled in bed beside her, he said, 'I don't think I've ever, ever been this happy.' He drew her close. 'I don't want tonight to end.'

'Neither do I.' She pressed a kiss into his chest. 'But I have to go home tomorrow.'

Back to real life. Yeah, he knew that.

But she'd said the words he'd needed to hear. She felt the same way as he did.

And he could risk a future with her.

CHAPTER TWELVE

THE next morning, after breakfast, Louisa was surprised when Dominic took a slightly different route from the one she'd expected.

'Aren't we going to pick Ty up?' she asked.

'Yes—but there's something I need to sort out on the way. I promise this will only take ten minutes.'

Fair enough, she thought—until she recognised the road. 'We're going to the stables?'

'Yup.'

'Dominic, you haven't ignored everything I said and arranged to meet Tyler here, have you?'

'No. This is just you and me. Ten minutes.' He parked, and took her over to the stable yard. 'Would I be right in thinking that you're just a little bit nervous of horses—and I mean in addition to the fact that you're terrified Ty's going to get hurt again?'

'Well—yes,' she admitted.

'And you've never ridden a horse?'

'Never.'

'So you don't actually know what he sees in them, do you?'

She wrapped her arms round herself. 'Why are we here?'

'Because I want to demonstrate something to you. Do you trust me?'

'Of course I do.'

'Good. Because you're going to ride my horse.'

Her mouth fell open in shock. 'But Pegasus is huge!'

'He's a gentle giant, and he's absolutely not going to hurt you. And I'm not going to let anything happen to you.'

'But I'm not dressed for horse-riding.'

'Your boots are low-heeled and you're wearing jeans and a sweater. That's fine.' He let his gaze travel all the way down from her eyes to her toes, and all the way up again. 'You look as sexy as hell, but I promise not to let myself get distracted by what I want to do to you in a quiet corner of a hayloft.'

'Dominic!' She felt the colour shoot into her face.

He grinned. 'Just giving you some ideas.' He took her to the tack room, picked up his bridle and saddle, and took her over to Pegasus's loose box. Swiftly, he put the bridle and saddle on the horse, checked the girth, and led the horse out into the yard. 'All righty. Let me help you up. Put your left foot in the stirrup, here,' he directed. 'On the count of three, I'll help lift you up—just bring your right leg out behind you.'

The next thing she knew, she was sitting in the saddle; though she could still feel the warmth of Dominic's hands against her body, even through her clothes.

'Just relax,' he said. 'I'm leading him, so he's not going to rush off and you're not going to fall. Let yourself feel his rhythm and go along with him.'

In other words, she had to trust him.

She knew that he was a perfectionist and would never

let anything go wrong. And she knew him, soul-deep.
The slightly reserved and formidable doctor whose mind
worked so quickly and who was so good with patients;
the wild horseman with a dangerous, thrill-seeking
hobby; the kind, considerate man who saw what needed
fixing and just did it without a fuss; the man who treated
her son as someone who was special on his own terms,
not just a boy with special needs.

She loved him. Of course she trusted him.

As he slowly led her round the field, her confidence
grew; and suddenly she could understand why he did
this. It was a feeling like nothing else, a bond between
human and horse. Shyly, she reached out to pat the horse's
neck.

When they were back to their starting point, Dominic
helped her down from the saddle. 'Well?'

'I get it,' she said. 'OK. You win. Ty can come back
to lessons—and to the Christmas party at the stables.'

'It's not a question of winning,' Dominic said gently.
'It's about the fact that you're scared and I wanted to
take the fear away. I understand why you're worried, but
I wanted you to see the other side of the argument for
yourself. So you could make an informed decision. The
person I want to win is *you*. I don't want you all tense
and worrying yourself sick every time Tyler goes on a
horse—or hating yourself for being so scared about the
risks that you're stopping him doing something he loves.
And it occurred to me this morning that the way to beat
a fear is to face it.'

'I think I'm always going to have my heart in my
mouth,' she said. 'When you ride, as well as Tyler. But I
understand where you're coming from now. And I'll do
my best to fight the fear. To trust you'll both be safe.'

He stole a kiss. 'Good.' He made a fuss of his horse, then removed his tack and put him back in the loosebox before scooping up the saddle again. 'I'll put this back in the tack room for now. And I'll be back later to give you a proper workout,' he told Pegasus.

The horse whickered, then nosed Louisa.

Gently, she stroked his nose. 'Oh! He feels like velvet.' Entranced, she stroked him again, and the horse gave a small whicker of pleasure.

'He's an old softie.' Dominic stole a kiss. 'Come on. We need to get you back to Ty.'

On the day of the Christmas party, Dominic took Tyler and Louisa over to the stables. The yard looked amazingly festive, with a beautiful Christmas tree in the corner covered with lights.

'No tinsel, mind. It's too tempting for the ponies,' Bea said, 'and I'm not risking any holly leaves getting between a saddle and pony's back, so the tree's the only thing we do here.'

'It looks lovely, though.' Louisa produced a box. 'Sausage rolls and brownies, as promised by Dominic.'

'I helped make them,' Tyler added. 'No nuts and lots of chocolate. In the brownies, that is. The sausage rolls just have sausage in them.'

'Excellent,' Bea said, smiling. 'Thank you very much.' She led them over to the table and added the food to the already mountainous spread.

'Wow. Nobody's going to want to eat for a week afterwards,' Louisa said.

'Don't you believe it,' Bea told her, laughing. 'We always use disposable plates and cups. I know it's not as eco-friendly as washing things up, but if someone drops something it's not a problem and we don't have to worry that we've missed a bit of glass or china that'll go straight through a dog's paw or a horse's foot.'

'Very sensible.'

Bea hugged Tyler. 'Great to see you back. Polo missed you—and so did we. Your mum tells me you're starting again just after Christmas. Cool.'

'I can't wait,' Tyler said. 'And Mum says I'm allowed to do what everyone else does today.'

'Glad to hear it.'

When the party started, Louisa was absolutely charmed. Just as Dominic had described, all the children were wearing foam antlers on top of their hard hats, and they all had a turn riding the ponies round the paddock, their little antlers nodding as they rode. And Tyler's smile was the brightest of all. She was glad she'd come; she wouldn't have missed this for the world.

'This is the best Christmas party I've ever been to,' Tyler confided when everyone was happily munching mince pies. He hugged her. 'I love you, Mum.'

She felt the tears well up. Tyler didn't often make emotional statements, but when he did they always went straight to her heart. 'I love you, too,' she said, hugging him back equally hard.

'And I love Dominic.'

She went very still.

'He loves me, too. He told me when I was ill after the accident,' Tyler said. 'Where's he gone?'

'I don't know. Probably to see Pegasus.'

But then she heard the sound of sleigh bells and she realised exactly where Dominic was. Something else he'd forgotten to mention, but something that was utterly perfect: his own role in the Christmas party.

'Father Christmas, I presume?' she asked Bea.

'Absolutely,' Bea said with a smile. 'And you wait to see what he comes in on.'

Louisa was expecting a sleigh, and maybe Bea and Ric knew someone who could bring reindeer for the children to ooh and aah over—but what she saw at the far end of the paddock was Father Christmas riding on...

'A unicorn?' she asked in disbelief. It was a pure white horse with a rippling mane and tail that looked as if it was bathed in moonlight, shimmering, and an iridescent horn coming out of his head.

Of course it wasn't a unicorn—she knew unicorns didn't exist.

But this one looked so real.

'How?' she asked in wonder.

'State secret,' Bea said with a grin. 'It's more than my life's worth to say.'

As Father Christmas rode nearer, Louisa recognised the horse as Pegasus. And when Father Christmas asked for a helper, she stepped forward. 'Will I do?'

'Perfectly,' Dominic said, handing her the first present from his sack.

There was a present for every child from the horse they rode; and Louisa loved the gift tags, which were pictures of the horses wearing Santa hats, obviously done with the help of a computer programme. The children were delighted with their gifts—all horse related—and Tyler was thrilled to bits to be given his own grooming mitt. 'This is the best Christmas ever,' he said, beaming.

Much later that evening, when Tyler was in bed, Dominic sat on the sofa with Louisa on his lap, their arms wrapped round each other.

'He's right, you know—this is going to be the best

Christmas ever. Because you're in my life. You fit every bit of me: work, the stables, home. All of it.' He paused. 'What I said, the night of the wedding: I meant it. You're amazing. And I love you. And I want to be a family with you—you *and* Tyler.'

'That's what I want, too,' she said.

'But it's only going to work,' he said, 'if Tyler's happy about it.'

'He told me today that he loved you. And that you'd told him you loved him, when he was ill.' She stroked his face. 'I had no idea. Why didn't you say?'

'Because I didn't want to pressure you,' Dominic said simply. 'And, I know it's selfish, but I needed to know that you loved me for *me*, not because of the bond between me and your son.'

'I love you for both reasons. But primarily for you,' she confirmed, kissing him. 'In fact…let me show you.'

They ended up falling off the sofa, their clothing in utter disarray, but both of them were laughing.

'I feel like a teenager,' Dominic said. 'Even though I'm half a lifetime away from that.'

'Half your life ago, you were in your mid-teens,' she pointed out. 'As was I. We're both older and wiser now.'

'Mmm, and you're gorgeous. You'll still be gorgeous when we're eighty. You'll still make my knees weak and my heart beat faster. Always.' He stole a kiss. 'I meant it. I love Ty as well. I look at him, and I see you. And I see a bright, quirky little boy who loves all the things I love. And I want to be his father. I mean, I know I can't take the place of Jack, but—'

She pressed a finger to his lips. 'Believe me, simple biology doesn't make someone a father. It's a lot more than that. Ty doesn't even remember Jack. You've done more with Tyler in the past couple of months than his father has done in years. You've helped him with swimming and riding, you've taught him to play chess, you listen to him when he comes home from school, you talk to him about his artwork and horses and knights. And I know he thinks a lot of you because he spends almost as much time talking about you as he does about horses.'

'So, if Ty's happy with the idea, would you consider marrying me?'

She smiled, a teasing light in her eyes. 'Ask me properly, Dr Hurst, and I'll give you your answer.'

'Then I'll talk to him,' Dominic said. 'Man to man.' He smiled. 'In the normal scheme of things, I would be asking your father for your hand in marriage. But, in this case, I think I need to ask your son.'

She stroked his face. 'That's another thing I love about you. You're thoughtful. You consider other people's feelings. Oh, and for the record, my parents think you're wonderful and my mum's already given us their blessing. She guessed a long time ago how I feel about you.'

'Then let's hope,' Dominic said, 'that Ty feels the same.'

The following evening, Dominic was playing chess with Tyler while Louisa was pottering about in the kitchen. His mouth was dry, his skin was prickling, and he could never, ever remember feeling this nervous before. Not when he'd been sitting exams or taking his driving test, because he'd had a fair idea what he was doing and had been able to judge whether he was getting it right. Not when he'd started his first job, because back then he'd known that he still had a lot to learn and it was fine to ask questions as long as you put the patient's needs first.

Right here and now, he felt all at sea.

Because, even though he thought he knew how Tyler would react to his question, he didn't know for certain. And it scared him to death that he might be wrong.

'You're letting me win, aren't you?' Tyler asked, moving his knight. 'Check.'

'I wouldn't insult you like that,' Dominic said. 'But, I admit, I'm not giving the game my full attention.'

'Why not?'

'Because there's something I need to talk to you about. Something serious. Man to man.'

Tyler frowned. 'What?'

This was the biggie. Dominic took a deep breath. 'How would you feel about your mum getting married?'

'Would that mean I'd have a new dad?' Tyler asked carefully.

'Yes. One who'd love you every bit as much as if he'd always been your dad.'

Tyler thought about it. 'Do you mean you?'

Dominic nodded. 'But I'm not going to ask your mum to marry me unless you're happy about the idea. So I'm asking your permission to propose to your mum.'

'You mean, like a knight used to ask the king?' Tyler said reflectively. 'Except you're a knight and I'm your page. So I'm not really the king.'

'True,' Dominic said, 'but this is your mum we're talking about, so this is a special case. It means I need to ask you first.'

'Are you going to have a baby?'

Dominic coughed. 'No.' But the idea of Louisa's belly

all rounded with his child sent a shaft of pure longing through him.

Tyler looked thoughtful. 'I'd like a little brother. Or a sister. And a puppy.'

Dominic laughed. 'I'll see what I can do. Not a wolf-hound,' he was quick to add, 'but I think we could talk your mum round on the puppy front.' He paused. 'So was that a yes?'

'My mum smiles a lot more when you're around. And I think I'd like you to be my dad—as long as I can still be your page.' His brow furrowed. 'Because knights used to send their son to be someone else's page, didn't they?'

'Not in this case. You'll be my son *and* my page,' Dominic promised. 'And, in case you were wondering, I don't approve of the old knightly custom of sending your son to grow up in someone else's castle. You'll be with your mum and me.' He smiled. 'Though my parents live in a castle, so you might get to stay there from time to time. Probably in my old bedroom, in the turret.'

'That's way cool,' Tyler breathed, his eyes wide.

'So do I have your permission to ask your mum to marry me?'

Tyler nodded. 'When are you going to ask her?'

'I was waiting to see how you felt about it first.' He smiled. 'If you've got any ideas about the best time, I'm all ears.'

'Christmas,' Tyler said. 'Because she'll say yes. And I'll have a dad for Christmas—the best present ever.'

Dominic hugged him. 'You,' he said, 'are going to grow up to be my joint-best friend with Ric. As well as a son I'm going to be very, very proud of.'

'And I get to call you Dad instead of Dominic?'

'Absolutely.' His heart felt as if it was full to over-flowing.

'Good. Because I love you. Dad.' He tested the word and smiled. 'Dad.'

'I love you, too.' Dominic held him close. 'Son.'

And when he went into the kitchen on the pretext of fetching drinks while Tyler dealt the cards, he saw that Louisa's lashes were wet.

'OK, honey?' he asked, concerned.

She cuddled in to him. 'I was eavesdropping. At the end. And…' Tears choked off the rest of her sentence, but he knew they were happy tears.

'I know,' he said softly. 'Me, too. And I can't wait until Christmas.'

The rest of the week flew by. Dominic was working on Christmas Day, but he'd taken Tyler to help him choose a very special present during the week and had sworn his new son to utter secrecy.

His shift was busy, with the expected patients who'd scratched their eyes on Christmas tree branches while retrieving presents, people who'd cut themselves carving the turkey—and one whose knife had slipped off an avocado and into his hand—and children with bits of toys stuck up their noses. But obviously his joy shone through because his patients ended up relaxing and smiling back at him, losing their misery and stress as he treated them.

And at last it was the end of his shift. He drove over to Gillian and Matt Austin's house, where Louisa and Tyler had spent the day, along with her brother Stewart, his wife, Marie, and their twin daughters.

'Merry Christmas.' Louisa met him at the door and kissed him soundly. 'How was your day?'

'Better now I'm with you.' He lifted her up and spun her round.

'Put the girl down,' Gillian teased. She kissed him warmly on the cheek. 'Happy Christmas, love. And thank you for those beautiful lace bobbins. They're perfect.'

'I'm glad you like them. Though I have to admit, I did have a bit of help choosing them,' he admitted. 'From your wonderful daughter.'

He had a mug of coffee and a turkey salad sandwich with the Austins, wished everyone a merry Christmas, and then put Louisa and Tyler's overnight bags into the back of his car before driving them to Amberhurst.

Fairy-lights were threaded through the trees on the approach to the castle.

'It's magical,' Tyler breathed.

'It certainly is.' Dominic exchanged a smile with Louisa.

Milly met them at the door, surrounded by bouncing dogs, and Tyler was utterly delighted by them. He was even more thrilled when he discovered that his bedroom was indeed going to be in one of the turrets.

'We've left your presents under the tree. But I'm afraid we've been terribly rude and already opened ours,' Milly said. 'Thank you so much for the photograph.'

As they went into the drawing room, Louisa could see the silver photo frame she'd bought for Milly, containing the picture of Dominic, Tyler, herself and Pegasus, in pride of place on the mantelpiece.

Milly sorted out a glass of orange juice for Tyler— one with no bits, on Dominic's advice—and Buck's

Fizz for Dominic and Louisa, and made sure they were comfortably seated.

'Dominic, can you do the presents, darling?' she asked.

Tyler was thrilled to discover that Milly and Roderick had bought him a deep velvet cloak like Dominic's, and was almost beside himself with joy when he opened Dominic's present. 'It's a real knight's helmet! Thank you so much.'

Oliver and Mina had bought Tyler some more art supplies; and Louisa adored the cashmere sweater that Milly and Roderick had bought her and the silver bracelet from Oliver and Mina.

Dominic handed over a box to Louisa with a slight smile. She opened it, then kissed him soundly. 'Thanks. My camera was on its last legs.' And the one he'd bought her was state of the art.

'What about the other present?' Tyler asked. 'Aren't you going to give her that now?'

Dominic had intended to ask Louisa to marry him, later, under the stars in the garden. But when he saw the expectant look in Tyler's eyes—reflected on the rest of his family's faces—he realised that right here, right now, would be the perfect place and time.

'That isn't actually a Christmas present,' Dominic said. 'But, since you mention it...' He dropped onto one knee in front of Louisa, and fished the velvet-covered box out of his pocket to reveal the perfect solitaire he and Tyler had chosen together, in a simple but pretty platinum setting. 'Tyler's given me his blessing to ask you, and now feels the right moment. I love you very, very much and I want to spend the rest of my life with you. I want to make a family with you. So please will you do me the honour of becoming my wife and making Tyler my son?'

She stared at him, a sheen of tears in her eyes, then wrapped her arms round him. 'I love you, too. Yes. Yes.' She kissed him. 'Most definitely, yes.'

EPILOGUE

Six months later

On a hot, sunny day in June, Louisa walked down the aisle of the church at Amberhurst Castle on her father's arm, with Mina, Bea and Mel as her bridesmaids, Tyler as her pageboy and her twin nieces as her flower girls.

Dominic turned round to watch his bride walking towards him. She could see the joy on his face—a joy that was mirrored through the whole congregation. Dominic's mother and her own were both brushing away a tear, her father and Dominic's were both looking proud, Oliver was looking adoringly at his wife, Ric was looking equally adoringly at his own wife, and her brother Stewart was holding hands with Marie, giving Tyler and the twins encouraging smiles.

Life didn't get more perfect than this. Making her wedding vows to Dominic in the place where his family had exchanged those same vows for hundreds of years, and knowing that they had enough love between them to get through anything.

As they signed the register, the tenor who had sung at Oliver and Mina's wedding sang 'You Raise Me Up'.

Dominic's hands tightened on his new wife's. 'You make me more than I am,' he said softly.

'Just as you do me,' she said, smiling at him. 'Always.'

'I love you, Mrs Hurst.' And, not caring that it wasn't quite the traditional place to do so in the wedding ceremony, he kissed her.

THE NURSE
WHO SAVED
CHRISTMAS

BY
JANICE LYNN

*To my children, who bring Christmas alive
and are life's greatest gifts. I love you.*

First published in Great Britain 2010
Harlequin Mills & Boon Limited,
Eton House, 18-24 Paradise Road, Richmond, Surrey TW9 1SR

© Janice Lynn 2010

ISBN: 978 0 263 87933 9

Harlequin Mills & Boon policy is to use papers that are natural,
renewable and recyclable products and made from wood grown in
sustainable forests. The logging and manufacturing process conform
to the legal environmental regulations of the country of origin.

Printed and bound in Spain
by Litografia Rosés, S.A., Barcelona

Dear Reader

Some of my favourite memories are of my children waking up on Christmas morning—of seeing their faces as they first catch sight of the goodies beneath the tree, of their laughter as they tear into packages, of watching the excitement in their eyes. Other wonderful memories are of going to my parents', sampling my mom's homemade goodies, enjoying time with my rather large extended family, looking around and seeing people treat others with love and generosity, making an extra effort to make the world a better place for others. All those things are what make up Christmas, but other not so happy memories can hit hard at the holidays as well. Memories of loved ones who are no longer with us, in particular.

In THE NURSE WHO SAVED CHRISTMAS I wanted to capture the warmth of the holidays, but also the pain of when your heart's not whole. Abby and Dirk have to learn the true meaning of the holidays, and of love. I hope you enjoy their story, and that you have a wonderful Christmas filled with all the magic of the season.

I love to hear from readers. Please e-mail me at Janice@janicelynn.net, write to me care of Harlequin Mills & Boon, or visit me at my website: www.janicelynn.net

Janice Lynn

Janice Lynn has a Masters in Nursing from Vanderbilt University, and works as a nurse practitioner in a family practice. She lives in the southern United States with her husband, their four children, their Jack Russell—appropriately named Trouble—and a lot of unnamed dust bunnies that have moved in since she started her writing career. To find out more about Janice and her writing, visit www.janicelynn.com

CHAPTER ONE

Nurse Abby Arnold hid her smile behind her hand as Santa Claus grimaced at the squirming kid sitting in his lap at the children's advocacy Christmas community outreach in downtown Philadelphia.

"Smile for the picture," she said sweetly, standing a few feet from the elaborate thronelike chair and Christmas tree being used for "Pictures with Santa."

Santa Claus's deep blue eyes narrowed behind his gold-rimmed glasses, but his lips curved in a smile hopefully only she could tell was forced.

How had she talked Dr. Dirk Kelley into helping when the Santa she'd arranged for the event canceled at the last minute, leaving her desperate for a replacement? So desperate she'd asked a man she'd treated as if they were just friendly colleagues for the past two months and not more, all the while walking on eggshells at the sharp undercurrents between them.

"Ho, ho, ho, what do you want for Christmas this year, little boy?" Santa asked, sounding more like the Abominable Snowman than a jolly old man full of Christmas spirit.

Despite her awkward physical awareness of the man beneath the suit, it was all Abby could do not to snort. Did Dirk really believe that voice sounded Santa-ish? Hadn't he sat on Santa's knee as a kid? Watched Christmas television shows about jolly Saint Nick? Anything that would clue him in that Christmas was the most magical time of the year and that for these kids he was part of that magic? Something they'd always remember?

For all she knew, he hadn't.

Although they'd started out with a bang the night they'd first worked together, she really didn't know much about the handsome doctor who'd knocked her socks off from the moment she'd met him.

She knew very little about him or his past. Although, thanks to *that* morning, she spent way too much of her present thinking about him and how much she'd like to feature in his future.

The kid on Dirk's lap, around five, wiped the back of his pudgy hand across his runny nose. "An Xbox, and a cellphone, and a digital voice enhancer, and a…"

The list went on. And on. Even Abby's eyes widened at some of the items the kid listed. What had happened to a baseball glove or a bicycle?

Santa's bushy white brow rose as he regarded the kid. "Have you been that good this year?"

Another wipe of the face, then a nod. "I have. Extra-good."

"I'll see what I can do." At the mother's frantic look, Santa diplomatically added, "But Santa's on a budget. To be fair to the other good little boys and girls, I'll have to prioritize and just bring one or two of your list items."

The mother heaved a relieved sigh.

Santa set the boy off his lap but, rather than walk away, the kid wrapped his arms around Dirk's neck and planted a noisy kiss on a high cheekbone Abby had doctored earlier with rosy rouge. "I love you, Santa."

Abby's insides melted. How sweet! This was why she'd volunteered to organize this event. Why she volunteered with so many Christmas events. To help bring holiday magic alive for others.

Only Dirk looked more like he was being cooked alive than feeling the magic.

"I…uh…" His eyes cut to her with a distressed plea for rescue. He didn't have to say anything aloud. Abby got the message loud and clear.

Not in a million years could she deny him. Not when his gaze held hers and she had a resurgence of the connection she'd instantaneously felt with him, had a resurgence of the connection they'd shared *that* morning. One so real, so tangible, she'd felt in sync with him, had comforted and been comforted.

No, she couldn't deny Dirk much of anything within her power to give. Obviously. Besides, she was good at helping others, giving to others. It's what she did. What she'd always done. What was expected of her by all who knew her, especially this time of year.

Wondering at Dirk's evident rising unease, she put her hand on the boy's back and gave him a gentle pat. "Santa loves you, too. Don't forget to keep being extra-good between now and Christmas. He'll be watching."

At the last, the kid shot a wary glance toward Santa, his face contorting in shock. "Even when I'm in the bathtub?"

"No, not then. Just when you're being good or bad." Sending an apologetic smile, the boy's mother took his hand and led him away. Several times he glanced over his shoulder, waving goodbye.

Standing to tower above her five feet, six inches, Dirk bent to whisper in her ear. "Santa needs a break. Stat."

His rush of warm breath tickling her ear filled her with Christmas magic, from her head to the tippy-tips of her toes. This so wasn't the place to be getting hot and bothered by Dirk and his overabundant male magnetism.

In a Santa costume, for goodness' sake.

How could she possibly be turned on by a man dressed in her deceased father's treasured Santa suit? Although she loved Christmas, she wasn't prone to Christmas fetishes. Then again, it wasn't the suit but the man inside it lighting up her world like the most overdecorated house in the neighborhood.

He was playing Santa as a favor to her—she had no choice but to get her feelings under control and not attack the man's lips with hers in front of all these children.

She gave a calm nod and told the waiting crowd, "Sorry, kids, but Santa needs to check in with his elves to make sure all the toys are being made just right." She smiled brilliantly at the children and their parents. "We'll be back in ten minutes."

As expected, moans and groans greeted them from the families in the long line. Despite Dirk's obvious need for a reprieve, she sensed his hesitation, liked him all the more for it. Still, he'd said he needed a break and she'd seen in his eyes that he really did.

"Come on, Santa." Smiling brightly, Abby looped her arm in a red-velvet-covered one and spoke loudly. "Follow me, and I'll take you to where you can use your special Santa phone to call the North Pole and put in the requests for presents you've heard so far. There's only two more weeks until Christmas, so they need to get started filling the orders right away."

Gratitude shining in his eyes, Dirk nodded, pasted on a fake smile, and waved at the crowd.

"I can't believe I let you talk me into this," he mumbled under his breath while allowing her to lead him away from the masses gathered at the community center just to meet him. "This is madness. Pure commercialized madness."

She still couldn't believe he'd said yes, either. Sure, he was the one man capable of delivering her Christmas wish, but long and lean Dr. Dirk Kelley playing the role of Santa to dozens of children was another matter altogether. They'd worked together long enough for her to realize kids made him uncomfortable, that he was quiet and kept to himself. Her friend and fellow nurse Danielle called him Dr. Dreamboat. Abby called him what she most wanted for Christmas, but had never said the words out loud, not even to her tabby cat, Mistletoe.

Regardless, Dirk was doing her a huge favor and she was grateful. Smiling, she quirked a brow in his direction. "Ah, Santa, where's your Christmas spirit?"

He snorted. "I lost it somewhere between demands for a new computer and the kid who wanted a Mercedes-Benz." He shook his red and white hat and white wig topped head in dismay. "What happened to kids wanting Tinkertoys and tricycles?"

Although he pretty much echoed her earlier thoughts, Abby just shrugged. "Now, Santa, stay with the times. It's high tech and electronics these days. You'll have to get your elves with the program."

"Apparently," he said wryly. The moment they stepped out of the main walkway of the community center and into the privacy of the employee break room where they'd left their things earlier, his broad shoulders sagged. "I'm not sure I'm going to last another hour. Christmas just isn't my thing, Abs."

"Bah, humbug, Mr. Scrooge." While trying to decide if he was serious about the Christmas comment, she gave an internal sigh at his use of his pet name for her. Did he have any idea how that sent shivers through her? That every time she heard it she was instantly taken back to being in his arms, to the first time he'd whispered the name when they'd been tangled together beneath her bedsheets? "Surely you can make it another hour." She sighed theatrically. "Guess men of endurance are a thing of the past, too."

"Don't you believe it," he warned, grinning for real for the first time in over an hour, his eyes taking on a dangerous gleam despite his costume and obvious dislike of his role. "My endurance is just fine. Better than fine."

She raked her gaze over his red fur-covered body. The padding beneath the suit didn't begin to hide the wide shoulders and abundant male charisma. Not really. Abby had caught more than one mom in line eyeing Santa as if they'd like to sit on his knee and ask for him in their Christmas stockings… If they knew Santa was none other than scrumptious Dr. Dirk Kelley, Santa would have had to beat the women off with a giant candy cane.

Besides, thanks to the particularly rough night they'd first worked together, Abby did know all about Dirk's endurance. If only she could forget what amazing stamina the man wielded at the tips of those magical fingers. What stamina the rest of him had delivered. Twice.

Dirk Kelley didn't need a sleigh and flying reindeer to take a woman to soaring heights.

Maybe somebody should thwack *her* with a giant candy cane for even letting memories of *that* morning creep into her thoughts. Hadn't they agreed they'd made a mistake? Memories like those could only cause her to want to sit on Santa's lap and tell him what she'd like to find under her tree on Christmas morning.

And that was a family.

Kids anxiously waiting to rip into brightly colored packages.

Aunts, uncles, cousins, parents and grandparents to fuss and carry on about everything from setting the table for Christmas morning breakfast to who was the most surprised by their gift.

A man to share her life with, to love her, and surprise her with something special just for her. Not necessarily something expensive, just something with meaning, something from his heart.

Like the beloved Christmas village pieces her father used to give to her mother before they'd been killed in a house fire when Abby had been seven. She wanted to experience what her parents had shared, to open a package and glance up with excitement, not at the physical gift but with the love with which it had been chosen. She wanted to see that love reflected back at her in the glow of twinkling Christmas morning lights.

But on top of all that, she wanted Dirk.

Abby sighed.

Other than her very busy volunteer schedule and long work hours, Abby led a lonely life. Oh, she had friends, lots of friends, amazing friends like Danielle, but she didn't have someone to come home to, someone to whom she was the most important person in their life, someone to love and be loved by. Only her tabby cat Mistletoe cared whether or not she came home in the mornings after working the emergency department night shift.

Oblivious to her onset of melancholy, Dirk adjusted his belly padding, scratched at his glued-on beard. "I'll never complain about a monkey suit again. After this getup, wearing a tuxedo will feel like a real treat."

Pulling herself from her unwanted self-pitying thoughts and trying not to think about how handsome Dirk would look in a tux, *out of a tux*, Abby focused on the here and now. She had a great life, a great job and great friends. She was a needed, productive member of society. At the moment she was needed to give downtown Philadelphia children a magical visit with Santa.

Abby wasn't the kind of woman to disappoint. Not when she had any say in the matter and never when it came to children and Christmas.

"Better let me adjust your beard there, Santa." She tugged on Dirk's fake white beard, soothing down the coarse lifelike hair he'd ruffled with his scratching.

Just touching him prickled her skin with goose bumps.

Glancing everywhere but at her, he fanned his face. "Man, this thing is hot."

He was what was hot. Hot as a roaring fire she'd like to warm herself next to. Oh, my! Abby turned away before she had to fan her face, too.

"You think that's why Santa's cheeks stay red?" She reached into the break room's refrigerator and pulled out a cold bottle of water.

"I thought it was from kissing all the mommies under the mistletoe," he surprised her by saying.

Abby blinked at him, at how the corners of his mouth hitched upward ever so slightly. Was he flirting with her?

Laughing a bit nervously, she handed him the water. "Well, there is that."

Twisting off the top and taking a long swig, Dirk sagged into a chair, his blue gaze lifting to hers. "Tell me I don't really have to go back out there."

"You don't have to, but you will, anyway."

He would, too. In the short time since he'd arrived in Philadelphia, just a couple of weeks prior to Halloween, Dirk had proved himself the type of man who didn't shirk a commitment. Even one he so obviously regretted having made. Why had he? Guilt at what had happened between them? At his hasty retreat into "This never should have happened" immediately afterward? She'd hid her hurt. She knew she had. And she'd told herself she should be relieved—workplace romances never seemed to end well.

"You're right." Even for a guy dressed like Santa Claus his sigh was a bit too melodramatic. "I will, but you owe me, Abs. Big-time. Any time. Any place. Any thing. You owe me. Take note."

Despite how her heart tattooed a funky beat at his unexpected words, wondering if maybe that morning haunted him, too, Abby placed her hands on her hips. Or maybe it was because of his words she felt the need to stand her ground. "I think 'any' is a bit too general."

"Nope." He shook his Santafied head. "Any it is."

She sighed. How bad could owing him be? They'd both agreed falling into bed together had been a mistake, the result of a particularly bad night in the E.R. where three people had died due to trauma received in a multicar accident. Although they'd done everything medically possible, the internal injuries had been too extensive. An elderly man had suffered a heart attack and hit another car head-on. He'd died instantly, but a two-year-old girl and her mother had been alive, barely, when paramedics had rushed them into the emergency room. The mother had died within minutes, the child soon thereafter. Abby's heart had felt ripped out by shift change. Surprisingly, Dirk had been just as devastated. It had been the only time she'd seen his E.R. physician armor crack.

They'd ended up at her house, clinging to each other for comfort. That's all *that* morning had been. Comfort sex between two normal, healthy adults who found each other attractive.

Not that comfort sex with Dirk had been a bad thing. She supposed sex with any man of his probable experience would be fabulous. Definitely, Dirk had been fabulous. Practice made perfect, right?

Which meant there was no way his any thing, any time, any place would have anything to do with a repeat performance. He might have been well on his way to the perfect lover, but she'd been sorely lacking in practice.

As in a couple of not-so-perfect boyfriends.

So why had she asked Dirk in when he'd dropped her by her house when he'd caught her crying in the elevator and insisted on driving her home? How had him walking her to her front door ended with him carrying her to her bedroom, stripping her naked, and initiating her to the joys shared between a man and a woman that up to that point she'd only believed happened in romance novels?

"Abs?" He pulled her back to the present.

She blinked again, hoping more fervently than every kid on Christmas Eve that he couldn't read her thoughts.

He pushed the gold-rimmed glasses back against the straight slant of his nose. "Do we have a deal?"

She may as well agree. It wasn't as if Dirk would ever really need anything from her. He was gorgeous, and despite his grumblings about having to play the role of Santa, Dirk was good-hearted, an honorable man and an excellent doctor. The physical chemistry between them kept her from being a hundred percent comfortable in his presence—how could she be comfortable when she looked at him and remembered how delicious his kisses tasted, how his naked body felt gliding against hers?

Just thinking about him made her feel a little giddy. There was always a little extra bounce to her step on the nights her shift overlapped his emergency room duties.

"Fine." She met his gaze and wondered what he was up to. The man was brilliant. He was also the only Santa she had. She needed him. "For the kids. I owe you."

"Good," he said, standing. "Let's get this over with."

Dirk's smile scared her. Which felt wrong. How could a smiling Santa be intimidating? Yet, as his gloved hand clasped hers, her nervous system lit up like a twinkling Christmas tree.

CHAPTER TWO

FROM the moment his precious two-year-old daughter and his wife had been killed in a car accident on their way to an early-morning Christmas bargain sale, Dirk Kelley had hated Christmas.

He'd avoided anything to do with the holiday year after year. To the point that his family had held a well-intended but unnecessary intervention at last year's not-so-joyous festivities.

After their unwelcome confrontation, telling him he needed to deal with Sandra and Shelby's deaths, they'd continued to hound him, to try to set him up on dates, to beg him to live life. By early summer, he'd known he had to move away from Oak Park, where his family resided, before the next holiday season. Much to their disappointment, he'd accepted the job in Philadelphia, knowing he was far enough away to avoid holiday get-togethers and their piteous look, but not so far away that he couldn't make it home if there was an emergency. He loved them, just couldn't deal with the pity in their eyes, their interference in what was left of his life.

They were wrong. He hadn't needed the intervention. What he'd needed was for his wife and daughter to be alive, but that was impossible. He'd accepted that inevitability years ago, accepted that he had to move on with his life, and he had. But that didn't mean he'd ever want to be involved with another woman or would welcome the month of December and all the holiday hoopla that arrived with it.

If he could fast-forward December, he'd gladly do so. The lights, the smells, the sales, the noises, everything about the month ripped open his never-healing chest wound.

Abby's initial shocked expression must have mirrored his own when he'd agreed to be her Santa.

Mortification and panic had struggled for top seat. Yet he hadn't been able to take back his ill-fated yes. Not when the wariness she'd eyed him with since the morning after they'd met had finally disappeared, replaced with surprise and soft hazel-eyed gratitude. That look had done something to his insides. Something strange and foreign and despite knowing how difficult today was going to be, he hadn't retracted his agreement.

Not when doing so would disappoint Abby.

Thank God the deed was behind him and he could put Christmas nonsense behind him, where it belonged.

Thankfully de-Santafied, he wandered around Abby's living room. The room had been taken hostage by Christmas Past since the last time he'd been here, two months ago. He'd swear he'd stepped into a nostalgic Christmas movie scene from a couple of decades ago.

An ancient wreath hung over Abby's fireplace, a slightly thinning silver garland was draped over a doorway with faded red ribbons marking each corner. A small Christmas village complete with fake glittery snow and dozens of tiny trees and villagers was set up on a white cloth-covered table, clearly set up in a place of honor beside the tree. The nine main pieces of the village looked old, expensive.

Her live Christmas tree towered almost to the ceiling, a ceramic-faced angel's tinsel halo mere inches from it. What a crazy tradition. Trees indoors. The entire room smelt like the pine tree—like Christmas. Smells he didn't like. Smells that haunted him and took him to hellish places he didn't want to go.

There had been a Christmas tree in the waiting room of the emergency department the morning Sandra and Shelby had died. Amazing how the smell could take him back to sitting in that room, a broken man, a doctor who hadn't been able to do a damned thing to save his baby girl and her mother.

He walked over to the fireplace, eyeing the giant painted toy soldiers to each side, picking up a slightly worn wooden nutcracker. He shook his head, waiting for the nausea to hit him, waiting for the cold sweat to cover his skin, the grief to bring him to his knees.

Christmas did that to him. Sure, he'd learned to bury his pain beneath what most labeled as cynicism, but that didn't mean in private moments the past didn't sneak up to take a stab through his armor, to chip away another piece of what was left of him.

And yet, for the first time since Sandra and Shelby's deaths, he'd agreed to do something that fed into the whole commercialism of Christmas. All because pretty little nurse Abby Arnold had asked him. She'd lit up so brilliantly someone could stick a halo on her head and place her on top of a tree.

He'd definitely found a piece of heaven on earth in her arms. Had found solace he hadn't expected in the heat of her kisses.

Solace? After the first sweep of his mouth over her lush lips, he hadn't been seeking comfort but acting on the attraction he'd instantly felt for the pretty brunette nurse. He'd been on fire. With lust. With need. With the desire to be inside her curvy body.

He hadn't been remembering or forgetting. He'd been in the moment. With Abby.

He'd wanted her the second he'd laid eyes on her, but never had he experienced such all-consuming sex as that morning. So all-consuming he'd known they couldn't repeat it. Quite easily he could see himself getting obsessed with having her body wrapped around him, getting serious when he had no intention of ever having another serious relationship. Just look at how often he thought of Abby and they'd only had the one morning where they'd made love, twice, and collapsed into exhausted sleep.

Letting out a slow, controlled breath, Dirk placed the nutcracker back on her mantel. Any time, any place, any thing. Why had he teased her into making such an outlandish promise? Better yet, why had he asked for what he had?

He turned, planning to go and find Abby, to tell her he'd changed his mind and needed to go.

A fat tabby cat in a wicker basket at the end of the sofa caught his eye. They'd been formally introduced when the cat had jumped onto the bed, waking both Dirk and Abby in the middle of the afternoon that mid-October day. The cat had been observing his perusal of the room but other than watch him with boredom the cat never moved except to close its eyes.

Realizing another smell, one that was making his stomach grumble, was taking precedence over the pine and was coming through an open doorway, he followed his nose.

When he stepped into the kitchen, he stopped still at the sight that met him, wondering if he'd had one too many kids call him Santa. Because he certainly had the feeling that he'd stepped into an old Christmas movie again.

Singing to the soft Christmas music playing on the mounted under-the-counter player, Abby had on an apron that had Mr. and Mrs. Claus kissing under a sprig of mistletoe on the front. She'd pulled her thick hair back with a red ribbon and had kicked off her shoes for a pair of worn, fuzzy Rudolph slippers.

Stirring a mixture in a glass bowl, a whimsical smile played on her lips as she swayed to the beat of "Rocking Around the Christmas Tree." She looked happy. Like she belonged in this house with its hand-me-down decorations and cozy holiday atmosphere.

Not that he found any of this cozy.

Only there was something about Abby that made him feel warmth where only coldness had resided for so long. There was also something about her that made him want to hold mistletoe over her head and kiss her.

He'd need a thatched hut with a mistletoe roof over her head to justify all the places he wanted to kiss Abby Arnold.

He wanted to do more than kiss her. Lots more. Like take some of that fudge and smear it across her...

Her gaze lifting from the glass bowl she held, she smiled, knocking the breath from his lungs with her beauty and sincerity. "I can't believe you wanted home-made fudge as your any time, any place, any thing."

Her smile said he'd pleased her with his ravings about

the goodies she'd brought to the break room at the hospital and how he wanted another bite.

He wanted another bite all right.

Her dimples dug a little deeper into her lovely face. "Some men are so easy."

Smiling at him like that, she made him feel easy. Like he was cookie dough in her hands, waiting for her to mold him into whatever shape she wanted. So why was he still there? Why hadn't he told her he was leaving as he'd come in here to do?

Why was he smiling back at her? Why was he eyeing the pan of chocolate-chip cookies she'd taken out of the oven and feeling a pang of hunger in his belly? A pang that didn't begin to compare to the one below his belt caused by eyeing Abby.

"If they've tasted your homemade goodies, I understand why. Especially the peanut-butter fudge."

"Thank you." Her eyes sparkled like the silver tinsel draping her tree. "It was my mother's recipe."

"Was?"

A flicker of pain crossed her face. "She died."

"I'm sorry." He was. Death was never easy. If anyone knew that, he did. In spades. No, death wasn't easy. Not even when you were a highly trained doctor who'd been dealing with life and death on a daily basis for years.

Just look at how stupidly he'd behaved that first night he and Abby had worked together. Even now, his reaction to the motor vehicle accident victims bothered him, but he understood why, understood that when he'd been battling to save the mother and daughter, he'd been trying to save his wife, trying to save Shelby.

Only to fail.

But he'd held up fine, wearing the mask he'd perfected

in those months following their deaths. Pretending he was okay when inside all he'd felt was cold.

Until he'd run into Abby.

He'd been on his way out of the hospital, had caught the elevator just as the door had started closing, and been startled to see a red-eyed Abby eyeing him in surprise.

After shift change, she'd obviously slipped into the bathroom and had a good cry, was still fighting tears. She'd looked vulnerable, needy, way too distraught to be getting behind the wheel of a car.

Way too distraught for him to let her.

He'd insisted on driving her home.

Which was all fine and dandy.

Walking her to the door, going inside, staying, was where he'd messed up.

He didn't date hospital employees, wouldn't date hospital employees.

He hadn't really dated Abby. He'd just not been able to stand the sadness in her eyes, to stand the thought of her driving upset and possibly something happening to her. They'd ended up naked, in her bed, making love until they'd both collapsed in each other's arms and slept the day away.

He shouldn't have done that.

Shouldn't have agreed to be her Santa.

Shouldn't be here now.

So why was he pulling up a chair, willingly staying somewhere Christmas tunes played, instead of beating a path to the door?

Was her imagination running wild or was Dirk looking at her like he'd rather take a bite out of her instead of the peanut-butter fudge?

Abby turned away from his intense blue eyes and took a deep breath. Needing to do something with her hands, she twisted on the faucet and filled the sink with sudsy water to wash the dishes she'd used to make the cookies and two batches of fudge—one chocolate, one peanut butter.

"This is really great."

There was no doubting the sincerity in his voice. She'd swear she heard him moan a moment ago.

Without turning toward him, Abby began stacking the dishes into the hot water to let them soak a few minutes.

"My mother had tons of great recipes, but…" But most of them had been lost in the fire. Only her mother's Christmas recipes packed away in the crates in the basement had survived. The items stored in the basement had been the only items that had survived, period. Almost every box had contained precious Christmas items. "I always bring several big platters full of goodies to the hospital every Christmas."

"Like the fudge you brought the other day?"

"That, and more." She grabbed a dish towel, turned toward him and leaned against the sink. "I like to bake. I like how the house smells when I have cookies in the oven and candies going on the stovetop and…"

Realizing she was probably boring him, heat flushed her face. She wiped her hands more with the dish towel, wondering if the moisture was from the dishwater or from nervous clamminess. Dirk made her edgy.

"Sorry." She smiled wryly. "Christmas is my favorite holiday and I get carried away at times."

"Obviously."

Despite the amusement in his eyes, something about

the way he said the word struck her as wrong. "What's that supposed to mean?"

His grin stayed in place but, still, there was something off kilter, something a bit too brittle about him. "Just that it looks like Bing Crosby should be showing up any moment to start singing about a white Christmas."

"What would be so bad about that? He was a great singer. What's wrong with you anyway? All day you've acted like you really don't like Christmas."

He shrugged. "I don't."

"Say it isn't so!" Astounded, flabbergasted, shocked, her mouth dropped open and her palm flattened against her chest, dish towel and all.

"Why?" He shrugged, looking so serious it made Abby want to loosen her apron strings. "It's the truth. I'm surprised you buy into such a commercialized holiday."

"The business world commercializes every holiday but that doesn't lessen what the day is about."

"Which is?"

"Are you kidding me?" She eyed him, wondering if he was teasing her. When he'd first told her he didn't like Christmas, she'd thought he was just trying to get out of playing Santa. Could anyone really not like Christmas? Why wouldn't they? "Christmas is about everything good in life. It's a time when families come together and give of themselves to each other. A time when the world slows down and gives a helping hand to someone in need. It's—"

"It's a time when people run up credit-card debt they can't pay. It's a time of the highest rate of depression cases treated, the highest rate of suicide, the highest rate of—"

"How can you be such a cynic about Christmas?" Abby tossed the dish towel onto the countertop and frowned. How could someone not love Christmas? Not love the bright colors in the stores, the sounds of Christmas over the radio, the decorations along the streets? Abby even loved walking past the Salvation Army bellringers. Dropping money into their collection pails always made her feel warm and fuzzy inside.

Giving of oneself was the greatest joy of the holidays. Sure, it would be nice to have someone give to her, to share the moments with, but she'd already decided once today that she'd had enough self-pity.

"I'm not a cynic," he denied, but the more he talked, the more convinced she became that he was.

"I'm a realist," he clarified. "For most, Christmas is a major stressor with trying to come up with the perfect gift, trying to figure out how they're going to pay for that gift, and how they're going to fight the crowds to make sure they get their hands on that perfect gift."

"You're so negative," she pointed out, wondering what had given him such a slanted view of her favorite time of the year. "I see Christmas as at time when you get to search out that special gift to bring a smile to someone's face. A gift meant just for them from you that signifies who they are and how much you appreciate having them in your life."

"It's about rushing from one place to the next," he went on, as if she'd never interrupted his tirade. "Never quite satisfying family and friends with how much of your time you can allot for the festivities they planned without any consideration for your busy schedule. It's about high emotions and family bickering and—"

"Bah, humbug," she interrupted, pulling out a chair at

the table and sitting down beside him, positive she was staring at a complete stranger. Who would have thought the wonderful emergency doctor was such a Scrooge? The caring man who'd been as devastated by the deaths of two patients as she had? "Say what you will, but that's not what Christmas is about. Not to me, and you should be ashamed for being so…so…Grinchy!"

He eyed her for long, silent moments, studying her as if she were an oddity. Then, as if he'd not just dissed her favorite holiday, dissed her favorite childhood memories of perfect Christmas moments, his lips curved into a crooked smile. "If it's any consolation, I really like Christmas fudge."

Taking a deep breath, relaxing the tension that had tightened her neck muscles, Abby sighed. How could she stay annoyed at him when he gave her that boyish look that made her toes curl in her shoes?

"Good thing I didn't know all this about you when I asked you to be Santa," she said, smoothing out the edge of a plain red and green table placemat. "You, Dr. Kelley, are no Santa Claus."

"You asked me to be Santa because you couldn't get anyone else to agree." Still showing wry amusement, his gaze pinned hers. "Admit it."

An unexpected giggle rose up her throat. "Okay, you're right. Everyone else I asked claimed to be busy."

"Such classic examples of Christmas goodwill and cheer."

"They were probably busy," she said defensively, although she doubted any of them could match her holiday season schedule. Every year she took on as many projects as she could fit in.

"Sure they were." He popped the last piece of his fudge into his mouth. "But if they'd known they could maneuver their way into your kitchen, you'd have had to beat Santa-wannabes away with stockings filled with coal."

"I'm guessing you'd know a lot about those stockings filled with coal." At his mock look of horror, she smiled. "You should've tried my mother's Martha Washington candy."

Memories of standing on a chair beside her mother, carefully dipping rolled candies into melted chocolate, her mother smiling down at her, praising her efforts, filled Abby's heart. How she longed for a family to spend Christmas with.

Dirk reached for a second square of fudge. His sooty ashes swept across his cheeks as he bit into it. Was it shameful she'd like to see that blissful look on his face while he tasted her lips? Yes. Yes, it was. They'd agreed anything physical between them was a mistake. She'd agreed when he'd said that.

It had been a mistake. Hadn't it? Or had agreeing with him been the mistake?

Because looking at him, being here with him, denying the way she wanted him when she wanted him so badly sure felt like the bigger mistake.

CHAPTER THREE

"IF YOU'RE more into peanut butter, there's always peanut-butter balls and homemade peanut brittle," she rushed out, trying to redirect her mind away from the direction it was headed.

Eyes wide, his gaze lifted to hers. He looked like an eager little boy. *Like he'd looked that morning when he'd devoured her mouth.*

He placed his hand over his heart. "I've died and gone to heaven. You're right. I was too easy. I should have asked for peanut brittle."

She laughed out loud at his look of ecstasy.

Just as quickly her laughter faded as more memories of another time, another look of ecstasy had been on his handsome face.

When he'd been standing just inside her front door, awkwardly saying goodbye but making no move to leave. The only move he'd made had been to bend and gently kiss her lips.

Then he'd kissed her not so gently.

Oh, Lord, how he'd kissed her.

And kissed her.

No, she couldn't keep thinking of *that* morning. Not

with him here, alone, in her house, just the two of them and the bed where he'd made love to her.

No, not love. They'd just been two colleagues dealing poorly with a very stressful night in the emergency room.

Her gaze tangled with his and his good humor faded just as quickly as hers had. Was he remembering, too? Recalling that the last time he'd been in her house, he'd never seen the kitchen but had had an up-close-and-personal tour of her bedroom?

He stuck the remainder of his fudge in his mouth, stood and brushed his hands over the faded jeans he'd changed into in her guest bathroom after his shower. When he'd swallowed the mouthful, he took a step back. "I put your Santa suit on the sofa."

His words managed to pull her from memories of Dirk's last visit to further in the past. Her father's Santa suit. When Dirk had asked her about what he'd wear, she'd instantly offered her father's suit.

"Thanks for the fudge and for the loan of the suit."

"It was the least I could do as you filled in for Santa." True, but had anyone else agreed to play the role, she would have bought a cheap Santa costume from a department store. For Dirk, she'd dug out the treasured suit that had belonged to her father.

"Thanks all the same."

"If you hadn't agreed, I'd have had to play Santa." Not that her father's suit would have fit her, but she'd have made it work somehow. "I think the kids might have been scarred for life."

His gaze raked over the ample upper part of her body. "You're probably right about that. You're no Santa." He tossed her earlier words back at her.

Abby didn't know whether to be offended or flattered. Either way, heat crept into her face.

"I'll get a dish for you to take some home." She stood so rapidly her chair almost toppled. Pulling out a Christmas patterned storage tin, she placed a generous piece of plastic wrap inside, arranged as much as would fit of the fudge and cookies, and put the lid on. "There you go."

He'd moved over next to her, standing near the cabinets. His body heat radiated toward her, luring her nearer. "I feel guilty, coercing you to make this and then taking most of it."

"You should feel guiltier if you left it here," she teased a bit nervously, playfully elbowing him, the contact shooting stars through the pit of her belly.

His gaze dropped to where she'd touched his arm then his brow rose in question of her comment.

"If you left it, I'd eat it," she clarified, not lowering her gaze despite how her blood pumped through her body at warp speed and made her feel as if she needed to call time out so she could catch her breath.

Again his eyes ran over her features, taking their time and not seeming to mind the bumps and valleys along the journey. "That would be a bad thing?"

"I'm a woman who is constantly on a diet," she admitted, sucking in her waist reflexively as his gaze traveled lower. Not that holding her belly in would do much good.

"You have no reason to be on a diet." When his eyes met hers, they were blue fire, hot, lust-filled.

A thousand carolers began to sing in her soul, louder and louder until she might explode from the sheer beauty of it, until she was sure the sound must be able to be heard in heaven itself.

"No reason at all," he repeated, his gaze burning hotter. "You're perfect just as you are."

Um, right. Perfect. If you liked a woman who was busty and hippy, with a little extra thigh thrown in on the sides. But she couldn't look away from Dirk, because he was either the most talented fibber in the world or he meant what he said. And, darn, if those carolers hadn't gone up another octave in the pit of her belly, making every individual cell vibrate in a happy dance.

"I, uh…" What could she say when he was looking at her as if a slightly fuller figure really was perfection? She shoved the fudge at him. "Thank you, but I'm glad you're taking it, all the same."

He looked as if he wanted to say more, but must have decided against doing so as he took the candy, stared at her a few moments, his gaze going from fire to almost a sad smoldering. "Bye, Abs. You working tomorrow night?"

Abs. He really shouldn't say her name like that so carelessly! Holding her breath, she nodded.

"Are you planning to go to the hospital Christmas party this weekend?" Had he winced while asking that? Or after the words had left his mouth?

"Of course," she answered slowly, watching the play of conflicting emotions dance on his face. "I'm on the hospital's Christmas committee and helped put the party together. Are you going?"

"I hadn't planned to, but…" He paused, looked as if he needed to loosen his collar even though his black T-shirt was far from restricting at the neck.

"But?" she prompted, her eyes focusing on a bead of sweat she'd swear was forming on his brow.

He took a deep breath, as if he was about to embark on a dangerous quest he really didn't want to go on but had little choice. "If you'll go with me, I could probably tolerate it this once. When I didn't RSVP, the hospital administrator came by." Dirk sighed, looking almost as uncomfortable as he had when he'd been playing Santa. "He said it wouldn't look good for the newest member on the medical staff to not show for the hospital's biggest employee social event of the year."

Not the most enthusiastic invitation she'd ever received, but happiness spread through Abby.

Dirk had just asked her on a date to the hospital Christmas party.

Not that he really wanted to go, but he'd asked her to accompany him. On a date.

"I'd love to go to the Christmas party with you." There wasn't a man alive she'd rather attend with. Being at Dirk's side would make the party all the more special, made everything all the more special.

Would he please turn around a moment so she could happy-dance around the kitchen?

Dirk had asked her to the Christmas party! Their morning hadn't been a one-night stand after all. Er…a one-morning stand after all.

"Okay. Great." He sounded relieved at her answer.

Had he thought she'd say no or was it the Christmas party itself stressing him? Either way, Dirk had just asked her to go on a date.

Thinking this just might be the best Christmas ever, she bubbled with good cheer and found herself wanting to tease a smile out of him. "Do I need to have my father's Santa suit dry-cleaned or will you be providing your own wardrobe for the evening?"

He snorted, his mouth creeping up at the corners as she'd hoped. "You worry about what you're going to wear, Li'l Miss Christmas Spirit. I'll take care of my suit."

"So long as it's not green with pointy toes, Mr. Grinchy."

He laughed. "Deal."

They stared at each other long moments, so long Abby couldn't help but wonder what he was thinking, couldn't help but wonder what had prompted his invitation. Was it possible that she wasn't the only one with visions of more than sugar plums dancing through her dreams? Could he at this very moment want to whisk her off her feet and carry her back to her bed and have a repeat? Why bother going to the bedroom? Kitchens were always good for cooking up something hot.

He cleared his throat, coughed, shook his head a little. "See you tomorrow night at the hospital. Thanks again for the fudge."

With that, he took his goodies and left.

Abby wrapped her arms around her apron-covered waist and danced around the kitchen while singing along with one of her favorite Christmas tunes.

She was going to the hospital Christmas party with the most amazing, sexy, wonderful man she'd ever met.

God, she loved Christmastime and if she wasn't careful, she just might end up loving Dirk, too.

"Bay one has a probable UTI," Abby told Dirk when he stepped out of the exam area where he'd just been seeing a patient in. "White blood cell count is twelve thousand, with neutrophils slightly elevated. There's a trace of blood and plus four bacteria in the urine. The patient reports tenderness in the abdomen and in the mid-low back."

Dirk nodded, without glancing directly at her.

Abby sighed. He'd seemed a bit distant tonight. She'd been dreaming of dashing through the snow like lovers with him ever since he'd issued his invitation to the Christmas party. Okay, before then. Way before then. She'd been dreaming of Dirk since the morning they'd ended up in bed together. Hadn't she known not to get her hopes up after the way he'd *dashed* out of her house after they'd made love? But she just couldn't seem to help herself where Dirk was concerned.

Reminding herself that she was a registered nurse, a professional, and on the job, she followed Dirk into the bay, telling herself to keep her mind—and eyes!—off the man in front of her, even if he did look fab-u-lous in his hospital-issue scrubs.

Obviously, he didn't spend his days inside, baking. Not with the taut definition in his upper arms, the strength in his neck and shoulders, the taper of his waist, the… Abby gulped. *Focus! He is not a Christmas package waiting for you to unwrap him. He's a highly respected emergency physician.*

But she'd really like to unwrap Dirk.

Focus! Focus! Focus!

"Hello, Mrs. Youngblood," he greeted the thin lady with streaky brown-blond hair and pinched facial features. "The nurse was just telling me about your lab results. It appears you have a serious urinary-tract infection. Tell me what's been going on."

Dirk examined the patient while the lady told him of her symptoms, when they'd started and how they'd gotten much worse during the night to the point she'd decided she couldn't wait until morning to check in with her primary care provider.

"No history of kidney stones?"

Mrs. Youngblood shook her head, her expression easing very little. "My husband has them, but I never have. Are they contagious?"

"No. You can't catch kidney stones from another person." Dirk pressed on her thin abdomen, attempting to palpate organs. "Any vaginal symptoms?"

"I don't think so," she denied, her hand guarding her belly as Dirk examined her. "It just really burns when I urinate. And feels like my bladder is going to turn inside out when I go, too."

"Have the medications given since you've arrived helped?"

"Yes." Although you sure couldn't tell it by the woman's grimace. "When I first got here I was miserable. The pain hasn't completely eased, but I'm a lot better."

Dirk washed his hands then turned to his patient. "I'm going to write a prescription for some antibiotics. You'll need to follow up with your primary care provider within the next couple of days." He began writing out orders. "Do you need a note for work?"

The woman shook her head. "I work from home as a medical billing clerk."

"Great." Dirk turned to Abby, meeting her eyes for the first time since they'd entered the room, and he smiled.

A real smile that reached those gorgeous blue eyes and pierced right into her heart.

Relief flooded Abby. Did he have any idea as to the lethalness of his smile? Probably. She soaked up every drop of his potency, letting the intensity of her emotions flow through her veins.

"Mrs. Youngblood," he said, his gaze flicking back to his patient. "The nurse will get you ready for discharge. If you have any additional problems or get worse before morning, I'd suggest you return to the emergency department for a recheck."

An hour later, the emergency department was in full swing. Every bay was full. Both physicians and the nurse practitioner on duty were at full stretch.

Abby adjusted a breathing mask over an asthma patient's mouth and nose, preparing to administer a beta-agonist medication via a nebulizer to rapidly open up the restricted airways.

"You may feel a little shaky and jittery after the medication starts working," she warned her patient. "The process that causes the bronchial tubes to dilate also speeds up the heart rate. Don't let the reaction alarm you as that's a natural and expected response to the medicine."

She turned on the nebulizer and waited to make sure the patient's wheezing slowed before she stepped out of the bay to check on her next patient.

Dirk was with him—a morbidly obese man who'd woken up with a sharp tightness in his chest that took his breath. They'd started him on meds immediately on arrival, done tests, including an EKG that showed left ventricular hypertrophy and a possible blockage. They'd stabilized him while awaiting the results of his cardiac enzyme tests.

"I read your chest X-ray, Mr. Lytle. Your heart is enlarged, showing signs of your high blood pressure and congestive heart failure, but that shouldn't have caused you to wake up with chest pain. I don't see anything acute on the films, but your troponin level is slightly elevated. That's a myocardial muscle isoenzyme that elevates when the heart isn't getting enough oxygen. I'm going to admit you to the cardiac-care unit for close observation. The cardiologist on call has been notified you're here and will be by soon. He'll schedule you for a cardiac catheterization, likely for in the morning. That way, if there are any blockages, he can repair them immediately."

Abby began to prepare to have the patient transferred to the cardiac-care unit while Dirk answered the questions of the patient and his wife.

The rest of the night passed quickly. The E.R. was still bustling come shift change. An hour past time for her to have left, Abby clocked out, exhausted and feeling a little woozy.

Dirk had still been with an abdominal pain patient who'd come in minutes before shift change. Abby had offered to stay, but the day-shift nurse had taken over and had things under control.

She'd felt relieved at the reprieve, and surprised at how tired she was. The night had been busy, but no more so than dozens of others she'd worked, but she just wanted to go home, crawl into bed and pass out.

She rarely got sick, but definitely her stomach churned at the thought of breakfast. Maybe she'd just skip her usual light meal before going to bed. Hopefully, she'd feel better once she got some sleep.

She hoped she wasn't coming down with something, especially so close to Christmas.

Regardless, no way would she let a little nausea and fatigue get her down when she had a date with Dirk for the Christmas party on Saturday evening.

CHAPTER FOUR

"DON'T tell me you unwrapped a Christmas present early and found Dr. Kelley inside, because if that's the case, I'm changing what I put on my wish list for this year." Medical floor nurse Danielle Booker draped her arm around Abby's shoulder on Saturday night at the hospital Christmas party being held in the ballroom of a nearby hotel.

Abby glanced away from where she watched Dirk talk with a couple of other physicians. When the conversation had turned to golf, she'd excused herself. She'd needed a few moments to breathe. Dirk had been the perfect attentive date, but the tension between them was so palpable it threatened to cut off her windpipe. Between that and his obvious discomfort at being at the party, Abby was wound tighter than a spool of ribbon.

"I'm waiting." Danielle tapped her slinky black high heels against the ballroom floor. "Were you such a good girl this year that Santa arranged for Dr. Kelley to be in your stocking?"

"Now isn't the time for details about my relationship with Dirk." Not to mention that she didn't know how to define their relationship.

"You're admitting you have a relationship with *Dirk*?"

Her friend put emphasis on the use of his given name rather than his title of Dr. Kelley.

He'd been Dirk from the moment she'd glanced into his eyes and felt as if she were drowning in a blue sea of Christmas ribbon. With all her volunteering with the community outreach program, she hadn't found the time to call her best friend and they'd been on different shifts at the hospital. She hadn't told anyone about the morning she'd spent with Dirk. Perhaps if their relationship hadn't ended almost as fast as they'd started... And if they'd ended, what was tonight about? And why did she fluctuate between giddy and the need to protect her heart?

"I'm not admitting anything. Not here." Abby's gaze shifted to him again. Just looking at him made her feel as if she was all tangled up and would never be able to free herself. "But I like him, if that's what you're asking."

"You like him? Girl, that isn't 'like' I see in your eyes," Danielle teased, her grin growing bigger in direct proportion to Abby's face growing hotter. "You are so telling me everything soon."

"Everything," Abby agreed. Which was what? Dirk hadn't called or even talked to her at the hospital other than about patients and to confirm what time to pick her up. After his Santa debut and him asking her out for tonight, she'd jumped every time her phone had rung, hoping he'd call. She'd been disappointed every time. Disappointed that he hadn't made any effort to talk to her outside the parameters of work.

Until tonight.

Tonight, he'd been a considerate date, if quiet, taking her white faux-fur wrap and gloves to the designated coat room, ensuring she had everything she wanted to drink and eat, even making the comment that her goodies tasted better than the ones supplied by the party's caterer.

Yet that ever-present awkwardness, awareness, kept her slightly on edge, not letting her completely relax, making her stomach stay slightly knotted with tension. That's why she'd needed a breather. Being so close to Dirk, his hand occasionally resting possessively on her back, she'd been on the verge of swooning from lack of air.

On the verge of grabbing his hand and dragging him to a room and kissing him like crazy in hopes of abating whatever this burn inside her was.

Abby covered her mouth with her hand, biting back a slight smile at what Dirk would do, say, if she marched over to him and did just that. Bet that wouldn't do a thing to ease the edginess she'd sensed about him all evening. Because of her? Or the Christmas party?

Danielle eyed her a moment, taking note of exactly what Abby wasn't sure, just that her friend's smile faded. "You okay? You look flushed."

Any flush on her face was from her thoughts, not from not feeling okay. Actually, the bug that had been bothering her earlier in the week was sticking around. But, fortunately, by the time Dirk had arrived she'd been fine. When he'd looked at her as if she was more mouthwatering than any piece of peppermint candy, had told her she was beautiful, well, she'd been over the moon.

If she'd stop trying to label whatever was happening between them and could just enjoy the fact that something was happening, everything would be wonderful.

She visually sought out where he still stood with the

group of golfing physicians. He wasn't saying much, just listening to the others. Dirk didn't have to say much. The man would stand out in any crowd. Not just because of his height or his good looks or even his quick intelligence. No, he'd stand out because of the confident way he held himself, the pure aura of testosterone that clung to him and demanded women take notice, even though he seemed oblivious to the fact he was gorgeous.

Abby noticed. From his thick black hair to the tailored lines of his dinner jacket and trousers to the pointed toes of his Italian shoes, she noticed. And liked. She definitely liked.

"How could I not be okay?" she practically sighed, wondering if Danielle would scoop her up if she melted into an Abby puddle. Dirk liquefied her insides. Any moment she might slosh to the floor.

"Right," Danielle replied, her gaze following Abby's. "Got to admit, that man is fine. A little quiet and brooding for my taste, but he is easy on the eye."

Very easy on the eye. She'd seen more than one envious look her way when they entered the hotel ballroom.

"Just because he doesn't like Christmas doesn't mean he's brooding," Abby defended. "Plus, he isn't quiet once you get to know him. He has a great sense of humor."

Just recalling how he'd teased her made her insides toasty warm.

"I didn't know Dr. Dreamboat doesn't like Christmas and I still think he's brooding," Danielle pointed out.

Okay, so maybe a little brooding.

"The man keeps to himself, doesn't socialize, rarely talks to anyone outside anything to do with a patient or work. That's okay, mind you. He's probably just a

private person, but that's not my style. Although…"
she glanced toward where Dirk stood "…in his case,
I could be convinced to make an exception." Danielle
gave a little shake of her head. "Seriously, he doesn't
like Christmas? Talk about your opposites attracting.
Does he know you're the Queen of Holiday Cheer?"

"He knows." Recalling their conversation about the
holidays, Abby tried not to wince. She'd just focus on
the positive. "He likes my peanut-butter fudge."

"I'll just bet he does." Danielle snickered.

Abby rolled her eyes, but couldn't keep her smile
from her face. "He stepped in and played Santa the other
day at the community center, too."

See, there was another positive. Dirk had been there
when she'd needed him. How many people could she
say that of throughout her life so far?

"You're kidding! Dr. Kelley was Santa?" Danielle's
mouth dropped open. "Now I know I'm changing my
Christmas wish list. You should have told me. I could
have come and sat in his lap."

Um, no. If any grown-up had been going to sit in
Dirk's lap, Abby had dibs.

"My Santa canceled very last minute and I couldn't
find a replacement. He saved me from canceling the
event. Plus, he did a good job." Abby laughed at her
friend's amazed expression. "Seriously, he did."

Mostly. He hadn't seemed to enjoy himself, but he
had stayed until every kid in line had gotten their time
with Santa. Not every busy doctor would have given up
so much of his free time.

Okay, so he professed not to like Christmas. He was
here at the Christmas party. He'd played Santa. Next
thing you knew she'd have him out caroling or ringing

bells for charity donations. Hey, it could happen. She was here with him, wasn't she? He was taking her home, wasn't he?

As if sensing her gaze, Dirk looked up. Laser-blue fire flew from across the room, flooding her belly with the sensation of a curly Christmas ribbon having been stretched out and released.

Wow, but the man packed a wallop.

First saying something to the men he stood with, he headed toward her. Tall, handsome in his dark suit, his eyes solely trained on her, as if she were the only person in the room, the only person who mattered. His hand touched her elbow and her world shifted off its axis.

"Hi, Dr. Kelley. Great party, huh?" Danielle smiled at Dirk, taking a sip of her wine.

"I suppose." Dirk's gaze briefly touched on Danielle, but immediately returned to Abby. His eyes had the same look in them that he'd had at the "Pictures with Santa," a *rescue me, please* one. He held her gaze, his thumb stroking over her bare arm. Did he realize he was doing that? Would he please stop? The more he touched, the more she wanted him to touch. Not good. Her bosses were all here!

When she went to pull away, his hand enveloped hers, clasping her fingers in his slightly clammy ones.

Oblivious to Dirk's discomfort, Danielle sent Abby an impressed look, smiled widely, then excused herself under the pretense of getting another glass of wine.

"I'm not going to be able to stay much longer, Abby."

She nodded as if she understood, but she wasn't exactly clear. Had he gotten a call from the hospital? Due to the party, they were operating on a skeleton staff.

Both Dirk and Abby were on call, so it was a possibility. Although she couldn't imagine why that would make him nervous.

"I'm sorry."

"What are you sorry for?"

"Not wanting to stay at the party you planned."

Work hadn't called. He just didn't want to be there. Abby bit the inside of her cheek, studying him.

As his gaze skimmed over the Christmas decorations Abby had thought gave just the right touch, he winced. "If it were any other kind of party…"

Than Christmas. He didn't have to say the words.

There was something about the way his eyes darkened, the way his body tensed, that had her squeezing his hand. She didn't want to leave, but neither did she like the tortured expression in his eyes. "It's okay. We can go whenever you like. Most of the good stuff has already taken place."

"Good stuff?" He focused on her face as if using her as a focal point to stay grounded.

"When the administrators acknowledged all the hard work everyone does every day of the year, when they acknowledged what a great staff we have, and, of course, when they gave away the gifts donated by local businesses."

His expression not changing, he studied her. "Sorry you didn't win."

"That's okay." She smiled up at him, feeling petite despite her four-inch heels.

"You look like a winner." His gaze raked over her Santa Claus red dress, pausing at where the waist dipped in before flaring out just above the knees.

"Thank you." She'd seen the dress, added the white

wrap and the heels that were much more daring than anything she usually wore but couldn't resist, and known she had the perfect Christmas party ensemble.

She'd even splurged on new underwear. Not the granny whites like she usually wore. No, the tiny silk and lace garments beneath her dress kept up her Christmas red theme and made her feel less like that broken-down old toy and more like the shiny new one waiting to be played with under the Christmas tree.

Just in case.

As crazy as it was, she definitely wanted to relive all the things she and Dirk had done together, all the ways he'd touched her, kissed her, loved her body. She sighed in remembrance of the ways his hands and mouth had given her pleasure. So, so much pleasure.

"What are you thinking about?"

She glanced up, curious at the slight rasp to his voice. When her gaze collided with his, heat flushed her cheeks. She might not be able to read his mind, but he'd certainly read hers. He knew.

Knew exactly what she'd been thinking. Remembering.

It turned him on. Maybe as much as she was turned on. Could that be possible? Could he really feel the same?

"Earlier, when you asked, I promised to dance before the evening ended." His gaze never shifted from hers. "With you by my side, staying doesn't feel quite so impossible. Dance with me, Abby, then we'll go."

He was really going to dance with her? She'd already resigned herself that unless she danced with someone else, she wouldn't be making her way onto the dance floor.

Smiling, she let him lead her out. He took her into his arms and they swayed to the music in gentle rhythm.

"You're a good dancer." She'd imagined he hadn't wanted to dance because perhaps he couldn't. She should have known better about that, too. Dirk Kelley was a man of many talents.

"You sound surprised." He almost smiled. "It's been a while," he admitted, endearing himself even further, "but I guess it's like riding a bicycle. One of those things you don't really forget how to do."

"Why has it been a while since you've danced?"

Instantly, his arms stiffened.

"I just don't dance any more," he finally said.

Which wasn't really much of an answer and left her with a dozen questions he obviously wouldn't answer. Resisting a sigh, Abby laid her cheek against his chest, soaking in the warmth of being in his arms.

They danced, slow and in sync, their bodies touching, brushing against each other, his body heat melting her like a marshmallow in hot chocolate. Dirk made no motion to leave when one song turned into another.

"You smell good." He nuzzled her lightly, brushing his cheek against her hair. "Like fresh berries and cinnamon."

"You smell good, too," she admitted, amazed at her vocal cords' ability to make coherent sounds when her entire insides shook like she'd been trampled by stampeding reindeer.

"Are you having a good time?"

Nodding, she laid her cheek against his shoulder. From the corner of her eye, she saw Danielle give a thumbs-up and a suggestive eyebrow waggle and shake of her hips. She also noticed several of their colleagues watching them. Some with curiosity. Some with smiles.

A low, nervous chuckle rose up her throat.

"What?" he asked in a low voice, near her ear.

"Everyone thinks we're a couple."

His feet stilled a moment, as if he'd forgotten where they were, but his hands stayed at her waist. "I don't do couples, Abby."

She raised her head, stared at him. "Okay, we're not a couple." She took a deep breath. "What are we?"

He hesitated, looking torn. "I'm not sure."

Not the answer she'd hoped to hear. Then again, what had she expected? Feed the man a little fudge and he wouldn't be able to get enough of her?

She couldn't deal with his hot-cold attitude. Not and keep her sanity intact. Her heart intact.

"Then maybe you should get sure before we go any further, Dirk." Her heart banged against her rib cage in protest of her words. She wanted to go further. Lots further. But she wasn't a fool and wouldn't pretend to be one, not even for more time with Dirk. Regardless of how she felt, she deserved better than to be at his beck and call, available for comfort sex and Christmas parties. "I like you. A lot. But I don't want to end up with a broken heart and if you're not in this with me, then…" She shrugged. "Well, whatever this is needs to end now."

He studied her, his fingers splayed against her back, stroking over the material of her dress, possessively, distractingly. "I'd never hurt you, Abby."

"Not intentionally." Why were tears pricking her eyes? Why did she feel as if he was going to tell her goodbye? Why did that hurt so much? Technically, tonight was their first date. She would not cry. "But if I'm not careful where you're concerned, I will end up hurt."

Her heart protested it was way too late to start thinking about heart protection. She was crazy about Dirk. Way too crazy to walk away unscathed. Hadn't she fought tears more than once that he'd immediately had regrets about making love to her?

"You're right." He took a deep breath and she expected him to let her go, to push her away. Instead, his hands tightened at her waist, as if he wasn't willing to let go, as if he clung to her for support. "I shouldn't have asked you here tonight."

"Why did you?"

"I didn't want to be here alone."

Had he only asked because she was convenient? Because he'd known she'd say yes? She bit the inside of her lower lip to hold it steady. He'd not made any grand promises. All he'd done was ask her to attend a Christmas party with him. She'd been the one to attach all sorts of sentimental meaning to his invitation.

Just as she'd attached all sorts of sentimental meaning to their morning together. Lord, she was a fool.

"But mostly because I can't quit thinking about you."

A soft moan escaped. That was more along the lines of what she wanted to hear. More along the lines of how she felt about him. Her breath caught, knotting in her throat.

"About making love to you." He shifted against her, holding her more closely, pressing the length of her body to his. "I want you, Abby. I haven't stopped wanting you. Seeing you tonight, like this…" his gaze moved over the curve of her neck, her upswept hair "…touching you, I can't help but want to make love to you even though I know I shouldn't and you certainly shouldn't let me. Because regardless of how much I want you, I was serious when I said I don't do relationships."

"Why not?" She swallowed the knot, wondering at the raw emotions in his eyes. Emotions she wasn't positive had only to do with her, emotions he'd rarely bared, if ever.

He shook his head. "Not everyone wants the cozy Christmas fantasy of being part of a couple, Abby. That's not what I want."

The pain in his voice overshadowed his words, words she was sure were chosen to alienate her emotionally, revealed so much more than what he said. Did he realize how much he'd just exposed to her? That he'd given her a glimpse inside him? A glimpse that undid any resolve she might have had to walk away.

"What do you want?" She held his gaze, clinging to his shoulders to remain steady on her feet as she prepared to expose her heart. "Because I'm not asking for some cozy Christmas fantasy. I just want you. So much I forget to breathe when I look at you."

He inhaled sharply, closed his eyes.

"Oh, Abs," he whispered against her forehead, sounding tortured and pleased all in the same breath. His jaw flexed. His eyes darkened then closed again. When they opened, possession shone. Possession and something so primal and needy that desire swept through Abby. His eyes asked questions much more potent than any he could speak.

She toyed with the soft hair at his nape, twirling the silky black strands around her finger, wondering if it was bad that she felt just as wrapped around his finger. "Will you take me home now, Dirk?"

He placed his thumb beneath her chin, lifted her face. "I want to leave this monstrosity more than I can say, but are you sure?"

Concern flickered that he was calling what she'd thought a lovely Christmas party a monstrosity, but hormones ruled. That possessive look had her glutes tightening.

"Yes." She was sure she wanted to give him…everything. More. Needed to give him everything and more.

What the hell was he doing? Dirk wondered for the hundredth time that week.

Little Miss Merry Christmas was getting to him. And not just a little.

He'd been right when he'd told Abby she was beautiful earlier. She was. Absolutely stunning in her party dress.

But not as stunning as she'd been in nothing at all.

Dirk had been focusing on Abby to get through the party, had hung around the golf conversation just because it had been one of the few conversations going that had had nothing to do with the holidays.

Now, if he wanted to get out of the party without embarrassing himself, he had to keep his mind off Abby, off *that particular morning*, off how he'd lost himself in her body, how he'd felt whole inside for the first time in years. Even now, with her smiling up at him, he could lose himself in everything she was and almost forget the ever-present ache inside him at this time of year.

Her big hazel eyes were striking even without makeup accentuating them. Tonight they looked huge, like luminous stars guiding him to her. Her silky brown hair had been pulled up, but rather than the tighter style she wore for work, lots of strands hung loose, curling in loose tendrils. She wore a bright red dress that demanded attention and had captivated his from the moment she'd opened her front door, smiling at him as if he really was Santa come to fulfill her heart's every desire.

And those shoes.

He didn't know how she walked in the spindly red heels, how any woman walked in heels, but he appreciated how they pumped out Abby's calves, accented the toned lines of her legs. How they made his gaze want to keep traveling up those long lines, to unveil where they met, where he wanted to be. Oh, Abby.

Since his wife's death, he hadn't been a saint. He'd tried to ease the ache inside of him, only to realize he wasn't dating material any more.

But he'd never been as attracted to anyone as he was to Abby.

He knew better than to get involved, knew there could never be a relationship between them. Not one that would go anywhere. He'd suck the goodness right out of her life, weigh her down with his heavy heart. She was right to question him. Given the chance, he would break her heart.

Yet, he'd slept with her, figuratively and literally, after the first night they'd worked together. Sure, he'd backed off after that morning, but only because of how she'd looked at him with hope of a happy-ever-after. That look had had sweat prickling his skin and his heart fluttering in a panicked rhythm. Otherwise he'd have been burning up her sheets for the past two months.

He'd gotten out of her house stat and promised himself he'd keep his distance. So why had he agreed to be her Santa? Why had he asked her to come to this party with him? Sure, the administrator had questioned why he hadn't been going, but the guy would have gotten over it if he hadn't attended.

"Dirk?" Abby prompted when he failed to respond to her gutsy invitation to take her home.

He stared down into her blue-green eyes with their golden flecks, his hands around her waist, holding her to him while Christmas music played around them.

She was sweet and wonderful and giving. The more time he spent with her, the more he craved, the more he knew he should stay away. She believed in goodness and in the magic of Christmas. She gave of herself without asking for anything in return. Hadn't he just told her he didn't do relationships? Yet here she was, willing to give what he wanted. The truth was, he didn't want to go home alone, didn't want to face the demons of being at this party, just being alive during the holiday season, dredged up from his past, not when being with Abby made him feel better, less alone. She made him forget everything but her.

Just as on the morning they'd fallen into bed together, words weren't needed.

He was going to take all she'd give, knowing he had nothing to give in return and never would.

Bah, humbug. He really was a Scrooge.

CHAPTER FIVE

STANDING on her front porch, Abby fumbled twice before inserting the key into her door lock. Her hands shook like crazy.

She was crazy.

Hadn't Dirk told her he didn't do relationships? So why had they rushed from the Christmas party like teenagers? She laughed nervously. God, she felt like a teen on her way to a heated make-out session.

"Let me," he interrupted when, although she'd gotten the key into the lock, the release hadn't caught properly.

The lock clicked and Abby pushed the door open, practically falling into her foyer and dragging Dirk with her. He pushed the door closed with a resounding snap. The sound echoed through the darkness broken only by her Christmas lights, which cast a magical aura over the foyer and living room thanks to the timers she kept them on.

"Come here," he growled, pulling her to him, taking her mouth by storm as he worked off her wrap, letting the heavy faux fur fall to the floor.

Yes, Abby thought, this was exactly how she remembered Dirk kissing her. As if she tasted sweeter than

Christmas cookies and he was eager to go on a sugar binge.

He tasted just as sweet. Sweeter. His lips were marauding her mouth, his tongue tangling with hers as his hands slid over her body, touching, caressing, *claiming*.

Abby set about staking some claims of her own. Meeting him kiss for kiss, tangle for tangle. Tactically committing the hard lines of his body to memory, committing everything about him to memory.

"I want you so much."

She'd noticed. Oh, how she'd noticed!

"I want to savor every touch, every sigh that escapes from your lips." He nibbled at her throat, at the base of her neck. Hot kisses that scorched her skin, bringing her blood to a boil.

His fingers searched out her zipper, slowly parted the back of her dress as his tongue traced over her carotid pulse, licking at the raging beat on her throat.

When his hand rested on her lower back where the zip ended, he turned his attention to the thin red straps holding up her dress.

Eyes locked with hers in the flickering colors of the Christmas lights, he looped one finger beneath the thin satin and slid the string off her shoulder, letting it dangle against her deltoid. He kissed where the strap had been. A soft, gentle, stomach-knotting kiss that shot an arrow of pleasure straight to the apex of her being. He turned to the other side and repeated the seductive gesture, his lips lingering on her bare shoulder.

"You are so beautiful, Abby. So sweet and perfect."

"I'm not perfect." Surely he knew she wasn't without her having to tell him. Surely he was just spouting lines.

Although why he would when he already had her, she couldn't fathom. And, oh, how he had her!

He trailed more kisses over her shoulders, light, reverent. "You're the closest thing this side of heaven."

Dear Saint Nicholas alive! Did he have any idea what his praise was doing? What his kisses were doing?

Apparently, because he shimmied her dress over her hips to puddle in the floor around her feet.

She stood in her foyer, dressed only in the new red underwear she'd bought to match her dress and her high heels. If not for the blaze in Dirk's eyes, she might be cold, might be embarrassed. She was neither.

His gaze burned with desire. Deep, hot desire that told her everything. More. Desire that made her warm from the inside out. Hot.

She took his hand in hers. His eyebrow rose in question when she led him into the living room, rather than toward her bedroom. But she didn't explain herself, sensing that words would ruin the magical atmosphere. Instead, she took the throw blanket off the back of her sofa and tossed it into the floor in front of her fireplace, turned the knob that lit her gas logs, and met his gaze.

Swallowing audibly, he nodded, lay down with her on the blanket, pushing her back and staring down at her in the firelight. Wordlessly, his lips brushed her temples, her cheeks, her eyes, her throat. Slowly, his mouth worked over her skin.

She shifted, grasping at the buttons of his shirt, fumbling to undo them. She ran her hands inside the parted material of his crisp white shirt, loving the feel of his smooth chest against her fingertips, loving the rapid pounding of his heart beneath her palm.

She'd done that to him, made his heart beat wildly.

Like a snowman caught in a hothouse, Abby melted.

Dirk groaned, and gave up whatever hope he had of going slowly. He'd wanted to kiss every inch of her, to take things slowly, to do things right, instead of the desperate coupling they'd had last time. *Twice.* But where Abby was concerned he obviously could only go one speed. Head-on.

He shucked out of his shirt, groaned again at the feel of her hands rubbing over skin, over his shoulders, down his back. The pleasure Abby found in his body thrilled him, had him aching for more. She craned her neck to kiss his throat, his shoulders, his chest. Frantic, quick kisses that seared his flesh.

"So beautiful," he repeated, breathing in the spicy scent of her skin.

"If anyone in this room is beautiful, it's you," she whispered, pressing a kiss to his clavicle and reaching for his belt at the same time. "Hurry, Dirk."

If he hurried, everything would be over. Fast. She was driving him crazy. Each and every cell in his body had caught fire and burned with need.

Letting her pull his belt free, Dirk slid over her, pinning her beneath him, loving how she wrapped her arms around him, clinging to him.

"Hurry," she urged. "I need you."

Dirk kissed her until he thought he might explode, until their hands locked on to each other's rather than continue the frenzied exploration of each other's bodies.

"I need you, too, Abby." More than he'd ever imagined

possible. Rolling slightly to his side, he reached for his waistband, planning to strip off his pants.

That's when he heard the sound of cold reality.

His cellphone.

"Don't answer it," she moaned, taking over where he'd stopped undoing his zipper. Her fingers brushed against him, and he inhaled sharply.

He wanted to ignore the phone, but he wouldn't.

"I'm on call." How he wished he wasn't. "No one would call me this late unless there was an emergency."

Abby's face paled in the glow of the firelight. "Oh, God. I forgot."

He understood all too well. She made him forget, too.

Going into the foyer, he grabbed his jacket from the floor and removed his phone from the inside pocket. He listened to the caller for about thirty seconds then raked his fingers through his hair. "No problem. I'll be right there."

He hung up the phone and met Abby's soft, concerned gaze. She'd followed him into the foyer, stood next to him, her arms crossed protectively over her gorgeous body.

"It's okay. I understand," she said before he spoke. "My phone will likely ring at any moment."

"Probably." He went back to the living room, got his shirt, buttoned it with a lot less enthusiasm than he'd removed it, although with just as much haste. "There's been a gas leak in an apartment high-rise. One death. Dozens suffering inhalation injuries and respiratory distress. Patients are being diverted to several hospitals."

Stooping down and providing him with a delectable

view of her backside that tempted him to say to hell with everything, Abby plucked up the blanket from the floor. She wrapped it round her shoulders, as if she didn't want him to see her almost naked body now that they'd been interrupted. "I'll get changed."

He started to speak, to tell her to get some rest while she could, that perhaps they'd already called in enough nurses without her. But her phone started ringing from inside her purse.

She gave a shaky laugh. "Wonder who that is?"

While she took the call, Dirk finished dressing, got his coat. A gentleman would wait until she finished her call, but he didn't. He left.

She already knew he wasn't a gentleman. Hell, he'd slept with her the day they met and had been about to take advantage of her yet again.

Still wanted to take advantage so badly every cell in his body protested against the interruption.

She'd be wise to stay far, far away.

Perhaps that's why they'd been interrupted.

To give them both time to think about what they were doing. For Dirk to recall that Abby deserved better than what he'd give. For Abby to recall that she was young and beautiful and not bitter at the world, that she saw the goodness in life, the positive.

Things Dirk had quit doing long ago even if Abby had made him forget that for a short while.

Abby had put in eight hours of nonstop running from one patient to the next. Every bay had been full, with a rapid rate of turnover as patients were triaged into admission or treated and released.

The day shift would be arriving soon. Thank goodness.

Her lower back ached and she felt more tired than she recalled feeling in a long, long time.

Surprised to find there wasn't another patient waiting, she took advantage of the unexpected reprieve. Just a couple of minutes to disappear into the break room, lean against the wall and close her eyes, then she'd recheck the pneumonia patient in bay five.

"Things are starting to slow down. You should go home and get some rest. You look tired."

"Dirk." Abby's eyes shot open, surprised to see that he'd followed her. Not that she'd really expected otherwise, but he'd been the consummate professional all night. Not once had he let on that there was anything between them other than a doctor-nurse relationship, not once had he let on that had they not been interrupted they'd have made love most of the night.

Not once had he mentioned that when she'd come out of her bedroom, he'd left, breaking her heart into a thousand tiny shards that he'd left her without so much as a word.

"The others can handle the remainder of the shift." His tone was brusque, paternalistic. "Go home and get some rest, Abby. You look tired."

"I am tired, but I'll be fine until the end of shift." She would. Already, just looking at him, she could feel her energy level rising. Or maybe that was her hurt and anger coming to a head. "Are you coming back to my place?"

He sighed, raked his fingers through his dark hair, and glanced around the otherwise empty break room. "We need to talk."

Trying to read his expression, Abby searched his face. "I understand if you're too tired. It's just, well, I wanted you to know that if you want to come back, that's good by me. I could cook us something."

At least, she could cook him something. The thought of food made her stomach recoil. Or maybe it was the thought that he'd left her and she knew she wasn't going to like what he had to say.

His jaw worked back and forth. "I've been thinking about last night."

"Me, too," she admitted unsteadily. She couldn't quit thinking about last night, how they'd touched.

He grimaced. "Not like that, Abby. I've been thinking about what you said at the party about me needing to be sure before we went any further."

A feeling of impending doom crawled up her spine. Doom that made her stomach pitch so high it could have capsized a tanker.

"And?" she asked, not really wanting to hear his answer. Why was he backpedaling? She'd thought they'd come so far last night. Had everything only been physical? Was she really so naive as to have misread his looks, his touches so drastically?

"You were right to say that." He didn't meet her eyes, stared somewhere to her right at the wall. "If we continue on that path, I will hurt you and that's not what I want. I think we should just be friends."

"You're kidding, right?" She could tell by the look on his taut face that he wasn't. *Friends?* "If your phone hadn't rung, what we'd have been doing was a lot more than what just friends do," she pointed out, not willing to let him backtrack so easily.

"Which means we shouldn't have been doing what we were about to do. Fate stepped in."

Chin lifting, Abby's hands went to her hips. How

could he be so dense? "Fate had nothing to do with that gas leak."

"But fate did rescue you from making a mistake, Abby. I have nothing to offer you beyond friendship. Nothing."

Did he really believe that? Looking at him, she realized he did, but not because he didn't want to offer her more, just that he didn't believe himself capable. What had happened to make him so cynical? To make him see the glass as half-empty? How could she look at him and see so plainly that he had so much more to give? So much more life in him than he saw in himself?

Why was it that when she looked at him she saw a world full of good and amazing things? A world full of Christmas every single day just because he was a part of her life?

She closed her eyes and counted to ten. "Okay, if you want to just be friends, we'll just be friends."

She couldn't make him love her. Couldn't make him want to take a chance on loving her. She'd spent years living with her great-aunt, doing everything she could to earn the woman's love. In the end, she'd realized you can't make someone love you. Either they did or they didn't.

"I'm glad you understand." He let out a slow breath, looked relieved that she wasn't going to make a scene.

Had he expected her to stomp her feet and throw a fit? Wrong. But neither would she pretend everything was fine, when it wasn't.

"No." She shook her head. "I can't say that I understand, because I don't. Obviously I misread your feelings for me."

"Abs—"

"Don't," she interrupted, holding up her hand. "Don't say things you don't mean in the hope of making this easier. I like you, a lot. You obviously don't feel the same so, fine, end of story. We'll be friends."

So why didn't she believe he didn't feel the same? Why did she believe that something else had prompted him to back away? Something that ran so deeply through him he believed he had nothing to offer her but heartache? Something that had to do with his dislike of the holidays?

"You deserve better."

She nodded. "You're right. I do."

This time she was the one who left.

By the time she got home, she was throwing up. No doubt from the stress of the night and the sickening feeling that had crept in during their conversation.

Friends. He wanted to be friends. *Liar.* Who did he think he was kidding? He didn't look at her the way her *friends* looked at her.

Neither did she have sex with *friends.*

Or even almost have sex with her friends.

Really, she'd just like to know how it was possible for a man to look at her with fire in his eyes and ice on his tongue? Because his words had bit into her bitterly coldly. Frigidly. *Friends.*

Fine, if that's what he wanted, she'd be his friend.

She told herself all these things and more right up until that night, when she was scheduled to work with him.

Then she admitted the truth.

She couldn't be Dirk's friend. Not when she felt the way she did about him. If she didn't protect her heart, she'd end up wearing battle scars from their *friendship*. Scars that ran so deep she wouldn't ever recover.

No, she couldn't be his friend, but somehow she had to be his colleague, his nurse. She had to work with him and be the professional she was. Somehow.

Almost, she called in sick, but her illness had passed, had just been from a morning spent longing for what might have been. So she'd go to work and come face-to-face with a man who seemed determined to be *friendly*.

Seriously, it was enough to send her stomach into Churnville all over again.

CHAPTER SIX

DIRK hadn't slept much between ending his emergency call the morning following the Christmas party and reporting back in for a half-shift that evening. How could he when he couldn't stop thinking about Abby?

She'd agreed to his friend proposal, but he'd seen the hurt in her eyes. The confusion. She didn't understand.

Why had he let things get so out of control the evening before? Not that Abby had given him much choice. He'd looked into her eyes, heard the truth in her voice when she'd told him she wanted to make love, and he'd ignored all the reasons why they shouldn't.

Just as he'd ignored the reasons why he shouldn't have asked her to the Christmas party to begin with. Not that he'd meant to. The invitation had just slipped out of his mouth and she'd looked so happy when she'd said yes, he hadn't taken the words back.

Just as he hadn't taken them back when he'd agreed to be her Santa.

Seeing Abby happy did something to him, made him do things he ordinarily wouldn't do. Made him want things he shouldn't want.

When he had slept, he'd been haunted by treacherous

nightmares. Had they been triggered by attending the Christmas party? Or just by the season he could never escape? Or from walking away from Abby when she was the best thing to enter his life in years?

Regardless, he'd welcomed the evening and the start of his abbreviated—due to the holiday party—shift. Right or wrong, he'd also welcomed seeing Abby again, welcomed everything about her, including the tray of goodies she'd left on the break-room table.

Mostly he just wanted to make sure she was okay. During the night, as they'd worked on patients, he'd felt her gaze on him, felt her studying him, trying to see beneath his surface. If she only knew what darkness lay beneath, in the depths of his soul, she'd have turned away, never wanting to look again.

If he wasn't careful, he was going to hurt Abby.

That and that alone should accomplish what he hadn't previously had the willpower to do.

He would ignore the attraction between them before he hurt her. Otherwise he'd end up taking every drop of sweetness from her and leaving her with nothing more than a barren tree with a few empty hangers where shiny ornaments had once glistened.

Abby deserved fullness of life, color and brightness, glittery packages, and tinsel, and twinkling lights. All the things he wasn't.

Having finished with the patient he had been tending, he stepped into the next bay, pausing in mid-step. Abby was cleaning the room, preparing for the next patient. She had to know he stood there, but she didn't look up to acknowledge him.

He turned to go, but the fact she ignored him irked. She'd been polite all evening, courteous when discussing a patient. But other than regarding a patient, she hadn't spoken a word to him.

He didn't like it. They were friends, right?

"I saw you'd brought more goodies." He'd snagged a couple from the rapidly disappearing tray. "Those haystack things were great."

She nodded, not looking up from where she spread out a clean sheet. "I always bring lots of goodies this time of year. It's tradition."

She kept her tone even, but she was upset. She'd invited him to stay the day with her and he'd left her high and dry, told her he just wanted to be friends.

Idiot.

Dirk grabbed the corner of the sheet closest to where he stood and spread the material out, eliciting a surprised look from her. "You have a lot of Christmas traditions, don't you, Abby?"

"Yes." Taking a deep breath, she tucked the clean sheet in around the hospital bed. "Christmas traditions are important to me." She straightened, held his gaze then sighed. "Before you give me a lecture on all the woes of the holidays, let me just warn you that I'm a little cranky so you might not want to do that. Not tonight."

Dirk took a step back. Abby was cranky? Because of him. Because he'd refused to go with her. Because he'd said he just wanted to be friends.

"I'm sorry, Abby."

She snorted, rolling her eyes. "It's not that."

"Then what? Is Macy's all sold out of that gift you just have to buy still?" He tried to keep his tone light, to make a joke in the hope some of the usual sparkle would return to her eyes, but when he spoke of anything to do with Christmas a brittle edge always seemed to be present.

"Ha-ha. Too funny." Rather than sparkle, she rolled her eyes again. "For the record, I finished my shopping weeks ago."

She was probably one of those women who started next year's shopping the day after Christmas. That seemed like the kind of thing Abby would do.

"If you must know," she continued, smoothing out an imaginary wrinkle on the expertly made bed, "I haven't felt well."

Her hand popped over her mouth as if she hadn't meant to say that out loud, as if she regretted that she had.

"What's wrong?" All desire to keep the conversation light vanishing, Dirk studied her. She didn't look ill. She looked…beautiful, almost ethereal, like the delicate angel on top of a Christmas tree.

"Don't look at me like that. I shouldn't have said anything," she huffed, but when he only stared, waiting for her to elaborate, she continued. "I'm fine. Really. Just a virus."

But she didn't meet his eyes and he placed his hand on her forehead.

"I don't have a temperature." She gave an exasperated sigh.

"Tell me what's going on. I'm a doctor, remember?" Again, he strove to keep his tone light, but her evasiveness worried him. The thought of her being sick worried him. "Maybe I can help."

He wanted to help. As a doctor to a patient, he told himself, even as he acknowledged his concern went beyond that of doctor-patient. As a friend to another friend, he corrected, but even that didn't cover the protective feelings the idea of Abby being ill spurred within him.

"Fine. I'll tell you, but just remember you asked for this." She picked at the pristine bedding, rubbing her fingernail over the white material. "I've been feeling tired. A little nauseated at times to where my appetite just isn't what it should be. I threw up this morning, but that's because I crie—" She paused again, flushing.

She must have spent as restless a day in bed as he had. Guilt hit him. He didn't want Abby to suffer because of him. He'd wanted to keep from hurting her, but he'd waited too late.

"You should have taken sick leave tonight."

"Why? Nursing staff are almost always shorthanded as is." She frowned. "Besides, it's nothing much, really. I don't feel myself, but that's my own fault, isn't it?" Glancing up at him, her weak smile almost knocked him to his knees. "I do realize that I shouldn't have read so much into you asking me to the Christmas party, Dirk."

"I'm sorry I gave you the impression we could be more than friends." He wanted more than friendship. He wanted to be her lover. Without strings. Without having to worry about hurting her.

She lifted a shoulder in a mock shrug. "I should have known better."

"Why should you have known better, Abby? I was sending mixed signals." Saying one thing, wanting another. Why was he admitting this to her? Wasn't he only sending more mixed signals by doing so?

"Were you?" Her brow lifted. "I hadn't noticed."

The way she said it, so sarcastic, bugged Dirk. Abby

was happy, bubbly even. Not today. Nothing about this conversation felt right. Sure, he'd expected tonight to be awkward, but they'd done awkward before. Had done awkward for two months with only a break when he'd agreed to be Santa. This went beyond that.

Something was wrong with Abby.

He thought of the long hours she worked, of all the volunteer work he knew she did. No doubt she was spending the time she should be sleeping baking Christmas candies.

"You're not getting enough rest."

She pushed an empty IV stand against the wall, out of the way. "I slept eight hours each of the past couple of days. I'm getting plenty of rest, Dr. Kelley."

His name came out with emphasis, coated with annoyance.

He followed her around the room. "Obviously your body needs more rest."

"Obviously," she agreed wryly, picking up a stray alcohol pad package from the counter. "But it's choosing the wrong time of year to tucker out on me. I've got too much to do to get sick right now."

"Like what? More spreading Christmas cheer stuff?"

Her eyes narrowed into an outright glare. "I like spreading Christmas cheer. If anything, volunteering makes me feel better about life. Not worse. Maybe you should try it sometime instead of all that bah-humbug stuff."

"Maybe when you're healthy, but at end of shift, you need to go home and get some sleep. Doctor's orders."

"This morning, after my shift ends, I'm picking up boxes of food to deliver to the poor." Her expression dared him to say anything. "After I finish that, I'm de-livering fruit baskets to a nearby nursing home."

Boxes of food. Fruit baskets. Hadn't she mentioned something earlier in the week about volunteering in a soup kitchen, too? Plus, she'd been doing all this baking.

"Aren't you on schedule to work again tonight?" He knew she was. He knew each and every night they'd be working together. And the ones they wouldn't.

"I'm due here at seven. For the record, you're not my doctor and I didn't ask for your advice, neither do I want it."

He crossed his arms, pinning her beneath his gaze. "So when are you planning to sleep?"

"After I get the fruit baskets delivered." She winced, confirming what he already suspected. She hadn't left much time for sleep. "Normally, I can do this and more without so much as blinking my eyes. Getting called in to work on the night of the Christmas party threw off my rhythm a little, that's all."

She didn't comment that he'd played a role in her rhythm being thrown off. She didn't have to. She had to be on the verge of exhaustion and whether she wanted his advice or not, she was going to get it.

"No wonder you're coming down with something," he scolded. "Didn't they teach you anything about taking care of yourself while you were in nursing school? Sleep is important."

Said he who had slept very little over the past few weeks. How could he when every time he closed his eyes his dreams took him back to the morning he'd made love to Abby? A morning where he'd felt guilty for taking advantage of her goodness. After that, he'd done all he could to avoid her, to keep things completely professional between them. Abby hadn't pushed, hadn't asked anything of him. Not until she'd asked him to play Santa.

He should have said no.

None of this would be happening if he'd just said no.

"I do this every year," she insisted, sounding more and more annoyed. "I just have a light virus or something. It's no big deal and really none of your business."

Dirk gritted his teeth, took a steadying breath, and managed to keep from pulling her into his arms to shake some sense into her.

"Yeah, well, you might try to kill yourself every year, but I've never been here to watch you run yourself ragged in the past," he reminded her, moving in front of her, placing his fingers on her chin and lifting her face so she had to look at him. "I'm going with you."

Her forehead wrinkled as her brows lifted high on her heart-shaped face. "Do what?" she scoffed, her hands going to her hips.

Yeah, that's pretty much what Dirk was wondering, too. *Do what?* But the thought of her pushing herself all day after working such long shifts back to back bothered him. Especially knowing she planned to come in and work another long shift despite the fact that she wouldn't be able to squeeze in more than a few hours' sleep at most.

None of his business? That bothered him, too. Right or wrong, he cared about Abby, didn't want her pushing herself so much. Friends could care about friends, could want to help each other.

"I'm going with you," he repeated, his tone brooking

no argument. "You'll finish quicker and be able to get some of the rest you obviously need."

She regarded him a long moment, then her lips twisted into a rather sinister smile. "You're welcome to go with me, Dirk. Not because of me, but because you need a lesson in what Christmas is really about. Helping the needy is a great way to learn that lesson."

He didn't need to learn any such lesson.

"That's not why I'm going." He was going because she needed him, whether she was too stubborn to admit it or not. If easing Abby's self-imposed load counted as helping the needy, so be it.

"No, but it's definitely what you're going to learn. Come on, Scrooge. Let's finish our shifts so we can go make a difference in the world."

Abby snuck a glance at where Dirk helped pack more canned food and basic household supplies into a box that would later be given to a needy person.

She hadn't wanted him to come with her, didn't want him being nice to her, didn't want to be near him, period. How was she supposed to protect her heart when he insisted on helping her?

As much as she hated to admit it, he was right. She had overstretched herself, and appreciated his help so that she'd finish earlier. But there was so much to be done at this time of year. So much important work. Besides, sitting at home gave her too much time to contemplate that when she went home only Mistletoe cared. That she had no family to come home to, no family to share Christmas dinners, no family to sit around the tree with and open packages.

No one.

Her gaze lifted from the box she was packing, landing on the man across the table.

Why did looking at him bring how alone she was into focus so clearly? Why did looking at him make her see what she'd been able to hide from herself in the past? That, although she loved volunteering, she didn't do so selflessly. No, she also volunteered because doing so prevented her from thinking about how she'd spend another Christmas alone.

"You okay?"

Abby blinked at Dirk. Although he'd been terse when they'd first arrived, he had quickly impressed the other volunteers.

Volunteers who kept sending Abby sneaky smiles and suggestive eyebrow wiggles. After her first few attempts at convincing her longtime friends that she and Dirk were only coworkers, friends, she'd given up. After all, she didn't buy the friends bit any more than they did. Besides, the more she'd protested, the bigger their smiles had grown.

"Abs? You okay?" he repeated.

She glanced at where Dirk had finished with his box and had lifted another to fill. A wave of dizziness hit her and she grasped hold of the table. What was wrong with her? To get sick right now would be so unfair.

"I'm fine," she lied, hoping she was imagining the sweat beads popping out on her forehead.

Maybe she should have said no for once, asked the ladies to get someone else. Anything so she didn't get ill in front of Dirk.

What was she thinking? Of course she couldn't have done that. Not when it would mean that someone's Christmas wouldn't be as special, as magical.

When it would mean going home and being alone.

She was fine. Or would be if Dirk would get back to packing and quit staring at her. It wasn't as if he knew she was struggling to keep up. She would not let him know just how much effort she was putting into this.

"Maybe you should rest for a few minutes," he suggested, boxing up more canned goods. "I'll finish this."

Or maybe she didn't have to tell him how much effort she was putting in. Maybe he already knew. Somehow. Probably that crazy connection they shared. The one he insisted on calling friendship.

She sighed.

"Or better yet…" He stopped what he was doing to pin her beneath his azure gaze. "Let me take you home where you can get proper sleep before you drop."

The two volunteers elbowed each other. Abby bit back another sigh, this one from fatigue, and straightened her shoulders. "There's no reason I can't finish, Dirk."

How dared he tell her what to do? Try to tell her what she needed? The only reason she'd agreed to let him come with her was because he needed a lesson in helping others, on what Christmas really meant. She should have said no. Him being here obviously stressed her.

"No reason except you need to rest."

She ignored his comment. Drawing on all her inner strength to hide just how woozy she felt, she smiled at the ladies watching them curiously. "Once we get these packed, we'll divvy them up and take the ones on my list to deliver. Dr. Kelley can go home and rest."

Eyeing her like a kid studied a sole, tiny package labeled for him under the Christmas tree, Dirk frowned.

A tightly controlled muscle jumped at the corner of his mouth. "This is too much after working all night. Call and cancel the fruit basket delivery."

Tempting, but then who would deliver the baskets? Besides, she was pretty sure it was the stress of being near him making her feel so bad. That and the virus. If he'd just quit looking at her...

"No." She couldn't cancel her activities. Sure, she'd been a little out of sorts. That wasn't any reason to let down those depending on her. They needed her help to make their Christmas all it should be, all hers wouldn't be.

"Abby, if you're not feeling well, Joyce and I can finish this up," Judy, the lady in charge, offered, placing her hand on Abby's shoulder.

Dirk smiled smugly, obviously viewing the woman's offer as reinforcement that he was right, that she should do as he wanted. Enough was enough.

"Seriously." She made eye contact with the elderly lady she'd bonded with while still in nursing school on her first volunteer project. "I'm fine. I just made the mistake of mentioning to Dr. Overprotective—" she flicked her thumb toward Dirk, hoping how much he meant to her didn't show "—that I'd been feeling under the weather."

"Nothing serious, I hope," Judy said sympathetically, completely ignoring that Abby had said she was fine.

"Of course not. I've just had a little nausea and fatigue for a few days. No big deal." At the woman's look of concern, Abby added, "Nothing contagious."

At least, she didn't think so. If so, surely some of her coworkers would be having symptoms by now since she'd been fighting this for more than a week. For that matter, Dirk would be having symptoms. He'd definitely had up-close exposure the night of the Christmas party.

"I'm definitely not contagious," she repeated, hoping to reassure her friends.

Her face brightening, Joyce clapped her hands together gleefully. "Ooh, when you walked in today, I just knew there was something different about you. Beside the fact you brought this gorgeous man with you." The older woman sent a knowing smile Dirk's way then returned her attention to Abby. "Just look at how you're glowing."

"Glowing?" Abby's mouth dropped just as Dirk's can crashed to the concrete floor as the woman's meaning sank in. The sharp intake of his breath almost drowned out the loud clang. Abby was surprised the thunderous beat of her heart didn't deafen them all. "If you're implying... I think you're making a wrong assumption."

The two smiling volunteers looked at each other, then back at Abby and Dirk, their smiles fading as realization dawned. "You're not pregnant?"

"Uh, no." Abby coughed into her hand, trying to make sure she worded this correctly so she didn't end up as before, protesting to the point that she was only convincing her friends of the opposite. "Of course I'm not pregnant. I can't be."

Dirk had used a condom. Although she'd been wrapped up in what they'd been doing, she was sure he had used protection. She'd found two opened foil pouches.

She faked another cough, whether to show her symptoms were from something else entirely or just to buy a few more seconds to think of what to say she wasn't sure.

"You ladies are as bad as Dirk about overreacting." She laughed as if their suggestion was preposterous. It was preposterous. Pregnant. Her. No way. "I've just been pushing myself a little too hard with the holidays and have picked up a minor bug of some sort at work. You know how I'm exposed to everything in the emergency room. It's a wonder Dirk isn't sick, too."

But even as she gave the excuse she counted back the days since her last menstrual period and came up with a too-high number. Way too high a number. Oh. My.

This time she inhaled sharply, would have dropped a can if she'd been holding one. Her fingers curled into her palms, her nails digging painfully into the soft flesh.

Could she be? Was it possible? She'd never considered the possibility, hadn't dared to consider her lovemaking with Dirk might leave her pregnant. They were consenting adults who'd used a condom. Not overzealous teenagers who'd had unprepared-for sex.

She wasn't pregnant. Or was she?

She wanted kids. Someday, she wanted kids a lot. But not while unmarried and by a man who said he wanted to just be her friend. She wanted the dream. Snuggling in front of the fireplace together, sipping hot cocoa, enjoying each other's company. She'd take his hand and place it over her much, much thinner belly from where she'd finally stuck to that exercise routine and, with hope in his eyes, he'd ask if she was. She'd nod. They'd fall into each other's arms and be so happy together. A family. No more lonely Christmases. No more lonely ever.

But never had she imagined being pregnant, unwed and finding out while volunteering at a food bank with the prospective father having told her just the day before that they were only friends. By the look on Dirk's face, this obviously wasn't how he'd envisioned the moment, either.

Powerless to stop her hand, her palm settled over her abdomen. Was Dirk's baby growing inside her? Would she give birth to a little boy or girl with eyes so blue they left the sky envious? With hair so inky black the night paled in comparison?

If so, what in the world would she do about an un-planned pregnancy by a man who she technically barely knew, but felt as if she knew better than anyone she'd ever met? A man who said he only wanted to be friends and professed not to even like Christmas?

CHAPTER SEVEN

DIRK'S ears roared with the intensity of a jet taking off inside his head. Any moment he expected the backdraft to knock him off his feet and send him crashing against the wall.

Mentally, he was already thrashing about the room. Emotionally, he'd already crashed and gone up in flames.

Abby's big hazel eyes had widened with shock, had darkened with unwanted possibilities, with fear, then softened as her hand pressed her lower abdomen.

Hell, no. She couldn't be. He'd used a condom both times they'd made love. He always used a condom. Always.

But, hell, how old had the condoms in his wallet been? Although he hadn't lived the life of a monk over the past four years, he hadn't exactly had a high prophylactic turnover rate, either. He'd never considered checking the condoms' expiration date. They'd been, what? About a year old, maybe? God, it was possible they'd expired.

He should have checked. He should have known better. He was a doctor, trained not to make the mistakes a seventeen-year-old boy would make.

Abby might be pregnant, and it was his fault.

He didn't want her to be pregnant.

The two women who'd hovered over them both like mother hens were obviously drawing the same conclusions.

Despite her protest, Abby might be having a baby. His baby. The slightly stunned expression on her pretty little face said so.

Another woman, another pregnancy, swept through his memories. Sandra excitedly telling her news. Lord, he'd been scared. After all, he'd still had a few years of residency left. But he'd looked into her eyes and he'd hidden his fear, had swept her into his arms and spun her around. A baby. Shelby. And now, would there be another baby?

Sharp pain zigzagged across his chest at the thought.

Both volunteers turned to him, expectation and protectiveness of Abby in their eyes. He couldn't blame them. He felt like beating the crap out of him, too, for doing this. He deserved worse if he'd made her pregnant.

Judy crossed her arms over her chest, her head bent slightly to one side, as if to say, *Well?*

Uh-huh. He wasn't going to have that conversation with two strangers watching, listening to every word.

Abby wasn't pregnant. And if she was… Hell, he didn't know what they'd do if she was.

Regardless, that was a private conversation. Not one for women he'd just met, even if they were longtime friends of Abby's and treated her like a favorite niece.

Following Abby's lead, Dirk drew on acting skills he'd honed in the days following Sandra and Shelby's deaths, days in which he'd been dead inside but had had to go on, puting on a front for the world. Had put on a show for his friends and family who'd not been able to look at him without pity in their eyes. Pity he'd tired of and left behind. In late spring he'd started searching for another position, knowing he couldn't face another holiday season under their watchful gazes. In June he'd accepted the position in Philadelphia, finished up his Oak Park contract, and had started in the emergency room in October.

And met Abby. Possibly impregnated her.

"This is the last of the boxes, Abby. You ready to pack them into my truck so we can go?" God, he hoped so, because he wanted away from the prying eyes. "We've still got to go pick up those fruit baskets and get them delivered. Unless I can convince you to cancel out so you can rest and properly get over this *virus*."

Did his voice sound normal? Or could everyone in the room hear his panic? See how his insides quavered at the thought he might have made Abby pregnant?

"I, uh…" Her hand fell away from her belly. She turned to him, her expression so tentative and vulnerable that something fragile deep in his chest cracked open and bled freely, gushing, leaving him weak. "Yes, I'm ready. Let's get these loaded."

Stunned by the rush of emotions, Dirk just stood, unable to move, unable to put on a show, only able to watch Abby smile briefly at the other volunteers and walk over to a far corner of the room. She had a dolly in her competent little hands within minutes.

"It's not much," she said, rolling the dolly toward him. "But it will do at a pinch."

He would have welcomed any excuse to get away

from the mother hens' knowing looks. He hightailed it, boxes in tow, moving at record speed, leaving the three women alone.

Even before he'd made it out the door Judy's excited squeal echoed throughout the building, across the city, across his stampeding heart.

"Tell me the truth. You're pregnant, aren't you?"

He turned, waiting at the doorway to hear Abby's answer. The two women had practically pounced on her, were holding her hands and excitedly asking her questions.

As if sensing he still stood there, she glanced toward the doorway, met his gaze. Deep emotions shot across the room, deep pleas. Pleas for exactly what Dirk wasn't sure, neither was he sure he wanted to know.

Abby needed him. How could he be there for her when there wasn't anything left of him to give?

"Tell us." Judy wrapped her arm around Abby's shoulder in a motherly hug. "Are you pregnant or not?"

"Regardless, we love you and are here for you," Joyce added. "You know that."

Did they even know he still stood here? He held his breath, waiting, wondering, knowing it was impossible, knowing it was damned well possible. He'd made love to Abby quite vigorously. Twice.

"Don't be silly and start rumors," she said with a falsely bright voice, looking from one of the ladies to the other, then at him. Their gazes met, clung to each other.

Don't say it, Abby. Don't say that there is any possibility you might be pregnant.

"Of course I'm not pregnant."

Which should have relieved him, but her eyes told a different story.

All eight of Santa's reindeer drop-kicked Dirk in the gut at once, knocking his breath out of him and stomping him to smithereens while he was down.

Abby might be pregnant with his baby.

What had he done?

"This is crazy," Abby protested when Dirk pulled his truck into a parking space at the pharmacy.

After his terse "We'll talk when we've finished delivering" they'd continued in virtual silence. They'd delivered to the public housing residents on her list. They'd smiled and said all the appropriate things to the grateful recipients, but there had definitely been underlying tension.

Abby didn't feel tense. Not really.

She felt numb. Perhaps in denial. Yes, she'd missed her period. Two of them. But she'd been irregular on occasion in the past, so that was the likely explanation. Certainly, she hadn't thought anything of her missed periods. They'd always come and gone as they pleased.

Plus, there were the increased demands on her time with her Christmas volunteering. Although she loved what she did, believed one hundred percent in making the holidays brighter for others, the workload was stressful.

Stress. Stress did a lot of things to the body and could be the reason for the missed periods. She hoped it was. Really hoped it was.

Which was why she didn't want to walk into the drugstore and buy the item she knew he'd come for, although, from the moment he'd turned off the ignition, they'd just sat in silence.

What if she was pregnant? What if the test came back positive? Then what? Hadn't he already told her he didn't do relationships? Yet he'd gone with her today. God, the man confused her. She really couldn't be pregnant.

"I'm probably not." She battled the tightening of her throat that she might be. "You used condoms."

She was twenty-five years old. Why was her face on fire at saying the word "condom" out loud? Here they were discussing the possibility of having a baby and she was blushing over contraceptives?

Gripping the steering wheel, he stared out the windshield at some unknown object. "Women get pregnant all the time despite having used a condom."

God, he sounded so terse, so like he hoped she wasn't pregnant. Despite understanding and feeling exactly the same way, his reaction stung. No doubt having her pregnant with his child would be a nightmare to Dirk. After all, he'd only slept with her because they'd been grieving. Although, admittedly, the intensity of his grief had caught her off guard. But there had been sexual attraction between them, too. Lots of sexual attraction. She hadn't imagined the sparks, the way his gaze had lingered when they'd first made eye contact, the way he'd seemed shocked by the physical awareness zipping back and forth. But women used for sex weren't supposed to end up pregnant.

Oh, God. Dirk had used her. Two months had passed before he'd asked her out again. That had only been after she'd initiated contact outside work, after getting him to be Santa. The physical attraction was there, but obviously Dirk wasn't interested in a relationship.

The morning they'd made love, they'd shared a physical attraction, an emotionally wrenching work experience, sex, a budding *friendship*, and, possibly, made a baby.

Just the thought had her hand going back over her belly. Was Dirk's baby nestled inside her, growing and wanting to be loved? If she was pregnant, and, God, she hoped she wasn't, but if she was, she would love this baby. A baby she and Dirk had made.

Maybe made.

"Don't do that," he snapped.

"What?" Startled by his outburst, she jerked around in the passenger seat to look at him.

His blanched white fingers clenched the steering wheel. His face looked just as pale. "Cover your abdomen as if…as if you are."

Was the idea that repugnant to him? Of course it was. She was the one longing for a family, longing for someone to love, and the idea of an unplanned pregnancy left her in a cold sweat. No wonder Dirk was pale. Such a gorgeous man probably had loads of people to love, loads of people who loved him. A baby with a woman he'd used was the last thing he'd want or need.

Then another thought hit her. Was there someone already in his life?

Oh, God. Was that why he was so upset? Although she'd never heard of anyone special in his life, she wasn't privy to the intimate details of his life. Actually, his private life was just that. Private. She'd never heard anyone speak of outside work activities involving the man gripping the steering wheel so tightly there was likely to be finger impressions when he let go.

"Is there someone in your life, Dirk? Someone who will be upset if I'm pregnant?"

He didn't answer her, just gripped the steering-wheel all the tighter, his fingers digging into the dark leather. "*If* you're pregnant. We need to know what we're dealing with."

A baby. That's what they were dealing with. She wanted to scream at him. But she bit her tongue, reined in her anger. She couldn't lash out. Not when deep down she didn't want a pregnancy any more than he did. It was just…just what? She wanted him to be happy he'd made her pregnant when she wasn't happy about the idea herself?

Wasn't that irrational? Could she blame it on hormones? She winced. She could, but she wouldn't believe it. But if she wasn't pregnant, this was all immaterial, all stress and angst for nothing.

She sighed. As much as she didn't want to walk into the store and purchase a pregnancy test, he was right. They had to know. Had to figure out what they were going to do if she had gotten pregnant *that* morning.

There went the rest of her life, all riding on the results of a plastic stick.

She reached for the door handle, but Dirk's hand shot out, stopping her.

"No, that's not fair to you. I'll go and buy the test." He squeezed her hand, held on another few seconds, as if for his own reassurance. "I'm sorry I snapped at you, Abby. This isn't easy. Just…just wait here."

With that, he leapt out of the truck and flew into the store as if he'd been snacking on Santa's reindeers' magic corn.

* * *

Dirk supposed it was only appropriate that he be surrounded by Christmas hell while he waited on Abby's sofa to find out if he'd made her pregnant.

That he should be reminded of how he'd taken off her red dress, lain on the floor in front of her fireplace the last time he'd been in her house.

Had that really only been two nights ago?

Everything had seemed so right. But it hadn't been. Later, when not driven by surging testosterone, he'd been glad his phone had interrupted them. Too bad his phone hadn't rung the morning they'd had sex.

Abby might be pregnant.

His brain kept telling him the test would be negative. But his heart, his heart had seen the very realistic possibility on her face.

He suspected Abby didn't need the test to know the results, whether she'd admit as much to herself or not.

Hearing the bathroom door, he glanced up, waiting for her to reappear, to tell him the bad news.

Carrying the slender plastic test, she sat on the sofa beside him and placed the test on the coffee table.

"Well?" he asked, unable to wait another minute without knowing and unable to decipher her expression.

Her cheeks pink, she shrugged. "It's not been long enough. I came straight out here after doing the test. The instructions said to wait three minutes."

Three minutes. A hundred and eighty seconds. The difference between knowing and not knowing what the rest of his life entailed.

Knowing he was being a selfish bastard, he took a deep breath and clasped her hand. "Abs, I want you to know that regardless of what this test shows, I'll be here for you."

He didn't know how or what exactly he meant by his comment, but if he'd made her pregnant, he wouldn't abandon Abby. He might be a heartless bastard, but he'd do the right thing. Whatever the right thing was.

"I know you will." She sounded on the verge of tears. Her hand trembled and he clasped her fingers more tightly.

"If it's positive, I'll do whatever you want." What would she want? Marriage? An abortion? Child support? To castrate him for being so stupid as to get her pregnant?

"Okay, Dirk. That's fine."

Her voice was so flat his gaze lifted to hers. Unshed tears shone there and her lower lip quivered. Her fingers shook. Her whole body shook. He squeezed her hand, hoping to offer reassurance and wishing like hell someone would reassure him.

"Aw, honey, don't cry." He'd done this to her. It was his fault they were sitting here, wondering if they'd created a life. If only he'd not instantly been attracted to Abby. If only he'd not let the death of that little girl and her mother get to him. If only he hadn't found such comfort in Abby's arms. Sweet solace like none he'd known since Sandra and Shelby's deaths.

He could "if only" all day to no avail. If onlys wouldn't help them. Not at this point.

He wiped his finger along Abby's cheek, catching a runaway teardrop. "It'll be okay. One way or the other, it will be all right," he promised, although he wasn't sure he believed his words.

If Abby was pregnant, nothing would be all right.

She stared at him, opened her mouth, but no words left her tremulous lips.

"I'm sorry, Abs. So sorry." He leaned over and kissed her, gently, hoping to make the trembling stop, reminding himself that this was what had caused what they currently faced. Still, he wasn't able to stop.

Her mouth was warm and pliant, accepting his kiss, accepting him despite the fact he didn't deserve her.

"Oh, Abs, what have I done to you?" he whispered against her lips, threading his fingers into the soft waves of her hair.

"You didn't do anything to me, Dirk," she assured him, her voice catching slightly. "Nothing I didn't want."

"You didn't want this," he scoffed, gesturing toward the pregnancy kit.

"No, I didn't." She pulled back from him. Her eyes glistened with tears, but he'd never seen her look more sure of herself. "Not like this. Never like this. But if that test is positive, I will be okay."

"You'll keep the baby?"

She nodded.

"I'm sorry."

She stared him in the eyes, overflowing tears silently streaming down her cheeks. "For?"

"This. Taking advantage of you that morning."

"You didn't take advantage of me any more than I took advantage of you. We needed each other."

"What we did shouldn't have happened," he reminded her, so why was he holding her, leaning in to press another kiss to a teardrop on her cheek?

"No," she agreed, "but it did happen and we can't change the past."

"Or the consequences of that past." If only he could. Damn, there he went with another if only.

"True." She sighed, closing her eyes, opening them with strong resolve replacing her tears. "A baby wouldn't be the end of the world. Regardless of what the test shows, I will make the best of what life gives me."

She would, too. Dirk could see the determination and willpower reflected in her eyes. Knew enough about her to know Abby always made the best of any situation life presented. She was a glass half-full kind of woman.

Dirk had moved beyond glass half-empty years ago. His glass had been drained dry the moment his wife and daughter had taken their last breaths. After that, he'd tossed the cup against the wall, shattering the remains to bits.

"That's big of you, considering you're talking about the rest of your life." He couldn't keep the pain out of his voice. "A child is a big responsibility."

An odd expression on her face, Abby searched his eyes. "The biggest, really." She gripped his hand tightly in hers, a glimmer of uncertainty surfacing. "Promise me you'll try to be happy, too. Maybe it's crazy, but I need to hear you say that before we know, Dirk. Please."

Happy? She had no idea what she was asking of him. How could he be happy if he'd made her pregnant? He'd given all his love to his wife and a beautiful little girl with straw-colored hair and big blue eyes, and that love had been ripped from his soul. He couldn't do that again.

When he didn't answer, Abby sighed, dropped her forehead against his. "Maybe it'll be negative and all of this will have been for nothing. It's probably been three minutes."

Dirk was sure it had, but he didn't move away from where he stared into Abby's eyes. He wasn't a fool. He could see that she did need to hear him say he'd try to be happy. He didn't understand why, couldn't begin to fathom why, but in her eyes he saw beyond the happy front she put on to the world and saw real need. Need unlike any he'd ever experienced. Need that made him feel emotionally impotent and protective at the same time. Abby's need gutted him.

The thought of disappointing her filled him with mixed emotions. She was the kind of woman a man felt inclined to protect, a sweet, wonderful, generous woman who gave a hundred and ten percent of herself to those in her life.

She'd welcomed him into her bed when he'd needed her.

Sex with her had been phenomenal and had provided his first moments of peace in years. Yet he'd known Abby didn't give her body lightly, that if they continued, she might fall for him and want things he didn't.

But whether or not he wanted those things, if Abby was pregnant, he'd be forced to accept what fate dealt him.

She wanted him to say he'd try to be happy if the test was positive, if she was pregnant with his baby.

He couldn't do it.

"You read the test," she urged, her eyes searching his.

Without a word, he picked up the test, registered the unmistakable plus sign and felt his stomach drop down the chimney lickety-split. "You're pregnant."

"I am?" Abby grabbed the test from his hand, studied the results. "I'm pregnant."

He'd said that.

"I'm pregnant, Dirk." Dropping the test back onto

the coffee table as if the plastic had scalded her hand, she turned to him, wide-eyed and stunned, grabbed his hands and squeezed. "We're going to have a baby."

A baby. What could he say? He couldn't hurt Abby, couldn't suggest they consider their options, because even if he could ask, she wouldn't do that. He didn't have to hear the words to know that.

"Oh, God, I'm going to have a baby." Her chest rose and fell rapidly. Her eyes grew bigger and bigger. Her face grew paler and paler, as if she was on the verge of a panic attack. "What am I going to do with a baby?"

"You'll be fine." Had that really been his voice? Had he really sounded normal? He didn't feel normal. He felt as if he'd been dipped in ice water and stuck to the North Pole.

"Other than from nursing school, I don't know anything about babies. Nothing." Was she even talking to him? Or just thinking out loud? Talking to herself?

She grabbed his arm, shook it as if to get his attention. "What if I don't know how to take care of him or her? Then what?"

"You'll be fine," he repeated, unable to think of anything better. Unable to think, period. Abby was pregnant. With his baby. He was going to be a father again. He didn't want another baby.

Yet he couldn't look away from Abby's pleading eyes, couldn't shut out the need he saw there.

But he wanted to. He wanted to run from her Christmas-filled house and never look back. Never have to face the fact that he'd fathered another child when he didn't have a heart to love him or her with.

Leaving Oak Park to escape his family and friends

this holiday season had backfired. He'd jumped out of the frying pan and into the fire.

He pulled his hands free, turned from her to stare at her Christmas tree. God, he hated Christmas. Hated having to dredge up the past, but since she was having his baby, there were things Abby needed to know. Things she wouldn't like. By the time he was finished, she wouldn't like him. Which was fine. He hadn't liked himself in a long, long time either.

"I was married."

CHAPTER EIGHT

"MARRIED?" Jack Frost zapped a frigid coating of ice over Abby's spine. Surely she'd heard Dirk wrong. Hadn't she been thinking earlier about how little she really knew about him? For all she knew, he could still have a wife and family back in Oak Park where he'd come from.

How could she be pregnant by a virtual stranger?

Only when he'd kissed her, made love to her, he hadn't been a stranger. Far, far from it. He'd known her better than anyone, had touched her soul right along with her body. She'd looked at him and felt she'd known the essence of who he was, all she'd needed to know.

But she hadn't. She hadn't known he'd been married.

She was pregnant. Dirk had been married. Why wasn't he saying more? Why was he sitting there with his hands tightly fisted in his lap, with his jaw clenched and his eyes glazed over as if he were fighting demons? Had his marriage been that bad?

Was. That meant he wasn't still married, right? Why wasn't he explaining his bombshell statement?

"You were married?" she prompted.

He took a deep breath, raked his fingers through his

hair. "Sandra and I married too young. I was still in medical school, gone most of the time, didn't have two nickels to rub together, but we loved each other. Then Shelby came into the picture."

Another layer of ice settled over Abby's nerves.

"Shelby?" Was she a girlfriend? A mistress? A brief fling he'd had on the side? A—?

"My daughter."

His daughter? Abby blinked, sure she'd heard wrong. He had a daughter? Why hadn't he mentioned a daughter? How could she have not known such pertinent details?

Then again, why would she have known? She wasn't important to Dirk. Why would he have told her? Disgust filled her. How could she have been so foolish?

Outside work she'd spent a total of four—*four!*—days with him. The day she'd gotten pregnant, his Santa stint, the Christmas party, and today, the day they'd found out she was pregnant.

God, what must he think of her?

Then again, she hadn't been alone in that bed. She refused to abide by some double standard that said it was okay for him to sleep with a woman he barely knew, but that for her to do the same made her less of a woman.

He had a daughter. A wife, hopefully former wife, but the fact he'd not clarified that point worried her. He had a whole other life she knew nothing about. A whole other life he hadn't shared with her. Would he ever have if she hadn't gotten pregnant?

God, she was going to throw up.

"Do your wife and Shelby live in Oak Park?" She asked each word slowly, controlling each breath to keep from gasping air into her aching chest.

Was that why she occasionally saw the look of pain in his eyes when he treated a child? Was that why he never seemed completely comfortable in a child's presence? Because seeing children made him miss his daughter? Had he and his wife had problems? She should have suspected something the moment he admitted to not liking Christmas!

"No, Sandra and Shelby don't live in Oak Park. They don't live anywhere." His voice caught, his jaw flexed, he swallowed. "They died in a car accident four years ago. Shelby was only two years old."

"Oh, God." Which explained why he'd reacted so emotionally on the day they'd made love. The mother and daughter dying in the car accident must have stirred up memories of his own losses. Dirk had had a daughter who'd died. A wife who'd died. Abby's heart twisted inside out at the thought of how much that must hurt, at what he'd been through. "I'm so sorry, Dirk."

She placed her hand over his, hoping he sensed how she wanted to comfort him.

"It's not your fault." He pulled his hand free, raked his fingers through his hair, looked tormented, as if he was erecting every defensive wall around himself. "Just as this pregnancy isn't your fault. I'm the one who's sorry."

She had a thousand questions, things she wanted to know, to understand him better, really know this man whose baby grew inside her. But he'd closed his eyes and, she suspected, the subject of his past as well.

Still, she ached for him and, as awkward as she felt doing so given their current predicament, she wrapped her arms around him and gave him a hug. A big hug. She held on to him, hoping he knew how much she wanted to ease his burden. He sat stock still, never moving, never budging, never talking. Just sat.

"I don't blame you for my pregnancy," she assured him, "if that's what you're wondering. We're both consenting adults. We used protection. Neither of us could have known this would happen."

She traced her finger over his, laced their hands. Although she wasn't sure he welcomed her hold, she squeezed. "We'll figure this out, Dirk. Somehow, all this will work out okay."

But even as she said the words, Abby wondered if they were true. Wondered why she was having to play the role of the strong one when really she just wanted to curl up against him and cry. She wanted his arms to be wrapped around her, to have him holding her, giving comfort. She wanted to be the one taken care of, the one who got to let her emotions loose, and be comforted.

Instead, she'd be raising a baby, possibly by herself, and would never have the dreams she'd clung to since childhood.

Dreams of magical Christmases with a man who loved her and their happy family. Dreams of someday sharing the magical news of a pregnancy with a life partner who would rejoice with her at the news. Dreams of a happily ever after written just for her and her special Prince Charming.

From the first, she'd hoped Dirk would be that man, but not under these circumstances. Unable to hold back the erupting emotional volcano, Abby burst into tears.

And although Dirk wrapped his arms loosely around her, she found no solace in his embrace.

How could she when he was only holding her because

he was trying to do the right thing and not because he loved her or wanted her pregnant with his child?

Did Dirk really think no one was going to suspect something was up when he kept babying her? *Argh*. Abby was going to strangle him if didn't quit treating her so differently. Their coworkers weren't stupid.

And neither was she. After the halfhearted way he'd held her while she'd cried, she'd known she had to protect herself. After he'd left, she'd cried more, this time for the great grief rocking her insides, grief that she'd entangled her emotions so irreversibly with a man incapable of returning her sentiments. Even if he wanted to, he'd locked his heart away years ago and thrown away the key.

Dirk was a good man, but one without a heart to give, which meant she needed to guard hers with all her being.

"Here, let me do that." He stepped into her personal space, taking over where she was helping to transfer a patient from a gurney onto an exam table.

Biting her tongue because she didn't want to draw more attention to what he was doing, she shot him a back-off look and tried to continue with her job, to no avail since he didn't step away as they vied for a hold on the patient.

As their coworkers were looking back and forth between them, and even the patient had a curious look on her face, Abby held up her hands.

"Fine, Dr. Kelley. I'll go check on bay three's X-ray report." At least she sounded professional, even if he was making her look like an invalid.

What was wrong with him anyway? Why was he

acting like she couldn't do a thing for herself without his help? She was pregnant, not disabled.

"He's quite taken with you, isn't he?"

Abby spun to look at the medical assistant who'd only been working at the hospital for a few weeks. "Who?"

The girl, who couldn't be much older than high-school age, smiled. "Dr. Kelley, of course. I saw you together at the Christmas party. You make a lovely couple."

Abby swallowed the lump in her throat. She'd thought they made a lovely couple, too. Now, she knew they'd never be a couple. Perhaps if they'd had more time prior to her pregnancy, perhaps if they'd met years ago, before Dirk's marriage. Now it was too late.

"We're not a couple."

Dirk didn't do couples. Just because she was pregnant it did not mean she expected that to change. Neither did she want it to change because of her pregnancy.

She wanted Dirk to care enough for her to want to be a couple with her. Because of her. Because of his feelings for her.

She wanted him to love her.

The young girl frowned. "Really? I'm surprised. You looked like you were having a good time together."

That had been before they'd been interrupted and he'd said he wanted to just be friends. Before they'd known they were going to be parents. Before she'd realized Dirk was incapable of giving his heart to her.

"We were having a good time. As friends."

"Oh." The assistant didn't look as if she knew what else to say.

"No problem," she assured the girl, keeping an "it's no big deal" smile on her face in the hope of waylaying more curiosity. Particularly in light of Dirk's odd behavior since she'd clocked in. "Do you know if the X-ray reports are back on the fall patient in the next bay?"

Looking chastised, although Abby hadn't meant her to, the girl nodded. "They are."

No wonder the girl had thought they were a couple as they'd left in such a heated rush from the Christmas party and with the way Dirk had acted tonight.

She really was going to have it out with him the first private moment they got. Although they'd have to establish some type of relationship for the future, his overbearing, almost paternalistic attitude had to go. Besides, for now, Abby wanted a break from him. Later, after the holidays had passed, she'd figure out how she and Dirk could coexist in the world of parenthood.

"Hello, Mrs. Clifton," she greeted her patient, a friendly smile pasted on her face in the hope of reassuring the woman. "Dr. Kelley will be by in a few minutes to give your X-ray results." She pulled up the tests and flagged them for his attention. "How are you feeling?"

"Foolish." The woman in her early sixties gestured to the arm she held very still. "I still can't believe I slipped and did this."

"Unfortunately, falls happen." Abby lightly pinched each of the woman's fingertips, observing how quickly the blanched skin returned to its natural pink color. Almost immediately. Excellent.

"I guess this will teach me to be more careful of ice." The woman shifted, trying to get comfortable.

"Who knows, this might save you a much worse accident later down the line." Abby checked the automatic blood-pressure cuff that was wrapped around the woman's uninjured arm. One twenty-six over seventy-eight. Great. A normal reading.

The woman laughed lightly. "You're one of those positive people who always sees the best in everything, aren't you?"

"Usually." Only she hadn't been seeing the positive in her pregnancy. Only the negative. Only that her dreams for her future were undergoing a drastic transformation.

She was going to have a baby. A beautiful, precious baby that she and Dirk had made together. A baby to share her life with. To be a family with. To share Christmas with. Abby had never met anyone other than Dirk who she'd want to have a baby with. No one she'd want to share the rest of her Christmases with. Just Dirk.

If they weren't meant to be more than friends, then she'd deal with that, would love and cherish their baby without letting Dirk break her heart. Somehow.

"Nurse?" Mrs. Clifton eyed her curiously.

Pulling her thoughts together, Abby smiled at the elderly lady. "Thank you."

The woman's forehead creased. "What for?"

"For reminding me that it's much too wonderful a season to be down."

Especially over something that so many women would consider a blessing. She'd been given a gift, an unexpected, unplanned-for gift, but a gift all the same.

Just because that gift hadn't come at the time in her life she'd planned or in the way she'd hoped for didn't make a baby any less of a blessing.

Yes, there was still that part of her that didn't want

this, wanted her and Dirk to have the opportunity to get to know each other without a pregnancy shadowing their every thought and word. She didn't have that luxury.

She was going to be mother to Dirk's child.

"Were you down?"

Abby considered the question. "Not really. I just wasn't seeing the miracles of Christmas clearly."

"Christmas is the best time of year, isn't it?" Her patient's gaze fell on her immobilized arm. "Only this year someone else will have to do the cooking because I suspect I'm not going to be doing much of anything."

Helping reposition her pillow, Abby nodded her agreement. "I suspect you're right. I hope you have your shopping finished."

"Mercifully, yes. I'm one of those crazy women who gets up before dawn and does all my shopping on the day after Thanksgiving." The woman chuckled self-derisively. "Fighting the crowds is a bit rough at times, but the bargain buys are worth the effort."

"Aren't they just the best? I do the same thing."

Dirk stepped into the area, his face going pale.

Abby bit back a sigh. Did he really dislike Christmas so much that just hearing a discussion about shopping bothered him? How would she explain to her child that his or her father didn't like Christmas?

Avoiding looking at him, Abby entered her nurse's notes while Dirk went over the X-ray results with Mrs. Clifton, explaining that she needed to schedule an appointment with her primary care provider in addition to seeing the orthopedic surgeon the following day.

He left the room long enough to grab some patient education materials, flipped the pamphlet open to a page with a photo of magnified images of a normal bone and an osteoporotic one.

"Your arm broke more easily than it should have because your bones are thinning due to a condition called osteoporosis," Dirk explained, pointing out the difference in the bones in the pictures. "This happens when the bones lose mass, weakening, leaving them in a state where it takes much less force to cause a fracture. Sometimes even something as simple as taking a step can cause the bones to crush in on themselves when the bones have weakened."

"Crush in on themselves? The bones can break without me even falling?"

"Yes, it's possible in osteoporosis, but falling or taking a hit is much more likely to be the culprit of a break."

"I have this?"

"You do." He nodded. "Have you ever been told you have osteoporosis?"

"At my last physical, my nurse practitioner mentioned that I should be taking calcium." The woman gave a guilty shrug. "She tried to get me to go onto a medication to make my bones stronger."

Dirk's brow lifted. "Tried?"

The woman sighed, shrugged her good shoulder. "The medicine gave me bad indigestion so I only took a couple of doses."

Dirk frowned. "Did you let her know you'd stopped taking the medication?"

She shook her head, careful not to disturb her arm. "No, I figured I'd discuss it with her at my next visit." She gave him a thoughtful look. "If I'd been taking the medicine, would my bone have broken from falling tonight?"

"It's impossible to know for sure," Dirk replied. "Medications can add around ten percent back to the bone strength, which is a significant amount and can mean the difference between a break and no break." He pointed to the X-rays again. "The medicine rebuilds those tiny connections, adding strength. With bones as thin as yours are, you do need to be on some type of bisphosphonate."

"Putting up with a little heartburn would have been better than this." She gestured to her immobilized arm.

"You should discuss your options with your nurse practitioner. There are a wide range of treatments for osteoporosis, including a once-a-year intravenous infusion of medication. With the IV method, you wouldn't have to worry about taking a pill or having indigestion as that alternative would bypass that system and the side effects of pills."

The woman asked a few more questions which Dirk patiently answered. Watching him, watching his seemingly infinite patience when the woman became repetitious in her efforts to understand, gave Abby insight to Dirk. She'd witnessed his patience, his kindness, his caring time and again in the emergency room while he dealt with patients from all walks of life. Not once had he lost his temper or behaved unprofessionally.

She didn't have to wonder if he'd been a good father. He had. Although, no doubt, with completing his residency, he'd probably been so busy that he'd missed out on more of his daughter's short life than he'd have liked. Sandra Kelley had been a lucky woman to have

Dirk's love, to have had his baby, and experience the joys of pregnancy and motherhood with Dirk by her side, loving her.

Despite his aversion to Christmas, Dirk was a good man. The best Abby had ever met, really.

Honest, honorable, giving, strong in character.

Why didn't he like Christmas? Did the holidays remind him of all he'd lost? Of Christmases he'd shared with his wife and young daughter?

Would she and their child forever live in the shadow of his former life? God, she prayed not, but deep down she wondered if that wouldn't be the case.

If that happened, how would she prevent that over-shadowing their child's well-being? Just the thought of their child being made to feel inferior made her neck muscles ache and her stomach clench.

She finished her notes, left the bay and entered the next, determined to stay on task. A patient she'd tri-aged had discovered a large amount of blood in their urine and had been having tremendous back pain. She'd put him into the bay, and initiated protocol hematuria labs.

When Dirk stepped out of the fractured arm patient's bay, Abby caught him and without meeting his eyes gave him the stats on the patient. "Do you want to get a renal protocol CT scan?"

"Yes. Thanks." When she started to walk away, he grabbed her wrist, causing her to turn to look at him. "You holding up okay? You're not overdoing it, are you?"

That did it. She'd had enough of him interfering with her work.

"No." She pulled her arm free, hoping no one noticed.

"My back hurts. My feet hurt. I'm tired. My stomach hasn't felt right in days. But the main reason I'm not holding up is *you*."

His forehead wrinkled. "Me?"

"You're driving me crazy. You've got to stop treating me differently than you were before, well, you know."

His jaw worked back and forth slowly, as if he was trying to categorize her words and having difficulty knowing where to stick them. "I'm concerned."

"I appreciate your concern, but work isn't the place. I've got a job to do and if you keep making a difference, people are going to complain."

"People?"

"Our coworkers."

"I don't care what anyone thinks, except you, Abby."

He was saying all the right things, but Abby didn't want to hear them, could only hear his "let's just be friends" speech echoing through her head. She didn't want or need his overbearing behavior.

In his "concern," he was exposing her to her colleagues' curiosity. Her volunteer friends suspecting she was pregnant was one thing. Her coworkers another matter entirely. Not that they wouldn't know soon enough.

Everyone would know soon enough.

But she wanted a few weeks of having the knowledge to herself, to completely come to terms with her future plans prior to having to answer other people's questions.

"Well, I do care." It wasn't asking too much for him to give her time to work through this in privacy. "A lot of my closest friends work here. I won't have you undermining me."

His gaze narrowed. "No one would say anything if you needed an extra break."

Abby's jaw dropped. "Why wouldn't they?"

He looked away, guiltily, not answering her.

"Dirk?"

When his eyes met hers, a bit of arrogance she hadn't previously witnessed shone there. "I'm a doctor, Abby. If I give a nurse permission to take an extra break because I think she needs one, no one is going to deny that right."

Oh, no. That so wasn't going to happen. He'd do irreparable damage to her working environment. With a baby on the way, she needed her job.

"I can't take extra breaks just because you think I should." She paused, acutely aware they stood in the busy emergency room. No one was near them, but when Abby glanced around, the medical assistant was watching them curiously, a "yeah right, just friends" expression on her young face. "We can't discuss this here. Just let me do my job, okay? That's all I ask."

"Abby—"

"Dr. Kelley," an assistant interrupted, looking back and forth between them. "There's a myocardial infarction patient on his way in. The ambulance is en route and should arrive in two minutes."

Grateful for the interruption, Abby jumped into action. "I'll get the renal protocol CT scan entered into the computer and have everything ready for the MI arrival."

"Abby—"

"Take care of your patients, Dr. Kelley, and leave me alone. I can take care of myself and don't need or want your *friendship* after all." With that she spun on her heel and walked away from a man capable of breaking her heart.

When the paramedics rushed the man in, a team was ready in the emergency room to take over trying to save the man's life.

Abby stayed busy for the rest of her shift, working straight through her break, grateful for the mental reprieve from her personal life due to the intensity of their patients' needs.

Definitely meeting Danielle's definition of brooding, Dirk never said another word outside anything to do with their patients. However, when he realized she'd not taken a break, not eaten, he'd disappeared and come back with a cup of yogurt, bottled water and an apple, thrust them toward her and walked away without uttering a single word.

His expression hadn't been a pleased one. Actually, he'd looked irritated.

Part of her had wanted to toss the items at the back of his retreating, arrogant head. He deserved a good wake-up thwack. How dared he be so high-handed? Just because she was pregnant it did not give him the right to dictate what she should and shouldn't do. He'd said he just wanted to be friends, giving up any potential right to have a say in her life.

She was her own woman, could do this on her own, would forge a good life for her and her baby.

Abby desperately clung to that thought as a shield against the hurt Dirk's rejection had caused.

Clung to her mounting anger at his hot-cold attitude to prevent more pain from seeping through and jabbing at her vulnerable heart.

CHAPTER NINE

IF ABBY didn't open her door soon, Dirk was going to jemmy the lock. Or break down the door.

Was this his fourth round of knocks or his fifth?

Where was she?

Finally, he heard a scratching at the other side of the door. At least Mistletoe was up and about. Abby should be, too. If she'd gone home and gone to bed, she'd have had a good eight hours.

Was she okay? She'd looked so tired and pale when she'd left the hospital and hadn't acted like her normal self. He'd been tied up with a patient when she'd clocked out, hadn't been able to believe she'd left without telling him she was going.

As if she was truly angry with him. He'd have understood anger on the day they'd found out she was pregnant, would have understood if she'd beat his chest with her fists, but last night? Hell, he'd made a conscious effort to take care of her, to let her know he planned to be there for her and their baby even if the mere thought gave him hives. Didn't she understand how difficult this was for him? How hard he was trying?

The lock clicked, and the door swung open. Abby squinted, putting her hand up to block the fading sunlight filtering onto the porch. "Dirk? What are you doing here?"

"You look awful."

Standing in her doorway wearing baggy sweats, her hair wild, dark shadows bruising her eyes, Abby did look awful. Like she hadn't gone to bed after leaving work.

"Nice to see you, too," she mumbled. Her cat rubbing against her leg, meowing, she moved aside for Dirk to enter.

Carrying a bag of groceries he'd brought because he seriously doubted she was taking care of herself, he stepped into her foyer. He eyed her more closely, taking in the pallor of her skin, the redness in her eyes. "Did you volunteer somewhere after work this morning?"

She shut her front door, turned to face him. "You're not my boss. Not outside the emergency room. If I want to volunteer somewhere, I can."

"Which means you did." He let out an exasperated sigh, assessing her like a bug under a magnifying glass. "Why didn't you tell me? I would have gone with you."

"Have you considered that maybe I didn't tell you because I didn't want you to go?" She yawned, stretched her arms over her head, raising the shapeless sweat shirt up to expose a tiny sliver of ivory skin.

"No, I haven't considered that. Why wouldn't you want my help?" Forcing his gaze away from that glimpse of flesh, Dirk swallowed, shifted the groceries in his arms. How could he be looking at her one minute, thinking how tired she looked and wanting to throttle her for not taking better care of herself and the next be fighting the desire to pull that sweatshirt over her head to expose a whole lot more of her delectable body?

"Go away, Dirk," she continued, gratefully oblivious to the effect her stretch had had on his body and mind.

"No." After a few minutes of lying in his bed, thinking about Abby and her uncharacteristic snippiness, he had crashed into a dreamless sleep and awakened with only one thought. Seeing Abby, making sure she was okay. "You need someone to look after you."

"I can look after myself just fine." Her lower lip puckered in an almost pout.

His gaze zeroed in on that full bottom lip. He wanted to kiss her. To take her in his arms and kiss her until she sighed in contentment.

"Since when?" Dirk fought wincing at how brusque his tone was. Just because he was fighting sexual awareness he shouldn't be feeling when she looked exhausted, it didn't mean she'd understand that's what was causing his irritation. What was it about the woman that drove him so physically crazy? Taking a deep breath, he tried again in a calmer tone. "You pulled an exhausting twelve-hour shift, Abby. What was so important that you couldn't have rested first? Something to do with Christmas again?"

Mixed emotions flashed across her face, mostly irritation. "Just because you don't understand my love of Christmas, it doesn't mean you get to prioritize my activities. Volunteering is important to me."

Shifting the grocery bag, he gave her an exasperated look. "What about our baby's well-being? Doesn't that count for something?"

"I'm not going to dignify that with an answer." Turning away, she walked over to the sofa, sat and wrapped a blanket around herself. The same blanket she'd wrapped around her almost naked body just a few nights ago.

Dirk swallowed. Hard.

"Christmas makes me happy." She looked like a vulnerable child, one he wanted to take into his arms and hold. But she wasn't a child. And if she were in his arms, he'd want much more than to hold her. She was a grown woman, a woman who he'd thought about almost non-stop since the night they'd met, a woman he desperately wanted. Why did he get the feeling Christmas meant more to Abby than the obvious?

"Look, you don't have to check on me just because I'm pregnant." She pulled the blanket more tightly around herself, causing the cat, which had jumped up next to her, to look annoyed. She picked up the fat cat, placing the animal in her lap and stroking her fingers over his fur. "Actually, I'd prefer it if you didn't."

"Why not?" He moved into her line of sight, but didn't sit down, just stood, watching her, wondering why she was shutting him out. His reaction on the day they'd found out she was pregnant hadn't been the greatest, but the news had caught him off guard. Way off guard. He'd have sworn she understood, that she didn't want a baby any more than he did. Finding out she was having a baby, that the rest of her life was going to be vastly different than she'd thought couldn't have been any easier for her than it had been for him. Probably, the news had been more stressful to her. But he was trying. He was concerned, wanted what was best for her and their baby. Why was she being so difficult?

"We're not a couple, Dirk. We weren't before this and we aren't now," she pointed out, scratching behind her cat's ears. "People are getting the wrong idea."

"What?" Was she serious? "How could they get the wrong idea? You're pregnant with my baby."

"Neither of us wanted this baby."

He winced. What she said was true, and yet to hear the words come out of her sweet lips so bluntly felt wrong. He'd never considered having more children, never considered starting over. He didn't want to start over, but neither did he want to father an unwanted child.

"Whether or not we want to be parents, Abby, we're going to be. We have to do what's best for the baby." God, he sounded so logical, so clinical. Did she have any idea how awkward this was for him? Standing above her, holding the groceries he'd brought to make her something to eat, her refusing to even look at him.

Her gaze remained fixed on where she petted her purring cat, her long fingers stroking back and forth. Lucky cat.

"I'm not stupid, Dirk. I will do what's best for the baby. But for now I want time."

"We don't have to tell anyone for a while, but you won't be able to hide your pregnancy for long, Abby. Decisions will have to be made. Soon."

Looking unsure for the first time since he'd arrived, she pulled her knees up, dropped her head onto them, burying her face in the folds of the blanket. "I hate this."

Helplessness washed over him. She looked so alone, so stressed. He wanted to take her into his arms, to hold her and never let go. But he just stood there. Taking her into his arms would accomplish what? Other than send his libido through the roof? Besides, he wasn't so sure she'd welcome his embrace.

As if sensing his thoughts, sensing his need for her to look at him, she glanced up with red-rimmed, watery eyes. "You seem to be handling this fairly well this morning."

Dirk felt as if a string of Christmas lights had been twisted around his throat and cut off his air supply.

Looks could be deceiving. He wasn't handling anything. But not wanting to deal with something didn't mean one could just ignore life's realities. He'd learned that lesson well.

"There's really no choice. Which means we have to make plans."

She inhaled deeply and let her breath out slowly. "Plans?"

"To protect you and the baby."

"No." Her jaw dropped and she shook her head in short little jerks. "I'm not going to marry you, Dirk. Don't even ask. That would just be compounding our mistakes and, honestly, if you did I think...well, just don't."

Ouch. She had a way of striking beneath his armor. "I didn't plan to ask you to marry me, Abby. Although if that's what you wanted, I wouldn't deny your request under the circumstances."

"My request? Under the circumstances?" She snorted. "I'm pregnant, Dirk. Not dying. I'm a big girl. I can take care of myself and this baby, too. I don't need you."

Did she think he'd just walk away and forget she was having his baby? Then the truth hit him. For all her bravado, Abby was scared. She did want his concern, but didn't know the first thing about accepting that concern. He'd gotten the impression her family had been close before her parents' deaths. What had happened to her after that? Had she been taken care of? Loved?

"Yes," he said softly, "you do."

She glanced up again. Surprise flickered in her eyes. "How dare you presume you know what I need? You know nothing about me."

He knew she was a prickly little thing when she was on the defensive. But why was she on the defensive with him? It just didn't feel right. Didn't she know she could trust him? That he'd never hurt her?

What was that she'd said at the Christmas party?

Maybe not intentionally.

She'd been right. He had hurt her. They just hadn't known it at the time. But he refused to accept her assessment that he knew nothing about her.

"I know more than you think. You're a great nurse. A caring woman. A fantastic lover." Her lower lip disappeared into her mouth, vulnerability shining so brightly in her eyes it almost blinded him. "And I believe you're going to be a great mother to our baby."

The tears Abby had been fighting pricked her eyes. How dared he come into her house and spout off sweet words like that after the awful morning she'd spent tossing and turning on the sofa? The sofa because she hadn't been able to get comfortable in her bed, had given up and curled up in the living room, staring at her mother's Christmas village pieces, wishing she could lose herself in that happy little world. Finally, she'd dozed a little.

She loved nursing and liked to believe he was right, that she was a great nurse. She could also go with the caring woman. She did care about others. But a fantastic lover? What a joke.

"We both know I wasn't a fantastic lover." She snorted softly at the mere idea of him thinking her fantastic. Not that he'd complained but, still, she doubted she'd been fantastic or anywhere close.

"Yes, you were, Abby." He set the bag on her coffee table, squatted next to her and reached for her hand.

"So fantastic you couldn't run away fast enough." She stuck her hands under the blanket, anywhere to keep him from touching her. She couldn't think when he did that. Not that she was thinking clearly anyway. Not after discovering she was going to be a mother, not sleeping much, and crying a whole lot.

He touched her anyway, running his fingers along the side of her face, into the edges of her wild-about-her-head hair. "So fantastic just remembering takes my breath away."

Why did she want to lean against him? To toss the blanket away and fall into his arms and cry until there were no more tears left?

"Why are you here, Dirk?" she asked, wishing he'd go, would leave her to what so far had been a less than stellar day. "Just go home."

"Can't do," he said, shaking the burgeoning plastic bag he'd put on the coffee table. "I brought you breakfast. Or lunch." He glanced at his wristwatch. "Or dinner. Whatever you want to call it. Regardless, I'm going to make you a healthy meal."

Just the thought of breakfast made her stomach heave. She grimaced. "Food is the last thing I want right now."

"You have to eat."

She rolled her eyes. "What would be the point?"

He stared at her for long moments and when she met

his gaze, his were so intent she couldn't look away even though she desperately wanted to.

"Abby, you've got to stop arguing with me."

She bit the inside of her lip. "Who's arguing?"

Stroking his fingers along the side of her face, he sighed. "This is certainly a side of you I've never seen."

She was sure it was a side he wished he still hadn't seen. Unbrushed hair, makeup-less face, nauseated-all-morning pallor. She wouldn't win any beauty prizes on her best days. Today she might send small children running for the hills.

"No one invited you here or is making you stay," she reminded him, chin lifting.

But rather than take offense at her unusual surliness, he just smiled, as if he knew some secret she didn't.

"Go take a shower. You'll feel better." Another of those dazzling smiles that it really wasn't fair for him to be flashing when she felt so… What was it she felt? Hadn't she decided the other night at the hospital that their baby was a gift? One that she'd treasure? But right now Dirk's smile, his gorgeous face and body, just annoyed her. How dared he look so wonderful when she felt so awful?

"I'll slice fresh fruit and cook breakfast." He leaned forward, dropped a kiss at her temple, lingered a brief moment.

Oh, my. If she didn't know better she'd swear he was breathing in her scent.

"How do you like your eggs, Abby?" Oh, he'd definitely nuzzled her just then, his hot breath caressing her cheek, burning her all the way down to her toes.

"Have you not heard a word I've said? I don't want

breakfast. I don't want a shower." Well, a long shower would be nice and the hot water might ease her achy body. "I just want to be left alone."

He cupped her face, holding her gaze to his. "No."

Abby gawked, not believing his high-handedness. "No?"

"I'm not leaving, Abby." This time his lips brushed her face, trailing light kisses on her cheek. "Not when you're like this."

Shivering from his touch, she took a deep breath. "Like what? I'm fine."

He didn't laugh, but he could have. She was so far from fine that no one would have thought less of him if he'd had a good chuckle at her comment. She felt on the verge of screaming, crying, laughing hysterically, throwing herself into his arms and begging him to love her, an entire plethora of heightened emotions all surging at once through her hormonal system.

"It's going to be okay, Abby." He brushed her hair away from her face, stared into her eyes and warmed a place deep inside her that she hadn't realized had chilled the moment he'd said she was pregnant. "I'm as scared as you are about this, but somehow this is all going to be okay. We'll make it okay. Together."

When his lips covered hers, she let herself believe him. Let herself give in to the temptation of his touch, the warmth of his caresses, the power of the emotions between them.

She couldn't exactly recall how Mistletoe ended up in the floor and Dirk stretched out above her, his weight pressing her into the sofa, his mouth drawing out her every breath. She clung to him, loving the weight of him covering her, loving his strength, the need in his kisses, his touches.

Rather than the frantic way they'd made love on that morning, or even their desperation the night of the Christmas party, their touches were slower, more drawn out, more *everything*.

Her brain screamed in protest, reminding her she was supposed to be protecting her heart against him, not kissing him, not helping as he pulled her sweatshirt over her head, revealing her naked breasts to his eager inspection. His eager kisses.

"I want you, Abby," he breathed from between her breasts. "Let me love you."

Despite knowing she should stop him, should not expose her all too vulnerable heart, she couldn't deny Dirk, not when his hot mouth felt so good on her body, not when she suspected he already owned her heart. All of her heart.

She wanted his love. More than she'd ever dreamed of wanting anything in her whole life, she wanted this man. All of him. His mind, his body, his heart. Yes, she definitely wanted Dirk's heart.

She tugged his T-shirt free, helped pull the material over his head, bit back a groan at the beauty of his naked torso. He removed his jeans, her sweats, and was inside her in what seemed a single breath. No condom. What would be the point? Body to body. Soul to soul.

"Abby," he breathed against her mouth, staring into her eyes, moving inside her. "I'm not going to last long. Not like this. I—I need you so much. So much."

Clasping her hands with his, he drove deeper, so deep Abby lost where she ended and he began, gave herself over to the emotions flooding through her body, her heart.

Not her heart, Dirk's.

If she'd had any doubts before, she no longer did. Her heart, all of her, belonged to him, completely and irrevocably.

She wrapped her legs around him, drawing him deeper, deeper still. "I need you, too."

Saying the words out loud somehow made them more real, somehow made her feel more vulnerable. But looking into his eyes, seeing matching need, real need, she could only expose herself further.

I love you.

She wasn't sure if she said the words out loud or just in her heart. Regardless, she felt them with all her soul, with everything she was.

She loved Dirk.

Much later, Abby didn't eat any of the turkey bacon Dirk fried, but she did have a healthy portion of the freshly sliced cantaloupe, scrambled eggs and buttered toast. And didn't dry heave once.

Amazing what good sex did for a body. Not good sex. *Great* sex.

No, not sex. No way could what they'd just shared be called mere sex. No, what they'd just done transcended everything.

"Apparently—" she smiled, feeling a little shy "—I like your cooking better than my own."

"Impossible." His grin was contagious, complete. Real. "I've had your fudge, Abby. You're a whiz in the kitchen."

"Thanks." She watched him feed Mistletoe the

leftover bacon. The cat purred against his leg, brushing against him time and again. Mistletoe wasn't the only one wanting to rub against Dirk. "My cat will forever be begging for more."

Just like she worried she'd be begging for more of the attention he'd shown her this morning. Wow.

Lord help her! She loved him.

The man had cooked her breakfast, made wonderful love to her until they'd both cried out. Afterwards, he'd held her. Held her tightly to him, stroking his fingers across her belly. She'd wished she'd known what he'd been thinking, wished she'd known if his caress had been incidental or if he'd purposely touched her where their baby grew.

She stood, intending to help clear away the dishes, but Dirk motioned for her to sit.

"I'm pregnant, Dirk, not disabled. You cooked. I clean."

"No." He shook his head, pointing at her chair. "My treat."

Okay, part of her thrilled at the idea that he was pampering her. Had she ever been pampered in her life? She didn't think so. Not since her mom and dad had died.

"I can wash dirty dishes," she assured him, not wanting the way he'd treated her at work to extend into her home. She wasn't an invalid. "Besides, you really didn't make that much of a mess. It won't take but a jiffy to clean."

"Probably not, but today is my treat. Take a load off, Abby."

She stood next to her chair, eyeing him, yet again wishing she could read his thoughts. "Why?"

"What do you mean, why? Can't I do something nice for you without you questioning my motives?"

She bit into her lower lip. "Is it because you feel guilty?"

"I am guilty, but that's not why I'm here."

His blue eyes looked so sincere. "Then why?"

He leaned back in his chair, looked perplexed, then shrugged. "I want to spend time with you."

"Because I'm pregnant?"

He studied her a moment. "I've wanted to be with you from the moment we met, Abby. That's how you ended up pregnant."

"I'm pregnant because we had a horrible night in the E.R." She didn't remind him of the similarities to his own tragic losses. She understood why he hadn't wanted to be alone, forgave him for using her, found herself wanting to comfort him even more now that she understood why he'd been so deeply affected. But that wasn't what earlier had been about, was it?

"I've had horrible nights in the E.R. before and never slept with my nurse."

Why did that admission make her feel better, lighter, less used?

"If the attraction hadn't been so strong between us, no tragedy would have brought us together like that." His confident tone left no room for doubt. "I made love to you because I wanted to make love to you. Just as I wanted to make love to you today. When I look at you, I can't think about much of anything except having you."

Had he really just admitted that he wanted her? She'd thought so, but then the whole pregnancy issue had clouded her thinking yesterday and this morning.

But he had wanted her. He'd said made love, not have comfort sex or one-night-stand sex or guilt sex.

"And now?" she asked, grabbing at the rope he was throwing her, hoping it was long enough to save her, hoping she wasn't grasping at straws. "Months went by with you barely acknowledging I existed outside work."

"I want you, if that's what you're asking. I never stopped wanting you. After what we just shared, surely you don't doubt that." His eyes caressed her face. "You're beautiful, Abby."

"You told me I looked awful," she reminded him.

"That was pre-shower." His tone was teasing, but his eyes remained dark, stormy. "You're always beautiful, Abby. You must know that."

"Thank you," she said. How could she not believe him when his gaze echoed his words? Dirk really did find her beautiful. He really did want her and really had made love to her.

Christmas miracles never ceased.

"But we can't repeat what just happened. Not when we're just friends."

She stood corrected.

Apparently, Christmas miracles did cease.

CHAPTER TEN

HAVING made it clear that he planned to lighten her load whether Abby wanted him to or not, Dirk went with her to her volunteer stints, becoming more and more involved in her day-to-day life, more and more involved in her Christmas charity events.

Although he didn't pretend the Christmas aspect didn't bother him, he no longer winced when she told him what they'd be doing for the day.

As she'd just done.

He'd come over, insisted upon bringing bagels, cream cheese and fresh fruit. They'd eaten and addressed Christmas cards to be distributed to nursing-home residents. When they'd finished, running his finger over the steepled church to her mother's Christmas village, Abby's favorite piece, he'd asked what was next.

"It's called Toys for Toddlers. Various businesses have set up stations for people to donate toys to be given as Christmas gifts to needy children. Our job is to go by the various drop-off points and pick up the toys. We'll deliver them to the headquarters and volunteers will wrap them at a later time, probably tomorrow."

His face remained impassive as he picked up a village figure of a couple holding hands on a park bench. "When and how do the toys actually get to the kids?"

Purposely trying to look impish, Abby smiled. "Santa delivers them, of course."

His gaze narrowed suspiciously and she'd swear he'd have tugged on his collar if he had one. She bit back laughter, enjoying teasing him, enjoying this budding aspect to their relationship.

"Santa?"

Watching as he carefully replaced the figure where she'd had it, she gave in. "No worries." She placed her hand on his arm, loved the sinewy strength there, but wondered at herself for touching him when she usually so carefully avoided doing so. "You're safe. I'm not in charge of Santa."

At least he was safe from playing Santa. Safe from her was another matter altogether. The contact of their skin touching was frying her brain cells, making her want to push him down on the sofa and leap into his lap for a little Santa role playing. She had all kinds of things on her wish list—naughty and nice.

She wanted him to kiss her, believed he wanted to kiss her, too. As frustrating as she found his insistence that they were just friends, she believed he had his reasons. But if he didn't work through them soon, she was going to make herself a mistletoe halo and wear it at all times.

"That's good to know." He sighed with real relief.

She observed him closely, noted that his shoulders had relaxed with her answer. "I was teasing. Maybe I shouldn't have, but I couldn't resist. Was being my Santa really that bad?"

He closed his eyes and took a deep breath. When

he spoke, his voice was low. "Anything to do with Christmas is that bad."

His words startled like gunshots fired through a silent night. The true depth of his dislike of the holidays struck her with guilt that she'd teased him. Yes, she'd heard him say he didn't like Christmas, had seen his discomfort, but she hadn't truly appreciated how deep his dislike ran, hadn't fully appreciated that he repeatedly set that dislike aside to help her with holiday projects.

"Why?" Why didn't he like Christmas? Why was he willing to set aside that dislike for her? Even before they'd known she was pregnant, he'd played Santa. Because she'd asked him to. He'd also volunteered to help her at the food bank. Because he'd thought she was ill and needed his help.

Looking at him, his handsome face clouded, his eyes full of pain as he stared at the ceramic village, she wavered between reminding herself to protect her heart and risking his rejection by wrapping her arms around him. But she only held on to his arm.

"I don't like Christmas."

If she understood, maybe she could understand him, could understand why he insisted on calling them friends. Out of misplaced honor to his deceased wife and daughter?

"Tell me why you don't like Christmas. Please." She squeezed where she held his arm. "I want to understand you and can't fathom why anyone wouldn't love the holidays."

Silence. More silence.

With his free hand, he raked his fingers through his dark hair. His jaw rotated, then clenched. "Sandra and Shelby died on their way to a Christmas sale."

"Oh, God, no," she gasped. She'd known they'd died in a car crash, had known he professed to dislike the holidays. Why hadn't she put two and two together and come up with the right answer about why he didn't like Christmas?

"It was early morning, before dawn," he continued, staring straight ahead, but she suspected he saw nothing, that he was locked away in a different time. A time where he had endured a horrible tragedy. Had hurt in ways Abby couldn't fix with a little Christmas magic.

Her heart bled for him, at the pain still so evident on his face, at the hollowness in his eyes.

"I'd pulled an all-nighter at the hospital, was still there and didn't know she was going to the sale. When they wheeled her in, I couldn't believe it was her, couldn't fathom why she'd be out that early."

"Oh, Dirk." She wasn't sure he heard her. He didn't appear to even be in the same room with her, his mind was so far removed from the present.

"She'd dragged Shelby out at that godforsaken hour so she could go and buy my Christmas gift." Anger cracked his voice. Deep, hoarse anger that chilled Abby to the core.

She clasped his hand, squeezed. "I'm so sorry, Dirk."

"Yeah, me, too." He looked toward her, met her gaze, and possibly saw her, although she still wasn't sure he wasn't too far lost in the past. "I'd rather have had my wife and daughter than anything any store sold."

"I know you would." Beyond caring about protecting her heart, she moved to where she could wrap her arms around him, hold him close. "Of course, you would."

He remained stiff in her embrace, not relaxing, not

making any move to take her into his arms or acknowledge that she held him.

"There was a Christmas tree in the emergency department's office where they put me after…Christmas music played." His face twisted. "I felt as if Christmas mocked me. The best part of my life was being ripped away when the world was celebrating peace, love and happiness. It didn't seem right."

"What happened was an accident. A tragic accident." She reached up, brushed her fingers over his face, smoothing the tension lines at his temples. "But Sandra and Shelby wouldn't have wanted you to be unhappy, to lose the spirit of Christmas, the spirit of life."

He blinked. "You don't know that."

"Your wife was on her way to purchase a gift for you. Not because of whatever that gift was, but because she wanted to buy you something special. That doesn't sound like a woman who would want her husband to be lonely and miserable at the holidays."

But it wasn't just at the holidays, she realized. Dirk had closed off his heart. Permanently.

"As if my family would let me be lonely at the holidays," he snorted.

He'd never mentioned a family. Only Sandra and Shelby. "Your family?"

Why had Dirk mentioned his family? Just because his mother had called repeatedly over the past week wanting to know if he was coming home for Christmas, attempting to change his mind when he repeatedly said no.

Apparently, she'd also put his brother and sister on the task as well, as both had been using various technologies to insist he come home so the family could all be together for the holidays.

As if he'd want to set himself up for another miserable confrontation. As if he'd want to give them the opportunity to force him down memory lane with photos and movies like they had the year before until he'd had enough and walked out.

A Christmas intervention. Who ever heard of anything so foolish? Anything so humiliating and embarrassing? Anything so hurtful? He'd been emotionally ambushed and, no matter how well intentioned, they'd ripped away what little balm he'd coated his raw heart with.

They just didn't understand the ache inside him.

No one did.

How could they when they still lived inside their safe little world? Sure, they'd mourned Sandra and Shelby, but they'd moved on, forgotten. Only his mother seemed to have some understanding. She put up Christmas ornaments in honor of Shelby. A baby's first Christmas ornament that had his precious little girl's photo inside.

As much as he wanted his mother to keep Shelby's memory alive, being surrounded by family only brought home just how much he'd once had. How much he'd lost.

Why had he brought up this subject? He didn't talk about Sandra and Shelby. Neither did he discuss why he didn't like Christmas. Not with anyone. Ever.

He'd never told anyone the details of his wife and daughter's deaths. His family knew, of course. Sandra's sister had shared that they'd planned to meet early at the department store. So early another car had crashed into her head-on when the driver had fallen asleep behind the wheel. A driver who'd also been on her way to an early-morning Christmas sale. All for a few sale-priced items that the recipient hadn't needed to begin with.

If Christmas never came again, Dirk wouldn't care, would be glad to not have to face all the reminders, would be glad not to have his family put so much pressure on him to "live life." What did they think he was doing?

"Dirk?" Abby touched his face, pulling him to the present. Her palm was warm against his face. "Do you have a large family?"

Closing his eyes, trying to focus on the present, he sighed. "Huge."

When he opened his eyes, Abby's had widened with delight. "Really?"

His stomach ached. "Unfortunately, yes."

She blinked, clearly confused. "Unfortunately?"

"Obviously you've never had a big family."

Looking a little sad, she shook her head. "No, my parents were both only children of older parents. I sort of remember my grandmother, but she died when I was five and the others had passed before her. When my parents died, I went to live with my great-aunt. She died while I was in college. I always wanted a big family."

Dirk studied her, a woman who had no family, had lost a great deal, and thought of what a bright light she was to those who knew her. "How is it you remain so positive when you've had so much loss in your life?"

"Everyone faces loss, although certainly there are varying degrees. Attitude is a choice and I choose to be happy."

"Even though you're pregnant with my baby?" He hadn't meant his question to sound so negative. Neither had he meant to hold his breath while he waited for her answer.

A smile softened her expression. "This baby is a blessing. I might not have thought so when I first found out, but that was foolishness. Our baby is a miraculous gift. All babies are."

He let out the breath, relaxing a bit that their baby would be loved, that Abby would be able to wrap this baby in her goodness, that she'd make up for the hole where his heart used to be. "You're the gift, Abby."

Clasping his hand, she lifted it to her lips, pressed a soft kiss to his fingers. "I'm thankful for you, too."

Her eyes glittered with compassion, which usually sent him running for the hills, but there was more in Abby's gaze. So much more.

In her eyes he saw hope. Hope that he could be what she needed. Hope that was a waste of her goodness since her hope centered around him.

Dirk's apartment stood out in stark contrast to Abby's house. No brightly lit Christmas tree. No wrapped packages. No Christmas spice candles. No garland or bows. Nothing.

For that matter, his apartment was stark when not considering the Christmas season. The bare necessities interlaced with a few high-tech niceties. Nothing warm and inviting.

A sofa. A fully loaded entertainment center worthy of hosting all sporting events. A square coffee table with a few sporting and medicine magazines tossed onto it. The area of the room meant to hold a dining table held a weight bench and an elliptical stair machine instead. Two stools sat in front of the bar that divided the kitchen from the open floor plan. The kitchen looked just as barren as the rest of the apartment. As if he barely lived here.

He'd been here, what? Two? Three months? Not a real long time, but enough that a home should begin to reflect its owner. Perhaps this bare one did.

Glancing toward her, Dirk paused, obviously reading her expression. "It's a place to live, Abby."

She nodded, aching more for him than she had since the morning he'd told her about his wife and daughter's deaths. Emotionally, she'd continued to waver back and forth between her growing feelings for Dirk and the pending sense that she needed to ship her heart to the North Pole in the hope of keeping it out of Dirk's clutches.

"It's a nice building."

He threw his head back in laughter. "Which is your way of telling me my apartment is sadly lacking."

Glancing around the sparse rooms again, she shrugged. "Well, at least I know what to get you for Christmas."

Christmas was Tuesday, just a few short days away, and she'd not bought him anything, hadn't known what to get him. She'd figured she'd make him a tin full of peanut-butter goodies, but she wanted to give him something more.

His laughter faded. "I don't want you to get me anything, Abby."

"I know." She bit her lip. She hadn't meant to say that, hadn't meant to mention Christmas at all.

They'd just stopped by his apartment so he could grab a shower and clean clothes, then he'd promised to take her out for dinner. When she wasn't nauseated, she was starved. Today had been one of those days where she couldn't get enough to eat.

"I mean it, Abby. No presents." Of course, Dirk would say he didn't want anything. She understood that, planned to get him something anyway. After seeing his apartment for the first time today, she had a much better idea of things he could use.

"But—"

"No buts. I'm serious. Do not get me a present. I don't celebrate Christmas."

She didn't say anything. How could she? Dirk was the most important person in her life. She couldn't not get him a present.

He eyed her as if waiting for her to argue. When she didn't, he gestured toward the entertainment center. "Make yourself at home. Watch whatever you like. There's drinks in the refrigerator. I'll only be a few minutes."

Abby nodded, but rather than sit on the oversized leather sofa she wandered around the barren room. No pictures hung on the wall. No little knickknacks sat on the coffee table. Anyone could have lived here. But Dirk did.

Her heart ached for him all over again. He really had cut himself off from the world after his wife and daughter had died. If not for work, she wondered if he'd have any contact with others. Until her.

She'd definitely pushed him outside his comfort zone with her Santa requests and numerous volunteer stints.

Now they were going to be parents, which definitely pushed his limits. Dirk needed her. Needed this baby.

Maybe he didn't realize just how much but, looking around this apartment, Abby did realize.

A loud ring sounded throughout the room. Abby jumped, looked around and spotted Dirk's house phone.

Should she answer? Probably not.

But as the shrill ringing sounded time and again, she decided whoever was calling must really need to talk to him, could possibly even be the hospital as he wouldn't have heard his cell while in the shower.

"Hello?" she said, hoping she was doing the right thing by answering, but knowing at the moment she was the one outside her comfort zone.

Silence.

"Hello?" she repeated, guilt slamming her as surely as if she'd peeked inside a Christmas package. She should have just let the phone ring.

"I was trying to get in touch with Dirk Kelley," a female voice said, sounding a little uncertain.

Whoever the caller was, she hadn't said Dr. Kelley. She'd said Dirk. Abby's guilt over answering the phone skyrocketed. As did her curiosity and some other green monster taking hold in her chest.

"Um, this is Dirk's number. He's not available at the moment. Could I take a message?"

A woman was calling Dirk. Who was she? Why was she calling? What right did Abby have to answer his phone, to take a message?

Every right, her heart shouted. She was pregnant with his baby, had spent the past several days in his company, working, volunteering, getting to know him, and he her.

Silence, then, "Who is this?"

Just exactly what Abby wanted to know, in reverse. But she bit her tongue. Dirk had had another life in Oak Park. Although they'd talked a lot over the past several days, he'd shared very little of that life with her. Had there been someone special? Someone he'd left behind?

The hurt she'd felt when she'd discovered he'd been married, had had a child, and she hadn't known came back. Why had Dirk revealed so little of his past?

"Abby. I, uh, work with Dr Kelley." Why had she called him Dr. Kelley? "We're friends." Why had she added that last? What she really wanted was to insist on knowing who the caller was and why she was calling Dirk.

"Oh," the woman said, slowly, as if digesting Abby's answer. "That's nice. Where is my son that he can't answer his cell or his home phone?"

Her son? This was Dirk's mother!

"Uh," Abby hedged, her face flaming. "He's in the shower."

"Really? Or is he just trying to avoid me insisting on him coming home for Christmas?"

"Dirk's not planning to come home for Christmas?" Abby couldn't fathom having a family and not wanting to spend the holidays with them. Was he not going home because of her pregnancy? Or because of the past?

"He's volunteered to work on the holidays, hasn't he?"

"He's working on Christmas Eve," she admitted. They both were. "He gets off at seven on Christmas morning."

"I'd hoped..." His mother sighed. "No matter what I'd hoped. I'm going to have to face facts. If he refuses

to come home, we'll just have to bring Christmas to
him. Tell me, Abby, just what's your relationship with
my son and how good are you at planning surprises?"

CHAPTER ELEVEN

ON SATURDAY, December twenty-second, Abby watched Dirk spoon a helping of green beans onto a cheap paper plate held by a rough-looking, unshaven, dirty man wearing multiple layers and carrying a toboggan.

Was he the last person to be served lunch?

They'd fed over two hundred today. Too many people with no homes, no food, no family, no Christmas.

She glanced around the dining area of the shelter. Smiling faces. Lots of smiling faces. And chatter. Being warm and having food in their bellies seemed to have turned up the noise level. Along with gift packages that included several basic amenities, baths were being offered. Several had taken the shelter up on that offer, but most had declined.

"This was a good work."

Surprised at Dirk's comment, she turned to him. "Yes. All the charities I volunteer with are good works."

He met her gaze. "You're a good person, Abby."

Slightly uncomfortable at the intensity in his eyes, she shrugged. "I'm no different than anyone else."

The corner of his mouth hitched up in wry amusement. "You're the most giving woman I've ever met."

Ignoring the depth of his look because she quite

simply wasn't sure how to take it, she winked playfully. "Thank you. I try."

"Why is that?"

"Why is what?" She wiped the metallic serving area with a washcloth, more to busy her hands than because of any spilt food.

"Why do you do so much for others?"

Feeling her face go warm, she shrugged. "My parents worked for Second Harvest. Both of them. It's how they met. After they died, a lot of people did a lot of things to help me. I want to do my part to give back."

"And?"

And she didn't want to dig any deeper than that. Didn't want to look beyond the obvious reasons for volunteering. "And so I have."

"Why so focused on Christmas?"

She took in his confused expression. "My fondest memories of my parents all revolve around the holidays."

He nodded as if he understood, but she doubted he did. After all, he still had a family who loved him, a family who craved to spend time with him and celebrate special occasions. A family he held at arm's length despite their continued efforts to be close to him.

"The Santa suit you wore was my father's." She wiggled her fingers inside their plastic serving gloves.

"You mentioned that the day you loaned it to me."

"He played Santa every year for various charity groups." How she cherished memories of seeing her father dressed up, of him scooping her into his arms and telling her he was off to be Santa's helper. Once upon a time she'd believed he really was Santa and just couldn't tell her. The times she and her mother had gone with him had been magical. He'd always made her feel special, loved.

"Good for him," the man who'd also played Santa for her said a bit wryly.

Abby just smiled, continuing her blast from the past. "Every Christmas Eve my father would put the suit on and put out my presents. He didn't know I knew, but the last two years, I snuck up and watched."

"You snuck up?" That brought a smile to Dirk's face. "Okay, so you've not always been on the nice list."

"Of course I have always been on the nice list. No way would I ever be on Santa's naughty list." She gave him an innocent look. "When my father had finished putting out my presents, my mom would offer him the cookies we'd made. My last Christmas with them, he pulled her into his lap on the sofa instead. They laughed and giggled and…kissed."

"So you literally saw your mommy kissing Santa?"

She laughed. "Yes, I literally did. I thought it wonderful how much they loved each other, how much fun they had with Christmas. All I ever wanted was to grow up and be like them."

He didn't say anything for a few moments. "Yet you chose nursing instead of going to work in philanthropy?"

Abby stared at him, amazed at how much he saw. She had always planned to go into philanthropy. "My aunt was a nurse. She convinced me I needed career skills to see me through life. I wasn't sure at first, but once I started school, I loved nursing."

"And the philanthropy?"

"I love that, too. Nursing is philanthropic work in many ways. It makes me feel better inside."

"Because you feel closer to your parents when you're helping others?"

Abby wondered how he'd seen what she'd rarely acknowledged herself, that volunteering made her feel less alone. Particularly at the holidays, when she'd otherwise be trapped inside her house with nothing to distract her from the loneliness of having no family.

"Yes," she admitted, "I guess it does make me feel as if I still have a connection to them."

"That's why the mad rush at Christmas? Because you want to feel closer to your parents?"

"I, well, I don't know. Possibly." She bit the inside of her lower lip, not wanting to admit the depth of her reasons. "They were wonderful parents. I missed them so much after they were gone."

"How did they die?"

"A house fire. Electrical wiring gone bad, according to the fire report. I was at a schoolfriend's house for the night. Everything was destroyed except a few storage bins in the basement." She gave him a blurry-eyed smile. "Those bins had Christmas decorations in them."

His expression softened. "The decorations you have up in your house?"

She nodded, surprised that he'd made the connection, then mentally scolded herself. Of course Dirk would make the connection. The man was brilliant.

"I've added a few pieces over the years, especially to the Christmas village as it's my favorite, and I've had to repair things, but, yes, my decorations are mostly all items that were part of my childhood. The only tangible parts left, actually."

Which explained a lot about Abby's love of Christmas.

Dirk sighed, glanced up to see a latecomer standing in the food line, and forced a smile at the unkempt man.

"Green beans?" he asked the man, who was of indeterminate age. Could have been in his forties, could have been in his seventies. A lot of the homeless were like that. They lived such a rough life with exposure to the elements aging them more rapidly and were so rumpled that it was impossible to estimate an accurate age.

The man nodded, extending his plate. Dirk scooped a big spoonful onto the plate, which was already burgeoning with food.

"Roll?" Abby held one out with her tongs.

Again, the man flashed a toothless grin. "Thanks, pretty girl."

Abby blushed. "You're welcome."

"He's right, you know," Dirk commented when the man walked over to a vacant seat at a half-occupied table. "You are a pretty girl."

"Thanks." But rather than smile at him, as he'd expected, she averted her gaze, wiping at the counter again as if she wasn't quite sure how to take his compliment.

He understood. He didn't know quite how to take his compliment either. Wasn't he the one insisting that they were just friends? Yet he fought the desire to take her into his arms constantly.

She was right to be wary. He didn't want to hurt her, battled with the need to put distance between them.

But she was pregnant with his baby and he couldn't turn his back on her. Wouldn't even if he could.

Soon decisions would have to be made. Decisions

Dirk wasn't sure he was ready to make, but he had little choice given the circumstances.

Abby had cooked most of the previous day while Dirk had been at work at the hospital. She'd only had to do last-minute items that simply couldn't be done ahead of time for dinner to taste right.

He should be arriving any moment. Would he be upset with her? He had no idea what she had planned, just that he was coming over for dinner.

Nervously, she swept her gaze around her living room. The tree blinked in multicolored magic. Her village houses glowed invitingly, making Abby imagine strolling along between them, hand in hand with Dirk as they peeped into shop windows and snuggled together to stay warm.

Despite being on edge, she smiled at the memories attached to each one of the special pieces to her mother's Christmas village. She ran her hands over the church's steeple. The first piece her father had given to her mother because it had reminded him of the small church where they'd married.

Mistletoe was in his basket next to her lit fire. Candles burned on the mantel and coffee table, blending with the pine of her tree to add a spicy Christmas scent to the room. Dinner and company waited in the kitchen.

God, she hoped everything went as planned, that his mother hadn't been wrong. But deep in her heart Abby wondered if she'd made a mistake in going along with this Christmas surprise. What if Dirk was upset? What if he thought she'd overstepped her boundaries?

Which was the crux of the matter. What were the boundaries of their relationship? He kept insisting they were just friends, yet he looked at her with desire in his eyes, looked at her with possessiveness in his eyes. She was pregnant with his child, crazily in love with him, and wanted to share her life, their baby's life, with him. But the him she saw, not the broken man he saw reflected in his mirror. She deserved better than walking on emotional eggshells for the rest of their lives.

On cue, the doorbell rang, causing Mistletoe's eyes to open. He yawned, but didn't budge from his basket.

"Nothing fazes you, does it, big guy?" she said to the lazy cat as she walked into the foyer. Pasting a nervous smile on her face, she opened the front door.

A freshly shaven and showered Dirk stood there, looking more handsome than she'd ever seen. Perhaps because he was smiling and running his gaze up and down her.

He held up a bottle. "I'd have brought wine but I figured apple cider was more appropriate considering."

"Um, apple cider is fine." Casting a wary glance over her shoulder toward the kitchen, she motioned him inside, closing the door behind him to block out the cold air rushing in. It hadn't started snowing yet but the weather forecast predicted there was a good chance of it.

Abby took the bottle. "I'll just put this in the kitchen while you remove your coat."

Slipping his coat off, he glanced around the room. "Wow, you've really gone to a lot of trouble for just the two of us."

"About that…" She waited until his eyes connected with hers, trepidation bubbling in her belly.

Only his gaze shot past her to where he could see into the small dining area, could see the table set with eight place settings. His smile faded. "It's not going to be just the two of us? Did you invite some of your friends from the hospital?"

She shook her head. "No, I have a Christmas surprise for you."

Furrows dug into his forehead. "You know how I feel about Christmas."

"I do know." *Please don't let him be upset that she'd gone along with his mother's suggestion. Please.*

"Okay." He exhaled slowly, moving close to her, close enough to touch. "I'm trying to deal with your Christmas excitement, but no more surprises."

Cupping his handsome face, she stared into his eyes, knowing she loved him, knowing she wanted him for ever, to spend all her Christmases with him and their child, and any future children that might come along. "Dirk, I—"

"Dirk! You're here!"

His expression instantly transformed to terseness, instantly tightened with cold accusation before turning toward the woman who'd entered the room.

What the—? Dirk rotated his jaw, counted to ten, inhaled and exhaled, anything to try to keep his mounting anger under control.

"Hello, Mother." He'd never mentioned Abby to his family, so his mother couldn't have been the one to make contact. But how? Surely Abby wouldn't have gone behind his back? This would explain why his mother's calls had eased.

Clearly having no clue as to the enormity of what she'd done, Abby's fingers clasped his arm. "Dirk?"

Seeing the stricken look in her eyes, he fought the

need to reassure her. How could he reassure her when panic gripped his throat, cutting off his airways?

"I'm surprised to see you here, Mother."

She walked to him, turned her cheek up to him. Automatically, he bent to kiss her in spite of his displeasure at her invading his holidays. God, he wasn't up for Christmas Intervention II.

"I can see why you like Philadelphia so much." His mother beamed in Abby's direction. "Your Abby is quite lovely."

"She's not my Abby." But she was quite pale, looking back and forth between them, clearly trying to size up the dynamics taking place. How could she have done this?

"Are the rest of the crew here?" But he could hear that they were. Over the sounds of the Christmas music playing, he could hear his nephews chatting back and forth, hear his sister shushing them.

"Holidays are meant to be shared with your family. We wanted to spend ours with you, Dirk, because we love you."

He raked his fingers through his hair. "So you invited yourself to Abby's?"

"No," his mother laughed, wrapping her arms around him to give him a hug. "I mentioned how much we wanted to see you over the holidays, that we planned to surprise you with a visit, and asked your lovely Abby to help. She invited us here. Such a good girl, Dirk. I like her."

Dirk struggled to process his mother's words. "When did you talk to Abby?"

His mother gave him one last squeeze, starting to

look a little nervous herself. "We've talked several times over the past week. She's absolutely lovely, son."

"Yes, you've mentioned that a time or two," he bit out tersely. God, what were they up to? If they brought out video tapes and photo albums again, he was out of there.

"I'll, uh, I'll go check on dinner." Abby gave him one last look, her lower lip trembled, then she disappeared into the kitchen, the low rumble of his brother's voice greeting her.

Abby had had no right to invite his family, to plan a Christmas dinner with them behind his back. Just what had his family told her? That he was a broken man? Pathetic and weak at the loss of his wife and child? That he might as well have died in that car wreck, too?

He should have. Sandra and Shelby should have lived. He should have been the one taken that morning.

"Dirk." His mother gave him a look that would have stopped him in his tracks during his younger years. "When I spoke with Abby, I'd hoped Philadelphia had been good for you, had removed the blinkers you've worn for the last four years. It's time you dealt with this."

Something inside Dirk snapped.

"Have you ever considered that I have dealt with this, only not to everyone else's satisfaction? Guess what, Mother, I'm the one who has to wake up every single day knowing that I will never look into my wife's eyes again, that I will never feel Shelby's fingers wrapped around mine again. You should respect that I've dealt with this and let me be."

"If you'd dealt with this, we wouldn't be having this

conversation, would we? Because you would have come home for Christmas."

"What? And be put through the hell of last year? I don't think so."

"We hired a top psychiatrist, Dirk. We followed her recommendations to the letter—"

"A psychiatrist?" Oh, God, that was rich. "I'm not crazy."

"No one thinks you are."

He paced across the room, spun to meet her gaze. "I was ambushed last Christmas."

She took a deep breath and didn't back down. "You were surrounded by people who love you and want what's best for you. People who want you to enjoy life again."

"What was best for me is lying in a cemetery in Oak Park." Dirk couldn't stop the words from streaming out of his mouth. Couldn't stop the feelings of hurt and betrayal streaming through him. "Something you conveniently forgot when you planned last year's fiasco. Tell me, what Christmas torture do you have in store for me tonight? Pictures? Home movies? Personal recollections of my wife and daughter? Because if that's the case, you should leave now, and take the rest of the family with you."

A loud gasp caused both Dirk and his mother to spin toward the kitchen door. Abby held on to the door frame as if she might slide to the floor if she didn't.

Sharp pain zig-zagged across her face.

Hell. He raked his fingers through his hair. What was wrong with him? He'd never verbally attacked his mother before. Not even last year during the worst of the intervention, right before he'd walked out on them.

No, he'd just calmly gotten up, informed them that they were mistaken about him and that he was leaving. And he'd left.

His mother recovered before he did, pasting a weak smile to her face as she regarded Abby. "I'm sorry, dear. It's rude of us to come into your house and squabble over family disagreements."

Family disagreements? Dirk wanted to laugh. Was that what they were calling invading his life?

"I came to tell you dinner was finished if you're ready to eat." Disillusionment shone on her face and when their eyes met, she quickly averted her gaze from his.

"Dinner would be lovely." His mother took him by the elbow, gave him a look meant to put him in his place. "Everything smells wonderful. Right, son?"

Dirk gritted his teeth, seeing right through his mother's ploy. She wanted to pretend everything was okay for Abby's sake. If they'd cared about him, or Abby, they'd have stayed in Oak Park, wouldn't have come to stir up the past.

"Right," he finally agreed, knowing this was going to be a long, long night.

Abby's face hurt from keeping her fake smile in place, just as she'd kept her smile in place all evening.

"It was so lovely to meet you, dear." Dirk's mother leaned forward, engulfing Abby in a giant bear hug. One so real and heartfelt Abby wanted to cry. "At least we know Dirk has someone to look out for him here in Philly."

Right. But during the terse evening Abby had realized she didn't want to look out for Dirk. Not under the current circumstances.

Having watched him with his family had only made obvious what she'd admitted to herself weeks ago but had shoved aside, hoping that Dirk could love her. He couldn't. He had closed off his heart to the world.

If he wasn't willing to let his own mother in, how was Abby supposed to believe he'd ever let her?

Which was the crux of the matter. After tonight, she didn't believe.

Dirk had stolen her belief in happily-ever-after, her belief in Christmas miracles. Her belief, period.

In place of the hope-filled woman she'd once been was a disillusioned woman but one determined to be strong woman who'd do what was best for her child.

"Dinner was lovely," said the next woman in line to head out the front door. A tall, dark-haired woman with eyes identical to Dirk's. His sister, Jolene. She held a well-bundled toddler in her arms. A toddler who shared the Kelley eyes. Would Abby's own baby have a similar blue gaze? Would she forever be haunted by the man she'd loved but who hadn't been able to love her in return?

"Thanks so much for inviting us." The woman leaned over and kissed Abby's cheek. "I hope to see you again soon. Maybe Dirk will bring you to Oak Park."

Abby felt tears pop into her eyes. What kind of man could have a family like this and shut them out?

Oh, he'd lightened up a bit as the evening had progressed, but he'd been out-and-out rude when he'd first arrived. So much so that Abby had planted the fake smile on her face and tried to make his family feel welcome despite his cold regard. Even now, as his mother pulled him into her arms, he wore a slight grimace, stood stiffly rather than embracing her in return.

Abby wanted to hit him. He had this beautiful family, her baby's family, and he ignored them, held them at arm's length.

No doubt after his wife and daughter's deaths things had been rough, but shouldn't he have leaned on his family, not shut them out?

His brother shook his hand, pulled him into a half-embrace. "Good to see you, man. If you can swing it, we'd love to have you at Christmas."

Dirk didn't comment. By his brother's sigh, Abby figured John knew Dirk had no intention of showing up in Oak Park on Christmas Day.

"He'll probably sleep most of the day. After all, he'll have just pulled twenty-four hours in the emergency room." Why was she defending him? This was his family. Not hers. She shouldn't be the one working so hard to make things go smoothly. "Driving long distances after working such a long shift really wouldn't be wise."

"You're right, of course." His mother's chest rose and fell beneath her heavy coat. "At least he won't be spending Christmas alone." She sent Abby a warm smile. "It really was lovely to meet you. Come on, children. Let's get this show on the road so Abby can prop her feet up. She looks tired."

Something in the way Dirk's mother said the words made Abby meet the woman's gaze, made her look away because she was sure the woman could see into her soul and see all her secrets.

Besides, she *was* tired. After pulling a twelve-hour shift at the hospital, coming home and grabbing only a few hours' sleep then finishing dinner, she was tuckered out.

It took Dirk's family another five minutes to completely get out the door, between more goodbyes, hugs, kisses to the cheeks, and kids dashing back in for a cookie for the road.

When the door closed, Abby sagged and didn't bother to try to hide her fatigue from Dirk. As his family had exited, she'd sensed his mounting tension, had seen the building fire in his eyes, had known they'd argue and was ready to get it over with.

"How could you treat your family that way, Dirk? They love you, drove all that way to spend the evening with you, and you lashed out at them every chance you got." Her heart had ached for the whole lot of them. Even Dirk. Because in his grief he'd lost much more than his wife and daughter. He'd lost everything that mattered and had no one to blame but himself.

"They had no right to show up here. How could you have invited them without discussing it with me first?"

"This is my house. I can invite whomever I want," she reminded him, chin lifting a notch. "Besides, your mother wanted to surprise you. I thought you'd be happy to see your family over the holidays."

"Well, I wasn't. You want to know why? Because I'm not you. I'm not little Miss Christmas Spirit, spreading good tidings to the whole world. I'm a man who lost his wife and daughter and the world, including his family who should understand, expects him to go on and forget."

"You weren't the only one who lost someone they loved when Shelby and Sandra died. Your family loved them, too."

"You have no idea what you're talking about," he scoffed.

"Whose fault is that, Dirk? I'm pregnant with your baby and yet you'd never introduced me to your family. Even tonight, you acted as if I was no one special."

"How did you want me to act? You went behind my back."

"It was supposed to be a pleasant surprise! Something to give you good memories to replace the ones you refuse to let go of."

"You'd have me forget my wife and daughter?" His eyes blazed, the veins on his neck bulged, his breath hissed.

Needing to put distance between them, Abby turned away, walked over to her Christmas village table, hoping to find comfort in the heirlooms she loved.

"Answer me." Dirk followed her, gripped her arm, turned her toward his angry face. "Is that what this was about? Making me forget Sandra and Shelby for your own purposes? Being pregnant doesn't give you the right to go behind my back, Abby."

"My only purpose was to give you a special Christmas memory, which you ruined for everyone by closing yourself off to any possibility of having a good time."

"I have all the special Christmas memories I need."

"Well, good for you, Dirk," she bit out, tired, frustrated, hurt, angry at him for his callous attitude. "Maybe you should stop to think about everyone else who might still want new special Christmas memories instead of being such a selfish jerk!"

She jerked back, freeing herself from his grasp and losing her balance. She stumbled, reached out to steady herself. And failed.

CHAPTER TWELVE

IN HORRID slow motion Dirk watched disaster unfold, unable to stop what had been set into play, only able to do damage control by reacting quickly.

Reaching out to keep from falling back, Abby had grabbed hold of the table her village sat on. Only she didn't catch the table. She caught the steeple of the church and kept going, the church traveling with her, knocking pieces of the village left and right.

"No," she cried as she kept going back, too off balance to do a thing to stop the pending catastrophe as the table tipped. "My mother's village!"

But rather than saving her houses, Dirk caught hold of her, righting her while the table and its contents crashed to the floor.

The sound of glass crashing into glass sent her cat tearing from the room with a screech.

"Are you okay?" he asked, visually checking her, grateful not to see any blood as she could easily have cut herself on the broken pieces.

"My mother's village!" She pulled free of him and dropped to her knees, picking up the pieces.

"Those are just things. Are you okay? The baby?"

When he'd watched her falling back, his anger had

dissipated into fear. Fear that she might be hurt, that she might lose the baby.

Abby ignored his questions about her well-being and righted the table. She picked up the church first, noted the missing steeple, the chip at the base. She dug her fingernail into the chipped area and took a deep breath, then continued to pick up piece after piece.

Dirk knew that she connected the decorations with her family, with the connection the three of them had once shared.

He bent to help her, picking up the pieces of the train set and placing them back on the righted table, carefully reconnecting the track, the train engine and cars. Two of the houses were intact, so was the schoolhouse. The carousel had a tiny chip at the base. All the other village houses had larger breaks.

Dirk took her hands into his. "Sit down, Abby. This is only upsetting you. I'll do the rest, save what can be salvaged."

"No. I think you've already done enough, don't you?" Her chin lifted. Her eyes blazed, blazed so intently that Dirk winced. He'd never seen that anguish, that pain, that accusation in Abby's eyes before.

"I didn't do this, Abby." But he hadn't been innocent. He'd been so wrapped up in his own emotions over his family's "surprise" that he hadn't considered Abby's emotions, hadn't acknowledged that she'd been trying to do something good by having his family there. Instead, he'd attacked the moment they'd walked out the door.

"No, I did this," she admitted, glaring at him. "I ruined my mother's Christmas village."

A coldness had crept into Abby's voice. A coldness he'd never heard from her. A coldness that held finality.

Her fingers clasped tightly the church steeple she held. She looked ready to snap into as many pieces as the village collection had.

She looked like she wanted to snap him into a zillion pieces and toss him out with the trash.

Abby didn't say anything more. She couldn't. Her throat had swollen shut with emotion. Her voice gone. Perhaps for ever.

She stared at the church's steeple in her shaking hands. Her entire insides shook. Her mother's Christmas village. Broken.

How could she have been so stupid as to fall into the table? How could she have been so stupid as to fall in love with a man who could never love her back?

"Abby?"

She sucked in a breath, knowing she couldn't just keep sitting here, staring at the shattered remains of the only tangible things she had of happier times, of her childhood.

The damage was done. There was no undoing it. She'd make do with the best she could, to repair the pieces she could repair. Try not to wonder if fate wasn't trying to tell her something.

That she might dream of the wonderful Christmas village scenario with Dirk, but all she was going to get was shattered dreams, and the sooner she accepted that, the less she'd have her hopes crushed.

"These are just things. You still have your memories of the Christmases with your parents. That's what's important."

Hearing Dirk say that made something snap inside Abby. Something that perhaps had been on edge from the moment she'd found out she was pregnant. From the moment she'd realized she'd never have her happily-ever-after dream. Never have magical Christmases of her own. Never have what her parents had had. Tonight, watching him with his family, had shattered all hope.

"How dare you call my mother's Christmas village 'things'?" she accused. "You, the man who could care less about his family."

"I care about my family."

She rolled her eyes at him. "You have an odd way of showing it."

"You don't understand my relationship with my family."

"Your family doesn't understand your relationship with them. Nor do they like it. God, you are so lucky to have a family to love you, but you know what? You don't deserve them, Dirk."

His jaw worked as he regarded her. "My relationship with my family is none of your business."

Unable to sit still another moment, she stood, glared down at him. "You're right. It's not. I'm just pregnant you're your child. A fact you haven't bothered to share with your family."

He stood, did some glaring of his own. "I thought you didn't want anyone to know."

"Great excuse, but we're not talking about anyone. We're talking about your family. Our baby's family." She'd never wanted to shake another human being before, but at that moment she wanted to shake Dirk. To jar some sense into him. "Are you embarrassed by me? Or were you not planning on telling them about me ever?"

Oh, God. Was that what the problem had been tonight? Dirk hadn't wanted his family to know about her? Hadn't wanted them to know he'd knocked up some naive nurse who'd fallen in love with him at first sight? Oh, God. She had fallen in love at first sight. Just as her parents had. Only Dirk hadn't fallen in love with her. He didn't even want his family to know she existed, had been a jerk because she'd invited them for Christmas dinner.

"It's not like that." He looked as if he'd like to wrap his fingers around her and do some shaking of his own.

"They don't understand how I feel. No one does."

Which said it all. Said exactly where she fit into the grand scheme of things. She'd given and given to him. Of her time and her heart. And although Dirk had given of his time, had helped her at her volunteer stints, he hadn't given her of his heart. Not once.

"Maybe it's because you keep your heart locked up inside and won't let anyone close, including your family."

"You don't know what you're talking about."

Abby just stared at him.

His look of annoyance grew. "You have no idea how much trouble you've caused me by inviting them here."

Trouble as in they'd be asking about her?

"Well, I'm sorry to inconvenience you."

His jaw clenched, and he exhaled slowly. "Quit misreading everything I say."

"Or maybe, for the first time, I'm reading everything

the right way," she said, knowing in her heart that it was true. She'd believed in Dirk's inner goodness. Had even believed that he'd come around regarding Christmas.

She really had been naive.

If not for her pregnancy, Dirk wouldn't be there. It was only his sense of responsibility that kept him coming round. Which wasn't nearly enough to base a future on.

Not nearly enough for her heart.

Abby longed to sob at her loss, but she wouldn't cry in front of him, wouldn't let him see how much she hurt. Instead, she turned her back toward him and went to the sofa and collapsed onto the plush upholstery.

"Leave, Dirk. I don't want you here." She hadn't known she was going to say the words, but once they left her lips she knew they were right, the only words she could say. Just like the Christmas village, her dreams, any hope of a future between them was shattered.

Silent, he walked over and sat down on the opposite end of the sofa. "You don't want me to go."

She gawked at his audacity. "Actually, I do. I saw a side of you tonight I never want to see again. You have no idea how lucky you are to have those people. They love you and want to be a part of your life."

"They are a part of my life."

"On the periphery perhaps."

"I've already told you, I talk to them routinely."

"About what? The weather? Sports? What is it you talk to them about? Because I got the impression they didn't know quite what to say to you tonight."

"There were no conversational lulls."

"No, there weren't, but no thanks to you."

"I warned you that I wasn't big on company."

"Family is not the same thing as company. Family is everything." But not to Dirk. He'd lost the only family that mattered to him, couldn't see what was within his reach. And Abby had had enough. More than enough. She leapt from her sofa, flung open her front door. "Get out of my house, Dirk."

"Abby—"

"Leave!" she shouted. "And don't ever bother me again."

Without another word, he gave her one last angry look, then left.

Abby started a hep lock while Dirk shined a light into their patient's eyes.

Since he'd left her house the night before, she'd been fighting melancholy. She'd hoped he'd say he wanted to change, that he wouldn't leave, that he planned to spend Christmas Day with her. Every day with her for the rest of his life. But she'd known better.

With as much time as they'd spent together over the last week, she'd thought she wouldn't be alone this Christmas, had believed deep in her heart that she'd spend the day with Dirk. How could she have been so foolish as to get her hopes up? Her hopes had been higher than the North Pole.

What would Dirk do today? Sleep? Flip through television channels? Pretend it was no different from any other day of the year? He wouldn't be driving to his mother's for Christmas, wouldn't be embracing the wonderful family she envied. More the pity for him.

But that wasn't her problem. Not any more. She'd meant what she'd told him. She didn't want him in her life. Not when he refused to acknowledge that what they'd shared had been more than friendship. Not when he refused to open his heart to love again. To open his heart to his family.

Which was why she'd ignored his phone calls today. Why she'd ignored his attempts to talk to her tonight. What was left to be said between them?

She loved Christmas.

He hated Christmas.

She loved family.

He'd shut his out.

Could they be any further apart? She didn't think so.

"How did you fall?" Dirk asked the patient, pulling Abby back to the present. She bit the inside of her lip. She had to stay focused just a little while longer. Her shift was almost at an end. She could do this. Would do this. Then she'd talk to the nurse supervisor about having her schedule changed, changed to dates when she wouldn't have to work with Dirk.

"My wife was complaining about the angle of the star on top of the Christmas tree. I climbed a stepladder, and it tipped."

Dirk's lips compressed into a tight line. Clearly, he blamed Christmas for the man's tragedy. Was it easier for him to blame the holidays than to accept that accidents happened? He'd sure been quick enough to point out that accidents occurred when it had been her village pieces involved.

Village pieces that she'd painstakingly spent the day trying to glue back together.

"Do you recall how you landed? What you hit? How your weight was distributed?"

"It happened kind of fast, Doc." The man scratched

his head with the hand Abby didn't have stabilized. "I know I hit my head." The pump knot on his forehead attested to that. "And my right ribs are sore."

"This happened about eight last night?"

The man nodded.

"What made you decide to come to the hospital this morning?"

"I woke up and couldn't breathe. I think that's what woke me."

"Are you still short of breath?"

The man nodded. "Not as badly as at the house. My wife says I had a panic attack."

"Your oxygen saturation is ninety-two percent. That's not too bad," Dirk explained. "But it's not as high as it should be in an otherwise healthy person either. I'm going to order a few tests just to check you out and make sure you haven't fractured any ribs or worse."

"Worse?"

"Fall injuries can result in serious damage to a person's body."

The man nodded. "Tell me something I don't know."

As always, Dirk responded to his patient, making Abby wonder how he could smile so sincerely at a virtual stranger and not his own kin. "Maybe you should stay off ladders for a while, too. Ask someone to help you with anything that requires climbing."

"Tell that to my wife. She has no patience and had to have that star straightened before the kids and grandkids show up in the morning for Christmas celebrations."

Finishing what she was doing, Abby excused herself and disappeared out of the bay.

The moment she finished giving report, she rushed

away, determined to somehow find joy in the most magical day of the year.

Her favorite day of the year.

His least favorite day of the year.

A day she'd spend alone yet again.

Christmas Eve shouldn't be a busy night in the emergency room, but this one was. Midnight had come and gone, so technically Christmas morning had arrived.

The only thing Dirk liked about Christmas was it meant the end was near. The end of the season, the decorations, the smells, the aggravation and harassment from family.

Yes, the signal that the end of the season was near was the best part of Christmas Day.

Or it had been.

Now he wasn't so sure. Somehow he'd tangled thoughts of Abby up with Christmas and the thought of the end put his insides in a viselike grip.

The end of Christmas. The end of his relationship with Abby. No, he wouldn't accept that. Not under the circumstances.

God, his family would be ecstatic when they found out she was pregnant. How many times had they attempted to set him up with someone when he'd lived in Oak Park? How many times had they told him to find someone new and start over? How many times had they called to say how much they'd liked Abby, what a great cook she was, what a warm house she'd had, what a generous person she'd seemed? And he'd let them, because Abby's accusations had kept playing over and over in his head.

None of his family had understood that he hadn't

wanted a new start, that he'd wanted his old life, a life that had been snatched away.

A life that had ended on the day his wife and daughter had died. Dirk had buried himself right along with them.

He hadn't been happy in years. Hadn't even really wanted to be. He'd preferred to wallow in his grief.

Until Abby.

In moving away, he had started over.

Quite frankly, that had scared the hell out of him. Had put him on the defensive. Had caused mixed emotions to surge. Emotions that made him want to cling to Abby and the hope she gave him. Emotions that made him want to pack up his bags and get out of Dodge. Emotions that had made him hold her at arm's length, just as she'd nailed him for doing to his family.

But he and Abby had a baby on the way.

A baby.

A precious new life that he and Abby had made.

When she'd fallen into her Christmas village table, he'd only been able to think of her safety, their baby's safety. Maybe he could have righted the table had he gone for it instead, but all he'd been concerned about had been keeping Abby from falling to the floor.

Because he wanted to keep her safe. Wanted to keep their baby safe.

He'd left when she'd asked him to, seeing she had been too upset to have the talk they needed to have, sensing that the emotions of both of them had been running too high. He'd been fine on his drive home. Fine when he'd walked through the front door. But when he'd crawled into his bed, alone, he'd done what he hadn't done in years. Not since right after Sandra and Shelby's accident. He'd been fairly positive there were no tears left inside him. The night the woman and her daughter died in the E.R. had been his first clue he might be wrong. He'd felt a crack in the protective wall that guarded his heart. Making love with Abby had sent a whole lot of bricks tumbling to the ground. Bricks he'd needed to keep himself safe.

But with Abby, she came first. Her and their baby. In that, she'd bulldozed right through the barriers around his heart, leaving him vulnerable.

Leaving him exposed to her warmth. Exposed to needing her. He'd been fighting to keep from making love to her every second they were together but as much as he'd enjoyed the passion they'd shared, he hadn't enjoyed how much he'd needed her, how connected he'd felt to her, how much he'd hurt if something happened to Abby.

She'd been right about him. He had kept his family at a distance. Had kept them at arm's length. How could he not? He'd always been the strong one in the family, but after Sandra and Shelby's deaths, he hadn't been strong.

He'd hated them seeing him that way.

Hated anyone seeing him that way.

So he'd shut them out.

No wonder they'd held an intervention.

He'd needed one. And more.

He'd needed Abby, so much so that he'd tried to hold her at arm's length, too, for fear of loving again, of possibly losing that love again.

Need had won out. Need and so much more.

He loved Abby. And wanted to risk holding her and the baby they'd made close to his heart.

But judging by the way she hadn't returned his calls, had all but ignored him since her arrival at shift change, he might have realized too late.

God, he couldn't lose Abby. In her, he'd found his salvation. Had found himself again.

If he'd lost her, he had no one to blame except himself. But he refused to accept that she wouldn't forgive his ignorance.

It was Christmas. A day of miracles. A day meant to be with the ones you loved. Somehow, he'd show Abby he could be the man she and their child needed.

A man who could be whole and start living again.

A man he desperately wanted to be.

Abby's man.

If he had to go to drastic measures to make that happen, then so be it.

CHAPTER THIRTEEN

IF EVER Abby would forgive him, this had to be the way. Hell, he hoped he wasn't wrong. Otherwise he was going to look like the biggest idiot who'd ever walked the face of the earth.

Which didn't bother him near as much as the thought of not winning Abby's forgiveness, of winning her love and trust.

It had taken him several hours to make arrangements for what he wanted to do.

But, finally, here he stood. Most likely she'd already gone to bed, would sleep for several hours.

Maybe it was wrong of him, but Dirk helped himself to the hide-a-key she'd told him where to find on the day he'd knocked and knocked without her answering.

Her house was quiet. Just as he'd expected it to be.

Not even Mistletoe was anywhere to be seen.

Quietly, closing the front door behind him, Dirk set into play what he hoped would show Abby everything in his heart.

"Meow."

Abby groaned, rubbed her face at where a paw

swatted at her. "Go back to sleep, Mistletoe. Didn't you get the memo? I'm going to sleep through Christmas this year."

"Meow." Another swat at her face.

Abby rolled onto her side, pulled her pillow over her head, hoping to gain a few more minutes of sleep before having to get up and face the reality of another Christmas spent alone.

That's when she heard another noise.

What was that? Music? Singing?

She stretched, pushing the pillow away from her head and straining to hear.

Definitely Christmas music.

Coming from somewhere in her house.

She had not left music on.

She knew she hadn't.

Someone was in her house.

Panic squeezed at her throat. Then, climbing out of her bed, she laughed at herself. What? A burglar had broken in and put on Christmas music? Right.

She must still be asleep, be dreaming.

Either that or Dirk had used the hide-a-key and if that was the case, she knew she was dreaming.

Dirk wouldn't be playing Christmas music.

But apparently someone would. Maybe Danielle had taken pity on her and come over to surprise her.

Tiptoeing down the hallway, Abby rubbed her eyes, certain she wasn't seeing clearly. Mixed emotions hit her at the sight of the man arranging Christmas packages under her tree.

The man she'd told to get out and not to come back.

How dared he come into her house and, well, whatever it was he was doing?

"I should have you arrested for breaking and entering."

At the sound of Abby's voice, Dirk turned from where he worked. Hell, he hadn't finished with what he'd wanted to do.

Still, he'd made great headway.

"Ho. Ho. Ho." Yes, he sounded stupid even to himself, but he had a lot riding on this. He'd seen the look in Abby's eyes, had seen that she'd given up on him. It was going to take a desperate act to win her back. This stunt was about as desperate as desperate got. He wished he'd been able to finish. "You're not supposed to be out of bed yet."

Her glare didn't let up. "You need to leave."

He'd meant to change into her father's Santa suit, had meant to give her the kind of Christmas Day she longed for, one like her parents had shared. "I will, but let me finish what I came to do first."

She crossed her arms over her flannel-pajama-covered chest. She glanced around the room, took in the presents he'd arranged, the Santa suit he had draped across the back of the sofa.

"What are you doing?"

"Delivering presents." Lots and lots of presents. Packages of various shapes and sizes were brightly wrapped and overflowing beneath the tree. It had cost him a small fortune to hire the personal shoppers to find stores open on Christmas morning, but if you were willing to spend enough, a person could do most anything.

Even do major Christmas shopping on the great day itself.

"Why would you do that? You don't even like Christmas." She stood in the doorway, staring at him as if she really had caught Dr. Seuss's Grinch stealing her Christmas rather than him in jeans and a T-shirt and a bundle of good intentions.

Obviously, he'd become overzealous when he'd turned on the Christmas tunes, thinking she was tired enough that the low music wouldn't disturb her and she'd sleep a few more hours. He'd just have to go forward as things were and pray for the best, pray for Abby to love him.

"Women aren't the only ones allowed to change their minds. Apparently I just needed to be reminded of the real meaning of the holiday."

"Oh, you needed that all right," she scoffed, eyeing him suspiciously. "So you've supposedly changed your mind about Christmas? Why?"

"You."

"Me?" This time she laughed with a great deal of irony. "I changed your mind about Christmas?"

"You changed my mind about everything, Abby. About life. My life. And the life I want with you."

This had to work. If Christmas magic didn't open Abby's eyes to the man he wanted to be for her, nothing would.

Abby crossed the room, stood next to him, but didn't sit, just stared at him with her forehead creased. "What about Sandra? Shelby? You still love them."

"You'd have me not love them?"

"No," she began hesitantly.

"I realize that part of my life is in the past, Abby.

I've accepted that. I'm ready to move on to the future. With you."

She glanced away, closed her eyes. "That's too bad, Dirk, because I don't trust you with my future."

He winced, but wasn't ready to admit defeat. Not when he was battling for the most important part of his life.

"Someone once told me that Christmas Day was the most magical day of the year. A day when miracles can happen." He prayed some of that Christmas magic would shine on him, would help Abby to see how much he loved her. "Trust me, Abby. I won't let you down. Never again."

She didn't say anything for a few moments then met his gaze warily. "How can I believe you? How can I know this isn't some ploy out of a sense of responsibility because I'm pregnant?"

Dirk's ribs squeezed his lungs. He'd hoped she'd say that she did trust him with her heart. That she wanted him and wanted to be a family with him and their baby.

Instead she looked at him with distrust shining in her hazel eyes. God, he'd been such a fool. How many times had Abby opened up her heart to him and he'd pushed her away out of fear? Fear of feeling again. Fear of loving and losing that love. Fear of feeling because with feeling came the risk of pain.

But there came a point when a man had to overcome his fears, had to risk that pain, had to risk rejection, because the alternative wasn't acceptable. Regardless of the risk of pain, not telling Abby the truth wasn't acceptable.

He took her hand in his. "You've had me from the

moment we met, Abby. I tried fighting it, but I think I fell for you in the E.R. that first night. I know I wanted you in that instance. And every instance since."

Her gaze lowered to their interlocked hands, then lifted back to his. "Why are you saying these things? Why now?"

"Because I can't bear the thought that I might have lost you. Tell me you'll give me a chance to prove to you that I can be the man of your dreams."

A tear trickling down her cheek, she closed her eyes. "I didn't really wake up, did I? I'm still asleep and am dreaming."

Dirk lifted her hand to his lips, pressed a kiss to her fingertips. "Then don't wake up quite yet, because this dream is far from over. You have a lot of presents to open."

As if hearing Dirk say he wanted to be the man of her dreams wasn't enough to convince Abby that she was dreaming, the number of packages under her tree clinched the deal.

Never in her life had she had so many presents.

But why was he doing this?

Sitting on the floor, she picked up a box, shook it prior to carefully unwrapping it to reveal a beautiful aqua-colored baby blanket.

He'd bought a gift for their baby. For her. God, could he be serious about wanting to share a future?

Running her fingers over the soft, fuzzy material, she lifted her gaze to his. "This is beautiful."

He reached for the next present and handed it to her. They repeated the process until she was surrounded with baby items. Some pink. Some blue. Some a mixture of pastels.

"You've been busy," she mused, biting into her lower lip, trying to decipher the meaning behind his gifts.

"I had help, but don't hold that against me." He gave a crooked grin. "Even Santa utilizes elves."

"Ah," she said, not quite believing he'd gone to so much trouble to bring her Christmas alive, to give her a magical day despite the fact they'd argued the last time they'd really talked, that she'd told him to leave. "Thank you, Dirk. I love everything."

She did. Not only because these were the first baby items for their child but because they'd come from Dirk. But what did all this mean? Why was he here? Giving her presents?

"Do you, Abby?"

She lifted her gaze to his in question.

"Love everything, that is?"

Abby's breath caught at the intensity in his blue eyes. At the vulnerability she saw shining there.

No protective walls. No barriers. No hanging on to the past. Just a man asking if she loved him.

A man who she loved with all her heart, but...

Glancing away when she didn't immediately answer, Dirk scratched his chin. "Um..." His voice broke slightly. "Better let me check my bag. Seems like there might be another present for you."

Abby wanted to stop him, to explain her pause, to ease what had put that break in his voice, but the moment had passed and she wondered if some of those fallen walls had been re-erected.

"You shouldn't have."

"Might not want to shake this one," he warned,

causing Abby's curiosity to grow as she took the package.

She unwrapped the present, lifted her gaze to his, and caught her breath at what she saw reflected in his eyes.

He hadn't re-erected any walls, had left his heart bare for her to see, for her to take if she wanted.

She swallowed, glancing back down at the gift in her hands. "I can't believe you had someone find this for me."

"Actually, I had this one in my truck on Saturday night," he explained. "I'd meant to give it to you after our quiet dinner."

"Only we didn't have a quiet dinner." She pulled the piece from the box, carefully removed the protective wrapping, stared in amazement at the antique village piece. A piece that matched her mother's pieces. How had he known? And that he'd bought it before the crash made it all the more special. He wasn't trying to replace something he felt responsible for breaking. He was giving her something from the heart, giving her something because he'd known it would mean something to her, would make her happy.

"I love it," she whispered, leaning forward to kiss his cheek and hoping he couldn't tell she was choking back tears.

"And I love you, Abby."

She almost dropped the house. "Dirk?"

"I love you, Abby," He repeated words sweeter than any melody. "With all my heart. I didn't think I'd ever love again, that I could ever love. But I do. I love you. And our baby. Please forgive me. I've been such a fool, wasted so much time we could have been together."

Taking a moment to steady her nerves, she put the house back into its box, took a deep breath. "Tell me again."

"I've been a fool—"

"Not that part," she interrupted, meeting his gaze, amazed at the emotion reflected there. "Tell me you love me again, Dirk. Please."

Eyes shining with everything Abby had ever hoped to see in a man's gaze, he took her hand into his, lifted it to his lips. "I love you, Abby. Completely. Always. For ever."

"I love you, too." She wrapped her arms around him, leaned in to kiss him, to show him everything in her heart.

But rather than take her into his arms and kiss her, he held her hands and stared into her eyes, looking almost nervous as he slid his hands into a jeans pocket and pulled out a small box, snapped it open. "Marry me, Abby."

"What?" An earthquake hit right in the pit of Abby's stomach. One whose aftershocks caused wave after wave of emotion to crash through her.

She stared in awe at the marquis-cut diamond reflecting the multicolored lights from the tree.

"Agree to be my wife. To share your life with me. To share all your Christmases with me. Always."

Abby couldn't believe her ears but, looking into his sincere eyes, she knew he was serious, knew he really did love her. No way would Dirk Kelley be pulling that ring free of its box and slipping it onto the third finger of her left hand otherwise.

She stared down at the ring, at where he held her hand. Could this really be happening?

"What about Sandra? Shelby?" she asked, not quite able to accept that her dreams might be coming true.

"They'll always be a part of my past, a part of who I am. But you are my future, Abby. You and our baby."

"I would never ask you to forget them, Dirk."

"I know you wouldn't, Abby. That's just one of the many reasons I love you. That and how you see the good in everything, including a man who'd lost track that there was anything good left in him."

"There's so much good in you, Dirk. Anyone who'd ever seen you with a patient would know that." She brushed her fingers across his cheek.

"But only you saw. Only you believed in me when I didn't believe in myself. All I knew was that from the moment we met I felt different, alive for the first time in years. You put breath back into my dying body, Abby. Say you'll let me love you always."

"Yes," she whispered, tears brimming in her eyes. "Oh, yes, Dirk."

This time Dirk took her into his arms, kissed her so thoroughly she'd have sworn she must be wearing that halo made of mistletoe, made love to her so thoroughly she'd swear they rocked the Christmas tree.

"Hey, Abs?" Dirk said much later, holding her against him.

"Hmm?"

A sheepish look shone on his face. "Your house wasn't the only place on Santa's list."

Realization hit her and Abby's heart swelled with love and pride of this wonderful man who'd truly opened his heart. "We're going to your family's for Christmas?"

He nodded. "I've got some making up for the past to do. Especially to my mother."

"What time are we supposed to be there?"

He brushed her hair away from her face, pressed a kiss against her temple. "They don't know we're coming, so whenever we arrive will be okay."

She wrapped her arms around him, kissed the corner of his mouth, excited at the magic filling the day. "Your mother is going to be so happy when you walk through that door, Dirk."

"She's going to be even happier when I tell her our news."

"That we're getting married?"

"That she's getting a new grandbaby for Christmas." He smiled wryly then shrugged. "And that she's getting her son back, along with a daughter-in-law who he loves more than life itself."

She hugged him, so proud of how far Dirk had come. "Your family is going to be so excited to see you."

All her dreams were coming true. She was getting a family. Dirk's family. And most importantly, she was getting the man she loved and who loved her. Dirk.

He grinned. "Yeah, and you know what? I'm going to be excited to see them, too, and to see their faces when I hand out their gifts."

"Gifts?" Abby raised her brow in question. "What did you get them?"

"Bought each one of them a *Dummies Guide to Holding an Intervention* and wrote a message, letting them know how much I appreciate them and that they have my permission to intervene anytime deemed necessary."

Abby laughed. "Oh, Dirk, you really are serious about this, aren't you?"

His brow lifted. "Did you doubt me?"

Had she? No, she trusted him with her heart, with their baby's heart. He loved them. She could see that truth in his eyes, feel it in his touch, in the way he'd cherished her while they'd made love. "Not in the slightest. You're a good man."

"I'm your man, Abby." He smiled in a way that reached in and touched her very being. "I'll always be your man. Merry Christmas, sweetheart."

"The best." But she suspected only the beginning of even happier times when she and Dirk celebrated the holidays with their baby, with his family—their family. "Merry Christmas to you, too. You've given me so much."

"Not nearly as much as you've given me. You gave me back my life, my heart, my family, my belief in Christmas." He placed his palm over her belly, caressing her there. "I love you and our baby."

Knowing Dirk had made her Christmas dreams come true, would continue to make them come true every day for the rest of their lives, Abby rolled over to kiss her very own Santa all over again.

1210/03a

Medical Romance™

SHEIKH, CHILDREN'S DOCTOR…HUSBAND
by Meredith Webber

Leader and dedicated children's doctor Sheikh Azzam has ordered Dr Alexandra Conroy to his royal palace. Then disaster strikes his beloved land. Not only must Azzam and Alex work together—but also temporarily marry…

SIX-WEEK MARRIAGE MIRACLE
by Jessica Matthews

When nurse Leah couldn't give her husband, Dr Gabe Montgomery, a family it broke her heart to walk away. Now, persuaded by Gabe to work with him in rural Mexico, Leah falls for the man who vowed to love her no matter what…all over again!

RESCUED BY THE DREAMY DOC
by Amy Andrews

Nurse Callie Duncan is putting her life back together when gorgeous returning army hero Sebastian Walker arrives at her hospital! Nights spent in Seb's arms mend Callie's broken heart.
If independent Callie can just let this dreamy doc deliver a fairytale ending…

NAVY OFFICER TO FAMILY MAN
by Emily Forbes

Juliet's ex-husband, naval officer Sam Taylor, can still make her heart flutter. But Juliet needs medical treatment—and it's Sam's wake-up call. He'll take the helm at home, and hope he can give his kids and the woman he loves a happy-ever-after…

On sale from 7th January 2011
Don't miss out!

Available at WHSmith, Tesco, ASDA, Eason and all good bookshops
www.millsandboon.co.uk

MILLS & BOON®

are proud to present our...

Book of the Month

St Piran's: Penhally's Wedding of the Year & St Piran's: Rescued Pregnant Cinderella

from Mills & Boon® Medical™ Romance 2-in-1

ST PIRAN'S: THE WEDDING OF THE YEAR
by Caroline Anderson
GP Nick Tremayne and midwife Kate Althorp have an unfulfilled love that's lasted a lifetime. Now, with their little boy fighting for his life in St Piran's Hospital…can they find their way back to one another?

ST PIRAN'S: RESCUING PREGNANT CINDERELLA
by Carol Marinelli
Dr Izzy Bailey is single and pregnant when she meets the gorgeous neo-natal nurse Diego Ramirez. When she goes into labour dangerously early Diego is there to rescue her… Could this be the start of her fairytale?

Available 3rd December

Something to say about our Book of the Month?
Tell us what you think!

millsandboon.co.uk/community
facebook.com/romancehq
twitter.com/millsandboonuk

A Christmas bride for the cowboy

Two classic love stories by bestselling author
Diana Palmer in one Christmas collection!

Featuring

Sutton's Way
and
Coltrain's Proposal

Available 3rd December 2010

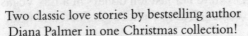

"Did you say I won almost two million dollars?"

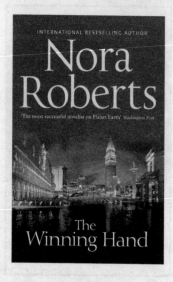

Down to her last ten dollars in a Las Vegas casino, Darcy Wallace gambled and won!

Suddenly the small-town girl was big news— and needing protection. Robert MacGregor Blade, the casino owner, was determined to make sure Darcy could enjoy her good fortune. But Darcy knew what she wanted; Mac himself. Surely her luck was in?

Available 3rd December 2010

www.millsandboon.co.uk

2 FREE BOOKS
AND A SURPRISE GIFT

We would like to take this opportunity to thank you for reading this Mills & Boon® book by offering you the chance to take TWO more specially selected books from the Medical™ series absolutely FREE! We're also making this offer to introduce you to the benefits of the Mills & Boon® Book Club™—

- **FREE home delivery**
- **FREE gifts and competitions**
- **FREE monthly Newsletter**
- **Exclusive Mills & Boon Book Club offers**
- **Books available before they're in the shops**

Accepting these FREE books and gift places you under no obligation to buy, you may cancel at any time, even after receiving your free books. Simply complete your details below and return the entire page to the address below. You don't even need a stamp!

YES Please send me 2 free Medical books and a surprise gift. I understand that unless you hear from me, I will receive 5 superb new stories every month including two 2-in-1 books priced at £5.30 each and a single book priced at £3.30, postage and packing free. I am under no obligation to purchase any books and may cancel my subscription at any time. The free books and gift will be mine to keep in any case.

Ms/Mrs/Miss/Mr _____ Initials _____

_____

Surname _____

Address _____

_____

_____ Postcode _____

E-mail _____

Send this whole page to: Mills & Boon Book Club, Free Book Offer, FREEPOST NAT 10298, Richmond, TW9 1BR